A Novel

QUEEN BESS

A TUDOR COMES TO SAVE AMERICA

MARIA VETRANO

A REGALO PRESS BOOK
ISBN: 979-8-88845-689-7
ISBN (eBook): 979-8-88845-690-3

Queen Bess:
A Tudor Comes to Save America
© 2024 by Maria Vetrano
All Rights Reserved

Cover Design by Jim Villaflores
Cover Photography by The Hatfield House

Publishing Team:
Founder and Publisher – Gretchen Young
Editorial Assistant – Caitlyn Limbaugh
Managing Editor – Aleigha Koss
Production Manager – Alana Mills
Production Editor – Rachel Hoge
Associate Production Manager – Kate Harris

As part of the mission of Regalo Press, a donation is being made to Silent Spring Institute, as chosen by the author. To learn more please visit: https://silentspring.org/

Regalo Press
New York • Nashville
regalopress.com

Published in the United States of America
1 2 3 4 5 6 7 8 9 10

For my mother Camille,
who was a woman ahead of her time.

PRELUDE

April 9, 2027, Charlestown, Massachusetts

"Art thou a woman? Where is thy hair?"

Dakota recoiled as if electrocuted. *That's the first thing she says to me?*

Queen Elizabeth's chest heaved in and out, her breath coming in short bursts, her eyes blinking rapidly. The queen looked around the room as she lay on a cot, then brought a bejeweled hand to the top of the duvet and pulled down, revealing a semi-crushed Elizabethan ruff of intricately patterned white lace. In the soothing light of the recovery room, Dakota studied Her Majesty's appearance. Her gold-brown eyes were bloodshot. Her face was angular, with high cheekbones and a prominent nose. And her bodice of black velvet embroidered with gold flower petals was resplendent. Pearl-drop earrings brushed against the light-gold fabric of her puffy sleeves.

Dakota startled as the queen opened her mouth as if to speak, but relaxed when her much hoped-for champion closed it again and her eyes rolled back and shut. The queen gave a loud sigh, and her chest rose and fell more slowly, settling into a rhythmic pace.

A few seconds later, the creases in the queen's forehead dissolved back into white paint, and the lines around her mouth softened. *Gloriana. The Virgin Queen. Good Queen Bess.* The many names for Queen Elizabeth I—who'd ruled England, Ireland, and Wales from 1558 to her death in 1603—captured different aspects of her persona. As Gloriana, she was royal and divine, the muse of poets and playwrights, and more likely to look down from the heavens than gaze up at them. As the Virgin Queen, she sacrificed intimate relations to retain her full power as a monarch. As Good Queen Bess, she was a beloved mother to her people, not just their ruler. Both virgin and mother, she was Mary, mother of God, in royal form.

From all that Dakota had read about her, Queen Elizabeth I was like the first reality star, adored by fans who wore miniature portraits of her as jewelry or who lined the streets for a glimpse of her on horseback as she traveled through the countryside each summer. Despite the grand scale of her royal progress, a procession that included dozens of courtiers and hundreds of carts towing provisions, the queen always took time to greet her subjects. She was offered small gifts, serenaded with poems, and even invited to take refreshment as she traveled to the next great estate.

Elizabeth was the sixteenth-century equivalent of a celebrity who took selfies with her fans. She was that kind of famous person, who would sit down and have a beer with a constituent, a comforting perception that would be critical to her upcoming campaign.

Had it only been five months since Dakota dreamed up an audacious plan to save both the country and the cybersecurity company that she founded twenty-six years before?

Was she crazy to think that she could convince a woman who had lived and died more than four centuries ago that she could become the most powerful figure in history…again? But this time, the great English queen's job would be more straightforward. She wouldn't have to defeat Europe's largest naval power, maintain control of the state religion, or thwart domestic or foreign assassins. Instead, she would be tasked with running against the vile incumbent president, who was an imminent threat to democracy and to the private ownership of Dakota's company.

If her Elizabeth were anything like what Dakota imagined, by this time next year, a Tudor would be sitting in the Oval Office, KODA would remain under her control, the US would be much more stable, women's rights would be restored, and all humanity would feel relieved that the nuclear football was no longer in the hands of an imbecile. That wasn't too much to hope for, was it? Maybe for someone else, but not for Dakota Wynfred. She'd never set a goal she couldn't meet.

Sure, she was making a bold move, but it wasn't just for her own benefit. She was doing it for a higher purpose. Just as her parents had always taught her. *The most important thing any person can do is to improve the lives of others.*

Though she'd never hear her parents say the words again, she hoped they would be proud of her choices.

It was still so important that they were proud of her.

She would do whatever it took to make it so.

CHAPTER 1

November 26, 2026, Cambridge, Massachusetts

"Where are you, Dakota? It's three o'clock, and we're eating in an hour. Aren't you having Thanksgiving with us?"

CeCe sounded pissed. And with good reason. For the past two weeks, Dakota had been blowing off her best friend from her undergraduate days at MIT. Avoiding CeCe's calls, texts, and emails had seemed easier than telling CeCe the truth, that she'd traveled through time to visit her forty-one-year-old mother on her own fifty-fourth birthday. There was no way CeCe would believe her since Dakota had yet to reveal she'd been funding a secret time-travel lab at her cybersecurity company KODA for the past seventeen years.

That little chestnut would either make CeCe madder, because Dakota had kept a life-changing event from her oldest friend, or it would convince CeCe, a practicing doctor of psychology, that Dakota needed immediate psychiatric treatment. *Ugh.*

Dakota bit her lip and answered. "I totally am, CeCe," she said. "I guess I lost track of time."

"Like you did about a thousand times in college," CeCe said with a harumph. "You'd work day and night on some computer science problem until you practically fainted with hunger. I remember this one time when I brought you a pizza, and your room stunk to high heaven." *Oh hell. Not the pizza story again.*

"I was in a competition, CeCe, you know that." Dakota rolled her eyes at the ceiling. "I didn't have time to shower."

"Well, be that as it may, Mom made your favorite pie so you better get your ass out of whatever chair to which it is glued," she said.

"I'm leaving home now," Dakota said. "I just need to do one more thing."

"No 'one more thing.' Just get here or no pie for you." CeCe hung up.

Dakota pulled off her MIT sweatshirt as she ran into her voluminous walk-in closet. She threw her favorite chocolate-brown cashmere maxi cardigan over her camisole, checked the floor-length mirror to make sure she didn't have a peanut butter smudge on her black jeans, and grabbed a pair of limestone suede lace-up sneakers from her Ecco collection. She needed to get out the door in two minutes if she was going to make the trip from her river-view condo in Cambridge to CeCe's parents in Milton. If she didn't hit traffic on Route 93 South, she could get there in twenty-five minutes. Who was she kidding? There was always traffic on Route 93.

A fine sheen of sweat glazed Dakota's forehead as she hopped into her cherry-red BMW iX M70 and exited the garage of her building. There was so much bubbling in her brain—between her visit to her mother, and her plan to save the country and KODA by mining the past to change the future—that she felt like she'd explode if she didn't share it soon. She'd try to get some time with her old friend after dessert. *If CeCe's in a food coma when I tell her I saw Mommy, maybe I'll be able to get some distance on her before she tackles me and tells me I've become delusional and need immediate treatment.*

As she drove across the Longfellow Bridge so she could pick up the highway in Boston, Dakota's thoughts drifted back to her recent conversation with her mother. When her mission changed from saving her mother to saving the world.

CHAPTER 2

November 10, 1984, Cambridge, Massachusetts

Dakota stood at the front door of her childhood home, a two-bedroom apartment on the top floor of a rundown triple-decker in East Cambridge. Her heart hammered in her chest as she anticipated the moment when she'd come face-to-face with the mother she'd not seen in decades. *She'll never recognize me. I'm older now than she was when she died. Oh God, how am I going to explain myself?*

The smell of baking bread that wafted into the hall made her mouth water. She'd almost forgotten how good her mother's fresh-baked bread tasted.

Dakota pressed her ear against the door to listen, but she couldn't hear anything over her pounding heart. It was still hard to believe that she'd been planning this visit since 2008, when she'd first seen Hoshi Kisai present his research at MIT's emerging technologies conference. Though a top theoretical physicist at Tohoku, Japan's most prestigious university for science and technology, Dr. Kisai had almost been laughed off the podium when he claimed to have discovered the key to human time travel. "Exotic matter," he said. Which was a new class of matter that can bend time-space backwards and forwards—or so other physicists had theorized. But since no other physicist in history had claimed real-world experience with exotic matter, most viewed it as fantastical. Unruffled by the skeptics in the audience—who expressed their disapproval through a din of gasps and coughs—Kisai explained that he'd successfully manipulated exotic matter to create wormholes that would allow a person to travel through time. Dakota knew genius when she saw it, and by 2009, Kisai and his research team were busy working in the underground lab in the bowels of her company's building in Charlestown, Massachusetts.

It took until January 2026 for Kisai to send his first team into the past. And while those early trips weren't quite perfect, she wasn't going to nitpick a discrepancy of a few hours—or days—when the overall platform generally worked as intended. Travelers arrived at the targeted location in the correct year, and they didn't come back like a bowl of cytoplasm. She also knew that Kisai and his brilliant nucleus of scientists had refined the platform over the past eleven months until it was ready for Dakota.

She had carefully planned the timing of this trip. Her father always took her to the Cambridge Public Library on Saturdays while her mother baked bread, so there was no danger of her meeting her younger self. What a wonderful childhood routine. She'd bound up the stairs with a fresh pile of books, her father following and laughing, her mother setting the butterscotch-yellow Formica tabletop with three plates, a butter dish, and butter knives on napkins for a pre-lunch snack. But now, Dakota's head throbbed at near-migraine level. Was it because she'd traveled four decades back in time? Or was it her anxiety that she would scare the hell out of her mother, who would be meeting her only child as a middle-aged adult?

It wasn't just that she wanted to save her mother. If she was being honest with herself, she was desperate for her mother's advice. Both of her parents were social activists, but her mother was her moral compass. It didn't matter how many years ago her mother had died, she was a constant presence in Dakota's inner life. Before every major decision, she conjured her mother's guidance. Which was easy when the decision was black or white, but when she found herself somewhere in the gray, she tended to feel a bit lost. She'd ping-pong ideas off her friends, but it wasn't the same as having a heart-to-heart with someone who understood you at a cellular level, and who would love you for all eternity.

And her father? He'd died of a massive heart attack at fifty-seven, which made zero sense because he'd always been in excellent physical condition. No smoking—except some weed—and he rode his bicycle everywhere, even when it was cold or dark or the weather was cruddy. He ate fresh vegetables and drank green tea, way before it was fashionable. Given his lifestyle, she always thought he would live to ninety, but she was wrong.

His emotional well-being, on the other hand, was a different story. From Dakota's perspective, her father wasn't the same man after he lost his wife. When she was still alive, he used to bounce around the apartment, playing little jokes on his family. Like the time he gathered Dakota and her mother at the kitchen table and told them he was going to work for his father—an investment banker. At first, Dakota's mother had rolled her eyes, saying that he was "very funny." But her father had kept up the joke for a good five or ten minutes— until Dakota's mother clamped a hand to her chest and said she didn't want to live with a capitalist. He caved immediately, at which point her mother screamed with laughter because she had called his bluff.

With no heart problems in his medical history, Dakota had always assumed that the actual cause of his death was a broken heart.

She supposed hers had mostly recovered. Yet here she was, having moved heaven and earth to reconnect with the mother she'd lost so young. Dakota couldn't predict whether her mother would agree to time-travel with her father to a new life in 2026, but she would do her damnedest to convince her mother it was for the best.

It's now or never. Dakota reached for the door knocker and rapped it a few times.

"Just a minute," her mother's sing-song voice called out. Then the door opened.

"Hello, there. Can I help you with something?" her mother said. She used a flour-dusted hand to brush her dark brown bangs out of her eyes.

"Could I come in for a moment, please?" Dakota's voice came out sounding strangled.

"Umm…. Do I know you?" Her mother frowned. "Damn if you don't look familiar." Her chocolate-pudding eyes locked on Dakota's.

"I've traveled a very long way to see you again, but you're going to find it almost impossible to believe." Dakota exhaled audibly through a small opening in her mouth, almost as if she would whistle. "Still, what I'm about to tell you isn't nearly as dreadful as that *Somewhere in Time* movie you took me to see at The Brattle Square Theater. I remember you buying me Junior Mints and Milk Duds to placate me."

"How could you possibly know that?" Her mother put her hands on her hips and leaned in toward Dakota. "And if you've done anything to my daughter, touched a single hair on her head, I will have your head on a platter."

Dakota grinned. "You go, girl."

"I'm not kidding, goddamn it," she growled. "Where is my child?"

"I'm pretty sure she's with her father at the library." Dakota reached for her mother's hand in slow motion. Her voice was now breaking. "Because that's where I was pretty much every Saturday for most of my childhood."

Her mother's mouth fell open as she clutched her chest. Seconds passed. She backed away from the door.

"Let's sit in the living room, okay?" said Dakota. The color had drained from her mother's face. "I'll get you a drink of water and check on the bread."

She edged through the door and walked her mother over to the royal blue leather sofa that they'd found three years ago on "Allston

Christmas," which took place on the first of September when thousands of college students moved from old to new apartments, leaving unwanted furniture on the curb. Her mother looked smaller than she remembered, sitting on the knife-edge of the sofa, her hands clasped in her lap like a child who'd been told to sit still in church. Dakota had reached her full height of five foot ten, standing a good four inches taller than her thirteen-year-old self. But her mother hadn't grown at all.

Dakota returned to the living room with a cool glass of water, which she handed to her mother with care. Then she sat down on a tufted orange recliner with matching ottoman, a well-preserved mid-century modern set that would have fetched at least $3,000 from that posh vintage store near her best friend Jeremy's place in Huron Village. Which was funny because her parents had probably picked it up at Goodwill for a pittance.

"Everything I thought I'd say to you. I mean, I rehearsed it in my head a million times, but now, it's all gone out of my head." Dakota stared down at her hands.

"And I'm wondering what's wrong with *my* head, to have let a strange woman—who intimates that she's an older, a *much* older, version of my thirteen-year-old daughter—into my home." Dakota lifted her gaze. Her mother's eyes looked like saucers. "I only did it once."

"Did what once?"

"Acid," she whispered. "Jax and I were at an off-campus party our senior year. We didn't even know about the side effects in those days. But I'll tell you this. I wasn't a fan. I remember staring at a big glass fish tank that was in the room. Then I was in the fish tank, and I felt like I was drowning. I was gasping for air." She moved a hand to her throat. "I didn't think there would be long-term effects, but clearly I'm experiencing them because I'm having a psychotic episode."

"You're not having a psychotic break, Mom," Dakota said. "This is real. I'm real." Dakota fixed her gaze on her mother. "I *am* your daughter, Dakota. And I've come a very long way to see you again." *Don't cry. You don't want to overwhelm her…oh God. I'm already overwhelming her.*

"I need your father…I mean Jax. I need him home." She was quivering.

Dakota moved to the sofa and rubbed her mother's back. "I know this is scary. In fact, no one at my company, except the brilliant scientist who got me here and the people who work for him, knows about the time travel." She touched her knee to her mother's. "And if I did tell them about it, they would think *I'm* the one having a psychotic break. Especially my friend Jeremy. He would freak the hell out."

"So not everyone travels from the future to visit their mother in the past?" Her mother bit her lower lip. "Though I'm not conceding anything, mind you, because you're claiming the impossible."

Dakota twisted the MIT Brass Rat ring on her right hand. "How can I convince you I'm telling the truth?"

"Why don't we start over?" Her mother slid away from Dakota. "First, prove you're my daughter and not an FBI agent who has me and my husband on some un-American activities list."

"I assure you I am not the reincarnation of J. Edgar Hoover."

"Not a spy then."

"Definitely not a spy," Dakota said. "And I can corroborate that with facts. You and Daddy met at Brown University in 1965 during an anti-Vietnam rally."

"You could have found that on microfilm."

She heaved a sigh. "Daddy liked to say he'd fallen in love at first sight when you wrapped yourself in an American flag—and then you burned it." Her mother's eyes bulged. *Okay, I've got her interested.* "You told me I wasn't planned but you were delighted to learn you were pregnant."

"Any mother worth her salt would say that."

"Right. But would any mother say it was a minor miracle that my grandparents weren't at each other's throats for the first time in history when you brought me home from the hospital?"

"Oh God. They're still like that." Her mother laughed.

"Well, Daddy's parents were Boston Brahmins who were hoping he'd marry a girl from Vassar who wore pearls at all hours of the day."

"And night. Except perhaps to bed."

"But they ended up with you instead. A radical peacenik who liked to rail against the establishment," Dakota said.

"I still do, you know," her mother said, smiling. "Bring on the socialists. To hell with the rich." She pumped her fist.

"You might want to rethink that last part."

"What do you care about the rich?" She blinked her eyes fast.

"I'm sorry to tell you this, Mom, but I guess I'm pretty rich."

"You mean rich in spirit?" She looked hopeful.

"Gosh, I sure hope so." Dakota played with her wristwatch. "But I also mean rich on a financial level."

"Could you buy a Cadillac?"

"Yes."

"Could you buy this building?"

"Yup."

"A villa in France?"

"I have one in Italy. I'd love to bring you and Daddy there."

"Are you richer than the Vatican?"

"You got me on that one." Dakota snorted. "I think the Vatican's richer. But not by that much."

"I imagine the Michelangelo on the Sistine Chapel is worth a pretty penny," her mother said.

"And that ceiling wouldn't fit in my condo so I'm not that interested." Dakota chuckled.

"I'm still not convinced you're my daughter." Her mother scratched her chin. "But as a concerned citizen, I'm curious. How did you acquire such wealth? I hope you didn't rob a bank."

"Nope. I founded a cybersecurity company named KODA after I graduated from MIT with a PhD in cybercryptography," Dakota said. "That was in 2001."

"Forgive my language, but what the hell is cybercryptography?"

"You've heard of computers, right?"

"Of course." She frowned. "Your father thinks everyone will have a Macintosh computer before we know it."

"Good call, Dad. Too bad he never bought stock in Apple," she said. "You're slipping up, by the way. You called him my father."

"If you were actually my daughter, you'd know we would never invest in the stock market."

"I am your daughter." Dakota looked her mother in the eye. "I remember you calling it a form of gambling."

"It's a cultural ill, dear."

Dakota ignored her. "Can I tell you why I've come?"

"Couldn't get tickets to Disneyland?" Her mother raised her left eyebrow like Spock.

"Oh, this is hard. I've wanted to see you every day since I last… saw you. But I'm not sure I can say what I came here to say." Dakota ran her hands over her face. Her mother touched Dakota's sleeve with powdery fingers.

"You do tug at my heart, I must admit." Her mother tilted her head to the side and stared at Dakota. "And it's disturbing how familiar you look," she said. "You remind me of my aunt Helen. Your nose, your mouth too."

Dakota brushed her lips against her mother's temple. "I'd forgotten your smell." Dakota closed her eyes and inhaled. "Like fresh-baked bread," she said, her voice trembling.

"There are worse smells, I suppose," her mother said. Her gaze was so soft and warm, Dakota's breath caught in her throat.

"Let's recap where we are." Her mother brought her fingertips to her chin. "You say you're my daughter, though you're what…twelve years older than I am now because you've traveled back in time to have an important conversation with me. I don't know what you've come to say, but it can't be easy because your eyebrows are scrunched in that worry-face that reminds me of my thirteen-year-old daughter." She paused for a breath. "Who is at the library at this very moment while I look at you and wonder what in God's name is happening." She tilted her head, continuing her visual scrutiny.

"I have to tell you why I came, Mommy." Dakota blinked back tears until her nostrils burned. "I'm just not sure I can do it."

"You're very emotional for a stranger." Her mother placed a hand on Dakota's wrist and rubbed it gently. Then she backed away. "I can't for the life of me understand why a woman your age, who bears an odd resemblance to my child, would knock on my door and tell me she's my grown daughter, come from the future to visit me."

"I always told myself I would move heaven and earth to see you again," Dakota said, her chin trembling. "And now I've done it. Please believe that I am here with you."

"I might as well believe in unicorns or space aliens." Her eyes bore into Dakota's. If they'd been in a staring contest, her mother would have obliterated her.

"I have proof," Dakota said. She pulled her driver's license from her wallet and handed it to her mother.

"Dakota Wynfred. Birthday, November 10, 1972. We'll have to see about that." She took a quick glance at Dakota. "Height, five feet, ten inches." She whistled. "Jeezus, you're tall." Then she giggled.

"I must have gotten my height from Daddy." She winked at her mother. "Because you're what? Five foot four?"

"Five foot *five*." She narrowed her eyes at Dakota.

Dakota's breath felt jagged. *Oh. There's that look. The one she gave me and Daddy when she was really ticked off.*

"My mistake," Dakota said. "It says so on your license, right?" With a six foot three husband and a thirteen-year-old who already had four inches on her, Dakota's mother always fibbed about her height. It was one of her few expressions of vanity.

"*My* license is a matter of public record." Her mother crossed her arms. "But yours might be a fake, for all we know." She nibbled on her fingernail. "But the question is: Why would you make the effort?"

"Telling you that is the hard part." A wave of sorrow swelled in Dakota's chest and rose toward her eyes. But she refused to cry. Too soon. Too soon.

"Then I will have to guess." Her mother drummed her fingers against her thigh. "I'm not conceding that you're my daughter, but I do want to get to the bottom of this. So, for the sake of argument, I will *pretend* you're my daughter as I ask some probing questions." She narrowed her eyes at Dakota. "Did I drive you crazy during adolescence, become one of those mothers who shamed their daughters for their beauty?"

Dakota rolled her eyes.

"Did your father's obsession with Bob Dylan cause you permanent damage?"

"No, but I do loathe Bob Dylan."

"Ditto." Her mother giggled. Then she went quiet for a moment. "I don't know what it is, but I must have done something." She shook her head.

"No, it's nothing that you did or didn't do. You weren't responsible for it. It just happened. It happened to all of us." Dakota gestured with open arms. "Some people call it an act of God. Although our family doesn't believe in God."

"Not a Judeo-Christian God, at any rate."

"Definitely not Judeo-Christian."

"Nor one from any organized religion."

"Then from a disorganized religion."

"Got it," her mother said. "An act of God from a disorganized religion caused something that inspired you to travel back in time to see me."

Dakota hoped she didn't look as sick as she felt.

"I'm a big girl, Dakota. You can tell me."

Dakota twirled the ends of her hair.

"You still do that?" Her mother smiled. "I find that so endearing."

Dakota shifted in her seat. "Mom," she said. "Remember two years ago when you had that breast biopsy come back benign?"

She nodded.

"And next week you have a doctor's appointment, right?"

Another nod.

"The doctor's going to find a lump in your left breast. He'll send you for a biopsy, and this time it's malignant." If she squeezed any closer to her mother, she'd be sitting on her lap.

"Just how malignant is it?"

"It's already metastasized." She grabbed her mother in a bear hug, then buried her head in the curve of her mother's neck.

"Oh shit," she said. "Shit, shit, shit and goddamn it all to hell."

"I'm so sorry, so terribly sorry to tell you this." Dakota pulled a sleeve across her face.

"How long do I have?"

"Not long, I'm afraid."

Her mother swallowed.

"But I have an idea." Dakota's eyes gleamed. "If you come with me soon, come to my time, that is, which is 2026, we'll get you to the best oncologists in the country. I'm sure we could cure you."

She shook her head. "I'm not leaving you or your father, Dakota…. I mean, I'm not going to just disappear on you. That would be even more scarring."

"Daddy can come too, Mom," she said. "You guys are going to love it. My condo overlooks the Charles, and it's big enough for all of us."

"And what would your father and I do in your future world?" she said.

"Anything you want, Mom," she said. "We'll start a foundation, and you and Daddy can run it."

"What kind of foundation?" Her mother tilted her head to the side.

"Anything you feel passionate about," Dakota said. "Voting rights. Climate change. Reproductive freedom. LGBTQ…I mean, gay rights."

"What's the problem with voting rights? And what do you mean climate change?" She pinched her lips. "And you can't be talking about a woman's right to choose, can you? You were just a baby, but your dad and I took you on a bus to Washington when the Supreme Court was hearing Roe versus Wade. Tell me that's not in jeopardy."

"Abortion is all but illegal in more than half of the country," Dakota said. Her mother gasped. "And voting rights have been in jeopardy for years because the Republicans have done everything humanly possible to disenfranchise people of color, especially Blacks."

"Yegads. That's horrendous."

"I'm also sorry to tell you that we've done a number on the environment," Dakota said. "Global warming is a massive problem. I give loads of money to the Sierra Club, and I drive an electric car. We've got to stop the polar ice caps melting."

"I think I'm going to throw up."

"Sorry. I'm chucking an awful lot at you."

"Back up," her mother said. "What does, LGB whatever-it-is-you-said, mean?"

"LGBTQ is the term." Dakota pronounced every letter clearly, sounding like a sixth-grade teacher in health-ed class. But not a teacher in states like Florida and Texas, where the most zealous Vlakians had banned any mention of LGBTQ in written or spoken form in public schools. Every day seemed to bring another vicious move from the house of Vlakas. She'd almost come to expect feeling her blood boil when she scanned the daily news.

Dakota felt a light tap on the arm. Her mother must have sensed her distraction.

"Sorry about that." Dakota gave a quick headshake. "I drifted off for a second." She resumed her lesson in pop nomenclature. "LGBTQ stands for lesbian gay bisexual transgender queer. But of course, you wouldn't know that because no one was using those words in your time."

"Nonsense." Her mother folded her arms across her chest. "Jax and I know plenty of gay men. And lesbians practically ran the commune." She would have rolled her eyes at Dakota if parents did that to their children and not vice versa. "We're hardly social conservatives." She looked askance at Dakota. "Do you have…someone, dear? Are you telling me you're gay?"

"Mom." Dakota drew the word out like an angry teenager. "We were talking about a foundation for you and Dad."

"That's right." Her mother nodded and paused for a moment. "Can we go back to the time-travel part again?"

"Of course."

"If your dad and I go to the future with you, what happens to you as a child?" She pulled on her earlobe.

"If Kisai's right—and he's been right about everything else when it comes to time-travel, so why doubt him now…." Dakota was speed-talking. "He believes that when you leave this time for 2026, that the you who lived this life will stay here while the traveling you lives a new life in the future."

"Who's Kisai?"

"Kisai is the most brilliant physicist on the planet. He's the pioneer in time travel, and he works for me." Dakota popped up from the sofa.

"And what does he say again?"

"He theorizes, and that's based on a ton of research, so I believe it…." She moved her hands like she'd just caught a big fish. "He says that during the picosecond when you and Daddy leave here with me and travel to the future, you will have lived your lives in their entirety. But your future selves get to live another life with me."

"Huh?"

"What Kisai means is you don't have to worry about leaving me here because by the time you and Dad reach 2026, the you who's with me today and the Dad who's at the library with me right now won't be plucked from 1984 in a way that leaves a gaping hole. You'll live the rest of your lives in this linear chronology." Dakota cleared her throat. "But by the time we reach 2026, your natural lifespans will have run their course…."

"Because both of us will have died by then…."

Dakota stared at the floor.

"Such a relief." Her mother ran her hands through the long tendrils of her hair. "I don't know why I might worry." She closed her eyes and sighed. Then she looked up at Dakota, her eyes full of tears. "Oh, Dakota. I love you so much, and it breaks my heart that I'm going to have to leave you when you're still young. But as much as I want to be with you, I don't want to leap into a future with melting polar ice caps, a disenfranchised population, and having to fight for a right that we secured for women in 1973." She took a long breath.

"Plus, you can't guarantee that your father and I won't be abandoning you as a thirteen-year-old, left to fend for yourself." Her chin began to tremble. "That's a chance I'm not willing to take because it would change history, your history, and I've read enough science fiction to know that the ramifications of such a move could be devastating for your future." Her mother crossed her arms.

"But, Mom. I know it'll work." Dakota felt like her throat was closing. "We won't take anything away from the me you already know. And you and Daddy can have a full life with me as an adult."

Her mother sucked in her breath. "I believe in fate, honeybun," she said. "Yours, mine, and Daddy's." Her voice was quiet. "You know what happens when people try to play God."

"I'm not trying to play God," Dakota said. "I just want you to have a good life."

"I've had a good life, darling." Her mother used a dish towel from her back pocket to dab her eyes. "I have a husband I love and a daughter I adore. And that's enough. It's been enough."

"Maybe you should sleep on it, and I'll come back again."

Her mother lowered her voice. "I wish that I could join you, truly," she said. "I wish that you would never know the grief of losing your mother at such a young age." She swallowed hard. "But what if that loss helped form you in ways that you don't even realize?" She touched Dakota's cheek. "And what if having me and Daddy with you now would alter the course of your life moving forward?"

"But I've been planning this for years." Dakota crouched in front of her mother and squeezed both her hands. "I literally have every-thing worked out."

"Please don't look like that, sweetheart, or you'll break my heart in two." She bent her head to kiss Dakota's hands. "I want to hear about your life now. Tell me. What have you been doing since adolescence?"

Dakota pulled away and collapsed onto the orange recliner. She pushed the side lever down until she was in full recline and stared at the ceiling. She tried to gather her thoughts.

"Don't be angry with me, Dakota," her mother said. "You're asking for too much. I don't know your world. I don't know *you* in your world." Her mother's voice grew quiet. "But know that I love you more than anything in *my* world. And in under an hour, your dad is coming home with the you I do know." Her mother's voice broke. "I will do everything in my power to care for that you for as long as I possibly can."

Dakota sat up, her face wet with tears. "My life isn't easy, Mommy," she managed to eke out. "I need you in it." She wiped her runny nose with her sleeve.

"Oh, sweetheart," her mother said. She found Dakota in the chair and wrapped her arms around her. Squeezing. Holding. Loving. Just as Dakota had wanted a thousand times throughout her life.

After a good rush of crocodile tears, Dakota took her head off her mother's shoulder. "I got snot all over the back of your shirt, I think."

"It's not the first time," her mother said.

"But it will be the last…at least for me now."

For a couple of minutes, Dakota sat quietly in the chair while her mother stayed crouched beside her. Then her mother broke the silence.

"Tell me what's hard in your life," she said. "Maybe I can help you, in the little time we have."

"You're going to get cramps if you stay in that squat," Dakota said. She guided her mother back to the sofa. "I don't need you to fix anything, Mom, because I'm a big girl now."

Her mother patted her on the leg. "I know you are, darling."

"My life is super stressful," Dakota said. "I've built this amazing company. It's world-class, Mommy. Seriously. We're making the world a better place."

"I couldn't ask anything more of you." Her mother beamed at her.

"Well, technologically speaking," Dakota said in a mumble.

"That's something at least," her mother said.

"But the thing is, we're hearing chatter that our asshole of a president wants to nationalize my company," she said. "That means he'll take ownership from me."

"That's awful, honey," her mother said, her eyes pools of sympathy.

"And that's not the only thing." Dakota's back and chest felt hot. "During the last administration, we thought things were getting better. But now, it's so much worse. Racism. Women's rights. Gay rights. The environment. It's a total mess." She swallowed hard. "I'm scared for the country," Dakota said. "And I'm scared for myself." She looked into her mother's eyes. "And I have no idea how to make it better. None at all."

"Now that won't do for my Dakota." Her mother had fire in her eyes. "Because Daddy and I always taught you that change starts with one person." She fixed her gaze on Dakota. "And from what I know about my daughter as a child, and from the adult sitting here with me now, I believe that the change you need, that everyone needs—it starts with you."

So much love from one person. And so much faith. It's almost hard to bear. Dakota's chest swelled like the Grinch when his heart grows three times larger.

Dakota wasn't sure what a geek like her could do to change the world. She only knew that she would try.

CHAPTER 3

November 8, 1984, Cambridge, Massachusetts

Dakota's mother handed her a cup of Swiss Miss hot chocolate, her comfort drink of choice when she was a girl. "Wait," her mother said. "Why is the president called the 'Pickle King' again?"

"I know, right? It's so ridiculous," Dakota said. "He didn't…still doesn't…know anything about politics." She huffed. "He didn't even build his own company. He inherited it from his father, and you'll never believe his biggest contribution to the business."

"I can't imagine."

"He increased the amount of ultra-high fructose corn syrup in Vlakas products. Increased," she said. "One ounce of Vlakas sweet pickles has something like eighty grams of sugar."

"And that's a lot, right?"

"It's more than a grande Starbucks Frappuccino." Dakota wrinkled her nose. "The steak sauce and ketchup are even worse."

"Um. What's Starbucks?" Her mother grimaced. "What's a Frappuccino?"

"I forgot. This is way before Starbucks." Dakota scratched her head. "Starbucks is like the Coffee Connection in Harvard Square except super corporate. And it's literally everywhere," she said. "It's like an alien lifeforce that reproduces when you're not looking." She shuddered.

"Sounds like a nice place." Her mother didn't skip a beat. "And the Frappuccino is?"

"A frozen coffee drink that has about nine million calories," Dakota said.

"And it gives you diabetes."

"At the very least, it would spike your insulin into the stratosphere."

"So this Vlakas is not a proponent of good health."

"His company motto is *Twice the Corn Syrup. Twice the Taste*®."

"Remind me, because this is after my time." Her mother smiled weakly. "When was this blockhead elected?"

"In 2024. But he didn't win fairly."

"Does anyone?"

"This guy had a lot of help from the Russians."

"You mean the Soviet Union?"

"The Soviet Union fell in around '90, I think. I'm talking about just Russia."

"I feel sick to my stomach."

"Sorry, Mom," Dakota said. "It's a lot to process."

"That's okay. I'm pretty sure I'll get through it." Her mother rubbed her temples. "I feel like I'm missing part of the picture. I understand that Vlakas is a leading cause of dental decay. Also, he's president. But why does he want your company?"

"Because KODA's the most successful cybersecurity firm in the world, and that makes us very powerful." Dakota raised her chin. "Mmm…and I may have said something to *The New York Times* about Vlakas being a moron of gargantuan proportions for using his iPhone to send work emails."

"What's an iPhone? What's email?"

Dakota giggled. "You must think I'm from *Star Trek*."

"I think you're giving me heart palpitations."

"Sorry, Mommy," she said. "An iPhone is a sophisticated portable phone that's like a miniature computer in your pocket. It also makes phone calls."

Her mother sighed.

"And email stands for electronic mail. It's like an instant messaging system that we use all the time." No response. "You can reach people all over the planet, twenty-four hours a day, three hundred and sixty-five days a year."

"Why would you want to do that?" her mother said. "Don't people ever take vacation anymore?" She smoothed her apron. "I wouldn't want to be reachable at all hours of the day and night."

"Mom." Dakota rolled her eyes. "Email has changed everything. You can communicate with friends and family—not just co-workers," she said. "Email really is amazing. You can send photos and stories or contracts. Whatever you want." She glanced at her mother, who still looked unimpressed. "Maybe it wouldn't be your cup of tea, but it's…" *How do I say this? Life-critical? Vital? Essential?* "It's essential in today's world, and my company delivers the industry's most secure email servers and clients."

"Huh?"

"My company protects our clients' business interests, whether those clients are national governments, commercial institutions, or secretive research and development."

"Now that sounds important." Her mother smiled. She sat down and squeezed close to Dakota.

"Tell me this," her mother said. "If Vlakas used your company— KODA, right?" Dakota nodded. "For his phone's email, then this vulnerability wouldn't have happened, and he wouldn't be after your company."

"I may have done one or two other things that annoyed him."

"Such as?"

"I was a major supporter of Jennifer Samson." *Whom she doesn't know.* "She was acting vice president in 2020, and I was her single biggest donor." Dakota grinned. "Even the private fundraiser I held for her set a record. Twelve million dollars in a single night, with movie stars and tons of CEOs from the tech industry and profes- sional athletes and…"

"Anyone from the public library or Harvest Co-op there?"

Dakota exhaled loudly. "I get the point, Mom. The rich and famous influence the people's choice of candidate."

"As they have always done." Her mother gave her a pat.

"As they will always do, I think." Dakota returned the pat. "Which doesn't make it right, but I did what I could within the con- straints of a flawed system."

"But Samson still lost."

"She did."

"The picture's becoming clearer," her mother said. "You insulted the president and championed his opponent, and he wants revenge."

"Yup."

Her mother gazed out the window for a moment. "You also said something about Vlakas tearing the country apart. What did you mean by that?"

Dakota clenched her jaw. "Vlakas is a xenophobic misogynist racist anti-science whackadoodle, who wants to make abortion pun- ishable by death." She paused for effect.

"You mean women who get abortions are going to get the death penalty?" Her mother's expression could have crumbled the Pyramids.

"No, doctors who perform abortions get the death penalty. The women just go to jail."

Her mother's mouth gaped.

"That's not exactly true in the blue states," Dakota said.

"What the hell are the blue states?" Her mother blinked in rapid succession.

"It's a symbolic thing," Dakota said. "One of the TV news sta- tions invented it around the early 2000s to show viewers at home which presidential candidate had won a particular state. Red was for Republican, and blue for Democrat. Now every news network colors the states this way on election night, and it's become part of the nomenclature to talk about red and blue states. You might say, 'I live in Cambridge, the bluest city in the bluest state in the country,' or, 'Hell no I'm not going to Texas, it's too red—unless, of course, you're talking about Austin, which is fine because it's in a blue bubble.'"

"We've always had geographic divisions around politics, back to before the Civil War." Her mother brushed her hand against her forehead, leaving white blobs of flour stuck in weird places.

"It's almost as bad as the Civil War," Dakota said. "Except most of the battles are fought with words, not weapons."

"Remember what Lincoln said: 'A house divided against itself cannot stand.'"

"Our house's foundation is made of sand," Dakota said. "It's a giant sinkhole. We could fall in at any moment."

"I get the picture," her mother said. "The country's falling apart, civil liberties are getting crushed, and Vlakas wants your business." Her mother tapped her fingers together. "Things are not so swell."

"Which is another reason I want you and Daddy to come back with me." Dakota looked into her mother's eyes. "I need your support."

"We've been through this." Her mother's voice was breaking. "I will be there with you in spirit."

Dakota dragged her foot in circles on the floor. Her mother took her by the hands.

"You're seeing injustice, Dakota, and you know what to do."

"I know, I know. It's my responsibility to change it."

"That's right." Her mother smiled. "And from what you're saying, you're in a privileged position, which makes you the kind of person who can effect change."

"I'm going to fight the administration with everything I've got." Dakota clenched her fists. "There's no precedent for an administration privatizing a company like mine."

"So they don't have a case?"

"There's no sound legal argument for what the Justice Department is attempting. That's true," she said. "But that's never stopped Vlakas. And if it goes to the Supreme Court, we're dead in the water."

"Because?"

"Because he's got six out of nine justices in his pocket." She shook her head. "I think we'd lose." She clamped her teeth together.

"Let's get creative." Her mother sprang out of her seat, like a cheerful Mary Poppins. "What can you do to save your company?"

"And save the world. Don't forget that." Dakota gave her mother a wide smile. "Remember the elephants?"

"Of course." Her mother gave her peck on the cheek. "I remember you going door to door, all over the neighborhood, to get signatures on your petition to ban the sale of ivory in the United States."

Dakota patted her chest. "I got over five hundred signatures."

"And that helped, right?"

"We did eventually ban ivory, but it's still a problem in Asia," she said. "I do fund an elephant sanctuary in Thailand. And one in Tennessee that cares for elephants rescued from circuses and private compounds."

"I'm proud of you, baby," her mother said. "And now, back to the problem at hand."

"Oh hell. I don't want to get into politics again." Dakota hunched her shoulders. "It's soul-crushing, but I don't know how to get away from it."

"You can't give up." Her mother stroked her daughter's cheek. "Why don't you try to get Samson elected again?"

"Because she was vilified by the Vlakas campaign. They annihilated her character. Called her an unfit mother for leaving her son's first birthday party because of a crisis in the Middle East." Dakota flexed her biceps. "You don't even want to know what happened when Fox News unearthed what Samson had written about Presidents' Day when she was still an undergrad at Harvard."

"Oh boy."

"Her op-ed in the student newspaper ran thirty years ago," Dakota shook her head in disgust. "Samson said that Presidents' Day dishonors the experience of Black Americans. That we should honor the contributions of Washington and Jefferson to the democratic *institution* of our political system, but we shouldn't call them heroes. They were unapologetic slave owners after all. Washington owned between three and four hundred enslaved Africans in his lifetime, and Jefferson had up to six hundred."

"Which included poor Sally Hemmings."

"Who let's not forget bore him seven children," said Dakota. "Samson included that little tidbit in her piece. And the Vlakas campaign, which still denies the existence of racism, called her a Black supremacist, who didn't have the same values as white Americans. Dakota tensed her jaw muscles. "Samson was the worst of woke, Vlakas said during every campaign rally. The label went viral, and Samson never recovered," she said. "Even the moderates were running for the hills by the time Vlakas finished with her."

"And people care about these things?"

"They do when they feel alienated by the other political party," Dakota said. "We call this 'identity politics.' You'll vote for your candidate even if they've committed a crime because they're your candidate." She snorted. "And race is as painful a topic as I can ever remember. Vlakas said Samson belonged on a bottle of maple syrup—not in the White House."

"Like Aunt Jemima?"

"Exactly," Dakota said. "Though Vlakas is too much of a navel-gazer to realize Quaker Oats finally took her off the packaging."

"Sickening." Her mother glowered. "It's like the Civil Rights movement never happened."

"Samson got so many death threats, she had to cancel the rest of her rallies," Dakota said.

"It's almost like we need someone with no past, so nothing they've said can be exploited," her mother said.

"And we need someone powerful," Dakota said.

"And politically astute," her mother said.

"Someone tough."

"But someone kind." Her mother touched her arm.

"Someone inspirational."

"Someone charming."

"Someone brilliant."

"Someone worldly," her mother said.

"But not quite of this world," Dakota said.

"You know who we need, don't you?"

Dakota shook her head.

"We need someone who's a legendary leader," her mother said. Then she fixed her gaze on Dakota and said, "I'm assuming you can use your time-travel thing to whisk someone from the past into the present."

"Like I wanted to do with you and Daddy," Dakota said, her voice just above a whisper.

Her mother's face dropped for an instant. Dakota would have missed it if she had blinked her eyes. "Buck up, honey. We'll figure it out." Her mother brushed her knuckles against Dakota's face, and Dakota leaned into her mother's hand. They sat like that for a moment without saying a thing.

Her mother broke the silence. "I think you need someone who died before there were photos," she said. "You couldn't bring back John Kennedy, or even Abraham Lincoln, and not have somebody recognize them. It'll be like they've come out of nowhere."

"That's brilliant," Dakota said, her mood lifting slightly.

"She'd be a complete unknown—except to you," her mother said.

"Except to me and a small circle of friends," Dakota said. "And Kisai. And some people that I don't know yet but will find."

"Let's come up with some names." Her mother gave a clap. "Who do you like?"

"How about Babe Didrikson?"

"Too butch."

"Harriet Tubman?" her mother said.

"Too Black," Dakota said, wincing.

"Anne Frank?"

"Too young."

"Marie Curie?"

"Too French."

"Amelia Earhart?" her mother said.

"Too flighty," Dakota said. She felt a punch on the arm.

"Walter Cronkite?"

"Too male," Dakota said.

"To sum up," her mother said. "We need an amazing woman who knew how to rule in a world of men, right?"

"We need a fearless woman who could lead troops into battle."

"Figuratively speaking, I guess," her mother said.

"Sure," Dakota said.

"How about one of our favorite women from history?" Her mother walked over to the aging wooden television console and plucked a video cassette box from the beige plastic case of VHS tapes stored on its top. Her smile was radiant as she handed it to Dakota.

"No."

"Yes." Her mother gave Dakota a tiny push. "We loved watching this together, remember?"

"Of course, I remember." Dakota took the box from her mother and hugged it to her chest. "*Elizabeth R* with Glenda Jackson. I adored it."

"I watched it with Daddy on Masterpiece Theatre in '71. It came out on VHS when you were ten or twelve," her mother said.

"I was eight." Dakota giggled. "What a history nerd." She looked at the white-faced woman with the pearl earrings, lace ruff, and bejeweled headdress.

"She ushered in the English Renaissance."

"She shored up the national treasury," Dakota said.

"She defeated the Spanish Armada," her mother said.

"She held her own, surrounded by powerful courtiers and wooed by foreign princes."

"She never married."

"I will have but one mistress."

"And no master."

"You are brilliant, Mom." Dakota dropped her head toward her shoulder. "You're also insane."

"Let's stick with brilliant." Her mother did a snort-laugh.

"Suppose I move ahead with this." Dakota drummed her fingers on her thigh. "There are heaps of impracticalities to conquer."

"That never stopped you as a child," her mother said. "And it's clearly never stopped you as an adult."

"Thanks for the vote of confidence," Dakota said. "But what would Kisai say?" Her eyes grew wide. "Hell, what would Jeremy say? He's going to blow a gasket."

"Jeremy will be fine," her mother said. "Whoever he is."

"He's the chief security officer at my company. He's something of a boy genius, actually. Started his freshman year at MIT when he was only sixteen," Dakota said. "And got his PhD seven years later, the year after I got mine."

"Perhaps he's just a very smart work friend?" her mother said.

"He's much more than that."

"Oh, I see." Her mother raised her eyebrows like she'd discovered something saucy.

"No, no, no. Erase the thought, please." Dakota held her hands up in the air. "I love Jeremy like a brother. A kind, funny, brilliant, younger—and gay—brother who's always by my side, though he sometimes drives me crazy…." She gave a half-laugh. "I wish you could meet him." Dakota felt like a powerlifter was squeezing the blood from her heart.

"It's good to have a best friend like that." Her mother's smile was like warm cocoa and Christmas cookies, s'mores by the fire, fresh cider donuts on a crisp October afternoon. All the best things that life had to offer. Dakota had missed it so much.

"I'm lucky to have friends like him," Dakota said quietly.

"Oh, my dear." Her mother clapped a hand to her mouth. "I don't even know…." She gazed into Dakota's eyes. "Do you have a family of your own? A husband? A child?"

"No, no." Dakota shook her head. "That wasn't part of my plan."

"Why not?" Her mother dropped the corners of her mouth. *That's her sad face. I don't want to make her sad.*

"I *could* tell you I don't have time for dating, though it's only partly true." Dakota picked at her fingernails. "I have dated in the past, some really nice guys, in fact." She looked up at her mother. "But I didn't think any of them could handle being with a CEO first…and a woman second."

"Well, don't give up, darling." Her mother furrowed her brow. "All you need is a confident man. A man who's successful in his own right, so he's not intimidated by your accomplishments."

"Mom." Dakota uttered an exaggerated sigh. "I do have one or two other fires to put out."

"I get it, honeybun." She did a slow blink. "Just don't give up. That's all I'm saying."

"I promise to consider it." Dakota crossed her arms in mock annoyance. "*After* I save the world." She winked at her mother. Who was staring at the clock on the wall.

"Dakota, it's almost eleven, and you—the younger you…" Her mother cleared her throat. "And Daddy are going to be home soon."

"I don't want to go yet." Dakota sniffled. *I can't believe I'm going to lose her again.*

"And I don't want you to either." Her mother grabbed her in a mama-bear hug. It was hard to breathe. "But you'd probably screw up the space-time continuum or do some other irreparable cosmic damage if you meet yourself at age thirteen, so I think you have to leave." Her mother bit her lip.

Dakota edged toward the door. "I guess I'll be going then." She sucked back her tears.

"Onto the next stop, darling," her mother said with false cheer.

"That's right, Mommy," Dakota said. "First to Cambridge, and then?"

"Tudor England."

"Tudor England it is."

Dakota bent down to hug her mother. She squeezed her and held on. It was almost impossible to let go.

Tearing herself away without stealing a look back, Dakota walked out the door and down the steps of her old Warren Street home. She made it down the block before she started sobbing, turning onto

Cambridge Street, where she passed the local "package" store—which meant liquor store in Massachusetts-speak at a time when you couldn't even buy beer or wine in a grocery store or minimart. She paused in front of the bakery closest to her house. The smell of the Portuguese sweet bread still made her mouth water. Though her eyes were as fuzzy as her torn-up heart, she observed more vacant signs than she remembered on the old brick buildings that then characterized East Cambridge.

Finally. Take 6th to Gore. She made the turns and stumbled her way to the back of the old hockey rink, intermittently wiping her face on her sleeve. She cried so hard, snot and tears spilled all over the ground. She sank into a squat, and stayed down until the wave of grief passed by.

This is awful. It's like I've lost her all over again. She licked her lips and tasted salty tears.

When she recovered enough to stand, she pulled a titanium box out of her pocket—Kisai had told her to hang onto it for dear life—and pressed her fingerprint to the top. When it opened, she held it up to her eye for the retinal scan. Before she could take another breath, she experienced that same lung-crushing, head-spinning, gut-screwing sensation that meant she was in transit. It was like being in a blender.

God, my mouth is dry. Now flat on her back, she heard the sound of feet running toward her. Dakota opened her eyes. A man with a white lab coat leaned over her. His bushy charcoal-gray hair was like a crown above his head. His gold wire-rimmed bifocals made his dark eyes look gigantic.

"Kisai." She choked out his name. Then she started to heave.

Kisai pulled a white handkerchief from his pocket and handed it to her. Her father used to do the same thing.

"Thanks." She wiped her face. "I think my mind is blown." She was struck by a fresh wave of sorrow.

Kisai bent down to take her hands. He'd never touched her before.

"I know your heart is hurting," Kisai said. "I hope this wasn't a mistake." His voice trailed off.

"Not at all." Dakota pushed herself to sitting. "It was the most amazing moment of my life, and I will always be grateful to you for giving me the experience," she said, her voice unsteady.

Kisai pushed his hand against the back of his head. He looked down at the floor.

Uh oh. I've embarrassed him. She stood up and gave him a head bow. He did the same.

"That was incredible, Kisai," she said. "And my mom helped me come up with an idea," she gave him a slow smile. "You'll never believe where we're going next."

CHAPTER 4

December 10, 2026, Charlestown, Massachusetts

"*Geuge Mwongmi*, Dakota." Her CSO and BFF, Jeremy Jiang, was swearing in Korean over the phone. Which was usually a bad sign. "It's already four o'clock, and you're nowhere to be found. You must be mucking about with Kisai in the secret lab yet again while I'm up here putting out fires. You've been so weird since your birthday." Jeremy was miffed. She imagined him as a cartoon character with a fire-engine-red face and smoke billowing from his ears.

"I know I've been leaning on you a lot lately. Which I appreciate, by the way," Dakota said.

"In case you've been wondering what I've been doing while you've been slurping down blender drinks in Kisai's lair, we've been tracking new chatter from Homeland Security, specifically CISA," Jeremy said, referring to Cybersecurity & Infrastructure Security's Cybersecurity Division, a ridiculous name that always made Dakota think of Monty Python's Department of Redundancy Department. "V is taking his fight with us public."

Jeremy didn't like using Vlakas's name on the odd chance his cryptophone got hacked.

"Oh crud."

"Crud is an understatement," Jeremy said, his voice dropping an octave. She imagined a scowl forming over those thick black eyebrows she so admired. "You already know that Justice is going to claim KODA is compromising national security by working with enemies of the United States."

"Which is completely absurd," Dakota spoke in a growl. "Justice knows we're not working with China, North Korea, Iran, Russia, or any other country unfriendly towards the US.

"Of course, they know, but they don't really care," Jeremy said. "They'd rather skewer those twin evil empires, France and Germany." He snorted in disgust.

She started to choke on her own spit. "How could this have happened?"

"First you pissed off V with that quote you gave *The New York Times* about him probably sending classified information from his iPhone's email."

"I said 'possibly sending' not 'probably,'" Dakota said. "I don't care how many shitty Instas he posted about me afterward. I had so much fun with that story." She cleared her throat. "But what does this have to do with France and Germany?"

"Remember that photo of the German chancellor and the French president laughing when V spoke at the G8?"

Dakota chuckled. "Hilarious. I saved some of the memes."

"It's no laughing matter, Dakota. V's minions are laying out a disinformation campaign about KODA. They're going to leak a story that a couple of young hackers broke into the VAULT˚ servers of the German and French trade ministries, exposing the naked data to the masses."

"And what exactly did those 'naked data' reveal? A ban on Brie exports? A trade deficiency in sauerbraten?" Dakota tittered.

"It's a bit bigger than that," Jeremy deadpanned. "They'll say France and Germany are planning a trade war, starting with a forty percent import tax on American cars. That's hundreds of billions in lost revenue for our auto manufacturers."

"That's a bold-faced lie on so many levels." Dakota felt her throat constrict. "First, no one's ever cracked one of our VAULTs. Second, no European country would start a trade war with the US. We'd dec-imate them." Beads of sweat pooled on her forehead. "Just because they say it, it doesn't make it true."

"Of course not, but the seventy-five million people who voted for V will believe it," Jeremy said. "And a few million other trusting souls around the world might hop on the bus with them." Jeremy cleared his throat. "The fact is, if the president of the United States is the source of the story, it'll damage our reputation."

"I need a minute." Dakota scooched back on the cushioned office chair in the conference room on the lab floor. Luckily, the team had just left the room, so she had a few minutes alone. Which she very much needed. She started doing jumping jacks, her latest remedy for dealing with her mounting anxiety. After she did fifty, she took a few seconds to catch her breath and said, "Have you vetted this?"

"I just got off the phone with DR," Jeremy said, referring to David Richmond, a longtime supporter of KODA who was near the top the food chain at NSA. "He just confirmed it. We've got to meet with counsel to discuss our approach because this is going to hap-pen." Jeremy gave a loud sigh. "We're having an emergency meeting with counsel in the Core at 3:00 p.m. tomorrow. Don't be late." He hung up before Dakota could respond.

Uh oh. They only met at the Core to discuss the most critical topics. Equidistant from both Dakota's and Jeremy's offices on the top floor of the building, the Core was a metallic enclosure with a copper ceiling and insulated walls. Shielded from acoustic and elec-tromagnetic interference to make it impervious to spying ears, the Core was secure enough to make NSA jealous. *If* they knew about it. *Which* they didn't.

Jeremy liked to say that the SCIF, which stood for "Sensitive Compartmented Information Facility" in the Vlakas White House, was like a lame-ass version of the Core. "Who else uses metal for their conference rooms?" He liked to say. "Just us."

When Dakota once pointed out she was sure the Israelis had something just as secure, she'd never seen him look so deflated.

Still, the Core was just one jewel in the crown of KODA HQ, the enormous nineteenth-century brick warehouse she'd purchased and renovated after closing her first big contract with NSA. While the building was stunning on the inside—architecturally designed with high ceilings and polished concrete floors and flooded with natural light—it was a modern-day fortress within Charlestown Navy Yard. Whether driving or biking to work, every KODA staff person had to pass through a biometric fingerprint scanner before driving or biking through the gate to reach the parking garage. Elevators or stairs from the garage led to the lobby and to the upper floors. The secret lab, of course, had more specialized entry points.

Client entry to KODA was equally secure. Clients could use a video kiosk at the outside gate, and a staff person would escort them inside. Or they could reach KODA by water after flying into Boston Logan Airport and taking a water taxi to the Charlestown pier. The latter was always the preferred option for the highly secretive, or the highly paranoid.

Dakota shook herself back to the present. That familiar flash of heat that started at her head and worked its way down had engulfed her body once again. She took a slow exhale through her mouth as she visualized the woman in those annoying Painless Perimenopause° YouTube videos. That model of middle-aged serenity brushed her hot flashes away with a few minutes of mindful breathing. *The hell with her. I'm having a freakin' hot flash, and I can't control it.*

Jeremy was right. She had been a little distracted lately, but she had good reason. She was planning something truly transformative, never-before attempted, never even conceived of by another human being. The back of her neck tingled with electricity.

So what if her friends would call her a nutball? Nutball. Genius. There was hardly a difference.

When she'd divulged her Elizabeth-saves-the-world idea to CeCe after Thanksgiving dinner—which had been right after she told CeCe she'd visited her long-deceased mother, which had been terrifying because it had literally made CeCe speechless, which had never before happened during their thirty-plus-year friendship—she felt instinctively that CeCe could be swayed by some sort of proof. Which Dakota had given her during a carefully orchestrated visit to the lab on the Sunday after Thanksgiving. CeCe had walked into her guided tour as a skeptic. By the time she walked out, she'd only called Dakota's *plan* "insane" but not Dakota herself. That was something at least.

Dakota was less sure how to tell Jeremy, but she'd figure that out when the time came.

She knew some things for sure. As founder and CEO of KODA, she had to fix the crisis at her company. But until last month's visit to mother, she hadn't realized it was also her responsibility to fix the crisis in America. All she needed was the right sort of help.

The truth was Americans couldn't save America from themselves. But Queen Elizabeth I? If she could command a country before the advent of national press, television, or social media, she could right the wrongs of the Vlakas administration. Sure, she'd need a little guidance, but that's nothing Dakota couldn't handle. After all, she was a helluva salesperson when the time called for it.

And this was that time.

CHAPTER 5

December 11, 2026, Charlestown, Massachusetts

"Dakota. You're scribbling away on that legal pad instead of getting ready to meet," Jeremy said from his perch in the Core. "What the hell are you working on?"

"I think I've figured it out." Dakota caught herself beaming at Jeremy.

"And exactly what is 'it'?" he said. "World peace? Solving the climate crisis?" He raised his eyebrows.

"Almost as major, but not quite," she said, grinning. "I'm building personalized AI into VAULT, so anyone using our Courier email client won't have to worry about spoofing."

Jeremy's mouth gaped. "Are you serious?" He walked around the curve of the table and looked over her shoulder.

"Very," she said. "The AI will understand each user so intimately that it'll stop email imposters dead in their tracks." Her words spilled out like a waterfall. "Imagine you're about to buy a house, and you receive an email from your spouse telling you to wire money to a different bank account."

"Except it's not your spouse," Jeremy said. "It's a cybercriminal."

Dakota nodded with vigor. "And the AI will alert you in near real time, saving you God knows how much money."

"I'm blown away, D. Seriously." He clapped her on the back.

"KODA will be so far ahead of the industry that no one will even try catching us," Dakota said.

It amazed her that twenty-six years after launching VAULT, it was still the only integrated platform with the world's only Very Good Privacy cloud email server, which she'd named the TOWER˚. Dakota and her inaugural team had soon added COURIER˚, the email reader that came with the package.

Impermeable, elegant, and protected by a small army of patent attorneys, VAULT had made her very rich. The day she first cracked *Forbes*'s list of the four hundred richest Americans, Jeremy said she was taking him and CeCe to Italy. That's when she bought her villa in Positano on the Amalfi Coast. That was ten years ago, and her life had seemed so simple. And now? Not so much.

"I'm glad you're so excited," she said. "I am too." She looked up at the lean-muscled man with thick hair the color of dark-roast coffee beans. Jeremy, her nerd-handsome second in command. "But first, we need a plan. That was a brutal meeting we just had with counsel."

"*Jen-jang*," Jeremy said, using the Korean word for "shit." He returned to his chair and leaned back with his hands clasped behind his head. "If I had to listen to one more word of legalistic jargon as they explained how they plan to protect us from the pitchfork-waving villagers from Justice at our gates, I was going to lose it."

They both laughed.

"I can't believe they would suggest moving HQ to Europe to avoid the battle before us." Dakota scowled. "As if we'd even leave this beautiful building."

"Or your condo in Cambridge," Jeremy said.

"Or your house in Huron Village."

"Or Chef Will," Jeremy said. "It's not easy poaching a Michelin-starred chef for corporate cuisine, but you did it."

"And I have the extra seven pounds to prove it," Dakota said.

"Such a random number, seven."

"I dare you to say another word." Dakota scowled at him. "You have the metabolism of a hummingbird."

"Time to change the subject, I think," Jeremy said. "It's already five-thirty. Let me check on Sumiko." He started texting.

"Why are we meeting with Sumiko anyway? You still haven't told me."

There was a tap on the door. "Ah, there she is now," Jeremy said, opening the door for his resident hacker.

Sumiko Hong entered the room headfirst, her long black hair sweeping over the front of her fashionable white-and-gray checkered sweater-coat as she continued typing on her keyboard without saying hello. Dakota always marveled at Sumiko's ability to work on her laptop as she walked through the office. Amazing that she'd never collided with a person—or a wall. It's like she had crash-detection sensor embedded on the top of her head. Dakota wouldn't put it past the twenty-something Taiwanese woman whom Jeremy had discovered when he read her senior thesis on ethical hacking.

"I ask you, Dakota, who gets published in *Science* as a twenty-year-old?" Jeremy had waved the magazine with Sumiko's article at Dakota's face like an exuberant child with his first baseball glove. And seven years later, Sumiko was still Jeremy's right-hand person. Kind of like Jeremy was Dakota's. Except he was also a best friend.

Jeremy broke the silence. "Dakota, I think you've met Sumiko, right?" Sumiko raised her head and blinked at Dakota. Her slender eyebrows formed elegant crescents over brown eyes that revealed neurons firing at light speed.

"Of course," Dakota said. She waved at Sumiko. "I'm still not sure why we're meeting, though. Nothing personal, of course."

Jeremy cleared his throat. "I thought you'd want to know Sumiko has been doing some digging on Vlakas and Russia."

Russia, Russia, Russia. Why are we talking about Russia? If Dakota squeezed her eyes tight, she could almost see it. A wispy tuft of Grecian Formula brown hair jumping out from Vlakas's receding hairline, his double-breasted navy suit with gold buttons stretching tight across his girth as he stared up at the massive Great Bear of Russia. The bear opened its gigantic maw, displayed its jagged, rotten teeth, and breathed down on Vlakas, who opened his giant-grouper mouth and sucked in deeply. And Kazimir Sokolov? Vlakas probably had a portrait of the Russian president on the ceiling above his bed.

"I'm not sure where this is going, but I trust your judgement." She looked at Jeremy. "And you've got me very curious."

"Do you remember how you asked me to research Vlakas's relationship with Sokolov after all the stories about Russian interference in the 2024 election?" Jeremy said. "Sumiko has been tapping her sources since then, and she's just made a discovery that will blow your socks off." Jeremy pulled a purple file folder out of his laptop bag.

"Your hunch about Vlakas and Sokolov was spot-on," he said. "We found a strong financial incentive. Two years before the election, Vlakas had been courting Sokolov because he wanted to build the world's biggest sweet-pickle-processing plant on the banks of the Neva River in St. Petersburg. Vlakas planned to buy Russian corn to make the corn syrup used not just in the St. Petersburg plant but in his US plants as well. The all-GMO Russian corn is really cheap, about one-quarter the price of American-grown corn. Since the Vlakas products use more corn syrup per ounce than any other comestible in the world, Vlakas could make a lot of money. He also planned to divert a share of the profits directly to Sokolov."

"I'm not surprised by any of this. Vlakas cozied up to Sokolov for financial gain." Dakota drummed her fingers on the table. "I'm mystified, though. Why would Vlakas bother campaigning for president if his focus was on personal wealth?"

"It wasn't Vlakas's idea to be president." Sumiko locked her eyes on Dakota's. "It was Sokolov's."

Mic drop.

"This is where it gets really interesting." Jeremy wiggled his eyebrows. "Sokolov did not, under any circumstance, want Jennifer Samson to be president. She'd sanction Russia for territorial invasions and call them out on human rights' violations. And she'd get tough on the trade imbalance." Jeremy leaned toward Dakota. "Did you know that the US imported forty billion dollars of Russian goods last year but only exported ten billion dollars to Russia? And the number one import?" He paused for effect. "Russian steel."

Dakota shook her head in disgust. "I had no idea."

"That's because it was never made public," Jeremy said. "We found it in some classified State Department documents."

"And you won't believe this next part." Sumiko sprang from her seat. "Sokolov has serious dirt on Vlakas."

"I wish that were unbelievable." Dakota licked her lips as all moisture drained from her body. "I feel sick."

"That's because it's sickening," Jeremy said.

"When Vlakas secretly met with Sokolov in Moscow in 2022, Sokolov arranged for a lovely lady to have a private 'dinner' with Vlakas in his suite at Lotte Hotel Moscow." Sumiko used air quotes around "dinner."

"Oh God." Dakota flexed her jaw muscles.

"Ekaterina Pavlova. She was a twenty-three-year-old Russian model," Sumiko said, her eyes gleaming. "She spent four hours with Vlakas on May 22nd of that year. Just a little longer than your average dinner, wouldn't you say? One month later, Vlakas announced his candidacy for president."

"Do I want to know what happened in that hotel room?" Dakota said.

"I sincerely doubt it. But we must tell you because it's relevant," Jeremy said. "Sokolov had planted security cameras in Vlakas's suite. Sumiko hacked into the footage, which was archived on the hotel's server, if you can believe it. Sloppy work."

"It shows Vlakas wearing an olive-green army uniform with blue and gold epaulets, golden stars, a double-headed golden eagle. Now this part is incredible." Sumiko was speaking faster and louder. "That's the parade uniform of a Russian army general."

"And then what?" Dakota leaned toward Sumiko.

"Then he yells commands at Pavlova and tells her to undress and obey," Jeremy said. "She takes off her clothes and straddles him. He lies down on the bed and unzips. It's all over in one minute and five seconds. We counted." He smirked. "Then he falls asleep for an hour, wakes up, and asks her if it's the best sex she's ever had."

Dakota choked on a sip of water. "Yuck."

"We found an executable file with the video footage, sent to Vlakas's iPhone," Sumiko said. "It was embedded in an invitation from the Russian ambassador to the president of the United States. It said, 'Shall we meet?'"

"So Sokolov blackmailed Vlakas," Dakota said. "That's why Vlakas had to run for president. But that's not all. He gets to build his plant in St. Petersburg, making tons of money off Russian corn. And Sokolov gets kickbacks."

"And he owns Vlakas," Jeremy said. "He can get Vlakas to do whatever he wants."

"Okay. We know why Vlakas ran, and why Russia is his number one ally. That doesn't answer the question of whether Russia interfered in the election," Dakota said.

"You bet your booty they interfered," Jeremy said. "They were like the uninvited uncle who never leaves your party or the pushy grandmother who wants to set you up with the shopkeeper's daughter, who was missing her front teeth, by the way, or, or…" He shut his eyes and shivered.

"You're getting lost in weird examples," Dakota said.

"Right." He rose to write on the smart board. "Let me show you what they did."

Jeremy outlined Russia's involvement, from fake news on Facebook to hacking the Democratic National Committee's email server to siphoning campaign funds into the America Over All Super PAC. America Over All had poured $300 million into attack ads running on Fox News in some of the key battleground states, including Pennsylvania, Michigan, Ohio, Iowa, and Florida. Winning those states had helped Vlakas clinch the election.

Dakota turned toward her CSO. "What can I do with this information, legally speaking, and does it relate in some way to the Vlakas administration coming for KODA?"

"To answer the first part of your question, you'd have to go to the FBI. And I have some idea about how they'd receive it," Jeremy said, with eyes that could burn holes into furniture. "As we know from our work with NSA and DoD, the US government tends to value stability more than anything. The idea that a foreign country could not just influence a US presidential election but could also blackmail the person sitting in the Oval Office into doing their bidding would seriously undermine the perception of our country around the world.

"Not just that," he said. "If known, it could dismantle the foundation of our democracy. It could erode American faith in the electoral system. It would make our country look weak, and the FBI would consider that a death knell. And they might want to shoot the messenger."

CHAPTER 6

December 11, 2026, Charlestown, Massachusetts

*O*w. Dakota placed her palms on her chest as she leaned against the stall door. She needed a moment of privacy in the women's bathroom before returning to the Core for some one-on-one time with Jeremy. Damned heart palpitations. Sometimes the warmth from her hands eased the pain of her squeezing heart.

Later she'd call Hazel Robinson, a sixty-something Englishwoman who had been her personal physician for the past fifteen years, to talk about her hot flashes. You'd think Hazel was a high-priced concierge doctor, she was so responsive. But that wasn't the case at all. Hazel was like one of those old-time doctors that opened her doors to everyone, from people on MassHealth, which was Massachusetts's state-sponsored health insurance, to the very affluent. Serving patients from a small office on the second floor of a two-story, red-brick building overlooking Main Street in Concord center—just as she had been for the past thirty years—Hazel treated all her patients with equal care. Dakota had been drawn to Hazel's warmth from the start, and over the past few years, they'd become personal friends as well.

Dakota tried not to take advantage of that friendship, but when she was in hot-flash hell, like she was this morning, she knew that a call to Hazel would bring her some relief. Too many doctors were still telling women to "suck it up" when their perimenopausal symptoms hit. Hazel wasn't one of them. "There's no prize for suffering more," Hazel had once said to her. "And if I can use my medical training to help my patients suffer less, I will do everything in my power to make it so."

Maybe Dakota just needed a bump in her Effexor? *As long as I don't have to give up wine or chocolate, I'll be good to go.*

She peeked into the mirror as she washed her hands in the sink. *Bummer.* She used her finger to wipe the mascara smudge from underneath her eyes. *Jeezus. We've solved time travel. Why can't someone make a water-resistant mascara that lasts all day?*

She rapped on the door so she wouldn't surprise Jeremy. But she needn't have worried. He was bent over his laptop, plugging a Cat8 Ethernet cable into his machine. No Wi-Fi in the Core or in any of their offices. What's the point of cybersecurity if you're sharing all your data over Wi-Fi?

"You know how we thought Vlakas was targeting KODA just because it was personal for him?" Jeremy looked up at her.

"Yes." Dakota took her seat at the large round walnut table in the center of the room. "I'm not expecting a dinner invitation anytime soon." She examined her fingernails for a few seconds, then looked up at Jeremy. "Weren't you going to make a big reveal?" she said.

"I was just getting to that." He tapped his fingers together and wiggled his eyebrows like a mustachioed villain from a silent movie. "We've been doing more digging. Sokolov is the man behind the curtain. He is not happy that we've been thwarting his attempts to penetrate our clients' servers." He opened his laptop and pointed to a timeline on a PowerPoint slide. "Check this out. In May of this year, we stopped the GRU from worming their way into NATO's technical infrastructure. In September, we crushed them at the gates of NSA. And three weeks ago…" He started speaking louder. "…we put a blockade around Treasury. Squashed them like a bug."

"That was stellar work, Jeremy." Dakota patted his arm. "Your team has been killing it."

"That's right, baby." Jeremy grinned. "We are shutting them down." He flexed his biceps like a bodybuilder in a muscle-pose. "We beat that *tto-ra-i* Sokolov at his own game. What a nutjob."

"Which puts us directly in his crosshairs." Dakota noticed her fists clenching. She stood and paced around the room. "I'm glad to finally know what's motivating Vlakas." She stopped in her tracks. "But as we've already discussed with counsel, there's still no legal justification for nationalizing KODA." She returned to her chair.

"We do a lot of work with federal government institutions," Jeremy said. "NSA, DoD, Treasury."

"And government contractors," Dakota said.

"And US embassies," Jeremy said. "Justice could argue that our platform makes the US government vulnerable to cyber incursions that could endanger national security, and if they were to assume control of KODA by nationalizing it as a division of CISA, they could better preserve the integrity of their agencies and the ecosystems in which they play."

"You are effing…" Dakota slammed her palms on the table. "You can't mean that." She sat down next to Jeremy. "What if we disclosed the attempted power play to NSA and DoD? Threaten to air the dirty laundry on Vlakas unless they get the administration to back off."

"I don't think so. If the Russians got wind of it, you'd be in mortal danger," Jeremy said, gritting his teeth. "We both know they've killed for less."

"What if we head off the leaks by contacting the French and the Germans?" Dakota said.

"Very risky," Jeremy said. "I could think of a dozen ways that could go wrong, none of them pretty."

"We could distract Justice by corrupting their servers. Nothing fatal, of course." Dakota twiddled her thumbs.

"That would be treason, Dakota, and I don't want you going to federal prison," Jeremy said. "And I'm not too crazy about going either."

"Which is why counsel recommended we sue Justice for libel," Dakota said.

"And that suit could take years," Jeremy said. "It's a classic Vlakas strategy that I'm thrilled to use against him. Hopefully by the time our suit is heard, Vlakas will be out of office."

"And the new president could get Justice to back the hell off." Dakota crossed her arms over her chest.

"I like that last one," Jeremy said. "Especially since there's no chance of me ending up in a tacky orange jumpsuit surrounded by scary guys who bench-press three hundred and fifty pounds for fun while the only thing I have to protect myself with is a plastic spork."

"Let's set up another meeting with counsel," Dakota said to Jeremy. "We need them to map out our strategy and tell me what it will take to pursue it, best-case, worst-case. You know the drill."

"You got it, boss." Jeremy's eyes glittered with ferocity. "I'll get the legal eagles on it, so you can run the business without worrying."

"Thanks for running point on this."

Jeremy always came through in a clinch. Which was a good thing because she had more than one tight spot to squeeze through in the very near future.

CHAPTER 7

December 18, 2026, Cambridge, Massachusetts

"New Age spiritualists." That's what Dakota's parents called themselves when she came home from second grade one day asking about her religion. Dakota didn't understand what they meant at the time, but since her family always celebrated Christmas—which her parents said was rooted in pagan traditions—she didn't really care. To this day, she still looked forward to the Christmas season, with its twinkling lights and Christmas cookies, its cheesy Hallmark Channel holiday movies, and its celebratory buzz. But this holiday season was different. It was one week before her annual Christmas Eve dinner party, and all she could think about was Elizabeth Tudor.

When it came to matters of state, Elizabeth had leaned on her chief adviser, William Cecil, Lord Burghley. When it came to securing her crown—and her life—Elizabeth had relied on her spymaster in chief, Sir Francis Walsingham. To Dakota, Jeremy was both men rolled into one. He safeguarded KODA as a company, and he always had Dakota's best interests in mind. Which is why she would need Jeremy's absolute support if she were to succeed on her next mission.

Dakota had seen it time and time again—Jeremy was unflappable in his professional life. He could thwart hackers, even cyberterrorists, without losing a night's sleep. But Dakota's new quest would stretch Jeremy beyond his comfort level. She was sorry she was about to push him to the brink.

As she stood in the foyer of her condo building on this frigid Friday morning, she played with the slim gold chain around her neck, feeling around for the puffy gold heart pendant that her parents had given her on her first day of middle school. "It's too expensive," Dakota had told them tearfully. "You'll have to take it back."

"We can afford it, Dakota." Her father had patted her arm. "Mom found it at this store by the river that sells estate jewelry."

"Don't you like it, honey?" Her mom had looked at her with knitted eyebrows.

"I don't like it. I love it. And I'm never taking it off."

Dakota remembered hugging them both. The feeling of their arms wrapped around her, the kisses on the top of her head, the warmth from their bodies, the smell of her mother's patchouli oil. Just pulling that little gold heart out of her jewelry box triggered her sensory memory like no other keepsake. And it had become a talisman of sorts, the object she wore when she felt anxious. Like that spring day twenty-six years ago, when she'd defended her dissertation before the faculty committee.

And like today, when she'd walk Jeremy into Kisai's subterranean laboratory.

Where was he, anyway? She checked the blue face of her clunky Breitling watch. Seven-thirty. *He's late.*

She watched the snow squall whirling outside. *He'll get here soon.* She zipped up her fluffy winter white Helly Hansen jacket and walked out the main entrance. Not a minute later, Jeremy's gleaming Rivian SUV pulled up to the curb. It was like a Range Rover for the environmentally minded, and he was madly in love with it.

Gripping her travel cup firmly in one hand, she silently pledged not to spill coffee on her jacket—which she seemed to do regularly despite her best efforts—then opened the door and sat next to her trusted friend and employee.

"Morning, Jeremy." She gave him an extra-long look. "Are you ready for today?"

"OMG. I am so ready," Jeremy said. "I can't believe after all these years you're finally taking me to see his work." He pulled away from the curb. "I can't imagine what he's got down there. Is Kisai working on space travel or something? If that's the project, I hope you've got a craft that works better than Elon Musk's moon rockets because I have no desire to combust before I go skiing next weekend."

"I'm not going to say another thing." Dakota brought her index finger to her lips. She turned on NPR as Jeremy made the eight-minute drive from the Esplanade condominium to KODA.

When they arrived at the Navy Yard, Jeremy opened the car window as he pulled up to the fingerprint reader outside the building's gun-metal gray gate. The big bay to the garage opened as usual, and he parked in his spot. Dakota suspected that solid, rational Jeremy would lose his mind during the tour that was about to happen. She already knew he long resented not knowing "what the hell Kisai actually does down there," and today he would learn the truth. Dakota gently took Jeremy's hand and walked him toward a part of the building to which he'd never had access.

They headed to the furthermost corner of the parking lot to the retinal scan positioned to the side of a metal door. Dakota placed her left eye in front of the scanner. The door opened into a small anteroom with a deadman door.

"Are we on a James Bond set, Dakota? Are we meeting Maxell Smart in here? Seriously. A deadman door?" He shook his head in disbelief. "How are we both going to get through it? And what's on the other side, Shangri La?"

Dakota spoke to him in a soothing voice. "I should have told you about this years ago," she said. "But I didn't know how you'd react. And I still don't know how you'll react." She gulped. "But you're going on a tour that only Kisai's staff have experienced. An even smaller number of people, me included, have gone one step further."

"What the hell are you talking about?" Jeremy said.

"Jeremy," she said. "Kisai has conquered time travel."

"*Ji-Ral.* That's bullshit." Jeremy scowled at her. "Why would you say something so outrageous?"

"I understand your skepticism. I really do." She reached for his hand, but he pulled away. "Kisai—and his team—have made the impossible possible. "I knew the only way you'd believe me…" Jeremy's eyes bulged out. "…is if you saw incontrovertible evidence. That's why I brought you here today."

"This must be some kind of bizarre test." Jeremy set his jaw. "To see if you can rattle me, to see if you can tell me any ridiculous thing, and I'll believe you. Not because I'm your CSO." His voice grew soft. "But because I'm your friend."

"My dear friend."

"Your dearest friend." He gave her a half-smile.

"Just follow me," Dakota said. She held her finger to a reader to the left of the deadman door, and it spun open. As she turned to look back, she said, "Don't worry. Kisai programmed it so both our fingerprints will open it. You go next."

Dakota shivered as she watched Jeremy pass through the door. It was the cold that always got her in this outer part of the lab. It was a chill that was hard to shake, even hours later.

"Jeezus, it's freezing down here." Jeremy ran his hands up and down over his crossed arms. "And it's really loud."

"I know. That deep buzzing sound is so exciting. It reminds me of the first time I visited CERN," Dakota said.

"It reminds me of the time I toured that IBM data center in Poughkeepsie," Jeremy said. "I bet Amazon has bigger ones now, though."

They took three steps up onto a white tiled walkway that led them into a cavernous space in which sat row upon row of refrigerator-sized open black cabinets with blue flashing lights. Yellow plastic ducts that housed all the cabling hung from the ceiling.

"I've never seen a data center this large," Jeremy said, swiveling his body around to take in the sight.

"It's a supercomputer, actually."

"Of course it is." Jeremy's voice sounded clipped. "Because that's what we've always needed at KODA, a supercomputer."

"We're going to need a second one for the personalized AI I'm working on." Dakota gave him a sideways glance. "Want to spec it out for me?"

"Yes, please." He did a fist pump. "You know how to make a guy feel better."

They walked down the path until they saw double-wide, elevator-style metallic doors about fifty yards from the entrance, a thick blue floormat in front of them. Dakota and Jeremy stepped onto the mat and found themselves stuck to it.

"There's Gorilla Glue on this welcome mat," he said, scowling.

"We'll get unstuck soon," Dakota said. "Kisai should be here in a second." *I hope he shows up soon.*

As if Kisai could hear her thoughts, the doors opened. And there he stood, all five feet, four inches of him, wearing a fitted white lab coat, his hair looking more unruly than usual. The man, the genius—Hoshi Kisai. He stood in an elevator-sized room with dull-gray metal walls.

"This much tungsten always blows me away," Dakota said. "I remember it costing a pretty penny." She ran her hands over the walls.

"Are you serious?" Jeremy clapped a hand to his cheek. "You had a whole room built with a rare earth metal?" he said. "What are you playing at?"

"Dakota hasn't told you what to expect, I take it?" Kisai said to Jeremy. "Given what we're doing here, that's logical. You'll only believe it if you see it for yourself." Kisai held his palm in front of his newest biometric gadget, a near infrared palm-vein scanner. What looked like a wall opened before them.

"That's very cool, sir." Jeremy said. He turned toward Dakota. "I want one."

The inner lab looked like a feng shui version of a NASA control room. Instead of rows of computer monitors facing a patchwork of video displays affixed to a wall, several clusters of white quartz-topped round tables circled by ergonomic-styled office chairs dotted the room. An eight-foot-long fish tank was set into the wall on the left, multi-colored fish gently swimming around. A light-oak farmhouse table with matching chairs looked inviting in the spacious kitchen area in the back-left corner of the lab. A small sitting area with midnight-blue Scandinavian recliners was off to the side of the dining area. Two glass-walled conference rooms ran the length of the right-hand side of the lab. And a massive video wall at the front of the room was powered on, displaying the gorgeous blue-blacks and purple-reds of the billowing cosmos in ultra-high-definition glory.

"I didn't expect it to look so Zen down here," Jeremy said.

Dakota watched the lines in Jeremy's forehead dissolve. *Let him relax while he can.*

Kisai interrupted her reverie. "Dakota, you already know these two." He motioned to two thirty-somethings in lab coats. "Jeremy, please meet Maeve O'Neill and Henry Endicott. Their research on relativity and quantum mechanics is foundational to the work we do here." Kisai looked at Jeremy for a response but got nada. He cleared his throat. "They shook the establishment at the World Congress for Quantum Physics in 2019 when they co-presented a new theory of quantum paradox. Perhaps you have read the conference proceedings." Jeremy scratched his head. Kisai's frown was almost indiscernible. He pushed his glasses over the bridge of his nose.

"May I interject?" Dakota said. Kisai nodded "yes." "Kisai went all out recruiting Maeve and Henry. Just like you did when you hired Sumiko."

"Ahh," Jeremy said. "Now I get it."

"We may be the only lab in the country to have two Oxford PhDs with a specialization in quantum materials and transport." Kisai sat up straighter. "In just six years, they have advanced our program immeasurably."

Henry smiled so hard his face must have hurt. Maeve blushed beet-red.

"And now, we would like to introduce you to Tempus Fujit." Henry opened his arms with a flourish like a ringmaster presenting his opening act.

"Tempus Fujit?" Jeremy squeezed his eyebrows so tight they looked like a furry black unibrow.

"Time flies, of course." Though not as tall as Jeremy, Henry had it going on. Big shoulders and muscular arms. A square chin and chestnut hair, he looked like that high school quarterback that drove all the girls crazy. Or maybe like a handsome vampire, with those long bicuspids of his. But Maeve didn't seem to mind them. As the couple pulled their chairs up to the small round table, Maeve sat so close to Henry that her strawberry-blonde ponytail flicked him on the chin whenever she turned her head.

I can't believe they've been here for six years already. Time was flying on so many levels. It made Dakota's head spin.

For the next twenty minutes, Kisai provided a fifty-thousand-foot overview of project Tempus Fugit "and how the science all came down to capturing and reproducing enough exotic matter to form wormholes large enough for human time travel." That was the first fifteen years of his work in Japan.

When he founded the lab at KODA in 2009, he and his team spent the next ten creating stable wormholes, and then three after that pinpointing locations in time and space, plus a few more returning an entity to the present within an acceptable period of time. Acceptable started at two weeks and was now down to minutes.

Jeremy leaned his head back and sighed. "I know what this is about." He turned to Dakota, his eyes boring holes into hers. "You wanted to see your mother," he said, his tone softening.

"I already saw her." Dakota held his gaze. "On my birthday this year."

Jeremy's mouth gaped.

"I promise to tell you all about it," she said, her voice soft. "But that's not why I brought you here today." She placed her hands on the table and made eye contact with each person seated. "Because what we're going to attempt is far bigger than my personal life. If we can pull this off, we'll save the company—and the country— from Vlakas."

"Oh no," Jeremy said. "Do you hear what you're saying?" He shifted his chair back. "I never thought you'd become a megalomaniac, but you sound like one. The all-powerful billionaire who will save the world." He looked like a statue. Rigid, as he sat in place.

"I'm not a megalomaniac." Dakota shook her head slowly. "I have a responsibility to fix this. All of it." Her voice began breaking. "And I'm one of the few people who can do it."

"I assure you. Her intentions are noble." Kisai's tone was serious. "And she cares deeply about your opinion." He looked at Jeremy. Then he stayed silent for a good thirty seconds. The classic pause in conversation with which the Japanese were so comfortable, and with which Americans were so uncomfortable.

"Let us show you why you are here." Kisai motioned with an open palm toward Henry and Maeve.

"It's go time." Henry said, his eyes sparkling. Even his upper-crust British demeanor couldn't hide his enthusiasm.

"Let's show them the footage, dear.... I mean, Henry," Maeve said. Her blue eyes were so light they were almost translucent. She pushed her chair against Henry's. "We have to smush in," she said. "Jeremy, come a little closer."

"This isn't Netflix, I take it," Jeremy said.

"I hope you like history," Dakota said. She scooched her chair closer to Jeremy's so their shoulders were touching. "Let's see what Brooklyn looked like in 1947."

CHAPTER 8

Still December 18, 2026, Charlestown, Massachusetts

"This is so completely crazy. It's off the charts." Jeremy flapped his hand at the video wall. "Are you claiming this actually happened? Because if you are…" He motioned to everyone else at the table. "…I am very concerned for your sanity. Very concerned." He squeezed his fingers against the side of his nose.

Dakota glanced at Jeremy. The man who had stared down bad actors from countless foreign governments and other malefactors attempting to hack into one system or another was glued to his seat, his left hand cupping his mouth.

"Wait a minute. You're telling me that Kisai has solved the space-time continuum, that the two of you…" Jeremy pointed to Maeve and Henry. "…just showed me spycam footage from your trip to Ebbets Field in 1947, where you watched Jackie Robinson play his first Major League baseball game?" Jeremy's voice rose so high that he sounded like Mickey Mouse. "And that Dakota visited her mother, who died in 1985?"

"We didn't actually get to see him play because the game was already sold out," Henry said, frowning.

"I think you're missing the point," Jeremy said.

"We need to stay on track, and we don't have a lot of time," Dakota said. "Kisai, Maeve, Henry, I need to run a couple of things by you. First, how soon can you host a couple of Harvard professors in the lab? They need to see the footage." She continued talking before anyone could answer. "I'm going to set something up for next week. Sound good? Okay, good."

"Wait." Jeremy tilted his head to the side. "Why are Harvard professors coming to the lab, and what does this have to do with Ebbets Field?"

"We need specialists in the Tudor period because we want Queen Elizabeth I of England to become our next president of the United States," Dakota said.

Jeremy stared at her blankly.

"The professors wrote a biography of Queen Elizabeth, and they're the best people to convince her to join us here." Dakota gestured at the room with open arms.

"What?" Jeremy raised his voice an octave. "Even if whatever convoluted idea you're concocting could work, you want someone who's moldering in her grave to run for president? What are you going to do, infuse her dead body with fluids and give her AI for a brain?"

"Of course not. That would be insane." Dakota's jaw muscles were starting to ache. She opened her mouth to stretch them. "The Queen will be fully alive when she gets here," she said. "Except that Elizabeth Tudor will have lived and died by the time *our* Elizabeth arrives." She gulped hard. "And Kisai says that's why she won't be able to go back home again."

Jeremy said nothing but his face was drained of color.

"Trust me, Jeremy." Dakota spoke more softly. "If we don't get creative, Vlakas is going to win again," she said. "And I know. I know this is drastic, but I believe she's the best person to defeat Vlakas in the 2028 election. We need a winner." Dakota was speed-talking. "You tell me if there's another candidate who could win because I can't think of anyone else. The Democratic Party is a mess." She felt like she'd just drunk two espressos. "The best person to beat Vlakas is a fire-tested politician who brings all the skills to the job but none of the typical baggage—whether it's real or invented." Dakota paused for effect. "We need a rock star, and I'm prepared to go back more than four centuries to get her.

"We need Queen Elizabeth I of England." Dakota pounded the table. "She was a brilliant political strategist and a phenomenal speaker. She was fearless, a woman in a world of men, who dodged multiple assassination attempts and kept her throne for forty-five years," she said. "Hell. She was as close to a pop icon as anyone could be in the sixteenth century. And that's what we need: a tough, smart politician with no known past to target."

"And the Harvard professors already know the plan?" Jeremy said.

"Not yet, but they will." *I must remember to breathe.* Dakota pulled a hefty book from her Tumi bag. *Heart and Stomach of a Lion: A Biography of Queen Elizabeth I.* "Here's the book they wrote. It's amazing." She gestured to the cover. A seated Elizabeth Tudor wore a jeweled headdress over intricately plated light-red hair—which by that time in the queen's life was one of her many wigs. An opulent gown studded with pearls and embroidered gold and silver designs billowed around her arms and lower body. Luxurious strands of pearls flowed from underneath her intricate lace collar to her bodice and her tiny, cinched waist. A golden crown decorated with rubies, sapphires, emeralds, diamonds, and pearls rested on a table near her right elbow. Her right palm cradled a globe, and paintings of a victorious English navy and a decimated Spanish armada were juxtaposed above her right and left shoulders, respectively. This Elizabeth was powerful, rich, and confident. It wasn't Dakota's favorite representation of her chosen candidate, but the Armada portrait of Queen Elizabeth I made a statement. She'd give it that.

"And was the book a big hit?" Jeremy said.

"It got a great review in the *Times,*" Dakota said.

"Another bestseller then?" Jeremy sniggered.

"I kind of doubt it," Dakota said. *Sometimes I feel like whacking him with a frying pan.* "But it's chock-full of useful information, explaining the protocols and cultural norms that *we* couldn't possibly understand."

"Such as?" Jeremy said.

"We should address her as Your Majesty instead of Queen Elizabeth. We should wait until she takes a bite of food before we do. We need to recognize that she believed she was chosen by God to become the queen of England."

"We already have a despot running the country," Jeremy said. "Do we really need another one?"

"We'll acculturate her to our time," Dakota said. "But she won't get there immediately."

Someone cleared his throat. *Oh right.* She'd been ignoring Henry, Maeve, and Kisai during her tête-à-tête with Jeremy. "I need everyone in this room to help us with the professors and get us ready to go back to England." Dakota swept a hand toward Henry, Maeve, and Kisai.

"What do you mean 'back to England?'" Jeremy said. "When did you go to England before now?"

Maeve pursed her lips. "We were there about seven months ago," she said.

Henry scratched a few numbers on a pad of paper. "Give or take four hundred and fifty years." He gave them his cheesiest grin.

"I'll explain everything, I promise." Dakota hoped she sounded calmer than she felt. "But the next step is to convince the professors that we're offering the opportunity of a lifetime. The chance to experience Tudor England. Not just to read about it or imagine it," she said.

"And how do you intend *not* to sound batshit crazy when you tell them what you're planning?" Jeremy's hands were tucked into his armpits. "I mean, I'm wondering about your sanity, and I already know and trust you."

"You hardly ever think I'm crazy?" Dakota's touch landed on his arm like a butterfly.

"I think you're crazy all the time, lady," Jeremy said with a chuckle. "But I'll help you anyway." He batted his eyelashes at her.

"I wouldn't be able to do it without you," she said to Jeremy. "Without all of you." She gestured to the others.

"You are not sending me to the sixteenth century," Jeremy said. "They didn't have 7G, so I'm not going." He crossed his arms.

"No need," Dakota said to him. "We're sending the professors, and one person from the lab to go with them, in case any technical issues come up." She tugged at her lip and mused aloud. "Maeve or Henry, I would think, since they're our experienced time-travelers."

"You mean you're not going too?" Jeremy said.

"I'm not a sixteenth-century kind of girl," Dakota said, her laugh weak. "You know how I am about fleas."

"I thought you were only phobic about cockroaches," Jeremy said.

"I'm generally not good with insects." She examined her fingernails. *Or with plague.* She shuddered at the thought.

"I'm comfortable with all types of fauna." Henry's voice rose above the others. "And I might point out that I'm still a British citizen." He touched his fingers to his chest. "I would sound the part."

"I'd say the accent is irrelevant unless you speak Early Modern English like William Shakespeare." Maeve smiled sweetly at him.

"Sorry to pull this one, but I'm a man," Henry said. "And it might be an advantage to have a man escort the professors in a time when women were more at risk." Maeve punched him in the arm.

"Sorry, but it was a patriarchal society." Henry's voice was just above a whisper.

"And ours isn't?" Maeve said, her face flushed. She cleared her throat. "But we need to ask Dakota, have you picked a date?"

"I think we should defer to the professors on that," Dakota said. "They're the experts, and we'll need them to choose the exact time and place," Dakota said. "But if I were just spitballing..." She gazed at the ceiling. "I'd say sometime just after the defeat of the Spanish Armada."

Henry did a fist pump, Maeve started typing, Kisai nodded— and Jeremy started to hyperventilate. Dakota looked around for a paper bag.

CHAPTER 9

December 21, 2026, Charlestown, Massachusetts

A side from reading biographies about Nikola Tesla (*a great visionary, and the true pioneer behind AC power*) and Thomas Edison (*a cruel inventor, he electrocuted stray dogs and an elephant to try to convince the world that AC power—which he later stole from Tesla—was dangerous*), Dakota wasn't a fan of biographies. But when she'd first seen *Heart and Stomach of a Lion: A Biography of Queen Elizabeth I* in the window of Porter Square Books around Labor Day, her heart had fluttered for a second. And not because of her hormones. Just seeing the cover had catapulted her back in time. She was sitting next to her mother on the living room sofa while her dad relaxed in the recliner, watching Glenda Jackson embody Queen Elizabeth I on the analog television that she thought was so modern because it had a remote control the size of a brick. *A nice memory.*

She'd brought the book home on a Wednesday and had finished it by Sunday night. The book was so full of vivid details, she'd found it hard to put down. She could almost feel the twenty-five-year-old Princess Elizabeth's relief when she was named queen upon her sister Mary Tudor's death.

For forty-five years, from 1558–1603, Elizabeth Tudor had ruled over England, Ireland, and Wales at a time when other women were rarely educated and had few legal rights.

Even queens were subject to the cultural restrictions of the day. Had Elizabeth married a man, her ability to produce heirs would have eclipsed her keen intelligence and natural ability to command a nation. She would have been in childbed during her fertile years, and England would have been the worse for it.

Elizabeth was remarkable in every conceivable way. She spoke seven languages, including ancient Greek and Latin, and even her private forms of relaxation often involved intellectual pursuits. When she wanted to withdraw from the world, she might retire to her quarters to do complex translations of works by ancient scholars like Cicero and Seneca or near-contemporaries like John Calvin and Petrarch. Or she might play one of the instruments at which she was proficient: lute, which was larger and had more strings than a mandolin, or virginals, a harpsichord-like instrument with a smaller keyboard. Many believed that Elizabeth's virginals had once belonged to her mother, Anne Boleyn, the second wife of King Henry VIII—whom he had beheaded at the age of twenty-nine on trumped-up charges of adultery—as they were decorated with the heraldic falcon badge of the Boleyn family. Dakota wondered if Elizabeth thought of her mother whenever she played it.

But music was just one of Elizabeth's pastimes. Bursting with physical energy, she loved to dance and walk, was an expert horseback rider, and hunted deer with a crossbow. God forbid that PETA ever found out—but according to her biographers, Elizabeth had no qualms about cutting the throat of a deer she'd just felled. *What's a little blood on the hands when you're living in the sixteenth century?*

It was a brutal historical period after all. When twenty-one-year-old Princess Elizabeth was taken to the Tower of London upon suspicion of treason, she was housed for two months in the same royal prison where her mother was beheaded at the decree of her father the king. And that was just one of her painful experiences. Elizabeth contracted smallpox at the age of twenty-nine, survived multiple assassination plots of both foreign and domestic origin, and thwarted a coup planned by her court favorite, the thirty-six-year-old Robert

Devereux, second earl of Essex, when she was sixty-seven years of age. Though it pained her personally to do so, Elizabeth honored the penalty for treason and had Devereux beheaded at the Tower of London.

As head of state, Elizabeth had led her country into war. Literally. On August 9, 1588, Elizabeth traveled to Tilbury to deliver one of her most famous speeches. Gleaming on horseback in a suit of shining armor, Elizabeth exhorted the British troops—a motley mix of volunteers and professional soldiers—to prepare for a land invasion by the Spanish. That the threat of an attack had passed by the time Elizabeth descended upon Tilbury didn't matter. Looking every bit the warrior-queen, Elizabeth had seized the opportunity to subvert her femaleness in favor of her kingly lineage while delivering one of Dakota's favorite lines: "I know I have the body but of a weak and feeble woman; but I have the heart and stomach of a king, and of a king of England too." It always gave Dakota chills.

The defeat of the awe-inspiring Spanish Armada was as much due to unfavorable weather, which blew the Spanish fleet out of formation and wrecked vessels onto the rocky English and Irish coastline, as to the skill of the much smaller British navy. But none of that mattered because the Elizabethans defeated the Spanish, initiating England as a world power.

And Elizabeth had proved her mettle as a courageous leader who could inspire men to greater things. If some of it was chutzpah, who cares? Dakota closed her eyes and imagined Vlakas trying to stalk Elizabeth across the stage as he had with Jennifer Samson during the 2024 presidential debates. *He wouldn't have the gall.* Her Elizabeth would spin on her heel to face the roly-poly blowhard, stopping him with a cutting stare, like a knife to the eyeball. *I can't wait to meet her.*

But then again, I'm also terrified to meet her. What if Dakota couldn't keep up with Elizabeth mentally, physically? She felt like she was swallowing marbles.

But fear had never stopped Dakota, and it wouldn't stop her now. But before she could move forward with her bold plan, she had to cultivate a relationship with the coauthors of *Heart and Stomach*, and fortunately, they could be found just a few miles away on the campus of Harvard University. Professor Janet Majors offered Renaissance and medieval British literature at the graduate level while Assistant Professor Gideon Horn taught introductory courses in medieval British history. After just a little online research, Dakota discovered that Majors had received tenure in 1992, was widely published in academic journals, and was a close friend of the university president. *Sounds like a cushy gig.*

Horn, on the other hand, had been an assistant professor for nine years. *Assistant*, not *Associate. That means he's not tenured.* She hoped that meant he was hungry as hell—and that despite having "made it" in academia, Professor Majors still had a fire in her belly for adventure.

Dakota rehearsed the words she'd say to invite them to KODA to discuss *Heart and Stomach* over lunch. "Not only is your book fascinating," she'd say, "it also made me wonder what Elizabeth would be like if she lived in the twenty-first century. What if she were a contemporary politician? How would she fare in our world? I'm most interested in your opinion—and in supporting your own research, of course. Are you available to have lunch with me this week?"

God, she hoped they'd say yes. It couldn't be every day that one of *Forbes*'s one hundred richest tech entrepreneurs invited them to a meeting. *But I'm not really that famous. What if they've never heard of me?* She bit her lower lip.

Coming from humble roots had influenced Dakota's choices, making her circumspect about her wealth. Other than her condo in The Esplanade and the little villa in Portofino, she owned no other real estate. No private islands and no yachts. She'd rather spend Saturday night having dinner with the people she loved most. That included her best college friend, CeCe Gibbons—or Dr. Gibbons, as she preferred to be called.

As a Black woman who'd earned her PhD in clinical psychology from prestigious Boston University, CcCc had busted the glass ceiling of academia—as well as her ass—earning that degree. She deserved some recognition for it.

They'd met as freshmen at MIT, and it had been a mutually beneficial—and effortless—relationship from the start. Dakota had always watched out for the shorter, leaner CeCe on the rugby field and had helped her friend pass first-year calculus. CeCe had introduced Dakota to people outside of her normal social circles, namely rugby players who thought it was funny to wear muddy, beer-soaked game jerseys to the library and mega-geeks who would rather get flesh-eating bacteria than experience human feelings. When CeCe had joined MIT's chapter of Alpha Kappa Alpha—better known as AKA, which was the country's oldest sorority for Black women— Dakota was thrilled because she knew she'd finally get an invitation to a decent party. God only knows what would have happened to Dakota's social development had she never met CeCe.

By sophomore year, Dakota had thrown herself headfirst into ever more challenging mathematics and computer science classes, while CeCe became one of the few MIT undergrads to pursue a curriculum in brain and cognitive sciences. Though their professional interests had set them down different educational paths, they'd remained good friends over the years. Dakota felt comfortable reaching out to her emotionally astute friend whenever she needed advice on human beings, and CeCe never hesitated to call Dakota for tech support.

But their relationship went far beyond mere problem-solving. Having honed her shopping skills searching for deals at Filene's Basement, where savvy Bostonians could buy classy outfits at bargain prices, CeCe was one of the few people who could entice Dakota to go clothes-shopping. It was a task Dakota pretty much loathed, unless they were going to REI, Helly Hansen, or Fjällräven, but CeCe somehow made it seem fun. Even when Dakota begrudgingly joined CeCe at Saks on Boylston Street, CeCe's favorite store of all.

Dakota had always admired that CeCe put her passion for helping others above monetary gain. Hell, CeCe could have been a CEO if she had wanted, but that's not the path she chose. Having grown up in a nice part of Milton—one of the few Boston-area towns where middle-class Black families could live a suburban life without sticking out in a sea of pale faces—CeCe had lived a sheltered life until college.

"I was living in a bubble until I came to MIT," she used to tell Dakota. Microaggressions around campus. Being overlooked in the classroom like she didn't exist. Experiences that never happened to Dakota happened to CeCe. No wonder her friend had pledged AKA within two weeks of starting college. CeCe's sorority sisters could understand what it felt like to have eyes watching them at a Harvard Square boutique, or worse, to have grown men catcall them on the streets of Cambridge.

In May of 2000, ten years after starting freshman year together, Dakota and CeCe earned doctorates at their respective universities within days of one another. With diplomas in hand, they had partied like it was 1999. For about three days. Then Dakota became a "hermit" as she was starting KODA from her tiny apartment in East Cambridge. CeCe moved on to a post-doc specialization in DBT, or dialectical behavior therapy, a newer therapeutic approach with proven success treating extreme emotion dysregulation in adolescents, with suicidality at the top of the list.

And which group of teens was at the highest risk of suicide?

"Black girls are like an invisible population in Boston," CeCe had told Dakota when she started at McLean Hospital in June of 2000. "They're not killing each other. They're killing themselves. And I will not watch from the sidelines."

As an early practitioner of DBT in the Boston area, CeCe could have opened a clinical practice in a wealthy white suburb like Newton or Concord. Or she could have returned to Milton. But she did neither. An entrepreneur in her own right, CeCe mined the powerful AKA network to raise funds for a subsidized clinic on Blue Hill Avenue in Dorchester, so she could bring DBT to an urban population of Black girls.

Two decades later, CeCe still had a hand in her clinic, but she'd turned day-to-day operations over to a capable executive director while she played a supervisory role. Along the way, CeCe also figured out how to make money. Executive coaching and a seat on the board of trustees at one of Boston's biggest medical conglomerates had brought CeCe the ability to afford the creature comforts, and the professional recognition, that she so desired.

Which is why CeCe was now on a first-name basis with pretty much everyone who worked at Saks.

CeCe was like the sister Dakota never had. Sure, CeCe would rather spend her Saturdays browsing the high-end boutiques of Newbury Street in Boston's Back Bay while Dakota would rather drag her old Enigma machine out of the closet so she could tinker with the only two World War II–era German messages that have never been decoded. But those things didn't matter. Dakota trusted CeCe. Period.

Dakota hadn't asked her yet, but she hoped that CeCe would join her as a member of Elizabeth's inner circle. God knows that the queen, no matter how steel-forged her heart, would have to navigate some hard transitions to manage life in the twenty-first century. And a resident psychologist could make all the difference to Her Majesty's mental health. But convincing CeCe to drop everything to help a privileged—really privileged—white woman was not going to be easy. A problem for another day.

Dakota had mused quite long enough. Time to call the professors. She took one last sip of her espresso, pulled her ultra-secure Bittium cryptophone out of her pocket, and dialed.

CHAPTER 10

January 29, 2027, Charlestown, Massachusetts

Dakota paced the lobby of KODA, glancing again at her watch. It was 12:10 p.m., and her professors were late. It had been over a month since she'd first spoken to Professor Janet Majors, who had just finished grading papers and was packing for a holiday trip to the Vineyard, followed by a "long-planned" fifteen-day Mediterranean Antiquities cruise on Viking with a "dear friend," when Dakota finally reached her.

Janet's schedule had caused a four-week delay to the overall project timeline, and Dakota was less than thrilled. But there was a silver lining. She finally had the time to explore bringing AI to VAULT. Had anyone published a paper on AI in captive email servers? *Not yet.* She might have found a new way to catapult KODA so far over the heads of the competition that no one could ever catch her. *Or, catch the company.*

And the call itself? It was super annoying. After telling Dakota she had just a few minutes to talk, Janet had said that she rarely received inquiries from the "general public" about her research. She was even more puzzled why such a well-known technologist was interested in the humanities. Promising to explain everything when they met in person, Dakota asked if she and Assistant Professor Gideon Horn could meet for lunch before Christmas. Their biography of Elizabeth I was fascinating--even life-changing—she'd told Janet, who'd failed to register the compliment.

Unfortunately, even after her extended vacation, Janet's professional obligations kept her extremely busy. Between research and teaching, her earliest availability was in late March. "So regrettable, but so unavoidable," she'd said over the phone.

Dakota had cranked up the flattery-meter because waiting until March just to learn *if* she could secure Janet and Gideon could have ended the quest for Elizabeth before it began. She had little time to lose. Calling Janet a "brilliant scholar of great renown," Dakota had told the professor she'd like to fund her research "in a significant way." She'd heard an intake of breath on the other end of the phone. *If I have to endow a chair at Harvard to get Janet Majors onboard, I'll do it.* Dakota would do almost anything to close the deal with the professors.

When Janet called Dakota back thirty minutes later, she said she had good news. She and Gideon could squeeze in a lunch with Dakota on January 29. *Which was better than late March.* Dakota said she'd send a car to pick them up and would have them back on campus within two hours of their arrival. Which was a white lie. If Janet and Gideon didn't think Dakota was certifiable after she introduced the time-travel concept, they'd have at least a few questions. Or a thousand. They'd be at KODA a helluva lot longer than two hours.

At 12:20 p.m. on January 29, a black BMW i5 company car stopped in front of KODA's front door. A tall silver-blonde wearing a calf-length camel coat exited the back seat. The wind blew her fine, straight hair behind her, making her look like a human version of an Afghan hound. Thin and elegant, with head held high, Janet was ten paces ahead of her traveling companion as she glided toward the front door.

Gideon, on the other hand, wasn't the least bit intimidating. His shoulder-length brown hair curled against the collar of his faded black pea coat. He plodded, rather than walked, and as he entered the building, he removed his tortoiseshell glasses to wipe away the condensation, revealing dark-green eyes.

Janet floated across the travertine floor as she strolled into the lobby. She planted herself in the center of the floor as she waited for Dakota to approach. When Dakota drew close, Janet extended a gloved hand without saying a word. She squeezed Dakota's hand upon contact, but Dakota squeezed back harder. And Gideon just stood there, gazing up at the KODA logo over the shiny copper elevator doors. The raised gold-leaf lettering of the company name emerged in three dimensions from a rectangle of solid obsidian, a carved scarab of sustainably sourced blue sapphire forming the "O" of the company name. The logo had been Dakota's idea, with the gold representing rarity, the obsidian conveying protection against negativity, and the scarab, immortality. It was a visual representation of her hopes for the company—solid, lasting, and highly valued.

"Welcome to KODA, professors. I'm thrilled that you could make it," Dakota said, like the gracious host she aimed to be.

"We are both delighted and intrigued," Janet said. "I am Professor Majors, and this is my associate, Professor Horn."

"Please call me Gideon," he said, taking Dakota's hand and shaking it up and down with vigor. "While I've heard of you, of course, I had no idea that you had heard of me—or our book, for that matter. It must be the book, I am sure." Gideon flashed a grin at Dakota, his eyes crinkling behind his glasses.

"Yes, it is a pleasure for me as well." Janet's gray eyes pierced Dakota's. It was like looking into klieg lights.

Dakota blinked. "I have much to discuss with you. I hope that you don't mind dining at our little company café. It's just this way."

Dakota took them to the first floor on the elevator. She got off first and escorted them through glass doors into an expansive space with soft lighting and thirty-foot ceilings, a wall of greenery, and polished concrete floors. Thirty or so round tables covered by white tablecloths were placed around the room, about half of them occupied. A rosy-cheeked man in a double-breasted white chef's coat greeted them as they entered.

"Here are our special guests, Chef Will. May I introduce Professor Janet Majors and Professor Gideon Horn of Harvard University," Dakota said.

Chef Will bowed slightly. "It's my pleasure to cook for you today." He held out his arm for Janet to take and escorted her to the table, which was set with blue-and-white ceramic plates, sparkling glassware, and real cutlery.

Nice touch. I did tell him to pour on the VIP treatment. Dakota thought she saw Janet's flicker of a smile.

Forty-five minutes later, after grilled salmon and risotto (for Janet and Dakota) and chicken cordon bleu with scalloped potatoes (for Gideon) plus a bottle of good Gewürztraminer, Dakota hoped her special guests felt sated.

Something of a rarity among brilliant technologists, Dakota had perfected the art of conversation. She credited that to her mother, who'd made it a rule that the family sat down to dinner together every night. "It's the one time when we get to ask each other about our day," she'd said. "I want to know how things are going for you and your father, Dakota, and perhaps you're curious about me every once in say…a million years." Then her mother would screw up her face in a pretend-frown and give a little laugh. Dakota had loved those dinners.

But today was no family dinner. Since she'd long known that people, Janet among them, as it turned out, loved to talk about themselves, Dakota asked the professors how they'd come to academia. Keeping both the conversation and the wine flowing for her guests, Dakota stayed mentally on task. This was a business meeting.

When she produced the NDAs, Janet and Gideon signed without hesitation. The Sicilian pistachio gelato that arrived just after Dakota pulled the documents from her padfolio might have sped the process ever so slightly. Dakota smiled to herself.

Now that the wine-and-dine was finished, it was time to lay it out there.

"Professors, I'm sure you're wondering why I was so eager to meet with you," Dakota said, taking a sip of water. "As Elizabethan scholars of some repute, you are uniquely qualified to help me with a project that's become my highest priority." She cleared her throat. "I would like to offer you the greatest adventure of your lifetime."

Gideon sat forward in his chair. Janet's hand wobbled slightly as she placed her cappuccino on the table.

"The thing is, I can't use words to describe it because you're going to find it so hard to believe," Dakota said. "I have to show you, or more specifically, my very specialized research team, has to show you what I'm going to propose."

"So that's why we signed an NDA," Janet said.

"I like the sound of adventure," Gideon said. "Is it going to be fun or scary?"

"A bit of both, I expect," Dakota said, looking at Janet for a response.

"My schedule is jam-packed this term, I must tell you." Janet waved her hand like she was dismissing a minion. "I've got four graduate students and a seminar to teach on the plays of Christopher Marlowe."

Dakota swallowed her pride. "I know how valuable your time is." She tried to keep her tone even. "I'd like to have my research team give you a tour of their lab before we discuss that further, if that's all right," she said. "We'd all like to introduce you to Project Tempus Fugit."

"Time flies. What a charming name for a project,'" Gideon said.

Janet squinted at Dakota. "What's this about?"

"I promise to explain everything when we get to the lab," Dakota said. *Damn. She's a tough nut.* "Just know that I'm inviting you to witness something that few others have seen. It represents the culmination of more than thirty years of dedicated research, seventeen of which have taken place right here, in the most secure part of our building," Dakota said. "You'll need to bear with me on the way there—access is a bit involved."

Janet took a slow sip of coffee. Then she checked her wristwatch. "I must admit that you have piqued my interest," she said. "I will make time for this exploration, so please lead on," she said. "If that's all right with you, Gideon." She flicked a crumb off her sleeve.

Gideon bowed with a flourish. "Where you go, I will follow."

"Good. Let me just inform our CSO Jeremy Jiang that our tour will begin now." Dakota typed into her phone.

"Interesting that you have your chief strategy officer joining us," Janet said. "Wherever it is that we're going."

"Actually, that's chief security officer, and here he comes," Dakota said as Jeremy approached the table, his black cashmere jacket draped over one arm.

"Please bring your coats with you," Jeremy said to the professors, even before Dakota could make introductions. "Kisai is ready for us, so we ought to be going."

Though he was ever the good solider, and she knew he was doing his best to exude confidence, Dakota thought Jeremy looked more nervous than usual. Poor guy. *I should take him to Positano for a week when this is all over. Or maybe I should have a bottle of Limoncello delivered to his house tonight.*

Dakota and Jeremy walked the professors back through the lobby, where they took the elevator to the ground floor and exited into the garage. Like ducklings in a line, they followed Dakota to the far wall. She opened her eye wide for the retinal scan, and the small group followed her through the outside door and into the anteroom. They crowded together in front of the deadman door.

"I'm not going to kid you guys. This part really freaks me out," Jeremy said. "Oh, and I'm Jeremy Jiang, by the way, and I know who you are." He nodded to the professors.

"Are you making nuclear warheads or something?" Gideon said.

"This is most unnerving," Janet said, looking pale.

"Just stay with me, please. It's going to be worth it." Dakota motioned them on. "Just a little farther now."

"Maybe more than a little," Jeremy said, glancing at the professors.

Janet's eyes were like saucers as she made the long walk by the blinking blue lights on the supercomputer. About halfway down the corridor, Janet stood erect and glared at Dakota. "Did you clear any of this with Harvard?"

"I did not, Professor. We really are almost there." Dakota gently pushed Janet onto the sticky mat in front of the double-wide metallic doors, which opened. Kisai now stood in front of them.

"Welcome to Tempus Fujit," he said.

CHAPTER 11

Still January 29, 2027, Charlestown

Two hours, six cups of strong Builder's tea from Henry's personal stash, and a dozen shortbread cookies later, Janet and Gideon sat before Dakota, stunned. She'd just asked them if they'd like to visit Elizabethan England to meet with John Dee, a renowned thinker of the Tudor period, who was a trusted advisor to Queen Elizabeth I for more than two decades.

"Assuming that we can still put sentences together if we make it back to Tudor England, why would we approach John Dee first and not go right to Elizabeth?" Janet said, frowning.

"It's because of what I read in your book," Dakota said. "You describe Dee as a natural philosopher, who was fascinated by the occult. He believed in what he could prove scientifically and mathematically. Yet as an astrologist who made predictions about the future, he was equally passionate about what he couldn't prove empirically." She sneaked a peak at Janet. *Good. She's paying attention.*

"As Elizabeth's astrologer, Dee had selected Elizabeth's coronation day in 1558," Dakota said. "He had accurately predicted the date that England would defeat the Spanish Armada. As a visionary who believed he could talk with angels, Dee's more likely to embrace the idea that three people from four hundred and thirty-eight years in the future want to speak with him about his famous patron."

"I must agree," Janet said. "We need John Dee to advocate for us to Elizabeth."

"And we'll be able to reach him much more easily than the queen." Gideon brushed a curl of his hair away from his eyes. "She was hardly ever alone, surrounded by an entourage of male courtiers, Privy Council members, various types of what we'd call 'ladies-in-waiting.' We need John Dee to come onboard if we have any hope of getting Queen Elizabeth to abandon everyone and everything she's ever known to journey to an unknown place and time."

"And we know where to find him because in 1588 he was at Mortlake, which is just down the Thames from central London. Isn't that right, Gideon?" Janet said, eyes brightening.

"Yes indeed," Gideon said, rubbing his hands together. "Dee's family home was a sprawling complex that included his laboratories and his library. And that library would have been something to see. It reportedly housed Europe's largest private collection of mathematical, scientific, and astrological texts. Also, magical ones. Alchemy. Astrology. Fascinating stuff. He even had a crystal ball and a scrying dish to help him make predictions.

"It would be the perfect place to speak with him," he said.

Peals of laughter echoed from across the lab, where a handful of white-coated staff members had gathered around a single computer monitor. Boy, they looked like they were having fun, even for scientists and engineers who'd probably graduated valedictorian from each of their colleges. Who said that nerds couldn't have fun? *What are they doing anyway? Watching funny cat videos?* "Kisai, it's a little busy here, with your other staff in the lab today. Could we move to a conference room?" Dakota said, figuring the professors might fare better if she could remove them from other distractions.

"I think I need a minute with Gideon first," Janet said. "Could we chat for a bit?"

"I know I could use a bathroom break. Or a spa day. A chakra realignment sounds nice about now," Jeremy said.

Dakota glanced sideways at him, slightly concerned that she was overtaxing his logical mind. *Definitely sending the Limoncello to Jeremy tonight. No, I'll bring it over instead. I'll ask Chef to prepare chicken and pesto over linguini for dinner. Jeremy would love that.*

"Why don't we give them a moment?" Dakota motioned to the group, which now included Maeve and Henry.

A few minutes later, Dakota glanced at herself in the bathroom mirror. *I don't look like a mad woman, do I?* She splashed water on her face, then applied some rose lipstick to her pursed lips. Her shoulder-length light-brown hair was kind of a mess, though she paid a small fortune to have it cut and colored monthly. Growing up she always hoped people focused on her big brown eyes and long lashes, not her angular face or her long, thin nose. Handsome, not pretty, but attractive in her own way, *she hoped.* Sighing, she tucked the tube of Dr. Hauschka into her front pocket and headed back to the conference room. She gave a soft knock on the door and peeked in.

The professors were hunched over pads of paper. *What are they doing?* Dakota turned around and saw Jeremy in the kitchen with Kisai, Maeve, and Henry. She waved them over.

Dakota knocked louder this time. "May we come in?"

"Yes, yes. Please do," Janet said, looking over the top of her reading glasses at Dakota. "Just so you know, I'm not a fanciful person." She clasped her hands in front of her. "I don't believe in fairies or unicorns. Even as a child, I thought Santa was ridiculous." She gave a small laugh. "But in this case, I'll hold my skepticism at bay because the prospect of seeing, of smelling even, Elizabethan England is too exciting to forgo." She twirled her pen as Dakota and the others entered the room and took their seats. "We're going to need a few things for our trip."

"We're starting to make a list, you see." Gideon pointed to scribbled lines in his notebook. "We also thought it wise to ask a question." He cleared his throat. "Henry and Maeve brought a newspaper back to the present. Have you ever tried to bring back anything well…living?"

"Would you like to see a photo of our puppy?" Henry said, his eyes dancing. "She's either four hundred and fifty or about four months, depending on how you look at it."

"When did you go to…let me do the math…1577? And why didn't I know about this, Kisai?" Dakota scowled at the brilliant physicist, who placed a hand behind his head. His face was contorted, as if in pain.

Oh no. I didn't mean to shame him. Dakota softened her features and offered a smile. "I'm sorry, Kisai, I was just surprised at the news."

Kisai picked up his head. "I approved the trip because I specifically wanted Maeve and Henry to return from the Tudor period with a living being," he said. "We needed to prove our hypothesis, that we could safely retrieve someone from the past in the same way that Maeve and Henry have traveled back and forth without ill effect."

"I understand now." Dakota bowed her head to Kisai. "That was a wise decision," she said.

"I have a teensy-tiny question for Maeve and Jeremy." Jeremy turned toward the couple. "What if you brought back the plague? Did you ever think of that? Fleas carried black plague. Fleas live on puppies. Not just rats. It's not just the damn rats. Did you check it for fleas?" He was practically yelling.

"Of course." Henry narrowed his eyes. "I checked her back in England."

"Well, that's a relief, guys," Jeremy said, extending his arms like Evita on steroids. "Except there was bubonic plague in 1577. Isn't that right, professors?" He stared at Majors and Horn.

"Actually, 1577, was a mild year for the bubonic plague," Gideon said. "But 1563, on the other hand—that was extremely bad."

"And 1665 was just atrocious," Janet said. "You've heard of the Great Fire of London, yes?" She'd morphed into a Dickensian teacher who'd rap their knuckles if they said "no." Dakota nodded "yes."

"One hundred thousand people died," Janet said. "And most of the rats that carried the fleas."

Jeremy snorted. "Now there's a macabre upside." He turned to Kisai. "If we're going to bring live things back from the sixteenth century, shouldn't we have a program in place to ensure we're not reintroducing some other horrific disease, like smallpox or polio, even if it's not the plague?"

"I am not as unaware of scientific protocols as you seem to believe." Kisai's voice sounded strained as he pushed his eyeglasses up on his nose. "Maeve and Henry received a polio booster and a smallpox vaccine before traveling. They each carried seventy percent ethyl alcohol hand sanitizer on their person. And we pre-treated their clothing with permethrin, which is highly effective at killing fleas, bedbugs, mosquitos, and other pests."

"I didn't mean to sound disrespectful, sir," Jeremy said. "I guess I panicked for a minute about the dog." Jeremy's ears had turned red. *So that's what he looks like when he's embarrassed.*

"I understand your concern." Kisai gave him a nod. "We are all doing our best to navigate through uncharted territory."

"And the dog is healthy, so there's nothing to worry about," Jeremy said to no one in particular.

"We took her to the vet the very next day, so she could start her vaccinations," Maeve said, her face pinched. "And our dog has a name. It's Rose for English Rose."

Henry brushed his hand across Maeve's forearm. "The odd part is that the vet said he'd never seen a dog like Rose," he said. "We told him she was a mixed breed from Tennessee." He gave Maeve a playful smirk. "Then we took a DNA sample and sent it off for analysis."

"She's one of a kind, our girl," Maeve said, eyes sparkling. "At least in our time."

"I'm afraid to ask what that means." Jeremy pinched the sides of his nose.

"The DNA panel couldn't place her. The report from BreedDNA said she could be some kind of spaniel mixed with Jack Russell Terrier," Henry said. "We called the company, and they said they'd never seen DNA quite like hers. They did tell us she'd have a long body and short legs, though."

"We think she's a turnspit dog." Maeve giggled. "If we hadn't rescued her, she would have run on a wheel ten to twelve hours a day to turn a piece of meat on a spit over a fire. And our Rose wouldn't have liked that at all." She held up her phone to display a small, floppy-eared, wire-haired dog with a white stripe down her face sleeping on a faux shearling dog bed.

"Please do not tell me you brought an extinct dog breed to the twenty-first century." Jeremy overenunciated every syllable. "Please. Do. Not. Say. It." He exhaled through an open mouth.

"Let's move on from the dog, shall we?" Janet said. "Gideon and I have started to compile a list of must-have items that we'll need for our trip back to 1588. Doxycycline in case someone gets Typhus. DEET for the fleas. Permethrin spray for the bedbugs. Hand sanitizer. Clorox wipes for God knows what. Lice combs. Tissues, since there was no toilet paper." She repeatedly clicked the top of her ballpoint pen. "And we'll also need to visit the Mount Auburn Travel Clinic for vaccines, although we'll need to say we're going somewhere where they still have polio and smallpox."

"Right. Professors, we'll provide whatever you need. You have my word," Dakota said. *Thank God she changed the subject.*

"I suppose you have access to many things." Janet turned to Dakota. "But how will you get sixteenth-century clothing for Gideon and me?"

"As you surmised, Professor Majors, I have the means to secure whatever you require." Dakota straightened in her chair and looked directly at Janet. "Name it, and it shall be done."

One hour later, there was a list on the conference room whiteboard that Dakota never could have imagined she'd see anywhere in her building. From doublets, hose, wide-cut coats with slashed sleeves, and feather-adorned hats for Henry and Gideon to a Tudor gown and Elizabethan ruff for Janet. That wasn't all for Janet. A seed pearl necklace, jeweled headdress, and fur wrap "were essential," she had said, for she must be perceived as a woman of means. Henry had but one single request. "We'll need period coinage," he'd said, "...in case we need to buy a snack."

"John Dee was a visionary, but he wasn't a fool," Janet had said. "We'll need to show him proof that we are who we say we are."

After another hour of brainstorming, they had a specific list of items that Janet and Gideon would bring to their meeting with John Dee. A biography of John Dee and a biography of Elizabeth. *Not hard to guess who wrote the biography.* Photos of Hampton Court, which was Henry VIII's favorite palace. An old drawing of the Tower of London juxtaposed with photos of it from modern times. A portable DVD player with one of the many TV shows or movies about Queen Elizabeth I.

Mmm...maybe not that last one. Moving pictures could wait until Elizabeth landed in the twenty-first century.

"I think we should appeal to Elizabeth's vanity," Janet said. "She was fifty-five in 1588. And that's not like being fifty-five today— or even in one's early sixties, when it's still possible to appear quite lovely." She smoothed her hair with her hand.

"Let's be more direct," Gideon said. "By her fifties, the queen's teeth were almost black from decay, and some molars were missing." He drew his eyebrows together. "And that white face that Elizabeth made so fashionable? It was made from ceruse, a mixture of lead, egg white, and water. She used it to cover her smallpox scars."

"Which were minor compared to the scars sustained by Mary Dudley, the Gentlewoman of the Privy Chamber who nursed Elizabeth when she almost died of smallpox in 1563," Janet said. "Elizabeth was very vain—"

"She believed that maintaining a glamorous appearance was critical to her influence," Gideon said, interrupting Janet. "A good example: she applied the 'Venetian ceruse' to cover the few pox marks she had." He cleared his throat. "Elizabeth, of course, had no idea that the lead could be poisonous." His voice dropped off.

"And by the time she was in her fifties, her once-resplendent red-gold hair was graying and cut short. She covered it with a variety of ornate red wigs," Janet said.

Jeremy snickered. "Sounds like she needed a makeover."

"Exactly. And we will appeal to that," Janet said. "We'll assure her that a woman of her age, once restored by modern beauty treatments, will look like a woman in her thirties.

"For someone who enjoyed the public admiration of her male courtiers—according to the tradition of courtly love to which she adhered—she was accustomed to handsome young men fawning over her. At her core, however, she must have known she was no longer a beauty. To have that beauty returned to her would seem very attractive."

"And how might we convey something so delicate?" Gideon said.

"I'll tell her my age," Janet said. "I'm sure her jaw will drop." She flashed a smile.

She is good-looking but leave it to Janet to say it out loud. Dakota said, "Aside from the beauty, what would she think about being called the most powerful woman, the most powerful person, in the world?"

"I think she'd embrace it," Janet said. "You must remember that she had to work extremely hard just to hold onto her throne. There were foreign threats, domestic threats. Her councilors didn't believe that a woman alone could secure the monarchy. They hounded her to marry, as did Parliament, for years. If Elizabeth were to become the president of the United States, she'd have no need for a man—other than that need which she may or may not have satisfied when she was living."

"Kick me if I ever get into sixteenth-century gossip," Jeremy whispered in Dakota's ear. She kicked him anyway.

"Ow," Jeremy exclaimed.

Janet gave them an icy stare.

Dakota cleared her throat. "When do you think you can be ready to travel?" she said.

"Gideon, could you please contact the Travel Clinic tomorrow? Ask how long it takes for the polio booster and smallpox vaccine to become effective?" Janet said.

"I think we need more than that." Dakota deepened her voice while addressing her team. "Given the complexity of traveling to and from Tudor England, I'd like to see a written protocol for all time-travelers. It would make me feel more comfortable for those of you who live here, and for Elizabeth, who will have a longer list of medical needs than any of our people."

"There is always value in advance preparation." Kisai brought a hand to his chin and remained quiet. Dakota bit her lip so she wouldn't jump in and interrupt his train of thought. After two or three minutes, he spoke again. "Maeve and Henry are our most experienced travelers." He nodded in their direction. "As such, they are best suited to outline the protocol," he said. "However, no one in our lab has the medical expertise required for optimal implementation."

"So we need a doctor?" Dakota said, her voice rising.

"I think that would be wise," Kisai said. "I will take responsibility for informing my trusted friend and personal physician, Doctor Abe Diamond, to serve us in this capacity. Would that be acceptable to you, Dakota?"

"As long as you trust him implicitly," Dakota said.

"And he signs the killer NDA that I gave the professors," Jeremy said.

"It is decided then," Kisai said. The others nodded assent.

"This is good," Dakota said. "Everyone has a role to play."

"And we are delighted to play ours. Isn't that right, Gideon?" Janet said. Her blue-gray eyes flickered with sparks of light.

"I'm still pinching myself that this is all real," Gideon said, beaming quiet happiness.

"Until today, I was worried that we wouldn't be able to pull this off," Dakota said, sounding more scared than she intended. "But now that the professors are with us…" She smiled warmly at Janet and Gideon. "…we have period experts who can guide us through the greatest adventure of our lives."

"*Almost* the greatest adventure," Jeremy said. "The greatest adventure is trying to find a parking spot in Harvard Square on a Saturday night."

"Why don't you just pay to park?" Dakota said.

"It's a matter of pride." Jeremy thrust his chin out.

"I think we need to refocus," Janet said.

"I think Dakota's getting hangry," Jeremy said.

"I'm going to ignore that." Dakota squinted at Jeremy. "Because Janet's right. We have a lot to do and not much time in which to do it." Dakota brought folded hands to her lips and paused. *Good. I have their attention.*

"The fact is we need everyone around this table—and a few others too—if we're going to change our future for the better," she said. "If we don't succeed, we may have another four years of Vlakas, and I cannot live with that." She shook her head. "Even if it weren't damaging to KODA, it would be damaging to everyone in this country."

"And the environment," Jeremy said.

"And so many things," Dakota said. "This is the most important mission of my life. Of all of our lives, I think." There were nods all around.

Would they still feel this way if it didn't work out? If it all went up in smoke because any one of a million things could go wrong? Dakota couldn't listen to such doubts. She had to be their fearless leader. No matter what.

CHAPTER 12

February 8, 2027, Cambridge

Dakota stuck to her sheets as she rolled over in bed. Hot flashes had kept her up half the night, so she was still groggy, but it was the stabbing pain in her chest that woke her. *I get how people confuse heart palpitations with a heart attack because these suck.*

She pressed her palms to her chest and glanced at her phone. Five in the morning. *Dang. Maybe I just need a vacation…or a spa day.* Who was she kidding? She had zero time for a spa day. Between work and planning the England trip, she'd barely had time to exercise. Which was a problem because she ran toward anxiety, and her workouts kept her grounded. She needed to hit something.

If I get up now, I can use the heavy bag before anyone else gets to Healthworks. She loved her all-women's gym in Porter Square where locker-room conversations often veered toward politics. She'd never forget going to the gym the day after Vlakas was elected. It was like going to a funeral wearing Lululemon.

Dakota removed her soggy pajamas and threw on her gym clothes. Usually, boxing kept her in the present like no other workout, but not today. All she could think about was Janet, Gideon, and Henry, and their intricate plan to convince John Dee that they were, in fact, from the future, and not candidates for the local asylum.

As she drove to the gym, Dakota's mind drifted back to their first major trip-planning meeting last Friday. Janet, Gideon, and Henry, a.k.a.: the travel team, and Kisai, Maeve, Dakota, and Jeremy, a.k.a.: the ground team, had done their first big walkthrough for *Go Day*, which they'd planned for Friday, March 5. After a painstaking discussion of various what-if scenarios, from total success to abject disaster, and a Magna Carta–sized description of each traveler's persona—Janet, for example, was the widow of a wealthy, but minor, lord, and as such, she used the Early Modern English that would be most familiar to John Dee—Dakota had turned the conversation toward the present chronology. If the travel team left at 10:00 a.m. on March 5, how soon would they return—and when would they be ready to debrief the ground team?

Dakota knew she had many attributes. Patience was not among them.

In this, Kisai was her antithesis. As someone who'd spent decades trying to solve time travel, Kisai was patience personified. And he would always do what was best for the cause.

For the trip to John Dee, Kisai would match the time lapse in the past to that in the present. For example, if the team left at 10:00 a.m. on March 5 and spent six hours with John Dee, the time-interval calculator would return them at 4:00 p.m. local time. Based on Kisai's observations, time-lapse intervals of just a few minutes caused more post-trip disorientation and exhaustion. Better to play it conservative with the professors' first trip.

The travel team would also spend twelve to sixteen hours in the recovery room for sleep, hydration, food, and mental relaxation before they met with the ground team. No one was to disturb the travelers before they were fully recovered. There would be no exceptions.

"But all I had was a bad headache when I returned from seeing my mother in 1984," Dakota had said in protest. "Do they really need that much time to recover?"

"I based my decision on Maeve and Henry's reports," said Kisai, his voice flat. "They expressed mild disorientation after their trips to Provincetown and Brooklyn, but their disorientation was more pronounced upon returning from Tudor England." He cleared his throat. "I hypothesize that there is a direct correlation between the number of years traveled and the toll on the traveler." For the first time in their relationship, Kisai made direct eye contact with Dakota. She backed down.

"The last recovery period was great for me." Maeve beamed from ear to ear. "Henry was so out of it, he proposed.

"Not such a bad thing, I think," she continued softly.

"No, not such a bad thing." Henry gave her a nudge.

Dakota couldn't help but notice how delighted Maeve and Henry were in each other's company. She may not have found that kind of romantic love in her own life, but she knew it when she saw it.

She snapped herself back to the present. Time to get to the gym.

Three-six, three-six, three-six, three-six, three-six, three-six, three-six, three-six. Dakota walloped the heavy bag with three-six punches—better known as right and left hooks to non-boxers—until she could do no more. Rivulets of sweat poured down her face, and her hair was sopping wet. She popped off her gloves so she could wipe a towel across her brow and grab a few sips of water.

Good. The endorphins were kicking in. God knows she needed something to make herself feel better. If Janet and Gideon couldn't woo John Dee—without scaring the hell out of him, or convincing him that they were not batshit crazy—her audacious plan to put a Tudor queen in the White House would go down the toilet before she could say "flush." That was a potential outcome that had been keeping her up nights—while making her uncharacteristically cranky during the day. She'd try to keep herself in check when she got to the office.

During her post-workout shower, Dakota thought back to *Gown-zilla*, her tongue-in-cheek name for the project to source the travel team's clothing. The garments had to be authentic enough to convince period-dwelling Elizabethans that Janet, Gideon, and Henry belonged in 1588. It had to be done with the greatest discretion. And it had to be done fast.

At Janet's request-slash-demand, Dakota had prioritized getting the right gown for the meeting with John Dee. But that was harder than she could have imagined.

She'd kicked off her quest last week by asking the British Museum to loan her a real Elizabethan gown, in exchange for a generous contribution to the Tudor collection. "Unfortunately," the curator had said, "an institution of our caliber would never risk a priceless artifact for a charitable donation—of any amount," she'd added for good measure. Dakota had hated playing the role of entitled American when she made that call, but she was willing to do whatever it took to make Janet look authentic.

Here it was February 8, and Dakota still didn't have a gown for Janet. It's not like she knew anyone in the fashion industry. She wasn't some rich celebrity broad who toodled off to New York or Paris for Fashion Week. Not that she was a slob, mind you. She looked damned good for a woman who wore so much Smartwool. She chuckled at the thought. But there were times when even Dakota had to dress up, and it was during those times that she'd go shopping with CeCe.

Tapping her fingers to her lips, she had a eureka moment. Saks! Last time she and CeCe had been there, they'd met a salesclerk who had made shopping less painful. Ashley Price. She was so unintimidating, she even tittered when Dakota and CeCe bantered about what looked good and what didn't.

But Ashley's girlish giggles belied a more substantive core. She'd assembled the perfect outfit for Dakota's upcoming keynote at the Grace Hopper Celebration, "the world's largest celebration of women and non-binary technologists." Dakota had to admit she looked attractive, statuesque even, in the Versace wide-leg wool pants with a Max Mara double-breasted velvet jacket that Ashley had found for her. But off the rack, the clothes didn't fit right. The pants were a bit snug at the waist, and the sleeves of the jacket gapped around Dakota's wrists. While Saks offered alterations through another department, Dakota was pushed for time as usual, so Ashley made a few measurements in the dressing room and told Dakota she did "at-home" tailoring for select clients. She'd even deliver the clothes to Dakota to make sure they fit perfectly.

Ashley seemed like a real go-getter. It was a trait Dakota could appreciate.

Dakota gazed into the magnifying mirror affixed to the wall above the vanity, quickly applying her "lotions and potions," a skincare regimen of facial toner, Vitamin C serum, eye cream, day lotion, and SPF30-tinted face lotion—a combination she hoped would keep her looking young. Then she threw on a coat of mascara and some blush and was out the door and back in her car.

Before starting the car's engine, she searched her phone's contacts for Ashley and sent her a text. Could they meet for coffee? She had a special project to discuss with her.

Five minutes down the road, and she hadn't heard back. Ten minutes. Twenty minutes. What the hell would she do if Ashley wasn't interested?

Before she deployed into full-blown panic mode, a phone call came in just as she was pulling into the garage at KODA.

A bubbly soprano voice came over the car's speakers. "Hi, Ms. Wynfred. It's Ashley Price calling. I was with a customer when your text came in or I would have responded more quickly."

Oh, thank heavens. "Hi, Ashley," Dakota said. "There's no need to apologize. I practically just texted you." *Though it had felt like an eternity.* "Is there any chance you can meet me tomorrow? I have a project I would like to run by you. I know a good breakfast place in Inman Square."

There was a microsecond's pause. "Yes. Yes, of course I can meet tomorrow," said Ashley. "Just tell me when and where, and I'll be there."

Smart girl. Dakota smiled to herself. Ambition properly channeled was almost always a good thing.

CHAPTER 13

March 5, 2027, Charlestown, Massachusetts

It was 9:00 a.m. on "Go Day." Dakota and Jeremy arrived at the lab to see clumps of lab-coated scientists seated at their workstations. Some typed ferociously on keyboards while others stared at the quadrants of changing data on the enormous video wall at the front of the room. Dakota tugged at the V-neck of her black-and-white Helmut Lang sweater vest—which she didn't care had come from the men's department of Saks—and received a slight electric shock. *Interesting.* The room was so charged with energy, it shouldn't have come as a surprise.

Dakota's stomach quivered as she waited for the Ashley-adorned travel team to arrive. She brushed her sweaty palms against her black jeans.

"There they are," Jeremy said, pointing to Kisai and Maeve exiting one of the inner-lab conference rooms.

A half-second later, a collective hush swept the room as Henry, Janet, and Gideon followed them in close succession. It was a shame that Ashley wasn't with them, but this mission was still on a need-to-know basis, and Ashley was able to do her job without knowing its true purpose. That would change, Dakota hoped, once Elizabeth arrived.

But first, Dakota wanted to witness Ashley's handiwork.

Janet was resplendent in a green silk gown embroidered with dainty yellow and red flowers. Her lace ruff made her long face look fuller, and her blue velvet cloak with faux-ermine trim draped over her shoulders with subtle elegance.

But how about Janet's hair? Fortunately for Dakota, Ashley had learned hair design in fashion school so she could give her models a complete look. And the look that Ashley devised for Janet was perfect, a Tudor-era twin-peak number that reminded Dakota of Lady Tremaine, the evil stepmother in *Cinderella*. Once Dakota stopped comparing Janet's look to a Disney villain—was she feeling a bit competitive with Janet?—she was free to admire Ashley's skillful updo: two sculpted mounds of silver hair at the front of Janet's head with a light-green silk coif covering the back. Ashley had hit the mark. Janet was a fashionable Tudor matron come to life.

"What doest thou think of mine own outfit, Lady?" Janet placed her hands on her hips as she addressed Dakota.

"I think I saw an outfit like yours on RuPaul's *Drag Race*," Jeremy said with a snigger. Janet looked like she was going to punch him.

"You look amazing, Janet," Dakota said. "Absolutely convincing—and quite stunning as well." She hoped her praise would help Janet forget Jeremy's quip sooner rather than later.

Gideon and Henry looked equally authentic. Each wore a fitted doublet with puffy sleeves, padded breaches and white stockings, and woolen caps with feathers. Ashley had designed and fabricated every piece of clothing except for their shoes—which were so close to the pointy leather shoes worn by fashionable Elizabethan men that it was impossible to tell they came from an upscale men's shoe store in Copley Plaza.

"Those shoes look just like yours, Jeremy," Dakota said when she saw them.

"Except mine are six-hundred-dollar Ferragamos," he whispered in her ear.

"And they would have cost only a few pence in Elizabethan England," Dakota whispered back. He narrowed his eyes at her.

Their clothing wasn't the only thing different about the two men. Each sported a manicured beard. When Dakota first glimpsed Gideon in his traveling garb, she almost did a double take. Without his glasses—she guessed he must have switched to contact lenses for the trip—and with his dark-brown beard and a thick head of hair curling against the edge of his jaw, Gideon reminded her of the portrait of Robert Dudley in *Heart and Stomach of Lion*. *Is it my imagination or does he look like a handsome pirate? I hope he doesn't catch Elizabeth's eye. Or Jeremy's. Either would be complicated.*

"Nice beards, guys," Jeremy said to Gideon and Henry. He touched his smooth-shaven face. *Is that envy or attraction?*

"Gentlemen," Dakota said. "You look like you stepped out of a Shakespeare play."

"As dashing as two of The Three Musketeers," Jeremy said. "In my humble opinion." He bowed to Gideon and Henry.

"I've never been so excited for anything in my life." Henry blazed a grin at Dakota and Jeremy.

"You look beyond debonaire," Maeve said to Henry. She whispered something else into his ear, causing his face to turn crimson.

While Ashley had designed the Tudor apparel to allow the travel team to pass for sixteenth-century nobles, their attire served another critical function. Unbeknownst to Ashley, Kisai's team had concealed miniscule spycams in the buttons of the men's doublets and hats. They'd hidden one of Janet's spycams in an enamel phoenix medallion that hung from a string of pearls around her neck. They'd embedded a second one in a scarlet jewel at the center of her English hood, an ornate head covering with pearl edging. Dakota couldn't wait to see the spycam footage, which would give her and the other non-travelers that fly-on-the-wall insight they craved.

Gideon vibrated excitement. Drumming his hands against his breeches, he turned to his professional colleague. "Are you ready for the greatest experience of your academic career, Janet?" He beamed at her. "I know I am."

"May I remind thee to speak properly, Sir Gideon, or thee may not be understood?" Janet raised her eyebrows at him.

"Certes," Gideon said. "I shall try to speak as thou dost, but should I forget myself while with John Dee, I hope thee will compensate."

"Quietus warranted." Janet nodded her head with as much grace as she could muster. "I have this well in hand."

"I feel like I'm watching Masterpiece Theatre," Jeremy grumbled under his breath, but Dakota could still hear him.

"Ahem." Kisai cleared his throat to get their attention. "We must meet with the operations team for a few minutes before departure."

"Houston. It's almost time for liftoff." Jeremy's eyes sparkled like black diamonds.

"Dakota. Jeremy. This is where we part for now," Kisai said, his tone solemn. He nodded to Maeve and the travelers. "Please follow me."

"I see how it is," Jeremy said. "We're not invited to the party." He crossed his arms.

Dakota motioned for Jeremy to follow her. "Our part is done for the moment," she said, leading him away from the others. "But believe me, we're going to need you a whole lot later on."

Now back in her office, Dakota spun around in her desk chair. *This waiting is brutal.* She twirled a piece of hair.

If Kisai's ground team had made accurate calculations—and the meeting went as expected—the travel team was scheduled to return at four o'clock that afternoon, although Dakota would have to wait hours more to see them. Time for distraction.

"Ooh." Her fingers danced across the keyboard. "IACR's challenge of the week: find a faster encryption algorithm than RSA. Now that's meaty."

While spending hours on the website of The International Association for Cryptologic Research was almost no one else's idea of fun, Dakota enjoyed challenging herself with the highly complex. She refused to become a CEO whom others called a visionary but also a "has-been." She wanted to be recognized for her achievements over the next several decades. Retirement was for other people. But even the very productive sometimes need a break from encryption algorithms, and she was suddenly famished. *I'll just head to the café for a snack.*

After schmoozing with Chef Will for a few minutes, she left the café with two double-chocolate brownies. One for her, and one for Jeremy. She ate both in the elevator.

She decided to visit Jeremy, nonetheless. Maybe he'd walk around the tourist part of the Navy Yard with her and look at the USS Constitution, the two-hundred-year-old battleship known as "Old Ironsides." It always made her feel better, seeing that old warship. So solid. So durable. Qualities she admired.

She knocked on Jeremy's door. "Hey there." Dakota peaked into his office. He was standing at his desk, which he could raise or lower according to preference.

"Hey there, yourself," he said. "How you holding up?"

"Not good," she said. "I'm sugar-loading, and you know how that goes." She gulped. "You know how I don't chew gum anymore?"

"It gives you a headache," he said.

"Big time," she said. "And today, I just don't care." She gave him a funny grimace. "I chewed at least ten pieces of Bazooka bubble gum. Before lunch." Jeremy rounded his mouth to feign shock.

"Oh, Dakota. Not the Bazooka," Jeremy said, now serious. "That's awful for your TMJ."

"I know, I know," Dakota hung her head.

"Let me check the time." Jeremy checked his TAG Heur Connected watch with extra flare. His newest luxury gadget, it was more glorified sports watch than smartwatch. Without email or web browsing, it passed KODA's rigorous security standards, which he himself had created. Jeremy had purchased it a few weeks ago and now took every opportunity to brandish it for others to admire.

Dakota played along. "So what time is it again?"

"Just after one," he said. "They're due back at four."

"But we won't see them until tomorrow." She heaved a sigh.

Jeremy walked over to Dakota. "Does somebody need a hug?" She put her head on his shoulder. She felt better…for approximately fifteen seconds.

Maybe she could cajole Jeremy into leaving work for a few hours to visit the Museum of Science with her. She was a patron of the place, after all, funding a STEM education program for urban youth and a computer lab that turned digital forensics into gameplay. And bonus, she could watch the gigantic Rube Goldberg machine, which always kept its balls in motion, no matter what was happening around it. She could relate. Install an interdependent operational structure— Kisai's lab. Watch the wheels in constant motion. Hold your breath until the end of the day that nothing came crashing down.

Would today be the day the machine stopped working? Like a bug in her code, she squashed the thought dead.

CHAPTER 14

Later that day, March 5, 2027, Charlestown,
Massachusetts

Aside from her visit with Jeremy to the Museum of Science, which had been a great distraction—they'd even seen the cute little cotton-top tamarins with their wonderfully expressive faces—it had been an agonizing day of worry. It was 6:45 p.m., and still no word from Kisai. Dakota and Jeremy had been entertaining themselves for the past half-hour playing hangman, using a yellow legal pad Jeremy had appropriated from in-house counsel. Their version of hangman was more like Wheel of Fortune because they allowed up to thirty-eight characters with spaces for their fill in the blanks. Jeremy had just spelled hypertext transfer protocol secure, better known as HTTPS. So easy with all those *E*s and *O*s. Dakota got it after just six guesses. He'd have to try harder.

Just before 7:00 p.m., Dakota had a good one. Supercalifragilisticexpialidocious. Jeremy would be pissed. He'd call it a nonsense word that didn't count. He was right, of course, but it would be fun to see him so ticked off.

Then her phone rang. Kisai at last. "The team has returned."

He should have sounded triumphant, but his voice sounded thin and strained.

"And is everyone okay?" Dakota said.

Jeremy elbowed her. "Put him on speaker." She did.

"We have verified their vital signs," Kisai said. His voice was flat.

"You never said that was part of the recovery protocol," Dakota said.

"We have subverted our protocol in this instance," Kisai said.

"And why would you do that?" Dakota's heart was thrumming.

"They were somewhat disheveled upon arrival." Kisai cleared his throat. "But you need not be overly concerned."

"You didn't send them to the Cretaceous period by mistake?" Jeremy said. Dakota flicked the side of his head with her thumb and forefinger. It was the ultimate gesture of annoyance between them.

"I think we should meet in the Core to discuss the team's status," Kisai said. "We will expect you at your earliest convenience." He hung up. What was happening here? Why did he sound so oddly formal if this wasn't serious?

Dakota and Jeremy rushed down to the Core. As they entered the room, Maeve ran toward them before they could sit down.

"They were crumpled in a pile on the floor," Maeve said. Her eyes were round and bright. "We saw it on the infrared, the outline of their bodies." She was practically panting.

Kisai approached. "We acted quickly, Dakota. I promise you." He blinked rapidly. *Is it my imagination, or is Kisai scared?*

"We sent in our reentry team immediately. They're very learned people. PhDs. And they've all had CPR." Kisai was stumbling over his words and talking so fast she wasn't sure he was breathing. "They checked for heartbeats. They checked for breathing. Everything was normal."

"They're alive," Maeve said. "But that doesn't mean they're normal."

"Oh my effing God. I need to talk to your doctor." Dakota strode toward the red button on the wall. Pressing it would override all security measures to open the deadman doors to the lab.

Kisai brought his palms together at his chest. "Please, Dakota. We believe their vital signs are fine."

"Glad their vital signs are fine," Dakota said, making air quotes around *vital signs*. "But how the hell are their brain waves?" She was yelling now. "We need to get them to the hospital as soon as possible," she said, her heart pounding in her ears.

"Abe Diamond will be here any minute," Kisai spoke quickly. "He's my doctor, remember?"

Did someone fry my cerebral cortex? I can't understand anything he's saying.

"Abe's here," Kisai said. "I'm sending someone to meet him at the gate."

"And will he have an EKG with him? Or an oxygen tank or whatever the hell they might need?" Dakota's breaths came fast and shallow.

Jeremy's hands were on her shoulders; his touch was firm but gentle. "D. You're panicking," he said. "Breathe with me."

Dakota focused on the rise and fall of his chest as she tried to match her breaths with his. "Thanks, Jeremy," she said. "Much better."

Kisai pulled his phone out of his pocket. "One moment, please," he said. "One of my people has just left the recovery room. He said the team's awake."

The four of them left the Core like it was on fire. When the door opened to the main part of the lab, they hurried past the few staff members who comprised the reentry team. Kisai collided with a table and howled while Dakota, Jeremy, and Maeve weaved through the furniture, arriving together at the recovery room. Maeve rapped on the door, and Henry opened it. She threw her arms around him, buried her head in his chest, and started sobbing.

Dakota walked toward Gideon, who was drinking a bottle of Coca-Cola.

"It's the best thing for jet lag," Gideon said, grinning at Dakota. Janet had wrapped a light-blue fleece blanket around her shoulders. She held a large ceramic mug with both hands and took tiny sips. "This tea is good," she said, sounding croaky.

Dakota fell to her knees in front of them. "Oh, dear God in heaven. How are you both?" She looked at them from side to side.

"Dear, dear, Dakota. There really is no need to worry," Janet said, beaming. "We've had the most incredible time. Though I'm exceedingly hungry."

"Let's get these people something to eat," Dakota said, looking at the reentry staffer who was wearing a hazmat suit. He, she—or they—jogged to the back of the recovery room and returned with a tray of cheese cubes, crackers, chocolate bars, coconut water, sodas, and apples. Gideon looked the most relaxed, alternating sips of Coke with bites of a chocolate bar.

He grinned and looked at Dakota. "I bet you'd like to know how it went."

Dakota walked over to Gideon and reached for his free hand, which she held ever so gently. "I would, Gideon, so much, but I want to make sure that the three of you feel well enough to talk with us. It sounds like it was one helluva tough trip home."

"I don't remember much of it, honestly," he said. "I remember Janet, Henry, and myself leaving Doctor Dee's office. We walked to the back of one of the outbuildings and held hands. Then it got really cold. I've never felt so cold." He started to shake.

"It was like diving into the Charles River in January, I imagine." Janet shivered. "But then I fainted or fell asleep, I'm not sure which." She gazed at the ceiling with a faraway look. "I remember seeing some lights, hoping I wasn't dead, and that's when I woke up, right here in the recovery room. And we did it, Dakota. We did it. You did it. Kisai and Maeve and Henry. It's a miracle. I have experienced a miracle." Janet's smile was blinding.

This is not like her at all, Dakota thought. Maybe we *should* get them brain scans.

"This was so much better than our first trip to Tudor England. I mean, that was amazing because Maeve was there with me," Henry said, looking at Maeve. "But this time, we met with a man, a brilliant man, who's been dead for hundreds of years."

"Four hundred and fifty, to be exact." Gideon took a swig of his soda. "That's how long he's been dead."

Were his pupils dilated? Was traveling centuries into the past like drinking a couple glasses of wine—or a couple of bottles?

"Abe will give the three of you a medical—and cognitive—assessment, similar to the one given to detect concussions." Kisai nodded to Maeve. "He'll be here any second," he said. "But first, a proper hot meal would help with your recovery." Henry's face lit up when Kisai said "hot meal."

"And if you don't mind, I'd like you to stay here overnight," Dakota interjected. "So Kisai's people can take turns keeping an eye on you," she said. "I'll order dinner and snacks for the three of you, also Maeve, so you can eat together. Maybe you can compare notes if you feel up to it." Dakota saw nods all around. "I know you have some of your own clothes put aside down here so I expect you can get comfortable."

"Can we get Netflix down here?" Henry's eyes were shiny. "That way, we can have a pajama party with movies."

"Henry dear, I'm just going to pop home to pick up Rose and her Porch Potty. We need our angel with us tonight." Maeve nuzzled Henry's cheek.

What the hell is a Porch Potty? Dakota coughed into her hand. "It's arranged then. You all get some rest, and Jeremy and I will see you tomorrow."

Dakota needed a moment to gather herself. She headed to the bathroom and locked herself in the stall. But her mind was still speeding like a bullet train hitting a brick wall. Transporting Elizabeth would be far more complex than moving the travel team through time and space. The queen would have zero frame of reference for what was to come. She'd lived way before HG Wells, so even the concept of a time machine hadn't been invented. What could they do to make her feel comfortable and safe? Maybe light sedation to prevent panic. And she'd need loads of vaccines. Polio. Measles, mumps, rubella. Tetanus, influenza, measles. *Wait. I already said measles.* Somehow, they had to get even the rare vaccines to the lab before Elizabeth arrived.

But that wasn't all. They'd need to transport Elizabeth to Dakota's condo without causing her trauma. Dakota's breathing was getting shallow as she realized the overwhelming immensity of this plan she had concocted.

She'd needed to read in a bunch more people. Hazel and Ashley. Her dentist. A cook who could make Elizabethan food. And CeCe. CeCe knew Dakota had visited her mother—or that she *claimed* to have visited her mother—but CeCe didn't know about Elizabeth. That was a secret Dakota no longer wanted to keep. She'd call CeCe first thing tomorrow, ask if she'd come to the office to meet with her about a science project. Just enough to get her curious. Then she'd whisk CeCe down to the lab to meet the team, see the new spycam footage, all of it. CeCe needed to know the truth because Dakota needed CeCe.

Dakota's phone buzzed. A call must have come in while she was worrying, but her phone's volume was so low, she didn't hear it, so it had gone to voicemail.

She listened to Maeve's message: "Hi, Dakota. Henry says he's very hungry. Could he please have some steak and a baked potato? Also pasta? And a salad and a few desserts? Gideon said he's peckish, and Janet says she feels like she's been skiing for two days on an empty stomach, so could you please get food down for six or eight, maybe ten? That should do it. Thanks! See you tomorrow."

Armageddon couldn't get between Henry and his appetite. It was a good sign that he felt normal. She pulled up a menu for Charlestown's historic Warren Tavern, delicious American pub food from a restaurant that claimed Paul Revere as a frequent patron. She called the restaurant and ordered. She'd ask Kisai if one of his staff could meet the delivery person outside the gate. Then she texted Jeremy. Could he bring over a pizza to her place later? She had a nice bottle of Sangiovese at the condo.

What would she do without Jeremy? When she was nervous, he was steady. And vice versa. Neither of them had a serious relationship, though Jeremy had confided that he'd like to find a nice man to marry. She knew it hurt him that he couldn't share that romantic part of his life with his family in Korea. But he could share it with her, and he did. Often.

As for Dakota, she'd had the odd fling over the years with a variety of bright, nice-looking men. Not one of them was serious. Not one of them would have understood that KODA, not he, was her priority in life. She'd never have a human baby, but she did have a baby. It was twenty-six years old and employed about three hundred people. A non-existent romantic life was the sacrifice she'd learned to live with.

She knew Jeremy wasn't completely onboard with her Elizabeth-to-the-rescue plan. He was so logical, and her vision, so not logical. Even to herself, its chief architect, her plan sometimes seemed too incredible to take seriously. But she did take it seriously, and this terrified her because so many things could go awry. What if Elizabeth never adjusted to twenty-first-century life? Or what if she learned to pass for a modern woman but remained a closeted divine-right monarch in her heart of hearts? What if she revealed that she was

Queen Elizabeth I, and people thought she was insane? What if people thought that Dakota was insane for publicly backing a politician who was obviously a nutball? What would happen to Dakota? What would happen to KODA?

If she wasn't careful, she'd be fending off doubt from now on. Then it hit her. She'd ask Jeremy to develop a response to his top three what-if scenarios. That would calm him down and reassure her. He was a whiz at developing tactical plans.

Although she loved and trusted Jeremy, she could never let him, or anyone else, know that she had fears of her own. She'd muscled through periods of self-doubt over the years by tapping into her extraordinary intellect and penchant for problem-solving. But this quest to bring Elizabeth to 2027 was more challenging than anything she'd ever attempted, and she couldn't fall back on proven paradigms that had worked for her in the past.

Knowing that her technical skills wouldn't save her, she employed a time-trusted approach to reaching her goals. Get the best people for the job and empower them to run. She was good at picking rising stars. And Elizabeth? She'd be the star no one else could anticipate. Like the brightest star in the firmament, Elizabeth would soar across the heavens, burning brighter than any president who'd come before her.

CHAPTER 15

March 6, 2027, Cambridge, Massachusetts

It was almost 4:30 p.m. on Saturday, and Dakota still felt like death warmed-over. Probably didn't help that she'd drunk two bottles of wine with Jeremy the night before. Though that wasn't the only reason she felt ill. She'd left after revealing to CeCe her master plan to retrieve Elizabeth Tudor from the sixteenth century until the eleventh hour. With CeCe about to arrive for a 5:30 p.m. meeting in Kisai's lab, that eleventh hour was almost here.

Dakota turned back to the digital forensics project that had occupied her mind since she'd arrived at the office a few hours ago. What a blast. She'd forgotten how much she enjoyed playing the role of cyber investigator as she searched for the digital footprints of nefarious malefactors. She was just about to crack the case when she felt her phone buzz. It was CeCe. Time to face the music.

"You look like *ton dongori*, CeCe," Jeremy said as Dakota and CeCe entered the recovery room at 5:45 p.m. "And you know what that means."

"I do not, in fact, know what that means, but I'm pretty sure I can guess." CeCe shuffled toward Jeremy like she was one hundred years old. Which wasn't too bad considering Dakota had explained the quest for Elizabeth while walking her from the garage to the secret lab.

"*Ton dongori*. It means 'piece of shit,' girl." He put his arms around CeCe, and she leaned her head on his shoulder. "You sit next to me," he said to her. "Because I can see Dakota's put you through the ringer."

Sometimes it sucks to be a leader. This is one of those times. Dakota gently placed her hand between CeCe's shoulder blades and said, "CeCe dear, I'd like you to meet some more people."

CeCe pulled away from Jeremy and uttered an "okay." She even managed a small wave after Dakota introduced her to Henry, who'd been staring at his laptop. Janet and Gideon stopped scribbling on the same notebook to acknowledge CeCe's presence. And Maeve moved from Kisai to Henry, whom she kissed on the cheek.

"Why don't we get started?" Dakota took a seat. "I'm sure we'd all like to hear about the trip."

Maeve left her post at Henry's shoulder to plug a cable from the SMART board into Henry's laptop. The image of a sprawling two-story stone house was frozen onto the screen.

"Oh my God, the suspense is killing me. Will one of you please say something?" Jeremy said, swiveling his head like an umpire at a tennis match.

"Let us begin," Janet said, pressing her palms together in a namaste move. "We have just a few things to show you." She dazzled them with her pearly whites. Dakota leaned forward in her chair.

"Henry, could you please start the footage?" Maeve said, scooching her chair close to Henry's.

"Here we go," Henry said, clicking his mouse. "This is just after we arrived."

"After a rather interesting detour," Janet said, eyes narrowed. "Because we arrived in Kensington, which is miles from Dee's home in Mortlake...."

"That was a laugh," Henry said. "Gideon and I used a bit of gold to hire a horseman to take us to Mortlake by carriage."

"I did not see the humor in it." Janet stiffened in her chair.

Gideon cleared his throat. "Let's have a look at Mortlake, shall we?" There was a murmur of collective affirmation.

Dakota saw a two-story building come into focus. The first floor was brick, and the second was white stucco with wide crisscrosses of painted brown planks. Two large chimneys emerged from opposite sides of the russet-tiled roof. *It looks straight out of Wellesley.* But this wasn't some faux Tudor house in a tony Boston suburb. It was the real thing.

She heard Henry's voice on the video. "This is remarkable," he said. Then birdsong and the clack of hard-soled shoes on the cobblestones that led from a grassy field to the front entrance. Blurry camera images caught a long, low one-story outbuilding to the left and a brown wooden barn to the right, with a couple of horses in a fenced paddock to the side of the barn. Dakota's stomach flipped, and it wasn't just from the night before. The video from the spycams bobbed up and down.

"Hallo, good fellow." That was Gideon's voice. She saw a young man, no, a boy, struggling to hold a reddish-brown pot with a thick handle and a large opening at the top. Ignoring Henry, the boy walked to the side of the barn and dumped the contents of the chamber pot on the ground. Henry approached the boy, then quickly backed up.

"That smelled horrible." Henry looked up at Maeve. "I don't know what those people ate."

"Everything smelled horrible in the Tudor period," Gideon said. "I had read about it, of course, but couldn't have imagined it would make me feel so ill."

"It was an assault on the senses. Body odor, human waste, animal waste. We live in an antiseptic world by comparison," Janet said. "Let's fast-forward to John Dee, shall we, Henry?"

"Of course," Henry said, clicking his mouse.

"This part is amazing." Maeve leaned in toward Henry so their cheeks touched. "You got to speak to someone who's been dead more than four hundred years."

Dakota clapped her hands. "They really did it, didn't they?" She smiled at the genius across the table. Not just any genius. *Her* genius. The brilliant mind who had conquered time. Kisai gave her a quick nod back.

"Dakota, you have to pay attention," Jeremy said. "I think we're getting to the good part."

"When Gideon told the servant we had a letter of introduction to give to Her Majesty, the boy took us right to Dee's office." Janet twirled her thumbs. "Turn up the volume, Henry, so everyone can hear."

On-camera Henry removed his hat and bowed to a tall man with an angular face framed by a long gray beard and caterpillar eyebrows.

"Good morrow, Doctor Dee. It is my life's greatest honor to meet you in person," Gideon said, bowing just his head this time. "We three have traveled far for the rare opportunity to converse with you. Prithee, may we have a few moments of your time, good sir?"

"It is not oft that I should'st have unannounced visitors," Dee said, frowning. "And yet I am told thou hast a letter of introduction from Her Majesty, Queen Elizabeth. If that be true, then thee possess the highest recommendation, for Her Majesty be the greatest queen in Christendom. I welcome thy visit, although I know not its purpose." Dee cleared his throat. "Nor do I know to whom I speak," he said, adjusting his black gown.

"Oh my good God. Certes, Doctor Dee, I am verily sorry for my lack of manners," Gideon said, placing a gloved hand to his mouth. "I am Doctor Gideon Horn. This is my assistant Master Henry Endicott, and this—he gestured to Janet—"is Doctor Janet Majors."

Dee turned to the camera, which must have been one of Janet's. *Is he looking at the camera on her hood or the one at her breast?*

"That is extraordinary, a woman doctor." Dee narrowed his eyes at Janet and gazed back at Gideon. "She must be the first in all o' Europe." *Ugh. He's talking to Gideon like Janet isn't even there. How typical.* Dee reminded her of the jerky professor who'd challenged her doctoral dissertation. Though she'd first met him in the fall of '91—when she was the only sophomore taking his Algorithms and Computation class—he never once acknowledged her during all her years at MIT. *I'm not sure he ever learned my name.*

"I find this a strange and surprising visit. Strange enough to interest me." Dee brought his hands together with an air of contemplation. "May I trouble thee for the aforementioned letter o' introduction?"

"Certes, Doctor Dee." *If I were the Elizabethan language police, I would arrest Gideon for the overuse of "certes." Oh my God. I'm spending too much time with Jeremy.* She was starting to sound like him. *Focus, Dakota.* "Here is the letter for your consideration." Gideon reached into a leather satchel and removed a piece of parchment, which he handed to Dee.

Dee broke the seal and read silently. "Though all appears in order, Her Majesty the Queen hath never mentioned thee by name." Dee stroked his beard for a moment. "She hath told me thou would'st like to converse on a subject o' great import. I should'st like to hear what thee hath come to say." Dee rubbed his hands over his black skullcap. "You are welcome to Mortlake, Doctor Horn, Master Endicott, Doctor Majors. I pray you be seated."

Dee gestured to several ornately carved but unmatching wooden chairs across from his desk. As the room spun around—whoever was filming must have done a three-sixty—Dakota glimpsed dozens, no, hundreds, of books stacked to the ceiling on uneven wooden shelves. *So this was the lost library of John Dee.* Gideon and Janet practically salivated whenever they talked about it, calling it "the greatest library of natural philosophy, mathematics, and occult in Europe at the time." Was "occult" like dark magic, Dakota had asked. "No," Janet had explained. "Occult encompasses alchemy and astrology, both of which were considered acceptable practices during Elizabeth's reign." *Ah, that's why Dee wasn't burned at the stake for practicing forbidden arts.*

Dee had built up serious street cred with Elizabeth over the years, which made him the best of her many counselors to approach with a concept that sounded bizarre. Even if he didn't believe the travel team at first, he was the least likely in the queen's inner circle to send them off to one of London's notorious lunatic asylums.

"Doctor Dee, we thank you again for seeing us without prior appointment," Gideon said. "We implore you to listen with an open heart and mind as what we are about to say may startle you."

"Gideon...rather, Doctor Horn, perhaps I could continue?" Janet said.

Dakota couldn't see Gideon, but Dee sat up straighter and leaned toward Janet.

"Doctor Horn hath told thee that we have traveled far to see thee, and that is true on two accounts," Janet said. We come from the new world, from a place called Massachusetts, which is hundreds o' mileth north o' the Virginia founded under Sir Walter Raleigh."

"Raleigh's colony is all deprivation and starvation, or so I have heard," Dee said. "How can this Massachusetts exist without mine own knowledge o' it?" Dee scowled at Janet.

"That, sir, is our second truth. Massachusetts was founded in 1630," Janet said. "But we come to thee from the year 2027."

Dee stood abruptly and threw his hands up toward Janet. Inside the voluminous arms of his cloak, his bony hands made him look like a Dementor. "You claim that which is impossible, that thou hast traveled hundreds o' years from a future place that doth not yet exist. Bah, this must be folly."

He leaned over his desk and looked down at Janet. "Forswear you speak the truth," Dee said with a growl. "Else I shall condemn thy words as falsity. Spoken by a serpent, not by the giant in female form I see before me." *Giant?*

Dakota couldn't see Janet's expression on the video, but she hoped Janet had done a better job disguising her emotions from Dee than she was doing right now. *Whoa. A glare like that could freeze the blood in your heart. Kill you in a millisecond.* Dakota refocused on the video.

Gideon jumped in with Dee. "We have come to you, Doctor Dee, because we know you are a learned man—and a forward-thinking one," Gideon said. "You are not constrained by that which you see before you. Your vision extends beyond us or the books in this room." He made a sweeping gesture with his arm. "It takes you to places that others can only imagine."

Ooh. He is good.

"Hmmm." Dee pulled at his beard. "I am in part persuaded by thy reasoning." He sat down again. "We cannot see angels, and yet they exist," he said. "But how can this be possible? And yet I see thee hither, sitting before me." He argued with himself like an archaic version of Tolkien's Golem.

"We do not expect you to apprehend what we say without considerable proof. Which is wherefore we have brought diverse items to share withal thee," Janet said. "Gid…Doctor Horn, could thee I pray you show him the first book?"

Gideon pulled a rust-colored leather-bound book from his satchel and placed it on Dee's desk. Dakota couldn't read the title.

"What is this thee offer me?" Dee stared down at the front cover.

"It is Benjamin Wooley's biography, *The Queen's Conjuror: The Science and Magic of Doctor Dee*," Gideon said, looking down at the book, and then at Dee.

"Is this sorcery? It cannot be. Or can it be? I find myself most confused," Dee said. He bent his head and placed his hands against his furry jaw.

Dakota could see his chest rise and fall.

Dee touched the cover of the book, running his fingers over printed words and the illustration of himself. He turned the book on its side to check its spine. He stared at it for a few minutes.

And then he picked it up and began to read.

CHAPTER 16

5:30 p.m., March 6, 2027, Charlestown, Massachusetts

"He just sat there and read, barely moving, for at least half an hour," Henry said.

"I would do the same and more, if travelers from the future presented me with a biography of myself, which described in detail years ahead of what I'd already lived," Jeremy said.

"Yes, you would do the same and more." Dakota laughed. "You would have thought you'd gone bonkers."

"Well, that's nice, Dakota. Thanks." Jeremy gave her a quick elbow. "I'm sure you would be all super-Zen Miss Equanimity. It wouldn't bother you in the slightest."

"Good point. I would totally panic." Dakota patted Jeremy's arm. "What did John Dee do? Did he just keep reading?"

"He was engrossed in the book for a good twenty minutes," Janet said.

"Watch this part." Henry pointed at the screen. "Gideon's about to show him a postcard of London Bridge." Dakota refocused on the video. She saw Gideon in Dee's study, pulling a postcard from his bag.

"Doctor Dee, I can scarce imagine your inner thoughts," Gideon said. "Shall we take respite, sir, or may we present the other gifts we have brought for you?"

Dee stroked his beard and looked directly at Gideon. "I am deeply puzzled, Doctor Horn, how you and your associates should'st come to possess this tome," Dee said. He placed his hand on the book's front cover. "Is it, as thee say, that thou hast journeyed from future centurieth hence? Or art thou sorcerers—and a sorceress—of the like I have naught encountered?"

"There is more of science than of sorcery about us, Doctor Dee," Gideon said. "That said, we come to you with higher purpose."

"Do thee come from the firmament above?" Dee pointed to the ceiling. "Are thee among the angels I have sought these many years?"

"Wait a minute." Jeremy interrupted the playback. "Why does he think you're angels? Didn't angels have golden halos and little wings in those days? Wouldn't you have been floating on fluffy little clouds if you were angels?" He put his chin on his hands and frowned. "And your cheeks aren't right at all. Not chubby. Not rosy. Sorry, but you just don't pass the angel test."

"That's not how Dee thought of angels." Janet gave Jeremy a stern look. "He believed that angels existed among us, as emissaries of God. Dee thought he could converse with angels through his long-time associate Edward Kelley, a so-called spiritual medium, who convinced Dee the angels wanted them to share everything, including their wives."

"So Kelley was a creep, and Dee was a loon," Jeremy said. He raised an eyebrow at Janet, who rolled her eyes and looked away. Dakota bit her lip to keep from laughing.

"Please, please, could we stop with the commentary and watch the footage?" Janet's face was now red, but her cheeks? Not plump at all.

Henry coughed into his hand. "Let's get back to it," he said, resuming the playback.

Dakota saw Gideon pull a postcard from his bag and give it to Dee.

"What a fine drawing o' London Bridge," Dee said.

The video zoomed in on the cream-colored postcard with a sepia line drawing of London Bridge as it must have appeared in Tudor times. More than two dozen stone arches supported the base of the bridge with several clumps of oddly angled Tudor buildings sprouting from that base. *Weird. It looks like a Dr. Seuss drawing.*

"I am glad you like it, Doctor Dee," Gideon said. "Now please let me show you what the bridge looks like in our time." Gideon removed a second postcard from his bag. It was a photographic image of Tower Bridge. Two massive multistoried stone columns with rows of ornate windows capped by Tudor-style turrets loomed high on either side of London's most famous drawbridge. On opposite sides of the columns facing each shore, thick teal cables sloped to the base of the bridge, where white cables crisscrossed in a suspension structure. Dakota could see a few skyscrapers under the uppermost part of the bridge between the columns. What must Dee have thought?

Dee gasped. "What marvel is this?" He held the postcard up close to his eyes. "Which architect designed it—which architect designed it—and how came it to be constructed? And wherefore, may I ask, doth this printed paper shine and shimmer? It looks resplendent to mine eye."

"I humbly regret my inability to answer your questions, as I am neither artist nor architect, but I promise to bring a book about the construction of the bridge upon our next visit." Dakota thought Gideon looked worried when he spoke. He probably didn't want to go down a rabbit hole about the bridge. "I hope that will suffice for now."

Dee squinted at the postcard, and then put both his hands around his head. "My head pains me," Dee said, looking up at the others. "Perhaps we should'st adjourn and meet upon the morrow."

"I wish that were possible," Gideon said. "Alas, we must return to our own time after our interview with you—but first, we have more for you to see."

Gideon retrieved another book from his travel bag. He was like some time-traveling Mary Poppins, pulling out remarkable items from a magical satchel at every turn. Dakota saw the famous Armada portrait of Queen Elizabeth I looking back at her from the book's cover.

"It is Her Majesty's likeness, thither can be no doubt." Dee picked up the book and read, "'*Heart and Stomach of a Lion: A Biography of Queen Elizabeth I.*' I like the title overmuch. But whose nameth are these? Gideon Horn and Janet Majors?" Dee looked back and forth at the professors. "You are author and authoress? How came this to be?"

"We are university scholars, Doctor Dee," Janet said. "We specialize in the literature and historical events o' sixteenth-century England, with a particular focus on Queen Elizabeth I. This biography represents the fruits o' our labor, years o' research on the woman we believe was…is…England's most important queen."

"Since we both work for Harvard University—which was founded in Cambridge, Massachusetts, in 1636, so you wouldn't have heard of it—we were able to collaborate on the writing," Gideon said. "Now that you have met us, we hope you will feel comfortable presenting the book to Her Majesty."

"Give the book to her?" Dee said. "Now wherefore would'st I do that?" Dee said. "Her Majesty hath been most tolerant o' mine own work these many years. This, this could be mine own undoing. At best, I might find myself a permanent resident o' the Tower o' London. At worst…" he cleared his throat. "…let me say that mine attachment to mine own neck is greater than mine attachment to this book."

"Oh, dear sir, I pray you. Thou art a renowned natural scientist and philosopher, a visionary, a courageous pursuer o' truth. We admire thee more than thee you know," Janet said.

"We are loath to put you, or anyone, in harm's way," Gideon said. "Rather, we have a critical and urgent need to…to bring Her Majesty to our time."

"What?" Dee jumped up from his desk and strode toward the window. He pressed his face to the glass pane and looked back at Gideon and Janet. "How canst thou take Her Majesty from us, where she is so keenly needed? Shalt thou pluck our Gloriana from the heart o' her people who love her? Wherefore, Her Majesty hath just led us to victory o'er England's gravest threat. Should'st thee know our history as thee say, hast thou ne'er heard of the Spanish Armada?"

Dakota could have sworn Dee's eyebrows grew ten times bushier as he scowled at the team.

"We have indeed heard of the Spanish Armada, good Doctor Dee," Gideon said, raising his hands in a classic calming motion. "England's defeat of the world's largest naval fleet helped to establish your country as a maritime power in her own right," Gideon said. "This event has oft been recognized as one of Her Majesty's major achievements."

"It will be far from her last achievement, I have confidence in it," Dee said. "Thusly, thee may not remove her from our time in favor o' thy own." He made a brushing gesture with his hands, as if sweeping them out of the room.

"Please be assured, Doctor Dee, that if Her Majesty leaves the year one thousand five hundred and eighty-eight anno Domini to join us, that the Queen Elizabeth who reigns here shall live all the days of her life in this time, without missing but a half-moment," Gideon said.

"How can I trust what you say, when all you have presented is beyond the realm of possibility?" Dee said. "If Her Majesty were to leave with you, then by all reason she would leave our England."

"I must give correction, Doctor Dee," Gideon said, but Janet jumped in.

"It may not make sense to thee now, sir, but what doth, at this moment?" Janet said. "Should'st Her Majesty leave with us during some future visit, by the time she hath left this time, she shall have lived her life in its entirety, her body laid to its eternal quietus."

"God's bodkin!" Dee said. "Have thee proof o' this outrageous claim?"

"It must be taken on faith," Gideon said.

"No actually, it must be taken on space-time continuum principles and on the science of exotic matter," Henry said. "Would it be helpful for me to explain it?"

"Are you a manservant or a mathematician?" Dee said.

"I suppose I'm both." Henry grinned. "How much time do we have?"

Jeremy waved a dismissive hand. "Please tell me that we don't have to listen to Henry's mathematical explanation of space-time continuum ad infinitum."

"Could we perhaps fast-forward through that part?" Dakota said.

"It's quite fascinating the way that Henry explains it," Maeve said, looking around at the others. No one looked back. "But have it your way, I suppose."

"We'll discuss every last detail later, darling. It's been so long since we've had 'date night.'" Henry winked at Maeve.

"Don't you still have to convince him why Elizabeth needs to leave the smelly old sixteenth century for our own?" Jeremy said.

"Yes, yes, let's keep going," Janet said.

"We have one more item for Her Majesty," Gideon said. "A pamphlet."

Dakota saw the camera focus on a printed booklet, bound together with leather ties. It read, "Greatest Queens in History."

"How came you upon this?" Dee said. "This compendium o' anointed queens."

"It is a popular work from o' time," Janet said. "People read it on what we have named the internet, a repository o' much o' the world's information, which is accessible to hundreds o' millions across the globe at any one time. I ask thee to open it."

"'BuzzFeed: The most influential queens in world history, ranked by order o' importance,'" Dee read. "'Number one: Queen Victoria of England (1819-1901). Number two: Catherine II of Russia (popularly known as Catherine the Great, 1762-1796). Number three: Isabela I of Castile (who co-ruled Spain with her husband, Ferdinand of Aragón, from 1474 up until her death in 1504). Number four: Empress Wu Zetian (the only woman emperor in Chinese history and the creator of the seventh-century Zhou dynasty). Number five: Queen Elizabeth I of England (1533-1603).'

"I cannot give a pamphlet to Her Majesty that lists her in the fifth position," Dee said. "She would'st take offence in extremis. And may I remind thee once more o' mine own attachment?" He placed his hand on his neck.

"Doctor Dee, this is exactly wherefore thee need to share the pamphlet with Her Majesty. In our eyes, thither ne'er wast nor e'er shall be a wiser, more accomplished queen who loveth her people more," Janet said. "But in the eyes o' world history, Queen Elizabeth I is sadly outranked by other lesser queens. This is a travesty and cannot be tolerated."

"Our impetus is of even higher purpose, Doctor Dee," Gideon said. "We have a horrid, incompetent ruler in our country."

"He is a nincompoop of enormous proportions," Henry said. "In fact, he is of enormous proportions."

"He is a dangerous idiot who puts his own people—and the majority o' the world's people, as well as other forms of life on the planet—at great risk," Janet said. "He personifieth corruption and malfeasance, malignancy and foolishness; a soulless, heartless shell o' a human being, he is evil incarnate."

"You go, girl," Jeremy whispered in Dakota's ear.

"In short, we need Her Majesty to rescue us...from ourselves," Gideon said. "We beseech you to speak with her about this opportunity, to share what we have brought, and to ask her to meet with us in sixty days' time, on your premises.

"If any man alive can invite Her Majesty's interest, without arousing equally her fear, it is you, good Doctor Dee. We are in your hands."

"If I approach Her Majesty with this opportunity, as thee have named it. If I show her the book about her life, or even the book about mine own life, she shall think mine own mind lost," Dee said. "I worry, too, that mine own head would'st anon join mine own mind."

"We shall bring assuranceth upon our return. We shall show her glimpseth o' what awaits her—richeth beyond compare. Full health and physical comfort. A restoration to youthful brow. Unimaginable power," Janet said.

"Riches, health, beauty, and power may attract," Dee said. "I shall convey these but shall leave her brow to thy own discussion because..."

"Because ay, thee value thy head," Janet said. "As we value ours."

"Let us choose the date o' thy return," Dee said. "Polish and prepare yourselveth as best thou canst. If all goeth well, thee shall meet Her Majesty in all her glory."

The recording stopped. Dakota looked around at the others. Except for CeCe, who still looked shell-shocked, why were they all smiling? She felt like an elephant was stomping on her chest. She found it hard to breathe. Her palms felt clammy, and her mouth felt dry. Then she began to sweat.

Isn't this what she wanted? Her dream, her vision, her quest to right the many wrongs already committed in the name of Vlakas—and to prevent those that would surely be committed in the future should he be reelected? And her company? She needed to save KODA from a hostile government takeover. So, the fate of the world and the fate of her company were at stake. Not such a big deal really. *Bullshit, Dakota.* If she were the size of a grain of sand, this goal of hers would be the size of North America. And South America. And Central America. And Europe. The walls were closing in on her, and her chest had started aching. She had to go home and process, but at the same time she didn't want to be alone.

Pizza and Pellegrino at the condo with Jeremy and CeCe? Maybe someone would sleep over in one of her guest rooms. She was alone so much of the time, sometimes it was a comfort to have another person home. She could just get a pet. Or maybe she should get a husband. *Oh hell.* All she ready needed right now was her best friends. She hoped she was still their best friend too.

CHAPTER 17

March 12, 2027, Charlestown, Massachusetts

Fifteen minutes.

Dakota had fifteen whole minutes before she met with her sales team and a prospective new client, a global investment firm based in London. She'd formed a relationship with the firm's CTO over the past few years, and now that Russia's most aggressive intelligence agency, GRU, was knocking hard at their door, she was pretty sure the company would become KODA's newest customer.

She stretched out on the sofa in her office, pulling the multicolored Christian Lacroix throw Jeremy had given her last Christmas underneath her chin. She closed her eyes and tried to relax, but there it was again, an image of Elizabeth floated across her closed eyelids. An imperious Elizabeth—adorned in an ornate pearl headdress and a neck-immobilizing lace ruff, a silver gown with swirling flower tendrils painted gold, a jeweled gold-and-pearl belt cinched around her waist, and a double strand of pearls draped across the embroidered fabric of her stomacher—stared down Dakota with a sideways look. *Was that the Darnley Portrait again?*

She shuddered.

Was she delusional for thinking she could pull off the most outrageous plan of the twenty-first century? There was a long way to go, and only a few weeks before the travel team was scheduled to meet with John Dee for the second time. But it wasn't just Dee they'd meet. If Dee succeeded in convincing the queen to grant them audience, Janet, Gideon, and Henry would meet Elizabeth Tudor herself.

Queen Elizabeth I. A.k.a.: Elizabeth the terrifying.

Why am I so damned scared of her?

She got up and checked her face in the decorative tile-framed mirror on her office wall. Monthly facials, plenty of water, and, if she were being honest, good genes, gave her a youthful complexion. Sure, she had her imperfections, but in her heart of hearts, in the quiet of her room—or the mirror at the gym—she was actually pretty attractive...for a geek. On a good day, one might say she resembled a movie star. Or a TV star. Yes, that was it. A powerhouse character from some Netflix or HBO series.

So what if she were a little vain?

Elizabeth will be much vainer, I'm sure.

My God, the woman had two thousand gowns and precious jewels galore. Dakota scooted forward in her desk chair and adjusted her reading glasses to get a better look at her screen. *Is this for real?* The email from her director of business development said that major customer inquiries were flooding the company. Alphabet, General Motors, Costco, and Qualcomm had all contacted KODA over the past week. Was it a coincidence that all their CEOs had endorsed her candidate Samson in the 2024 election? Dakota didn't think so.

She was glad to immerse herself in new business until it was time for the travel team meeting later that afternoon. It would be a relief to focus on what she knew so well. Cybersecurity as a practice was like a big, wonderful jigsaw puzzle. To make it work, you started with the edges and built your way into the middle, which was totally different from the way other cybersecurity companies approached things. They thought you needed this bullet-proof foundation, and you layered on top of it to provide better protection. Dakota, on the other hand, knew that the VAULT's client-specific tools were like the puzzle's framework. Put those in place around the edges, and whatever mess was happening in the middle didn't matter.

The day had sped by. The sales team was aglow after closing the deal with the investment firm that morning. KODA was doing well, and no power on Earth was going to take that away from her.

Just before 6:00 p.m. that evening, Dakota texted Jeremy to confirm that he'd met CeCe and Ashley at the gate to the parking garage, as he'd be escorting them to the Core.

She hoped CeCe was in better shape now than she had been last weekend, when Dakota and company had dropped a conceptual bomb on her head. CeCe did say she was coming tonight, though, so that was promising.

Telling Ashley had been an order of magnitude easier. Dakota and Kisai had brought Ashley to the lab yesterday since Thursday was her day off from Saks. What a piece of cake. It must have helped that Ashley was a big fan of *Outlander* because she had gleefully embraced the whole time-travel concept from the get-go. After Ashley had seen the John Dee footage, she seemed equally thrilled that Janet, Gideon, and Henry had put their period clothes to good use and wondered when she'd be asked to design more.

Dakota checked her watch. 6:05 p.m. *Whoops.* She'd lost ten minutes daydreaming. Everyone was probably there already. She'd always been so focused, and now she caught herself drifting off from time to time. Was her brain already aging? Was she low on B vitamins? Did she need to panic because she was five minutes late?

Make that ten. If she hustled, she could get to the Core by 6:10. Grace under pressure, that was Dakota. Calm in the eye of the storm. Peaceful when surrounded by chaos. That's how she wanted to deal with the maelstrom of life.

And sometimes she was able to pull it off.

CHAPTER 18

6:18 p.m., March 12, 2027, Charlestown, Massachusetts

"Sorry, everyone. I had to put out a fire," Dakota said, hoping the CEO's-so-busy card would buy her some good will. She slunk into an open seat that was farthest from the door.

A not-smiling Janet cast a hairy eyeball at Dakota as she cleared her throat to start the meeting. To the rest of the group, Janet opened her arms wide like a magnanimous host, saying, "Welcome to all. Gideon and I are so pleased that you could make it."

Gideon's smile spread unicorns and rainbows throughout the room. "As you may know, Professor Majors and I have been laying out a plan that would take us from our first meeting with Queen Elizabeth to her arrival here," he said. "We're looking at a multi-stage process. First, there's the convincing. Next, the journey and arrival. Then, we're going to need a transition period to ease her into the twenty-first century."

"This will be disorienting as hell for her," CeCe said. "In fact, it's going to be traumatic, and we'll need to prepare for a high-functioning individual who'll experience some of the symptoms of PTSD."

"Exactly, CeCe…" Janet began.

"Please call me Doctor Gibbons," CeCe said.

"Of course, Doctor Gibbons. We'll rely on your expertise to provide a therapeutically supportive environment for Elizabeth." Janet gave her a micro-squint. "Before we get to that piece, Gideon and I would like to present the stages of our plan for Elizabeth. May we proceed?" Janet looked over her mustard-colored reading glasses at CeCe. "Gideon, please begin."

Gideon projected a PowerPoint presentation from his laptop to the SMART board. Dakota read the title slide, "'From Past to Present: A Journey with Queen Elizabeth I.'"

"Let's assume that Her Majesty agrees to meet with us," Gideon said, clicking to the next slide. "'Stage I: Impress the Queen.'"

Dakota read the sub-bullets silently. "Preparatory phase: attire, gift acquisition, storybook." Over the next fifteen minutes, Dakota learned that the travel team would need new and more elegant clothing. That shouldn't be a problem. Ashley had a few weeks to get them ready. She watched the young woman now, writing furiously in a lined notebook.

Then came the gift list.

"Dakota, I'm sure you can understand that we will be dealing with a woman of sophisticated tastes," Janet said. "While Elizabeth may have lived four centuries ago, she was accustomed to the best of everything: the best clothing, the best food, the best accommodations. She had a dozen royal palaces, one more glorious than the next.

"She had a royal barge to transport her in style as she rode on the River Thames, her own stable of horses at the ready, court musicians, and the Lord Chamberlain's Men, a theater company that had Shakespeare as its principal playwright." Janet took a breath. "Elizabeth had royal servants to accommodate her every whim, gentlewoman of the bed chamber, gentlewomen of the privy chamber, a lord chamberlain, a lord steward. From the care of her linens to the preparation of her food, Elizabeth had servants for every task."

"Did she have a servant to wipe her ass?" Jeremy said.

Giggles broke out.

"I think she managed that on her own." Gideon gave them a bemused smile. "She did, however, have one of the first flush toilets. Her nephew invented it in 1596, and it was installed in Richmond Palace."

"Since she's leaving in 1588 and won't have experienced the flush toilet, perhaps that's what you should bring her? It could be very exciting for her," Jeremy said. Dakota used her thumb and middle finger to thwack him on the side of the head.

"May we move on from toilets, please?" Janet scowled at the others. "We cannot go empty-handed to meet with Elizabeth. We must bring a gift of great beauty—and of significant monetary value." She nodded at Gideon.

When Gideon clicked to the next slide, Dakota's mouth fell open. A necklace of rubies and diamonds rotated on the screen, allowing her to view it at all angles. A large ruby and diamond pendant formed the centerpiece of an intricate collar of rubies and diamonds that were joined at the back by a ruby-studded clasp. Dakota blinked to dull the sparkle of the precious gems. What could these people be thinking?

"This is the Bulgari Beating Heart, and we think it will convey our meaning: we're serious, we're respectful, and we understand her worth," Janet said.

"Holy shit," CeCe said. "How much does it cost?"

"Why don't we discuss its merit first? Isn't that what's most important?" Janet said.

"Hmmm…not sure." Jeremy tapped his fingers to his lips. "Does it cost as much as a private jet, or is it more like a single-family house in Cambridge?"

"How much is a single-family in Cambridge?" Gideon said.

"Very pricey, I'm sure. Hell, Dakota doesn't even own one," Jeremy said.

"It's not that I can't afford one, Jeremy dear. I just don't want one." Dakota squinted at him.

"Please, people." Janet raised her voice. "The necklace is much more affordable than a single-family in Cambridge. It's well under two million dollars."

"Well, that's a deal," Jeremy said, dripping sarcasm.

"I've never spent even close to that much on a piece of jewelry for myself," Dakota said. "But then again, I'm not known from my extravagant tastes." She closed her eyes, placed her hands together and touched them to her lips, pausing for a moment. "One question before we move forward: Why are we giving her jewelry when she must have precious jewels galore?"

"Like many rich people, I suppose more is better," Ashley said, looking somber.

"But not our Dakota," Jeremy winked at her. "She's the most grounded billionaire of anyone I've ever met."

"I'm the *only* billionaire you've ever met," Dakota said with a chuckle.

Janet turned to Dakota. "We wouldn't ask for this if we didn't believe it was important."

"It's an outrageous amount of money to spend on a bauble," Gideon said. "Yet, it was traditional for visiting courtiers, even those of royal blood, to present Elizabeth with expensive gifts when they sought an audience."

"If we don't give her something extraordinary, she won't take us seriously," Janet said.

"And we're making a very serious offer for a job with the potential to affect the lives of millions," Dakota said.

"More like billions of people. Then there's the environment," CeCe said. "As wrong as it is, an American president has the power to change almost everything…."

"For good or ill." Dakota finished her sentence. "Let's order the necklace tomorrow."

"Wonderful!" Janet clapped her hands. "Thank you, Dakota. I'm certain it will leave a lasting impression."

"Could we buy it soon so I can wear it for a few minutes? Just in the privacy of my own home, of course?" CeCe fluttered her lashes.

"Sorry, CeCe. When Ashley purchases it on my behalf, Jeremy will have it locked in KODA's vault," Dakota said.

"That's our actual vault, for those who don't know, not the product, VAULT," Jeremy said.

CeCe put her fist to her cheek. "It was just a passing thought."

"Could we please go back to the part that I'm the one buying the necklace?" All the color had drained from Ashley's face. *I hope she's not having a stroke.* "I have no idea how to handle that kind of money." Her voice got very quiet.

"Good point, Ashley," Dakota said, hoping she conveyed the warmth she was feeling. "I've only spent that kind of money on real estate until now—and I guess also on some of my causes, of course, because philanthropy is so important." She blinked at Ashley. "No matter. I'll ask my financial advisor to pull it from somewhere or another." She patted Ashley's hand.

"Let's get back to the gifts," Dakota said. "Do we need to send any other gifts? Hopefully ones that aren't quite as expensive."

"Just a few more much more modest items. Gideon, could you please move to the next slide?" Janet said.

Dakota had to remind herself to keep breathing as Gideon continued the presentation. When she saw the next slide, she exhaled.

"With the rest of the gifts, we're going for novelty," Janet said. "These include comestibles that weren't available in Tudor England. Chocolate bars, coffee—we'll bring some coffee beans, a grinder, and a French press. Also cashews, After Eight mint chocolate thins—"

"—ooh, I love those," CeCe said.

"—and Jelly Belly jelly beans," Janet said. "For her person, we're bringing a gift box of Gilchrist & Soames hand cream, probably lavender, since it will have a familiar scent, and an assortment of fragrance samples."

"I have a fragrance sensitivity," Jeremy said with a smirk.

Janet turned her back to Jeremy and said, "Gideon, you had one thing to add."

"Yes. I'd like to present her with a monogrammed Cross pen-and-pencil set," Gideon said. "My parents gave me a set like that when I earned my doctorate, and I still treasure it."

"Awww," Ashley said. "That's so sweet."

"Moving on," Jeremy said. "Looks like a complete list. Will dessert be here soon?"

"We need to talk about one last important item before we discuss our attire." Janet tapped her fingers on the table. "Don't worry, Jeremy. You don't need to stay for that part. We'll review it all with Ashley."

"But I'd love to talk about Renaissance frippery all night, Janet." Jeremy cocked his head to the side.

"It's a good thing I love you, darling, because sometimes you have the attention span of an eight-year-old." Dakota said to Jeremy, who blew her a kiss.

"Ahem." Gideon cleared his throat. "I've been thinking a lot about this, and of course, talking with Professor Majors all the time, about what we could do to help Queen Elizabeth envision what her life here could be like.

"I started thinking about artists storyboarding movies and believe we should do something similar. While we can't present the queen with an actual storyboard, we could present her with a book," he said.

He clicked to the next slide.

"The storybook introduces Queen Elizabeth to the people and places that will be important to her when she first arrives. We'll have photos of Boston and Cambridge, and Dakota's condo, since she'll be staying there during her initial transition," Gideon said.

"Of course. I've already started construction to make my condo fit for a queen." Dakota folded her hands in front of her.

"She'll need more than just Dakota." CeCe nibbled on the cherry from her Mai Tai. "She's going to need friends."

"So glad that you feel that way," Gideon said to CeCe. "Since the queen could be living with Dakota for a period of months, and you'll be needed close by. Best to move in."

"Say what?" CeCe said.

"As a psychologist, I'm sure you realize that Elizabeth is going to feel overwhelmed, no matter what we do," Janet said. "She may see you as a Gentlewoman of the Bed Chamber, Doctor Gibbons, but you will in fact be her personal therapist."

"I'm not changing anyone's linens." CeCe frowned. "But I like the idea of serving as her covert therapist. Of course, she will have no idea that therapists even exist, which is why she won't suspect when I use operant conditioning with her…. Ooh, this is going to be fun." She gave a small clap.

"This is no occasion for levity, I'm afraid," Janet said. "Many scholars, me included, believe that Elizabeth suffered from panic attacks. She was only twenty-one when her sister Queen Mary imprisoned her in the Tower of London for a few weeks, suspecting she'd played a role in trying to overthrow her."

"And she was just a child when her father, Henry VIII, had her mother Anne Boleyn beheaded, also at the Tower of London," Gideon said. "Just three years old at the time."

"Talk about trauma," CeCe said. "I'll plan a subtle course of trauma treatment."

"I suggest proceeding with extreme caution, Doctor Gibbons, at least until you get to know her better," Janet said. "She was accustomed to being in charge and may not wish to seem vulnerable to someone who is still foreign to her."

"Let's get back to the storybook, please. How are you planning to frame this opportunity, for Elizabeth to come to the rescue of twenty-first-century America?" Dakota said.

"We're going to play to her desire to claim a new and bigger place in history," Gideon said. "We'll describe the problem—that the most powerful country in the world is being run into the ground by an infantile ignoramus who doesn't care about his people."

"All of that will bother her," Janet said. "She was not one to suffer fools gladly. She was brilliant and highly educated, and she loved her people."

"Didn't she say she was married to her people?" Jeremy said, looking up from this laptop.

"So you *did* read the book," Dakota said. "I knew it."

"Yes, yes. Of course, I read it." Jeremy examined his fingernails.

"You ask an excellent question," Janet said, beaming at him. "Elizabeth once said to Parliament, 'I have already joined myself in marriage to a husband, namely the kingdom of England.' Married to her country, her people were like her children."

"We believe we can capitalize on gender politics as well," Gideon said. "From the time she acceded to the throne at age twenty-five until well into her mid-forties, when it was still deemed possible, albeit unlikely, that she could bear an heir, the English Parliament and some members of her Privy Council—particularly William Cecil, who served her for forty years—pressured her to marry. How could a woman rule England without a man to guide her?

"We're talking about a time when a married woman's property, including her children, belonged to her husband, when women didn't hold positions of power, were rarely educated at the level of men, couldn't attend university, and were barred from most professions—

except laundress, seamstress, agricultural worker…or prostitute." He looked down at his keyboard. "As a highly educated and incredibly powerful woman, Elizabeth was an outlier on so many levels. She succeeded despite being born a woman."

"We are convinced that she will take a visceral dislike to Robert Vlakas, if we do our job right," Janet said. "She will abhor the idea that an incompetent man defeated an articulate, well-educated, highly experienced woman for the highest position in the land. Elizabeth certainly wouldn't approve of what Vlakas says about women, criticizing their physical appearance or bragging about his predation. Elizabeth did not take kindly to bullies."

"Elizabeth was not faint-hearted when it came to confronting a powerful man," Gideon said. "In truth, it would be worth bringing her to our time just to see her debate him."

Janet looked directly at Dakota. "She will eviscerate him."

"Yes!" Dakota raised her fist in the air and grinned.

"We've not touched upon one little issue. And that is, what did Elizabeth think of Black people?" CeCe said.

"Don't forget Asian people," Jeremy said.

Janet's chest rose and fell a few times while the others stayed silent. "This is a delicate and complex issue." Janet stood, walked over to a sideboard, and picked up a sparkling water. She took a sip.

"Gideon and I have carefully considered this question as it will affect, at least initially, her response to you." Janet looked at CeCe. Then she cleared her throat.

"Do tell," CeCe said.

"May I, Professor?" Gideon asked Janet, who nodded back at him. He placed his hands on either side of his laptop and sat up in his chair. "From what personal accounts of this era tell us, Moors came from Spain to England in the late sixteenth century. Most were successful tradesmen and artisans. Educated people. It's likely that the queen would have received them at court at some point."

"That doesn't sound so bad," CeCe said. "But it gets worse, right?"

"It's a multi-faceted issue," Gideon said. "Because there was racism in Tudor England as there was in other parts of Europe at the time."

"What do you mean 'at the time?'" CeCe said. She gestured with a flourish. "There's plenty of racism right now, all over the world, including right here in America, in case you haven't been paying attention."

"I'm aware, Doctor Gibbons, although not in the same way that you are, I'm sure." Gideon blushed. "Queen Elizabeth most likely viewed Black people according to their economic class and level of education. She would have seen the Moors differently from say…"

"African slaves," Dakota said.

"Yes, from African slaves." Gideon bent his head down.

"She didn't own slaves, did she? Please tell me no," CeCe said.

"She didn't own African slaves, no. There were African entertainers in her court, but they were not slaves," Gideon said. "In fact, the English were not allowed to own slaves in England. There were some African servants in England at the time. They'd been taken from captured Spanish ships, but they would have been paid and…"

"Gideon, let me help." Janet tapped Gideon lightly on the arm. "Queen Elizabeth commissioned Sir John Hawkins's second voyage to Africa for the purpose of capturing and selling Africans."

"Oh, that bitch. I'm rethinking my whole role as therapist masquerading as a lady in waiting or gentlewoman of the whatever," CeCe said. She thwacked the table with the flat of her hand. The sound at impact was so loud that Dakota flinched in her seat. Though her eyes were still flashing, CeCe spoke again, "On the other hand, I think we should show the queen the nature of her wrongdoing. We'll start with a verbal brief, and then watch a series of movies. *Twelve Years a Slave. Amistad. The Hate U Give* will give her a feel for what it's like to be Black in today's America." CeCe clapped her hands. "I'm so looking forward to this."

"I don't blame you for being angry, Doctor Gibbons, or anyone else in this room. African slavery was a horror," Janet said. "The truth is that Elizabeth profited from Hawkins's second voyage, and though she didn't supply the ships for his future trips, the crown did benefit from the slave trade."

Dakota glared at Gideon and Janet. "Why don't I remember reading about this in your book?"

"Because we didn't include it," Gideon said. His Adam's apple bobbled as he gulped. "A few other historians have published entire papers about the queen's involvement in the African slave trade."

"Perhaps I was wrong in choosing her," Dakota felt queasy. There was no way she wanted a racist as president. *Another* racist, that is, because the a-hole they already had in the White House was in bed with the white supremacists.

"And there were African tradesmen and artisans who lived freely in England throughout Elizabeth's reign," Janet said, her voice weak.

"Is it off then, our journey to retrieve Elizabeth?" Gideon asked Dakota.

"CeCe, what do you think?" Dakota said.

"I think we should create and implement a robust cultural educa-tion program during her acclimation period," CeCe said, her hands clasped underneath her chin. "We will educate her about the ties between colonialism and racism—and about the lasting effects that these policies have had on America and other parts of the world," she said. "If we can change the perspectives of a sixteenth-century queen, we can do just about anything."

Gideon looked at Janet, who said, "Oh thank God. I'm so relieved."

"Just one more thing: she would have called Africans in England Blackamoors," Gideon said.

"Mmmm…I'm not feeling that," CeCe said.

"We'll add appropriate nomenclature to the storybook, I promise, and we'll cover it before you meet her," Gideon said.

"You might have to remind her, though," Janet said.

"Oh, not to worry. I'll be happy to remind her," CeCe said with a mischievous smile.

"Hey, good news. I ordered some cannoli," Henry said, picking up his buzzing phone.

"Excellent. I'm ready for something sweet," CeCe said. "I hope you ordered more than one cannoli apiece."

"This isn't our first rodeo," Maeve said. "Henry ordered extra everything."

"Can we please, please for the love of God, stop talking about food?" Janet looked like the top of her head was about to explode.

"I'd like to take a moment to remind everyone of the magnitude of what we're attempting." Dakota dropped her voice to her lowest-possible register. "And to emphasize that keeping everything we say in the strictest confidence is critical to our success."

"So I can't even tell my boyfriend?" Ashley said.

"You can't even hint at it," Dakota said. "For if the truth were to be exposed, the outcome would be almost unimaginable."

But then she imagined it. Kisai would win the Nobel Prize in physics, but only after the scientific community had dragged him head-first through the New York City sewer system. Academia would be no kinder to Janet, whose sterling reputation would be curdled by the accusations of jealous colleagues. Gideon would never get his tenure, and CeCe would lose her appointment at Harvard Med. Ashley would be exploited by reality television.

Dakota could protect Jeremy, Maeve, and Henry, but what of herself? She was a power-mad woman, the press would say, who'd rather be a kingmaker than a CEO. Like a million piranha feeding on the bloody carcass of her dream, the media would destroy Dakota, one tweet a time. And once her reputation was destroyed, KODA's would go down with it.

And Elizabeth? Oh dear lord, Elizabeth. She'd be the freak at the center of the circus. An oddity, a woman out of time; everyone would want to meet her, but none would be a true friend. They'd gnaw off little pieces of her until her authentic self was gone.

Dakota's mouth was so dry, she couldn't even wet her lips.

Get a hold of yourself. She took a good look at each person sitting around the table. Every one of them was bright-eyed and engaged, and so full of energy they could have powered a car battery. Even Jeremy was churning out 110 volts.

As they laid out a plan to woo the queen who might...who would...be president, Dakota saw that *her* inner circle would become Elizabeth's as well. She would have to trust them to honor Elizabeth's actual identity without ever disclosing it. And if one of them did? Dakota would throw that person to the wolves, for the good of the many outweighed the good of the one.

As the conversation flowed around her, she was struck with a thought: she might be a bit Machiavellian after all.

CHAPTER 19

6:00 a.m., April 9, 2027, Cambridge, Massachusetts

It had been the longest four weeks of Dakota's life, with the past week the worst of all. The travel team was supposed to arrive seven days ago, but April 2 had come and gone, and Janet, Gideon, and Henry were still missing. What had gone wrong? Did John Dee tell Elizabeth they were heretics of the worst sort? Or did Elizabeth decide that for herself? Were they rotting in the bowels of some horrid dungeon? She had no idea what had happened, nor did anyone else. All Dakota knew was that Kisai had 24-7 coverage in the lab with at least two of his staff watching for nanosecond energy blips that might indicate the arrival of ectoplasm, hopefully still living, in elevator central.

Dakota rolled out of bed and strolled to the master bathroom. One of her greatest extravagances—CeCe called it "palatial"—the bathroom sometimes made her feel guilty. It's not like she was an oligarch toodling around in a superyacht that burned more gas than the entire city of Cambridge. Still, there might be some who saw it as excessive.

"When I see your bathroom, I'm reminded that more than half the world's population doesn't even have a toilet at home," her mother might have said. "...which doesn't mean that your father and I aren't tremendously proud of your accomplishments, dear heart. It's just that we're interested in a more equitable distribution of wealth."

Dakota heaved a sigh as she sat on the heated toilet seat and surveyed her inner sanctum. After a stressful day at the office, she liked to come home and soak in her lava stone bathtub. She'd lay her head against the built-in headrest and look out at the night sky from the wall of windows—another advantage of living on the top floor. The feel of the radiant heat as she walked across the limestone tiles warmed her soul, and the hammam steam room, infused with eucalyptus, soothed her from the outside in. Thank God her bathroom wasn't under construction like the "wing" of her condo being renovated with haste for Elizabeth.

Once she came to grips with the necessity of Elizabeth living with her for some undefined period of time, she'd called in a design firm to make some modifications for a most particular houseguest. Since Dakota didn't have a castle, she'd need to make Elizabeth *feel* like her residence was opulent, even if her new home was a penthouse condo on the Charles, not a royal palace on the Thames.

Dakota licked a coating of fine dust off her teeth. *Eeww. What's on my toothbrush?* The construction had permeated every corner of her condo. Yesterday she'd even found dust inside her coffee cup, and that was *after* she'd already had a sip. Total sacrilege. She couldn't accept contaminated morning coffee under any circumstance.

She'd have the designer ask the contractor to do a better job sealing off Elizabeth's quarters. It was only a new bath and larger walk-in closet with internal sitting area and gas fireplace, for heaven's sake. It's not like she was gutting the place as she'd done ten years ago when she bought two adjacent condos to create her current home.

She bit a nail. *That's it. I'm going for a run.*

By 6:20 that morning, Dakota was running on the sidewalk along Memorial Drive. *That wind is brutal.* She brushed a few snowflakes out of her eyes and pulled her fleece beanie over her ears. It was early April so she shouldn't be surprised at the early-spring snowsquall, but that didn't mean she had to like it. She hoped the fierce weather didn't portend anything ominous. She glanced at her watch. Was it already 6:50? She hoped today would be the day her travel team would return with news of Elizabeth.

Hours later, Dakota leaned back in her office chair, hands behind her head. She'd been testing the inaugural prototype of Courier+˙, KODA's secure email reader with personalized AI. From all the data mining she'd done lately, she knew that no one else had anything like Courier+, not even in concept form. Time to give HR a heads-up. Start hiring more data scientists, more software developers, more hardware engineers with experience in supercomputers. KODA needed to increase staff well ahead of the product launch. *This is going to be fun.* A jolt of adrenaline ran through her body as she contemplated the next steps.

But first, she had a four o'clock with the Democratic National Committee, coming to see her for the third time since the 2024 election. Maybe this time the DNC would actually pony up to buy their own VAULT—which she planned to sell to them at a steeply discounted rate. The country simply couldn't afford more Russian interference in the next presidential election. Based on the extensive online sleuthing that Jeremy's group had done both before and after the last election, she knew for a fact that Sokolov had activated every weapon in his political arsenal to get Vlakas elected. Sokolov's operatives had waged a digital war against Jennifer Samson, annihilating the DNC's email server in the process. Coupled with the Republicans' assault of Samson in the conservative media, and their skillful use of fake news on Facebook and Instagram, Samson couldn't have won without divine intervention. Not even Dakota could have saved her.

A knock on the door interrupted her thoughts.

"Come in," Dakota said, rising from her desk.

"Thought you might need a little boost before our DNC meeting." Like Mufasa presenting his lion cub to the animals of the savan-

·nah, Jeremy held up a small brown bakery box tied with red and white twine.

"Oh, you didn't," Dakota said. "At least I ran this morning." She patted her stomach.

"I know when my boss needs her baklava," Jeremy said, holding his free hand to his heart. "I got it last night at that great Armenian market on Belmont Street. Time for a pick-me-up."

Twenty minutes later, Dakota and Jeremy were in the upstairs conference room sitting across from the DNC contingent. Her phone buzzed in her pocket. But she couldn't check it while three of the DNC's vice chairs—two US senators and the governor of one of the blue states in the Great Lakes region—were arguing with each other.

"How can KODA protect the DNC email server from cyberattacks when my colleague here…" said Senator Martin H. Harrison III of New York, a sixty-six-year-old with thinning brown hair pasted to his scalp, as he pointed to a wizened white-haired man, whose face was scrunched up like he'd just eaten something sour, "…uses AOL for his email?"

Senator John Bobbins of Ohio, who even progressives called Senator "Raisin," had served a mere forty-six years in the Senate. Raisin spun his chair around to face Harrison, the "young" upstart from New York, then used his feet to scoot closer. Dakota bit her lip to keep from laughing. "Why don't you quit your yappin' and listen to the computer whiz?" He pushed his reading glasses up the bridge of his nose and turned back to Dakota.

"Gentleman," said the baby of the bunch, Evelyn "Evie" Howard, a first-term governor with shimmering blonde hair and an easy smile. According to Dakota's sources, the buzz on the Hill was that Evie Howard was days away from declaring her candidacy for president. "I agree that we should listen to Ms. Wynfred. She is the expert among us, after all." *Uh oh. She's sane, attractive, and she has a nice voice. We better keep an eye on her.*

Evie's words seemed to pacify the others as the rest of the meeting passed altercation-free. The hard part for Dakota was staying focused when her phone kept buzzing. She was dying to glance at it, but there was no subtle way to take a peek. After what seemed like an eternity, she heard Raisin say they would "almost definitely be moving over to the VAULT as soon the rest of the committee approves the purchase." *I'm not holding my breath.*

Dakota stole a look at Jeremy, who was tapping his fingers on the conference room table. *Are we both getting texts? What the hell's going on?*

Just after 6:00 p.m., Dakota and Jeremy walked the DNCers to the elevator. She found herself taking baby steps so she wouldn't bolt ahead of Raisin. How old was that guy? Eighty-two? No wonder the Democrats were such a mess. Samson had been a rock star, in her opinion, but by and large, the Democrats were dominated by white men in their seventies and eighties. And it's not like the Republicans were any better. Look at Congress. Look at Vlakas, who'd landed the presidency at the youthful age of seventy-six. It seemed you had to have a dick and a decade of Medicare eligibility to hold higher office in the US government. Enough already. She hoped to hell the American people would agree with her.

With Bobbins and Raisin talking over each other during a long, drawn-out goodbye—Dakota thought she caught an eye-roll by Evie Howard—the three politicians got on the elevator. Finally. Like cowboys drawing their guns in an old-time shootout, she and Jeremy whipped out their phones just as soon as the doors closed. There must have been twenty text messages from Kisai, and few more from Maeve. She bit her lip. Then she started to sweat. What a shitty time for a hot flash.

"Jeezus Christ, Jeremy, I got a million texts from Kisai and Maeve during the meeting," Dakota said. "I'm terrified to find out what's happening in the lab." She rubbed the back of her neck.

"I was getting them too," Jeremy said. "Also Maeve just texted me. Ummm…I bet it's all good. Right? Probably nothing to worry about." He stared at his phone.

"There it is again." Dakota looked at her phone. "What the eff? Kisai says we need to get down to the lab NOW. I can't believe it. I've never seen him use all caps." Dakota's heart fluttered.

"I typed in all caps once," Jeremy said. "But that was good news because I'd just blown away the doctoral committee when I defended my dissertation, and I wanted to let my mother know that I wasn't a total failure."

"She doesn't think you're a failure, Jeremy. She's just very traditional." Dakota patted his back as they got onto the elevator.

Jeremy frowned. "I'll never marry a nice Korean girl."

"Let's survive the next five minutes, and then we'll talk about your mother's homophobia."

Dakota felt queasy as the elevator dropped. She rolled her shoulders back and took a few deep breaths. Maybe she was just overreacting. Maybe Maeve had ordered dinner for twenty and wanted Jeremy and her to eat some of it. Maybe Kisai wanted to tell her that the travel team had been delayed, but he thought they were all fine. Or maybe they'd found a bunch of bloody bits in Elevator Central. She pulled at the soft part under her chin.

She and Jeremy rode the elevator down to the garage. When they exited, she grabbed his hand. It was damp.

They walked over to the door that led to the Core, and Dakota scanned her way into the hallway.

"Whoa. Didn't expect to see you right here, Kisai," Dakota said. He stared ahead like a deer in the headlights, his hair even messier than usual.

"SHE'S HERE," Kisai said, gulping. "I know we didn't plan it this way, but they brought her back with them." He hung his head and stared at his feet.

"I don't understand. Who are you talking about, Kisai?" Dakota said. She placed her hand on the sleeve of his lab coat.

"She. Her. She's in the recovery room with the others," Kisai said, stammering. "I guess you'll meet her tomorrow." He blinked behind his glasses.

Dakota felt a stab in her gut. She looked at Kisai. She looked at Jeremy. And then she looked ahead, past the Core to the entrance of the lab. "What? You're kidding? Wait until tomorrow? Let's get real. I am so going in."

CHAPTER 20

Dakota's heart slammed against her chest cavity as she followed Kisai past the Core to the lab's side entrance. If Jeremy hadn't tugged the back of her sweater once she entered the lab area, Dakota would have squashed the back of Kisai's heels while beelining toward the recovery room. It was hard not to feel excited when she'd soon be mere feet away from Queen Elizabeth. The first. The original. Gloriana in the flesh.

She slammed on her brakes. *Who's that guy standing in front of the door?* Tall and angular, with wavy mahogany-brown hair, the stranger in the white lab coat huddled over a clipboard, writing furiously.

Kisai called out to him. "Abe. How is she?"

"Who's Abe again?" Jeremy whispered to Dakota as they followed Kisai into the lab.

"He's the doctor for our new health and safety protocol, remember?" Dakota whispered back. "Kisai had him check out Janet, Gideon, and Henry after the first John Dee visit, but we didn't meet him because we were at my place by then."

"Right. We drank a ton that night," Jeremy said.

"Yup. That we did."

As the trio reached Abe, he looked up from his clipboard. Beads of sweat pooled on his forehead, though the lab was cool as always. "She's very disoriented, Hoshi, but her vitals are good. Gideon's the most lucid of the four of them, so I asked why she was groggier than the others," Abe said. "As it turns out, he'd brought an Ativan with him in case someone panicked during the trip. He didn't want her getting anxious by the time she arrived, so he asked John Dee to give her the pill before they left."

"Gave it to who? The queen? Which 'her' are we talking about?" Dakota said, glaring at the man with whom she now made eye contact. His eyes were soft and brown. His shoulders, large and broad. His face, cleanly shaven. *Snap out of it, Dakota.*

"Hi, I'm Abe Diamond." He extended his hand to Dakota first, then to Jeremy.

"Forgive me for the lack of introduction," Kisai did a head-bow to Dakota and Jeremy. "Please meet my doctor and good friend, Doctor Abe Diamond." He angled his body toward Abe. "Abe, please meet my boss and benefactor, Dakota Wynfred, and her chief security officer, Jeremy Jiang."

"Doctor Diamond, please tell me how she's doing, and by 'she'—I can't believe I'm saying this—I mean Queen Elizabeth." Dakota's words spilled out. "What is your medical opinion of her?"

"Having never examined a Tudor before…" Abe gave a small laugh, showing his dazzling white teeth. "…I can only say that her blood pressure was excellent—one-twenty-five over eighty—her heartrate was good, and her lungs sounded clear. I did sneak a quick listen since she was sleeping," he said in a whisper, as if revealing that he'd cheated ever so slightly on a major exam. "Despite the good vitals, she looked awfully pale. If I could do a complete physical exam, I'd have a better answer for you."

Dakota shook her head. "Given that she's never had anything like a modern physical, that's out of the question," Dakota said. "She will need one, though, and soon, but a woman must do it. I hope you understand."

"Of course." Abe inclined his head toward Dakota. "Anything to reduce the shocks to her system, as I imagine there will be many shocks to come."

"We're going to try to minimize those as much as possible, but I'm sure you're right," Dakota said. She turned to Jeremy. "Could you please ask CeCe to get over here as fast as humanly possible? All that covert work she wants to do with Elizabeth is going to start much sooner than we thought."

"On it," Jeremy said. "By the way, we're getting Korean takeout tonight. It's going to be a hungry night, and I need my ribs."

"Good idea," Dakota said. "Let's get some fried rice and dumplings too, and include a Mai Tai for CeCe, with some extras for the crowd. It's going to be a thirsty night too." *I need to get myself in to see her, or I'm not sleeping tonight. Probably not sleeping anyway.*

"But first. Doctor Diamond. Could I go in to see her?" Dakota gave Abe her best puppy-dog eyes. "I promise not to wake her or otherwise disturb her. I just need a glimpse. Would that be acceptable?" Dakota stared at him unblinking.

"If you're going, I'm going," Jeremy said, reaching for Dakota's hand.

"I'm staying here, should anyone wish to know," Kisai said, shuffling his feet.

Huh. It's not like Kisai to act slighted. But then again, I suppose I've been taking him for granted, and it's not every day someone changes history.

"Before we go in, may I just say what a tremendous achievement this is, Kisai. And that goes for all the preceding trips and the many years of work you've invested in Tempus Fujit," Dakota said. "If we could tell the world what you've accomplished, you would have all the recognition you deserve. Since our project is of the utmost secrecy, however, I'll need to use this private venue to thank you for everything you've done to date." She shook his hand with vigor. "It's a privilege and a pleasure to work with you."

"It is with you as well." Kisai bowed and looked up with a smile, his eyes twinkling. "As long as Abe allows it, I think you may enter with care. Abe?"

"I won't make you put on HazMat suits, but you have to wear some protective gear," Abe said, handing them blue surgical masks and latex gloves.

Once adorned, Dakota took a few steps toward the recovery room door and ever so carefully opened it, not daring to make a sound. She squinted in the twilight of the room until her eyes adjusted to the low light. Reaching behind her for Jeremy's hand, she led him around the resting bodies covered with white duvets as they dozed on their cots. Henry was curled on his side, snoring. Janet mumbled something in her sleep, and Gideon had the covers tucked high around his neck. Protected for now. In the far-right corner of the room, a smaller shape shifted. Dakota tip-toed ahead, her breath shallow.

She let go of Jeremy's hand and drew close. One bejeweled hand rested on the top edge of the duvet. Tightly coiled copper hair was partially covered by an intricate headdress of pearls in a light lattice of gold. The queen was turned away from her. Dakota whispered a silent prayer. *Please, dear God, let me see her face.*

Wham!

"Oh, what the hell. I just smashed the shit out of my knee," Jeremy stage-whispered. And then quieter, he said, "I can't see a goddamn thing in here. Can you?"

"Shhh." Dakota turned and held one palm out toward Jeremy. "We promised not to disturb her." Dakota circled back around.

The figure was now turned on her side, facing Dakota. She bent over to get a closer look and was now just inches from the queen's face. *It's like someone brushed white oil paint all over her skin and then applied rounds of beet juice to her cheeks.* Dakota couldn't see any pockmarks. *I wonder if she even had them?*

Dakota realized she was holding her breath.

Then the queen's eyelids fluttered and opened.

CHAPTER 21

April 9, 2027, Charlestown, Massachusetts

"Art thou a woman? Where is thy hair?"

The Tudor in their midst must not have seen a woman with short hair before. Dakota ran a hand over her short shag, which at $185 a cut—plus color—was hardly inexpensive. *Who cares about my hair? Elizabeth the First is in the house.*

Queen Elizabeth propped herself up on her elbows and had a look around, but moments later, she slid down on her cot, laying her head against the pillow. She closed her eyes and fell back to sleep.

"Hey." Jeremy elbowed Dakota in the ribs. "I want to see too," he said, barely audible. Dakota shifted sideways to allow him to get closer.

Though the room itself was dim, the soft glow of a nearby night-light let Dakota make out the queen's features—the prominent nose and high cheekbones, the blotchy white makeup on her face, the fine curls of her copper wig still tightly coiled against her forehead, the crimson paint upon her lips. Dangling pearl-drop earrings, which must have been made of finest gold, hung from her delicate earlobes.

If Dakota put her ear close to the queen's mouth, could she hear her breathing? *Better not. I don't want to wake her.*

The queen was a miracle. She was all Dakota's hopes and dreams bundled into the body of a woman who had never heard of takeout food or had a hot shower or munched hot popcorn in a movie theater.

What would the queen think of her new world? Would she be terribly homesick, or would some modern convenience or form of entertainment take her mind off all the people and places she had known and loved? It was hard to stay in the present when all Dakota could think about was the future, but she would have to try.

Dakota straightened to standing and slowly backed away from the royal in repose. She motioned to Jeremy that it was time to leave. They crept out of the room like new parents who didn't want to wake their sleeping baby.

Now just outside the door, Dakota put a finger to her lips as she glanced at Abe, who was saying something to Kisai. Maeve sat nearby, staring at her laptop.

"Ahem." Dakota cleared her throat to get their attention. All eyes were on her, except for Maeve, who stayed glued to her post. *Makes sense. She doesn't want to stray too far from Henry.*

Dakota signaled to the others to follow her to the conference room on the opposite side of the lab. Looking over her shoulder to make sure they were behind her, she watched Jeremy, Kisai, and Abe line up like a brood of ducklings trailing their mother to the pond. She turned the doorknob ever so slowly, walked to the back of the room, and removed her mask and gloves as she waited for the others to come in. When Jeremy approached, she grabbed his hands and started jumping up and down.

"Holy effing God," she yelled at the ceiling. "Can you believe she's actually here? She might think I'm a man because I have short hair." She guffawed. "But who cares? I've never been so excited about anything in my life."

She dropped Jeremy's hands, then heard herself panting. Why was she gasping for air? She slid onto a chair. Before she knew it, a gentle hand tipped her forward, pushing her knees apart and guiding her head down through her legs.

"It's only natural to feel overwhelmed at a time like this." She heard Abe's smooth baritone telling her to breathe.

A few minutes later, Dakota was still taking small sips of the cranberry juice that Abe and given her. Her breath was returning to normal.

"Sorry about that," Dakota said, wiping some drool onto the sleeve of her midnight-blue cashmere crewneck.

"Don't worry about it. What's a meeting without a panic attack?" Jeremy said. She knew he was trying for levity, but his voice sounded strained. He must have been more worried than she realized.

"It wasn't a true panic attack," Abe said, his voice a low growl. "She just got overwhelmed." He smiled at Dakota, and she felt her face flush.

"CeCe and Ashley are pulling into the garage." Kisai looked up from his phone. "I've had them on alert in case something unexpected happened."

"And boy has it happened," Dakota said.

"I'll bring them through the side door." Kisai walked away to retrieve them.

Dakota couldn't wait to tell CeCe about Elizabeth. She'd think the short-hair quip was hilarious. When Dakota had shown up with that short shag on her fortieth birthday, CeCe had let her mouth drop open in mock horror. "Short hair makes you appear younger, CeCe, don't you know that?" Dakota had said. The hell with CeCe—and Elizabeth, in this case. Dakota liked her hair.

Just a few minutes later, present-day CeCe arrived. Ashley was almost on her heels.

"Girl, are you losing your mind over this, or what?" CeCe walked into the conference room like she owned it. *She never calls me "girl" unless she's sozzled, but I doubt she's been drinking. This is going to be a weird night.*

"Hi, CeCe. Hi, Ashley," Dakota said. "I'm sure Kisai told you about our surprise guest."

"He most certainly did," CeCe said. "But 'surprise' is more like a birthday party. This is closer to a bomb cyclone. Get ready for your own personal Blizzard of '78." CeCe put her hands on her hips.

"Okay, I get it. None of us expected this, not yet." Dakota brought her clasped hands to her chin. "We thought we had more time to prepare, but she's here now, and we can't exactly send her back just because my condo's under renovation," Dakota said.

"How about a nice cruise then?" Jeremy said. "Fourteen days in Italy and Greece. My ex and I did that a few years ago, and it was wonderful. I'd do it again in a minute, just not with him."

"Not helpful, Jeremy." Dakota gave him a schoolteacher scowl. "Why don't we all try to focus?"

"Good news." Jeremy grinned as he looked at his phone. "Dinner's here."

"Excellent timing," CeCe said. "I'm starving. Stress makes me so hungry."

"Me too," Maeve said. "I must have eaten a case of Pringles and a few dozen Snickers bars when Henry was away."

"I like Snickers, but I *love* Almond Joy," CeCe said.

"Those are good," Abe said, "but I'm a fair-trade dark chocolate bar guy."

"I like green tea mochi," Kisai said softly.

"Got it. We're going to need a bunch of candy bars," Dakota said. "And some mochi. Jeremy, isn't there some service we can use?"

"goPuff's good," Jeremy said.

"Isn't that an app for high people?" Maeve said, with a laugh.

Jeremy winced. "It's an app for *hungry* people, Maeve, just hungry people."

"Sometimes I feel like I'm working with third graders." Dakota shook her head. "We have a long list of things to do, and we're going to need to focus to get through them. Can we do that, please?"

"I focus better when I'm fed," Jeremy said.

"Me too," CeCe said.

"You know what they say, 'the quickest way to a man's heart is through his stomach,'" Abe said.

"And I am that kind of man," Jeremy said.

Dakota held up her hands. "I surrender. I'm sure all of us function better on full stomachs. That includes me. So let's eat first, and then we'll get down to work," Dakota said. "And Jeremy, put the goPuff on the company card."

It might seem nonsensical that they were so focused on food, but stress and eating somehow went together. At least they did for Dakota. Thirty minutes later, the pack of hungry lions was sated and watching Dakota intently as she began to write on the whiteboard walls of the conference room. Three hours, fourteen candy bars, and two dozen mochis later (because Dakota *knew* everyone would want at least one), Elizabeth's new council was still in animated discussion about how to best care for her. As they grew more excited, and high on sugar, their voices rose, and they forgot to take turns. It was getting hard to hear.

"Shhh." Dakota felt like a cop trying to slow traffic. "We're going in circles, and we need to get linear," Dakota said. "Let's start again at the top. Elizabeth needs a private and comfortable place to live."

"She's obviously living with you, Dakota. You may not have a single-family house in Cambridge…" Dakota punched Jeremy in the arm. "…but it's *pretty* nice, and you certainly have the room," he said with a smirk.

"It's stunning, Dakota. Don't let Jeremy egg you on." CeCe patted Dakota's forearm. "But I'm not sure what you're going to do about the contractors. I was at your place the other day, and it looks like they still have tons of work to do on Elizabeth's quarters. It was like *Love It or List It* when they go fifty thousand over budget because they have to replace all the electrical. What's your plan?" CeCe said.

"Before we go into my plan, and I do have one, of course, let's discuss who else is living with me." Dakota looked over the top of her reading glasses at CeCe and Ashley.

"You have got to be kidding me, Dakota. You actually want me to move in," CeCe said with a head roll. "I have a personal life, you know, including the occasional gentleman caller. What am I supposed to do about that?"

Jeremy raised his eyebrows and laughed. "Just take him back to your place if you need a booty call."

"Thank you for that pearl of wisdom," CeCe said with sarcasm. She turned to Dakota. "Let's get serious. Do you expect me to live with you so I can be at Elizabeth's beck and call? Just imagine. She'll ring a little silver bell, and I'll come running like some goddamned servant. Is that what you want?"

"That is *not* what I want, CeCe. I would never ask that of you, nor would I want it from anyone." Dakota bit her lip. "You know me better than that. I just need help," she said, her voice breaking.

CeCe reached across the table toward Dakota. "I'm sorry, my friend. I'm just very nervous. I've never been an incognito therapist to an old queen. Or any queen. Or someone who died centuries ago."

"There's no precedent for what we're doing," Dakota said. "We just have to make it up as we go along." She gazed at her dearest college friend. "CeCe, I would like you to live with me—with us. I'm going to need you there." CeCe touched her hand to her heart.

"You too, Ashley."

Ashley sat up in her chair. *She looks like a cute little elf with that heart-shaped face. Just adorable.* Dakota removed her glasses and focused on Ashley. "You'll play a critical role in Elizabeth's inner circle," Dakota said. "Elizabeth was used to having her gentlewomen dress her. They helped select her clothes and jewels. They cared for her wigs and washed her linens. They even applied makeup to her face. It's going to be a big job since you'll be taking the place of multiple servants."

"I thought I would be the queen's personal stylist, not a servant." Ashley nibbled the pen she was holding.

"Elizabeth's servants weren't inferiors exactly," Dakota said. "Well, only in the way that every person in the kingdom was her inferior."

Jeremy tapped his fingers. "Not helping."

"I'm not a servant either. I'm a professional," CeCe said, overenunciating each syllable of "professional" for effect.

That's CeCe's angry voice. I'd better figure this out fast. Dakota raised her palms in the air. "Please, everyone, understand that Elizabeth's most trusted servants were nobility in their own right," she said. "It was considered a great privilege to be among the queen's staff. Yes, that's a better word for them: her staff." Now she had their attention. "They were compensated in a variety of ways. Given money, lands, titles, estates, even exclusive licenses to import goods. If you stayed in Elizabeth's good graces, your fortune, and that of your children, even your children's children, was assured."

"And what if you didn't stay in her good graces?" Jeremy said. "I seem to recall her sending Sir Walter Raleigh off to the Tower at one point." He cocked his head to the side.

Dakota could have thwacked him. "It was only for a few months. And he lived there with his wife and baby in a comfortable apartment." She looked from side to side at the worried faces around the table.

"I hope their view of the Thames wasn't marred by the heads on pikes," Jeremy spit out.

"Jeremy!" Dakota shouted. She felt like her face was on fire. "Are you trying to frighten everyone now that she's here?"

"Sorry." Jeremy shrugged. "This whole thing is making me nervous. It's not logical, like computer code."

"Let's get back to the heads on pikes thing," CeCe said.

"I like my head where it is," Ashley said.

"Ditto," Abe said.

"Everyone's head will stay on his or her shoulders. I swear it." Dakota crossed her heart. "And let me explain about Queen Elizabeth. She was very hurt when Walter Raleigh married without her permission, which as one of her courtiers, he was sworn to seek. He also impregnated one of her most trusted ladies."

"Bess Throckmorton," Jeremy muttered.

"That's right. It was a shock to Elizabeth, and she acted out of temper."

"Somebody was in emotion-mind," CeCe said, looking thoughtful.

"Let's go back to our list," Dakota said. "CeCe and Ashley will live with Elizabeth and me during this immediate transition. I'm giving Elizabeth my bedroom."

"Oh my giddy aunt," Jeremy said. Dakota ignored him.

"CeCe, I think we're going to have to share the large guest bedroom so Ashley can have the smaller one," she said.

"Okay, Dakota." CeCe heaved a sigh. "But it's not a long-term thing. Just until we get her more adjusted to her life in the here and now."

"Thanks, CeCe," Dakota said. "Now, Ashley, I'm going to need more of your time. In fact, I'm going to need all of your time."

Ashley raised her eyebrows at Dakota. "So, what am I doing about my job at Saks?"

"I hope you don't mind giving them immediate notice, because I need you to make my room fit for a Tudor queen, and we don't have much time. We'll try to keep her comfortable in the recovery room for as long as possible, but I have this feeling that she's not a patient person."

"That's okay," Ashley said. "I'm used to demanding clients at work." Her eyes were like saucers. "I don't mean you, Dakota. I hope you know that."

"I wasn't at all worried." Dakota offered a grin.

"Why don't I take Ashley over to your place, so she can see your room and come up with some ideas?" Jeremy said. "Once we have a plan, we'll be ready to shop first thing and decorate tomorrow."

"That would be wonderful, thank you both," Dakota said. *Good. He's trying to redeem himself.*

"Mmmm…may I interject, please?" Abe said. "We need to talk about some medical issues before she goes much of anywhere."

"I'm listening," Dakota said.

"As a sixteenth-century woman, she won't have had any vaccinations, making her incredibly vulnerable to disease," Abe said. "She's going to need polio, DTaP, and MMR, to start. Like tomorrow. Before she leaves this building."

"We put that in the health and safety protocol for the queen," Kisai said. "But we weren't fully prepared for her early arrival."

"My GP Hazel teaches at Harvard Med, so she might be able to help. I'll call her first thing tomorrow. Errr…tonight," Dakota said, remembering that she'd never gotten around to telling Hazel about Elizabeth. "Unless you have a pipeline to vaccines, Doctor Diamond?" She tilted her head at him.

"Let me see." Abe scrunched his mouth to the side. "I used to date a virologist at Mass General," Abe said. "It's been a few years, but it all ended amicably, so I'll try her." He flashed a smile, displaying a gorgeous set of teeth framed by sumptuous lips. "And please call me Abe."

"You got it," Dakota said, feeling suddenly warm. Hot flash or something else? *Something else.* She put a hand to her chest as she recovered. *Not now, Dakota.* "There's a lot to do." She clapped her hands like a gym teacher. "So let's focus on what's critical for the next twenty-four hours."

"Food. We have to talk about food," Jeremy said.

Dakota scowled at him. "We just ate, for God's sake."

"For her, not for me," Jeremy said, rolling his eyes.

"Fortunately, I've already spoken to Chef about it," Dakota said. "I told him I was going to need a personal chef for a friend who'd be staying with me for a long time. He thought it was weird, but I know he's already started looking." Dakota noticed her breath getting shallow. She sat up straight and inhaled.

"It's getting late, everyone, and I still have calls to make tonight." Dakota placed her hands on the table. "We have much more to discuss tomorrow. Stress management, sensitivity training, cultural education, recreation, politics, modern English." She licked her lips, leaned back in her chair, and closed her eyes.

There was an insistent knocking at the door. It was Maeve, breathing hard like she'd just been running.

Dakota jumped out of her chair. "What is it? Is she awake?"

"Do we have a lute?" Maeve said. "She's asking for it."

"Oh shit," Dakota said.

"It seems that we are fresh out of lutes," Jeremy said.

CeCe guffawed.

"Well, we better get one soon because it sounds like she wants one now," Maeve said.

"Okay, we'll make it happen." Dakota turned to Ashley. "How are you at finding lutes?"

CHAPTER 22

*Y*uck.

Thick meat stew slid down the spoon into Dakota's mouth like a mouthful of mud. The potatoes, carrots, and parsnips were okay, and barley never hurt anyone, unless you had a gluten allergy—which she did not—but hunks of brown meat for breakfast? Not a fan.

A different story for Elizabeth.

Seated across from Elizabeth at the farmhouse table in Kisai's lab, Dakota stole a look at the queen. With each new spoonful of pottage, the queen visibly relaxed. And the brown bread Chef had made was delicious, and oh-so-good with the creamy butter Dakota usually avoided.

Elizabeth took measured sips of Coors Light from a tall glass. Gideon and Janet figured it was the closest thing to *small beer*, the weak version of ale that Elizabethans of all ages drank at every meal. Since the travel team had been drinking it every day for the past week while staying at John Dee's, they were all now familiar with it, although Gideon was the only team member to drink beer with his breakfast. Dakota hoped it was in solidarity with Elizabeth and not because his taste buds had gone to hell in a hand basket.

Mmmm. She licked the crema from her lips. Thank heaven the Nespresso machine worked. Dakota didn't know if Elizabeth had tried the coffee that the travel team had brought. She steeled herself. "Your Majesty, may I ask you a question?" Dakota said, with a nervous gulp.

Elizabeth raised her head to look at Dakota. Her eyes were penetrating. *She'd be killer at a staring contest.* Dakota blinked a few times.

"Aye, Lady Dakota. Thou art welcome to speak."

Dakota sat up straight in her chair. "Thank you, Madame." Elizabeth blinked hard at Dakota. *Whoops. Must have used the wrong form of address.* "Your Majesty, may I invite you to have a cup of coffee? I consider it one of life's small pleasures, but I'm not sure if you've had the opportunity to taste the coffee that I had sent to you in England." Dakota felt each thump of her heartbeat.

"Lady Dakota, I did indeed drink the coffee." When Elizabeth looked at Dakota this time, her brown eyes seemed warmer. "I sayeth to you that I liked it not upon the first taste. 'Twas acerb to mine own tongue. However, when Sir Henry added cream and sugar to the cup, I found the taste most pleasing." Elizabeth smiled, and it was as if there was no one else in the room. It was all brilliant sunshine raining on Dakota. *Wow. I wanted star power, and I got it.*

As if speaking in confidence, Elizabeth leaned toward Dakota. "'Twas not the flavor alone that wast unique," Elizabeth said. "Though in mine antique years, I felt enlivened by the brew, as if I wert a young woman again, with all her energy and spirit. I anon found I could not sit comfortably in company longer. I invited all to join me to walk, and walk we did, at a rigorous pace until I felt myself again."

Uh oh. I don't want her hyper before Hazel arrives. Dakota adored Hazel and hoped Elizabeth would feel the same way. Perhaps one day she could take them both to afternoon tea at SconeHenge, the cute little tea shop just around the corner from Hazel's office. But first, it was time for coffee. "My dear Majesty, I am delighted that you enjoy the taste of coffee," Dakota said. "I will make you a *'half-caf.'* It has all the taste of regular coffee but a little less of the caffeine, the ingredient that elevates the energy level."

As Elizabeth took dainty sips of coffee, Dakota stole a look down the table. Janet had dark circles under her eyes. She looked bedraggled in the Elizabethan clothing she must have worn all week. *I better make sure Janet and Gideon get home in time to shower and change before I need them back at my place.* And Henry should go home with Maeve to take a long—make that a short—break, Dakota concluded. There were errands to do. Dakota sighed and ate another bite of bread.

The sound of wind chimes rang out in even cadence.

"God 'a mercy. What is that?" Elizabeth looked at Dakota in alarm. "Whence cometh the music as thither is nay instrument on thy person?"

"It's just my phone ringing, Your Majesty," Dakota said. *Good thing it's wind chimes and not that annoying dolphin sound Jeremy downloaded for my ringtone.* She glanced at her phone and walked away from the table.

"Hi, Hazel. Thanks so much for calling me back," Dakota said. "Before I begin, let me assure you I am of sound mind and body. Please believe that I'm telling the truth and I desperately need your help…."

Elizabeth stood and walked toward Dakota, who was oh-so-quietly explaining that her team of scientists had brought Elizabeth Tudor to the present, and in fact, Elizabeth would be staying at her condo. But first, the fifty-five-year-old Elizabeth needed some medical care because she'd never had a vaccination or a modern physical exam.

"Pray pardon me, Lady Dakota. Wherefore speakest thou at the little musical box?" Elizabeth peered at the phone in Dakota's hand.

"Excuse me, please, Your Majesty," Dakota said. "I will do my best to explain this to you shortly, as soon as I finish my conversation with Doctor Robinson."

Elizabeth stood to her full five foot three inches and frowned at Dakota. "Prithee, Lady. Dost thou engage so for thy own amusement while I am held in obfuscation?"

Uh oh. Elizabeth was definitely miffed. *Not the most patient person on the planet.*

Gideon got up to help. He approached Elizabeth and smiled gently, saying a few words that Dakota couldn't hear. He then gently guided Elizabeth back to the breakfast table.

"Thank you, thank you, Hazel. So you can get the DTaP for the diphtheria, tetanus, and whooping cough, and the measles-mumps-rubella vaccine this morning, but you have to find out where to get the polio vaccine since you're not a pediatrician? Is that right?" Dakota tapped her finger to her lip. "Mmm hmmm. I understand," she said. "It takes time for the vaccines to percolate. We'll be very careful getting her to my condo and won't let her have contact with anyone outside our immediate circle until she's started the polio."

Dakota nodded and gave a weak laugh. "Of course. You can examine me too, to make sure that I'm not hallucinating. I expected nothing less," she said. "See you soon." She would need to remind herself to donate to the UU food pantry in Concord Center where Hazel volunteers on Saturdays. Then, if they were all still alive in a month, perhaps Hazel would want to interview Elizabeth about sixteenth-century medical care.

Dakota rolled her shoulders back as she walked over to Elizabeth.

"Your Majesty. Thank you for your forbearance. I will try to explain the telephone to you," Dakota said. "But first, I must retrieve another box that we call a 'computer.' It's very helpful with research and may make it easier for me to describe the phone's inner workings."

"Dakota, what are you thinking with the computer?" Janet hissed into her ear. "She's already boggled by your smartphone."

Dakota ignored her and pulled the laptop out of her bag. "I'm going to this wonderful place for information. We call it the *internet,*" Dakota said, like she was speaking to a three-year-old. "Let's see what HowStuffWorks says about phones."

Dakota scanned the web page about cell phones, which assumed that the reader understood the laundry list of underlying technologies that were invented in the late nineteenth and twentieth centuries. *This is way too advanced.* How about walkie-talkies? *Too confusing. How the hell am I going to explain this?* She couldn't go to circuit boards and wireless signals. Should she go to soundwaves and frequencies? *I know.* She pulled up a web page on Alexander Graham Bell and read for a bit. She felt sweaty. *All I know is that when I explain electricity, I'm going with Tesla not Edison.* Dakota put the laptop away.

"Majesty, may I ask you to accompany me to the room where you spent last night?" Dakota said. "There's a whiteboard on the wall. It's like a special kind of paper that makes it easy to share ideas, and I think I can use it to explain the principles behind the telephone."

Elizabeth walked slowly toward Dakota. "I am pleased to accompany thee, Lady, as I am all consternation and would'st prefer to have clarity. And yet, I have nay wish for longer confinement in the room where I have spent too many hours already." Elizabeth stretched her neck and flared her nostrils.

"I understand completely." Dakota nodded. "I promise we'll be in the room just so I can use the whiteboard. And just once more, when my personal physician Doctor Hazel Robinson comes to see you, which will be later this morning. She needs to make sure that it's safe for you to leave this area before we go to my house…which will be your house…which will have a beautiful apartment for you while you get settled in Cambridge."

"Hazel is a woman's name. Is't not?" Elizabeth cocked her head to the side. "I ne'er heard o' a female physician ere this. Hath she e'er treated one o' royal lineage?" she said.

"I don't think that Doctor Robinson has treated royalty before," Dakota played with her heart necklace. "But she is *my* doctor." She touched her palm to her breastbone. "And I only want the best for you."

Elizabeth inclined her head, but then she started to wobble. Gideon ran to her side and placed a steadying arm around her back. "Your Grace, are you unwell?" Gideon gazed into the queen's eyes.

"Perhaps I need a moment to reflect." Elizabeth put her hand to her stomach. "I correct myself. Where is the garderobe?" She looked straight at Dakota.

"And what is that, exactly?" Dakota said.

"It's a toilet, Dakota," Gideon said. "We've been using the commode at the far side of the recovery room since we got back, so this will be a new experience."

"Ah yes, of course. We have several of them in the lab," Dakota said. "Janet, could you please come with us? We may need your assistance."

Janet scowled at Dakota. *She may look like death warmed-over, but I've got to hand it to her, the woman still has attitude.* "Of course. It would be my pleasure," Janet said with an iron grin.

As the three women walked toward the restroom, Dakota hoped Janet would show Elizabeth how to flush for herself.

It wasn't even 9:00 a.m., but it already felt like midnight.

CHAPTER 23

April 10, 2027, Charlestown to Cambridge

Twenty miles per hour. Dakota had never driven that slowly from Charlestown to Cambridge. Luckily, Jeremy wasn't in the car, or she'd never hear the end of it. *What are you, like ninety-five years old? If you're going to drive like you're ancient, just put us out of our misery and turn on autopilot.* That's what he'd say—but she didn't care. She was driving with precious cargo.

Elizabeth dozed in the back seat, her head on Gideon's shoulder. Hazel had given her a light sedative before it was time to leave for the condo, later telling Dakota she was "pretty sure that Elizabeth didn't gad about Tudor England in a Rolls-Royce or a Bentley" so why terrify her by plopping her into a high-speed motorized vehicle when she was fully awake? *"Get her to your condo in the gentlest way possible,"* Hazel had said. So that's how the now-vaccinated Elizabeth made the trip from the lab to Dakota's place on Memorial Drive.

Janet sat in the front seat next to Dakota, speaking quietly as they drove. "I've only been away for a week, Dakota, and *I'm* feeling culture shock," Janet said. "You can't imagine how quiet it was there compared to here. No cars. No cell phones or television or even radio. Only the sound of crickets and birdsong at night. The world moved so slowly, and here, it's hyperactive by comparison. We need to slow the pace of life for Elizabeth in every conceivable way."

"I thought we'd have weeks to figure all this out, not hours," Dakota said. "Please do whatever you can to help the rest of us understand Elizabeth's previous reality. And thank you, by the way, for helping her in the bathroom. Even that was a new experience for her."

"Once we got in there, I didn't think we were ever going to get out," Janet said. "She must have flushed the toilet thirty times. And she asked me a million questions about the automated sink. I had to convince her that everyone washes their hands after using the toilet. It was clearly new information." Janet actually laughed.

"I appreciate you having a sense of humor about it," Dakota said. "I'm still not sure how to speak to her."

"It'll come with time," Janet said, patting Dakota's arm for the first time in their acquaintance. "She's very good with languages, you know, so she'll pick up colloquial English. Still, Gideon's going to work with her on it. In fact, we'll need to get started on her education program soon."

Dakota drove into the garage at The Esplanade and parked. She looked in the rearview mirror and saw Elizabeth and Gideon asleep in the back seat. They looked oddly comfortable, the disheveled queen and the professor. Then she did a double take. With his lush beard and mustache, and his brown hair in a ponytail, Gideon reminded her of a painting she'd seen of Sir Robert Dudley, the courtier from whom Elizabeth was rarely parted.

Elizabeth had had a long and passionate relationship with Dudley. In the early years, he was her Master of the Horse, which gave him charge over the many horses in the royal stable and which also made him responsible for court entertainments. What Elizabeth and Dudley did privately must have been the subject of conjecture, but whatever it was, Dudley's two marriages were secondary to his enduring relationship with Elizabeth, and she was able to preserve her reputation as the "virgin queen." If Dakota could see Gideon's resemblance to Dudley, wouldn't Elizabeth see it too?

Dakota leaned toward Janet. "Janet. Could you wake Gideon? He may need to carry Elizabeth to my place," Dakota said. "The elevator's at the end of the garage."

"Right," Janet said. "Umm...if anyone happens to see us en route to your place, will any of your neighbors find it strange that you're with three people dressed like we've just come from a Renaissance Faire?"

"We could use the Renaissance Faire idea, or we could say that you're in a Shakespeare troupe, and you've just come from a cast party," said Dakota.

"Let's go with cast party. It's more decorous," Janet said.

Five minutes later, the odd foursome arrived at Dakota's door. Elizabeth was awake, but only just, so it was up to Gideon to keep her upright. He didn't seem to mind.

Before Dakota could knock, the sound of wind chimes rang out. She picked up her phone. "Holy hell, Jeremy, are you on Psychic Friends Network? We're outside the door."

Just as CeCe opened the front door, Elizabeth woke and said, "A Blackamoore." She examined CeCe's face. "Doest thou know Sultan Al Mansur?"

If CeCe's head could have popped like a top, spun around sixteen times, and hit the ceiling, Dakota was sure it would have done so, but instead, she heard CeCe say, "It is a pleasure to meet you, Your Majesty. I do not know the Sultan. My name is Doctor CeCe Gibbons, and I look forward to us becoming good friends."

Dakota had no idea CeCe would be so good at playing lady of the manor.

Elizabeth raised her eyebrows, but then appeared to recover quickly. She extended her hand to CeCe, who proceeded to shake it instead of kiss it. "It is mine own heart's delight to meet thee, Doctor Gibbons, and I must say that in this new land I would'st be glad o' a friend." Elizabeth gave CeCe one of her beaming, black-toothed smiles. CeCe placed her hand over her heart and stepped back into the room.

"Well thanks for all the notice." Jeremy arched his eyebrows. "Welcome one and all, to the grand home of Dakota Winfred," he said with a bow.

"Pray pardon me, sir. I fear we have had nay introduction." Elizabeth sounded scarily formal.

"Your Majesty, please forgive the oversight," Dakota said. "Please meet Jeremy Jiang, my chief security officer."

"Ahh…Sir Jeremy is akin to mine own Francis Walsingham. Is this thy true meaning?" Elizabeth said, referring to her longtime spymaster.

"From what I've read about Sir Francis, Jeremy's role is quite different," Dakota said. "Jeremy ensures that other people do not compromise the integrity of my business interests."

"I disagree, Lady Dakota. I credit Sir Francis with preserving the security o' mine own realm on more than one occasion," she said. Then she placed a gentle arm on Dakota's sleeve and spoke in lowered voice. "Mayhap thou hast heard o' the Babington plot?" Before Dakota could respond, she said, "'Twas in Sir Gideon's book about mine own person. Thee may recall that Sir Francis preserved mine own kingdom upon discovering the aspirations o' the usurper, Mary Queen o' Scots.

"You must be a gentleman o' intellect and courage. And an Oriental too." Elizabeth held her hand out to Jeremy, who gasped but somehow recovered to press his lips to the top of her hand.

I can't believe he kept his cool, Dakota thought. *I am so hearing about this later.*

CeCe approached Elizabeth and said, "Your Majesty, we all bid you welcome. May I invite you to see your accommodations? We've been readying them for your arrival, and while we realize we have no palace to offer you, we hope you will find comfort here."

God, she's good. How did CeCe learn how to speak with Elizabeth? She must watch Masterpiece Theatre on the sly.

"I grammercy for thy kindness, Lady CeCe," Elizabeth said.

"Doctor Gibbons, please," CeCe said. Her voice was sweeter than sugar syrup. "And you are most welcome."

"Let us go together," Dakota said. She held out her arm for Elizabeth, so she could escort her to the bedroom.

Elizabeth took a step toward Dakota but then stopped short. She was staring at the toaster on the kitchen counter where a piece of toast had just popped up.

"What is this creation, may I ask?" Elizabeth walked into the kitchen and bent over to look at the machine.

"This is a toaster," CeCe said. "It makes toast."

"It toasts bread, Your Majesty," Janet said, removing the toast and handing it to Elizabeth, who turned it over in her hands and brought it to her nose to smell.

"Where is the fire in this magical box?" Elizabeth said, staring into the toaster's wire inners.

"It isn't magic. It uses an electric coil to toast bread," Jeremy said.

"What is a coil?" Elizabeth said. "And what is electric?"

Here we go again, Dakota thought. "Majesty, I will need some paper and a pen to explain electricity to you. I must think it through first, though."

"Please do take thy time," Elizabeth said to Dakota. "As I await thy explanation, I should'st like some bread to toast."

Twenty minutes later, burnt bits of toast lay in piles on the counter. Elizabeth had toasted every piece of bread in Dakota's kitchen several times over. There were crumbs in her hair, but she was smiling.

Oh no. Please do not look there. Elizabeth was staring with curiosity at the microwave over the range.

Dakota wondered if she would still be standing after lunch.

CHAPTER 24

April 10, 2027, Cambridge

"So where is our magnificent imperial Majesty, again?" Jeremy chomped into a raisin scone.

"For the love of God, Jeremy, please do not eat another scone before Elizabeth can try them," Dakota said. "Gideon went to La Saison after he left KODA, even before he went home for a nap."

"Fine. As long as you've got something decent to eat besides scones." Jeremy wrinkled his nose. "I heard about the delightful pottage you served for breakfast, and I'm worried for my palate."

"It's not like we can introduce her to Buk Kyung on her second night here." Dakota narrowed her eyes at him. "Nice pout, Jeremy."

"I know you wuv me," Jeremy said, making a little heart with his fingers.

"I adore you, dearest darling. Too bad you also drive me crazy," Dakota said, smiling. "But you make a good point about the food. It has to taste delicious to Elizabeth, and it has to work for us. Which brings me to an important role I would like you to play."

"Are you thinking knighthood? Because that's what I'm thinking," Jeremy said. "I read that Elizabeth named her knights to this Order of the Garter. Each new member would get a fashionable medallion with a special insignia to wear around his neck. I could be the first person knighted by her in like four hundred years."

Dakota chuckled. "If you could be slightly less snarky to her, you might have a chance."

"Ha ha, Dakota. You're hilarious. When I want to be charming, I can totally do it."

"I think somebody needs a hug," Dakota said. She put her arms around him and squeezed. He put his head on her shoulder.

"Oh, that is nice," Jeremy said. "So what special honor are you bestowing on me?"

"I'll give you a hint. It's near and dear to your heart."

He gave her his cheesiest grin. "A date with Zac Efron?"

"Not quite." Dakota raised her eyebrows. "It's about your other favorite subject—food," she said. "Given your passion for it, I'd like you to work with our new personal chef—who's on his way here. Our chef hired him to prepare and serve lunch and dinner daily, so he's going to be around a lot."

"Is he cute?"

"We can only hope," Dakota said. "But seriously, I'd like you to discuss menus with him. Come up with meals that everyone will like, or if there's something that will only work for her…"

"Like sheep's head in aspic?" Jeremy said.

"Exactly. That's one dish she can have on her own."

"I'm on it," Jeremy said, "but you still haven't told me where Her Royal-ness is at the moment."

"Are you kidding? It's almost noon." Dakota looked up from her watch. "That means Elizabeth's been in the bathroom with CeCe for two hours."

Jeremy chortled. "That's some serious constipation."

"I doubt she's been sitting on the toilet the whole time." Dakota rolled her eyes. "CeCe wanted to show her to the bedroom, but Elizabeth wanted to use the toilet, and that's the last I saw of them."

"You're saying your bathroom is like the Bermuda Triangle."

"Exactly. We'll send a search party if they're not out by one o'clock," Dakota said, grabbing a bite of Jeremy's scone.

A few minutes later, CeCe plodded into the kitchen, beads of sweat on her forehead. "We need two glasses of water pronto," she said. "Elizabeth's been in the bath so long she's getting dehydrated, and I'm getting dehydrated sitting in a steamy bathroom while fully dressed. I feel like a raisin."

"That's what she's been doing all this time?" Dakota said.

"Well," CeCe said. "She spent eons flushing the toilet, and that's before she used it. Then she actually wanted me to stay with her while she peed, which was gross, but I guess her maids of the bedchamber or whoever stayed with her while she performed every bodily function."

Dakota shook her head. "Oh, CeCe. I'm sorry you had to do that."

"It's not what I expected, that's for sure, but it is giving me the opportunity to get to know her in a less formal setting." CeCe offered a weak smile. "Getting that dress off her was hellacious, though. Eyes and hooks all over the place, layers of things I can't even name, and a corset that took forever to untie. When she eventually gets out of the bath, which I hope will be sometime before dinner, I'm not having her wear all those clothes. Do you know when Ashley's getting home with her new wardrobe?"

"Jeremy, could you please give Ashley a ring?" Dakota said.

"Why me?" Jeremy said. "Do I have nothing else to do?"

"It's because you've been working with her nonstop since last night," Dakota said. "When she texted me this morning to ask for a clothing budget, she said you'd been incredibly helpful."

"In that case, I will give her a call." He tucked himself into one of Dakota's Good Egg chairs after tossing a fluffy white shearling pillow onto the wood floor.

"I better get back in there with the water," CeCe said. "I'm also famished. Is it time for lunch yet?"

Dakota held her hands up to either side of her mouth, mock yelling to Jeremy. "Sweetness, after you call Ashley, could you contact our new personal chef? I'm texting his information now."

"Yes, my liege," Jeremy said in a commanding voice. "Should you need anything else—a date with the pope, a meeting on the moon, spinning straw into gold—just let me know. I am at your service."

"He really is very helpful." Dakota patted CeCe on the back while laughing. "Let me get you some water and a snack. I'll bring a tray with some cheese and crackers to the bathroom door. Just listen for my knock."

CeCe nodded and walked back to the bathroom. After popping some CALM gummies—*that extra magnesium is a stress-buster*, Hazel liked to say—Dakota checked the cheese drawer in her sub-zero refrigerator. Goat cheese, cheddar, and brie. Not a bad combination. *Hope Elizabeth will think so too.*

Returning to the kitchen after the cheese-tray delivery, Dakota found herself facing Jeremy.

"I got the scoop," Jeremy said. "Ashley should be here in fifteen or so. She's returning with clothing in three different sizes—boots, shoes, coats, undergarments, you name it…. Probably cleaned out Valentino's entire spring line.

Whoa. Elizabeth's going to be a fashionista on steroids while my favorite store is REI. I'm going to have to step up my game.

"She had three different salespeople at Saks with her the whole time, including one of the managers, who's coming here with her, by the way. She thinks he felt bad because she couldn't fit all the bags in her car. Get ready for the fun because two cars full of clothing for the family monarch will arrive soon. Want to know how much Ashley spent?" Jeremy slapped his hands against his cheeks.

"I'm not worried," Dakota said. "We'll return what she can't...or won't...wear. And I bet it pales compared to the price of the necklace I bought her."

"'Kay. That's the deal with Ashley. I also reached Teddy, our new personal chef. He sounded sexy so I looked him up on Snap. I saw photos in Ptown. Want to see?" He held his phone up for Dakota. A burly fellow with golden-blond hair and a beautifully manicured mustache smiled at the camera.

"I admit it. He's pretty cute," Dakota said with a smile.

"Gay or super gay?" Jeremy stared at the phone. "I'm thinking gay...only if he's single."

Dakota did a head roll. "Okay, Mario Andretti. Cool your jets," she said. "Please tell me honestly. Are you going to be too distracted to manage him?"

"I promise to be only pleasantly distracted." Jeremy crossed his heart, then checked his phone. "That's Teddy now. They put him in the freight elevator with the groceries. I'll go out to meet him." He headed for the door.

Dakota's smartphone and home phone rang simultaneously. "What the heck?" She picked up the home phone. "Yes, Ashley. I'll come down to meet you. Jeremy said you did a massive shop. Be right there."

Dakota hung up and answered her other call. "Oh my God, Maeve. I can't believe there's a Lute Society of America chapter in Boston," Dakota said. "What's that? I don't know how many strings Elizabeth's lute would have had. Since you're in touch with the experts, why don't you ask them what a wealthy Renaissance woman would have played? Just buy what seems best." Dakota nodded while listening. "Yes, she did play something like a harpsichord. They called it virginals in the book. Gideon and Janet's, that is. Not sure where to get one right now. Perhaps one of the professors would know."

Dakota's home phone rang again. *Just breathe, Dakota, just breathe.* "I've got to meet Ashley, Maeve. Call me if you have any more questions."

Dakota threw a sweater over her head and walked to the door. As she did, Jeremy texted to say he was just outside her condo with the hot chef, Elizabeth came into the kitchen wearing Dakota's Four Seasons bathrobe, the house phone rang again, Jeremy and a person Dakota had never seen before walked in lugging bags of groceries, and CeCe said, "Is lunch ready yet?"

All this and it was only 12:47 p.m.

CHAPTER 25

April 10, 2027, Cambridge

The smell of fried chicken and buttermilk biscuits wafted through the kitchen. Dakota's stomach rumbled.

Jeremy sat at the center island, his elbows resting on his hands, as he watched Teddy prepare lunch. CeCe napped in a chair, a rivulet of drool dripping down one side of her mouth. She'd handed Elizabeth off to Ashley after the longest bath in history. CeCe was taking a break while Ashley was on the hot seat, showing Elizabeth her new wardrobe choices. Gideon and Janet sat on the sectional, their heads together in quiet conversation.

It was quite a tableau, this New Privy Council of Elizabeth's. But if they were going to succeed, they'd have to put their pride aside to help Elizabeth acclimate, even if that meant teaching her how to use the toilet.

"Lunch will be served shortly," Jeremy announced from his perch. "Teddy has done a wonderful job with his first meal, don't you think, Dakota?"

"It smells amazing," Dakota said. "Could you please set the table, and I'll check in with Ashley?"

"Happy to help," Jeremy said with a grin.

No sarcasm. Weird. He must be trying to impress Teddy. Dakota headed down the wide hallway to her room.

Dakota knocked on her once-bedroom door. "Hello in there. How are things going?"

Ashley answered, her face flushed. "She has a nice figure for a woman of her age, so she's easy to dress. Or she would be easy if she didn't question every piece of clothing and ask me why I haven't brought her any gowns."

"Oh boy. I take it you won't be out for lunch."

"We might not be out by Christmas," Ashley said, rubbing her eyes. "She's the only person I've ever met who hates Prada. She said it must have been made by dullards, too lazy to embellish the fabric. Can you imagine?"

"That's harsh," Dakota said.

"Luckily, I bought some Valentino and some Alexander McQueen, and she likes some of those pieces, but she loves—loves— the Dolce & Gabbana. I'm going to purchase more D&G for her online because that's clearly her cup of tea."

"It sounds painstaking," Dakota said. "I can't imagine what it would be like to dress a sixteenth-century queen in twenty-first-century clothes, but that's exactly what you're doing."

"It could be the reality show to end all reality shows—or at least to end me." Ashley bowed her head.

"I know this is a big job, Ashley, and I so appreciate it. Is there anything at all I can do for you?"

"I would love some lunch, but since we're not leaving anytime soon, is it too much to ask if you could bring it to us?"

"You bet, Ashley. I'll bring a tray for you both. And tonight— you get to pick the wine for dinner." Dakota turned and walked back down the hall to her open-concept kitchen/dining area/living space.

Teddy was serving everyone individually from the kitchen island, where he'd arranged the food buffet-style. A heaping platter of fried chicken was surrounded by a plate of biscuits, a bowl of buttery haricot vert beans and baby carrots, and a crystal gravy boat. Dakota wanted to ask for a huge serving for herself (calories be damned!), but she gated her animal instincts and had Teddy make up two plates for Elizabeth and Ashley. She sighed as she carried lunch on the same silver tray she'd used earlier for the Elizabeth-CeCe bathroom snack. Now she had the Elizabeth-Ashley lunch delivery. Where—and with whom—would Elizabeth have her dinner?

Here's hoping it'll be at the table with the rest of us. I've just about had it with room service.

"Hello there, Elizabeth…Your Majesty, I mean, and Ashley. I've brought your luncheon," Dakota said, rapping on the door.

"Thee may enter," Elizabeth announced.

Dakota's hot flash flooded her back and chest with heat as she viewed the room formerly known as hers. Discarded clothing was everywhere. On her bed. On the loveseat and the ottoman. On the floor. A black bra was draped over her bedside lamp, for lord's sake.

"Ashley dear, could you help me find a clear surface for this tray?" Dakota said, swiveling her head like a fan at a tennis match.

"Of course. Let me help." Ashley moved a pile of clothes from the lacquered coffee table in front of the loveseat to the top of the ottoman, which already supported at least a dozen different coats.

After easing the tray onto the table, Dakota ran her fingers over a gorgeous bisque-toned shearling coat with a faux-fur trim. *Yech. That's not fake fur. It's real.* Dakota didn't care what Elizabeth was used to wearing. Someone would have to tell Elizabeth that fur wasn't just out of fashion. It was considered gauche.

Maybe Janet could explain the current cultural sentiment to Elizabeth. It might be a stretch for a woman who wore an ermine-trimmed cape on her coronation day, but Dakota had no doubt that Elizabeth would want people to see her as fashionable. But then again, Dakota ate beef and wore leather. Why was that so different?

"Lady Dakota," Elizabeth's sonorous voice reverberated across the room. "May we have thy conceit on mine attire?"

Huh? Does she want my opinion on my outfit?

Elizabeth held her arms out to the side and scowled. She looked like someone had asked her to wear a garbage bag. "I find it slight, ephemeral as a spider's web. 'Tis as if the quality o' the cloth, the intricacieth o' the design, have all been forgotten o'er time. What think thee?"

"I must ponder for a moment, Your Majesty," Dakota said. She surveyed the outfit—high-waisted flowing gray pants in some rich fabric, maybe silk? A fitted eggplant-hued turtleneck sweater. Elizabeth looked stunning—or she would have looked stunning if her short hair were more copper than gray, and well-styled, not sticking out in tufts. Maybe wearing wigs all the time had damaged her natural hair.

Dakota made a quick study of Elizabeth's face. She had a high brow with well-defined cheekbones, an angular face and Roman nose, a long and elegant neck, and golden-brown eyes that sparkled with intelligence. It was an elegant visage, fitting for a queen. With an extreme dental makeover and the repair of her skin from the pox marks that Dakota couldn't see through Elizabeth's heavy makeup, Elizabeth would be good-looking. Attractive enough to be president.

"Ahem." Elizabeth cleared her throat. "Your thoughts, I pray you, Lady Dakota. I must hear them."

"I have seen few casual outfits to rival it, in terms of quality and luxurious fabric," Dakota said. "I imagine, however, that it will take time for you to adjust to what we wear in this century. Our fashions are so different from the formal elegance of the clothing you wore all your life, before now."

"My gowns wert so beautiful," Elizabeth said, her lower lip trembling. "I should'st have prized them with greater zeal, had I known what wast attending for me hither."

"I am sorry for your loss," Dakota said as she approached Elizabeth. "I wish it were the last that you'll experience, but I am afraid that won't be the case." She looked with care into the queen's eyes.

"No matter." Elizabeth angled her head toward Dakota as she spoke. "I shall make do with what Mistress Ashley hath wrought as it would'st be unseemly to go 'round thy home in mine own natural state," Elizabeth said, with a slight laugh. "I have nay doubt these few things have been purchased on mine own behalf with the greatest o' care by someone who knows me not. O'er time, I hope that she shall better comprehend mine own taste, improving the result." *Now that's a backhanded way to say thanks if I ever heard it. I'll have to do damage-control with Ashley later. I hope she won't quit on her first day as stylist.*

"I should'st like to dine now," Elizabeth said. "When the repast is finished, I shall take some green air. " She looked at Ashley. "Mistress, could thee I pray you remove the habit that I disfavor—or which is simply too large, which much o' 'tis? I shall consider the other body coverings after mine own walk with Lady Dakota." *God, Ashley's face is red.* Dakota couldn't tell if Ashley was sad or angry, but she knew that Ashley needed a break. She'd tell Ashley to get some downtime when she went for a walk with Elizabeth. Maybe Ashley would nap… or rant with Jeremy. He was usually up for a good rant.

"I should'st like a dining table in mine own chambers, Lady Dakota," Elizabeth said. "It need not be grand—as it could scarcely fit in such a diminutive abode. Something simple would'st do." She pressed her lips together. "Could thee make the arrangement on the morrow?" Dakota gulped. Could such a small team manage the needs of one of history's greatest monarchs?

Dakota made her way back to the kitchen, where the rest of the team, Teddy included, was gathered in front of the television.

"I hope he goes straight to hell for this," CeCe growled from the overstuffed wool couch. Jeremy and Teddy had squeezed in next to her.

"I hope he goes straight to the *ninth* circle of hell. That's the worst one, you know." Jeremy shook his head.

"What's going on?" Dakota said.

"Vlakas just tweeted that he's closing the border with Mexico," CeCe said. "CNN's doing a breaking-news story on the tweet."

"Which totally amplifies it," Jeremy said. "They probably got Vlakas another million followers."

"Keep the Mexicans in Mexico," Dakota said. "I bet his people love that."

"It's not just the Mexicans, though," Jeremy said. "It's thousands of Central Americans fleeing the drug cartels."

"And the gangs," CeCe said.

"And sheer poverty," Teddy said.

"Even for him this is a low point," Jeremy said. "He's brought in over one hundred M-1 tanks to the US side of the border. They've got heavy artillery pointed at the refugees."

"So much for 'huddled masses yearning to breathe free,'" Dakota said.

"CNN reported that Vlakas was pushing for drones loaded with mustard gas. Can you believe it?" Jeremy clenched his fists. "The secretary of defense had to explain that we couldn't use chemical weapons against innocent people."

"It's horrible," Dakota said, frowning. "We need to treat these people with humanity."

"What do you mean, *these people*?" Jeremy glared at her. "I'm *these people*. I came here from Jeju because I thought I'd have a better life." He swallowed hard. "My mother was a Heanyeo. You know that, Dakota. She made less than twenty dollars a day free diving for shellfish. If she hadn't been able to hold her breath thirty feet under water, we wouldn't have had food on the table." His voice broke.

"Do you think our government would be acting this way if a bunch of desperate white Canadians were trying to cross our border?" CeCe grimaced. "No way. Vlakas would welcome them with open arms and ship them off to Idaho or something."

"I wish I could fix everything that's wrong in the world." Dakota clenched her jaw. "But I can't." Dakota's eyes felt misty. "At least not on my own."

CeCe put an arm around Dakota. "You're not on your own."

"The meal wast most pleasing," Elizabeth said to their backs as she walked into the room. "I have naught had poultry addressed in such a manner."

Dakota pivoted around, but the others stayed glued to CNN. "I'm so glad you enjoyed it."

"Pray tell. What manner o' magic is this?" Elizabeth's eyes grew wide. She walked over to the television and touched it. She stood in front of it for a few moments and placed her hands on her chest.

"We call this television, Your Majesty, and it's time to turn it off." Dakota picked up the remote from the ottoman and pressed the off button. She walked over to Elizabeth. "Television gives us information about our world, and it entertains us too."

"It started with moving pictures, over one hundred years ago," Jeremy said. "It's become much more sophisticated since then, and now we can transmit pictures and sound via digital images, all using satellites in space."

"TMI, Jeremy, but thanks," Dakota said. "I imagine television would be difficult to understand, Your Majesty, but I have an idea of how to explain it. And Jeremy will help."

Jeremy raised his eyebrows. "I will?"

"You are the right man for the job," Dakota said with a smile. "Could you please make a little flip-book? A person riding a horse would do it. I'd love to show it to Elizabeth…Her Majesty…after our walk. I think it will help."

"Yes, your bossiness," Jeremy said with a smirk. "It would be my greatest honor to make you said flip-book."

Snarky again. Good that he's recovered himself.

Elizabeth looked at Dakota. "Do thee advise it acceptable for staff to speak to their superiors in such a manner?"

"Jeremy's style of communication is not typical in a formal business relationship. That's true," Dakota said. "One thing that sets us apart is our friendship. He's like a brother to me, which is why he speaks to me without formality."

"Aww…Dakota, I'm moved by your explanation," Jeremy said. Dakota knew him well enough to see he was choked up. His sarcasm was cloud cover for a multitude of emotions.

"I am fascinated by these differences," Elizabeth said. "I suppose I have much to learn ere I become the leader of this country."

"We are here to help you with that, Your Majesty," Dakota said. "I've asked Janet and Gideon…we often call people with professional titles by their first names if we have close relationships with them… to serve as your cultural, linguistic, and historical advisors. In fact, at some point when you are ready, we will need to call you by your first name, as that is the accepted standard here."

Elizabeth waved her hand at Dakota. "I was anointed queen by God Himself," she said. "Thee say that I must forgo that recognition among thee?" She was silent for a moment. "I shall think on't, and I shall let thee know when the time o' change is upon us. Be warranted, that day is not this day," Elizabeth said.

So tell us how you really feel. Stop that, Dakota. Never respond to her with snarkiness.

"We recognize your need to acclimate to the many differences you will encounter in your life with us, Your Majesty," Dakota said. "Please, take your time." She gestured to the kitchen island. "Before we walk, I'll just take a few minutes to eat, as I've not had lunch. Perhaps Ashley could help you find a warm coat and gloves to wear before we go outside? It's still cold here in March."

"That is well and good, Lady Dakota," Elizabeth said. "I find myself curious about the moving pictureth on the television. The others showed themselveth distressed as they looked on. What did they see and hear? I should'st like an explanation while we walk."

Dakota nodded and walked over the island to fix herself a plate. She'd need her strength to explain the travesty unfolding at the border. She hoped beyond hope that Elizabeth would agree with her—and not with Vlakas.

CHAPTER 26

April 10, 2027, Cambridge

"What manner o' hellscape is this?" Elizabeth clutched her throat as she watched the cars driving down Memorial Drive, across from Dakota's building. "These horseless carriageth that bellow smoke. They are a malignancy upon nature, blighting mine eyne and mine ears. How come thee to live in such a place as this?"

Dakota feared Elizabeth would faint as the little color she had in her face evaporated, and she began to sway. She drew Elizabeth close as they stood on the sidewalk, steps from the crosswalk that would take them across the busy road toward the river.

"Should we go back inside?" Dakota said, tilting her head at Elizabeth. "I should have realized that a walk in the city could be jarring when you've only just arrived."

"Nay. I shall not forbear the weave o' daily life in this time and place, nay matter how disturbing to mine own tranquil nature." Elizabeth pulled away from Dakota. She seemed to refocus. "I oft traveled on the river, thee know. "'Twas the River Thameth. Hast thou heard o' it?"

"Yes, of course." Dakota nodded. "The Thames is very famous. I've not seen it in a long time, but some years ago I attended a performance of Shakespeare's *The Merchant of Venice* at the Globe Theatre in Southwark, which is very close to the Thames…as you may know."

"Certeth, I am most pleased—and surprised—to know that the people o' this time enjoy the plays o' Shakespeare, as did I. Didst thou know that I wast Shakespeare's patron?" Elizabeth bent her head toward Dakota. "I financed the Lord Chamberlain's Men, his acting company, and invited them on many occasions to perform at court. But what was the title of the play you so enjoyed, and why have I not heard of it?"

"It was *The Merchant of Venice*, Your Majesty. Let me check my phone to see when it was first performed." Dakota brought up her browser. "Ah…*The Merchant of Venice* was first performed in 1605, historians believe. That's why you haven't seen it yet."

Elizabeth frowned. "If 'tis performed in this age, I should'st like to see it ere long. I should'st be delighted if you could arrange it." Unblinking, she looked at Dakota.

"I would like to do so, Your Majesty." Dakota opened her palms to the air. "However in modern times, people, even queens and presidents, attend the theater when they want to see a live performance. And unfortunately, Shakespeare's plays are only performed in Boston a few times a year."

Elizabeth wrinkled her brow.

"But I will see if they are performed throughout the year in New York, just as they are in London."

"What is new about York? 'Tis an ancient town built by those cruel invaders from Rome," Elizabeth said. "I should'st like to see it again, though. When may we visit?"

Dakota shivered. They'd been standing on the sidewalk during the entire conversation, and the wind had picked up. "Let's walk, Your Majesty, if that suits you. When we return home, I will research where we can see a Shakespeare play. Shall we cross the street now?"

"Ay, I stand ready." Elizabeth raised herself to her full height and threaded her arm through Dakota's. Dakota pushed the pedestrian-activated crossing sign, which was about one hundred yards from her building. When the walk icon appeared, Dakota ushered

Elizabeth across Memorial Drive so they could walk on the path that ran along the river.

"The geese and ducks are plentiful, just as they are in London." Elizabeth stopped to look at the waterfowl on the river. "Praytell, dost thou also have horseth and dogs?"

"We have many dogs, even here in the city, but horses are only found in the country. We don't use them for transportation anymore."

Just then two cyclists in neon green whooshed past them on the right, causing Elizabeth to flinch. "What are these...wheel-riders?" Elizabeth drew close to Dakota. "Are they the soldiers o' this realm?"

Dakota shook her head. "No, Majesty, they are cyclists. That's the word for people who ride bicycles, either for exercise or transportation," she said. "Why would you think they were soldiers?"

"No person wears such a helmet unless he is a soldier in battle." Elizabeth seemed to lower her voice an octave. "But those people, they carried neither sword nor lance. If not in battle, these wheel-riders..."

"Cyclists," Dakota said.

"Yes, these cyclists," Elizabeth said, but she pronounced it like *seecle-eest*. "They must have a mission o' great importance to transport themselveth with such alacrity."

Dakota smiled. "Sometimes their mission is just to be on time for work."

The two walked together in silence for a few minutes. "Some o' the words thee speak are unknown to me. Thus, I look to their roots," Elizabeth said. "Television is from the Greek, *tele*, which means far, and the Latin, *visio*, which means sight. We have far vision. Bicycle is from the Latin, *bi*, which means two, and the Greek, *kyklos*, which means wheel or circle. We have two wheels." Elizabeth placed a gloved hand to her chin. "Do most o' the people o' thy time speak Latin and Greek?"

"They do not, Your Majesty," Dakota said. "Most Americans speak only English."

"Thee did doth not taketh an education." Elizabeth sniffed. "I did hath't an excellent education by tutors, and I did found Jesus College at Oxford University. Mayhap thee knoweth this." She leaned toward Dakota.

"I did receive an education." Dakota's face felt hot. "In fact, I have a doctorate degree—which is our highest academic degree—yet I only speak English fluently."

"American English, thee mean?" Elizabeth said.

"Yes, American English. But Janet and Gideon speak other languages, I'm sure, because they are academic scholars while I'm in the business world."

"Oh, I do hope that Doctor Horn speaks Greek and Latin as well as American English." Elizabeth looked dreamy. "If he doth not, we could converse in Italian or French. They are lovely languages, but not in Spanish. Ne'er Spanish." She grimaced. "Tell me, Lady. Must I convene soldiers and sailors anon so we may triumph o'er the Spaniards again, as mine own good English navy did a few months past? Mayhap thou hast heard about England's defeat o' the Spanish Armada?" Elizabeth looked askance at Dakota.

"England's defeat of the Spanish Armada is very famous, Your Majesty. It is often called one of the greatest achievements of your realm," Dakota said. "In fact, Gideon and Janet dedicated an entire chapter to it in their book."

"I found that chapter must elucidating." Elizabeth's eyes crinkled with pleasure. "'Twas a joyous time in England when we showed King Philip that our English backs would'st ne'er break. We are made o' stronger mettle than his beslubbering barnacles," she said. "Praytell, thou didst not answer mine own question. Must I guard mine own country against Spain when I am president?"

"They are no longer a threat, Your Majesty, to America or England," Dakota said. "I've found Spain a lovely country to visit. It has beautiful beaches and wonderful food and art."

Elizabeth paused mid-stride. "I can scarce imagine any person of good sense desirous o' traveling to Spain for his holiday." Elizabeth pursed her lips. "Spaniards are a somber people who adorn themselveth in black attire, without regard to season or state o' mourning. Didst thou not find it so?" Elizabeth went on without waiting for Dakota's answer. "Yond is not the end of 't. Spaniards have a steadfast dedication to papistry. They do honor to that mewling foot-licker in Rome, making him superior to their own God-anointed king and queen. It sours mine own stomach to think upon it."

"Spain is off the list." Dakota waved her hand. "Let's forget that I mentioned it."

Elizabeth nodded. "When methinks o' Spain, I recall mine own country. Mine own heart dwells thither still," Elizabeth said sadly.

"I can't imagine how homesick you must feel," Dakota said.

Elizabeth braced herself against the wind. "It is decided then, Lady. We must visit England anon. How many months shall it take reach her shores?"

"Not months. It only takes hours," Dakota said. "We can fly there in six hours."

Elizabeth stopped in her tracks. "Thee mock me, Lady," she said, jutting out her chin.

"I promise that I speak the truth—if we're talking about air travel. Which I realize is a big leap from traveling long-distance by water." Dakota froze at Elizabeth's scowl. "Up until about 1800, it would have taken months to travel by ship from Boston to London, but now, it only takes a week or ten days by boat because we have massive high-speed ships powered by engines, not wind."

"I should'st like to see these fast ships," Elizabeth said. "I had mine own row barge, thee may know. I spent many a pleasant afternoon on her, conversing with mine own favored courtiers, listening to the entertainments o' the most accomplished musicians. In the evening, the glow from the lanterns reflected off the water. Captured incandescence, she brought joy to those who saw her, not just to those carried by her."

"We could look for an image of her on my computer when we return home, if you like."

"I should like that overmuch." Elizabeth's eyes looked misty.

"I wonder how long we've been gone." Dakota pulled down her glove to look at her watch. "I can't believe it's four o'clock already." Dakota gasped. "We've been gone for more than an hour. We should turn back."

"What is this tiny timepiece?" Elizabeth touched Dakota's wrist. "I have many variety o' mechanical clocks but not a one this small and not a one with two hands."

Dakota raised her stainless-steel Breitling toward Elizabeth's face.

"The moon and stars it wears remind me o' the astrolabe Doctor Dee employed to interpret the influence o' heavenly bodieth." Elizabeth smiled at the watch and then at Dakota. "Do thee employ it in predictions?"

"No, Your Majesty. It merely tells the time," Dakota said. "It gives me the hour, the minute, and the second."

"I admire it greatly."

"I would be pleased to buy one for you. We will look at them together on my computer."

"The world is in thy computer, it seems to me," Elizabeth said. "There is much for me to learn, far more than I could have imagined." She looked away.

"Please rest assured, you don't need to learn it all at once. As we say here, all in good time."

As the two women turned back toward Dakota's condo, Elizabeth said, "I raise a query to thee. When I inquired about the trip to England, thee quoth it would'st take scant hours. I am not so overcome that I forget myself for long. Didst thou speak to me in jest?"

Dakota stopped to look at Elizabeth. "I wouldn't do that, Your Majesty. When you ask me a question, I will give you an honest answer," she said. "It's true that we could fly to England in hours. We'd go by airplane. As we've been walking, several airplanes have flown over us, but I didn't point them out because I didn't want to overwhelm you."

Elizabeth gave a mirthless laugh. "Thy generosity o' spirit is most welcome," she said. "'Tis true that I have come to walk an unknown path, but 'tis not the first rutted road on which I have traveled." She patted Dakota on the arm. "Do not worry overmuch. Though I am a woman and antique, I am born o' kings, and mine own spirit riseth to mountains when needs be."

Dakota gazed at Elizabeth in wonder. *My God. She's inspiring.* Then she heard a plane flying overhead and pointed it out to Elizabeth, "There's an airplane now."

Elizabeth saw the plane and grasped her chest, a blue vein pulsing at her neck.

"Are you alright?" Dakota asked, alarmed. *She's so white she looks almost translucent.*

"What noxious beast is this? Is God moving in the heavens above us?"

"I know this must seem shocking, Your Majesty, a machine that large flying through the air. Shall I explain it to you at home?"

Elizabeth stared into Dakota's eyes. "Explain it to me now."

Dakota did a slow inhale and exhale. "The airplane is a flying machine. That's what Leonardo da Vinci called it when he drew his version of it. It was much simpler than what we have today, of course," she said. "Ours is powered by engines—machines that produce energy, which is captured to propel a plane in the sky or a ship across the ocean." Elizabeth blinked. *Try again.* "We could start with a da Vinci drawing," Dakota said. "Do you know him?"

"Certes, I am acquainted withal the work o' Leonardo da Vinci. Mine own education did not want." Elizabeth appeared to bite back her words. "As he died ere the year o' my birth, we would'st not have met."

I am totally screwing up. "Of course, Your Majesty. That's what I meant to ask, that you knew of his work."

"Very good. We are of o' mind then," Elizabeth said. "When we are arrived at thy home, I should'st like a briefing on wherefore Doctor Gibbons, Sir Jeremy, and thee expressed much displeasure at thy television. Should'st I approve o' thy sentiments, shall it be in mine own power to correct what offends thee?"

What the hell does that mean—approve of our sentiments? "I would be glad to brief you on this serious issue," Dakota said. "We will set aside some time before dinner, should that meet with your approval."

"We are agreed on mine own schedule ere the evening meal," Elizabeth said. "Shall we have entertainment after we dine? Mayhap thou hast read that mine own court wast renowned throughout Europe for music and dancing. I should'st enjoy dancing a Galliard withal Doctor Horn."

Dakota's stomach lurched. "I don't think we have much space for dancing, so tonight we will invite you to experience the entertainment that comes to us on the television. I hope that will be alright."

"I will make do, Lady." Elizabeth sniffed. "I have withstood great difficultieth in mine own life ere this one. When I wast but one and twenty, mine own sister appeal'd me o' plotting treason against her person. By heaven! I ne'er did commit such treachery, yet I lived weeks in the Tower, not knowing which night would'st be mine own last. At nine and twenty, I wast assailed by smallpox. 'Tis proven by mine own scars." She pointed to a pockmark over her left eyebrow. "I have survived a multitude o' assassination assays by those who would'st send mine own soul to mine own heavenly Father. I have sat in conference withal the Spanish ambassador more timeth than I care to remember. He would'st beseech me to marry a Catholic king, to honor the 'one true religion'—for that is what they call it—or risk mine own soul to the fiery depths o' Hell." Her eyes looked black. "Fie. That fawning, fen-sucked minnow did not drive me to a lunatic asylum. I am all certainty that watching moving pictureth on thy television shall not end me."

Note to self: don't let Jeremy choose what we're watching.

CHAPTER 27

April 10, 2027, Cambridge

"As I understand it, thy president is enjoined to secure the borders of these United States of America," Elizabeth said. She'd been experimenting with the recliner during their conversation, so she was either sitting straight up or lying flat while addressing Dakota.

Dakota pinched the soft flesh between her thumb and index finger so she wouldn't laugh while Elizabeth was speaking.

"With such a mandate, is't not reasonable for him to protect the country's southern border from people who are not citizens nor do they have the education or wealth to improve the livelihoods o' those who are fully citizens?" Elizabeth—who was now upright for the moment—said.

Dakota nodded. "It's true the president has the legal responsibility to protect, or rather to help ensure the protection, of our citizens," she said. "It's also true that the United States of America—or just America, as we call it—was built by people moving here from other countries. Throughout the world, America is known as a melting pot, a country made of people from many different nations and cultures. Our diversity is our strength. We can't simply abandon desperate people seeking a better life."

"You protest against the president on moral principles, is that it?" Elizabeth rubbed her chin. "Do thee trow that thou art doing God's work, to ease the suffering o' others, and that thy president is not?"

"That's it in a sense, although not everyone in this room believes it's God's work…" Dakota looked over her shoulder at Jeremy, who was helping Teddy in the kitchen. CeCe was on the couch reading Gideon and Janet's book, *Heart and Stomach of a Lion*. Ashley was nowhere to be found, probably running for the hills—or back at Saks doing a million returns. "I, for example, was not raised in a particular religion, so I object for moral, not religious, reasons."

Elizabeth gasped, then reached for her decaf espresso on the side table. "How canst thou claim morality without religion?" She took a sip of coffee, then turned a steady gaze on Dakota. "Religion is the very foundation o' morality, for God hath determined what is right and what is wrong. 'Tis not for man to judge."

"I have a strong belief in what's right and wrong, I assure you." Dakota thrust out her chin. "I believe that those who are more fortunate should care for those who are less fortunate. This includes the poor, the sick, the old, children—those who are most vulnerable in society." Dakota smoothed her cashmere sweater. "The people now coming from Guatemala, Honduras, and El Salvador are desperate to get to America because it's their only path to a better life."

"Certes. I understand that they seek a better life. I do not relish suffering, but 'tis not reason enough to open the gateth to the kingdom."

"They are refugees, people who are fleeing abuse and hunger," Dakota said. "And the worst of all is that they're separating children from their parents and are putting them in cages." Dakota's stomach hurt.

"What mean thee by this?" Elizabeth leaned toward Dakota and lowered her voice. "Do thee speak in metaphor, about the encaged children?"

"No, I'm being literal," Dakota said. "The children are put in tall cage-like enclosures with bare floors. Some of them are very young, just toddlers."

"What is the age o' a 'toddler?' I know not this word."

"It's a child who's just learning to walk, one or two, I guess."

Elizabeth's gold-brown eyes grew two shades darker. "'Tis unconscionable in e'ry way." Her eyes flashed. "Even the Spanish, who burn heretics at the stake as a form o' entertainment, would'st not descend to such barbarity." She shook her head. "Are thee warranted that these people have nay intention o' subverting the power o' thy president or his government?"

"My understanding is that most of them are just regular people."

"Are they a threat to the sustenance of the people? Shall they take a man's ability to put food on his table for they have taken his job?"

"They're not a threat that way. Recent immigrants tend to take the jobs that Americans don't want. They pick our crops, maintain our gardens, clean our houses. And they do even more unpleasant jobs, like working in meat-processing plants."

"Meat processing? Is that an abattoir?" Elizabeth shrugged. "The English people are content to do such work as long as they can afford to buy grain. American citizens must have great personal wealth to deem such labor o' lesser value."

"Compared to the poor of even one hundred years ago, the American standard of living is high. Even the poorest families generally have shelter with running water, heat, and electricity."

"Praytell, do they starve in a bad harvest? It much pains me when thither is famine among mine own people."

"A poor harvest won't cause famine here."

"Remarkable." Elizabeth's mouth grew round. "Not one country in Europe—or anywhere in the world—could have offered as much to her citizens in my time. Fortune hath indeed smiled kindly upon thee." She scooched forward on the leather sectional and looked out at the river.

"Ding, ding, ding, ding," Jeremy called out. "I'm pleased to announce that dinner will be served shortly."

"Methinks Sir Jeremy maketh a fine herald." Elizabeth said, with a laugh. "Mayhap we should'st give to him a tambourine to play as 'twould be more pleasing than his sound o' music."

"Did you just say *The Sound of Music*?" Jeremy leaned over the sectional, putting his head between Dakota and Elizabeth. "I'm all about singing nuns." He giggled.

"My sister wast overfond o' nuns, papist that she wast, while I am overfond o' singing." Elizabeth looked merry. "Is thither chorale music in this time?"

"In abundance. I'm told the Boston Gay Men's Choir is very popular," Jeremy said, smirking.

Dakota flicked the side of his head with her fingers.

"'Tis a choir o'merry men then?" Elizabeth said.

"Some of them may be merry, but all of them are gay," Jeremy said. He walked around the sectional and faced Elizabeth and Dakota. "Which brings me to an important question, Your Majesty. In their biography of you, Janet and Gideon said that you imposed sodomy laws during your reign, and that the penalty of sodomy was death. As a gay man…"

"I find myself confused by thy choice o' words," Elizabeth said. "You are a merry man, a happy man? I am glad to hear it." She wrinkled her brow.

"Jeremy," Dakota said softly. "I believe our use of gay is a fairly modern term."

"What is the intent of thy question, Sir Jeremy? Its import, but not its meaning, is clear to me," Elizabeth said.

"If I were alive in the sixteenth century, would you have had me burned at the stake?" Jeremy's eyes glistened.

Elizabeth placed her hands on her heart. "Good sir. Thou hast given nay cause for such grave offense that I would'st have ordered thy demise. Wherefore ask thee this?"

Jeremy wiped his eyes on his sleeve and said nothing. Dakota rose to put her arm around his shoulders.

Elizabeth approached. "Thy inquiry about the sodomy laws. This hath upset thee."

"Yes, very much," Jeremy said, "because on Jeju, the island where I'm from, there were no gay people, not visible ones, anyway, and I knew that's what I was by the time I was twelve. That's also when I knew I had to leave." He watched for a response.

"Gay and sodomite. They are the same?" Elizabeth said.

"They are similar, Your Majesty, but not the same," Dakota said. "Gay is not a negative word. It's the word we use for a man who loves other another man. Sodomite, on the other hand, is both deeply offensive and archaic."

"A man can love another man for all to see. Is that thy meaning?" Elizabeth said.

"Yes. Men can love other men, and women can love other women. They can marry legally in the eyes of the state. They can have children together," Dakota said.

"A woman can impregnate another woman in this world?" Elizabeth's brought her fingers to her lips. "How can the laws o' God be changed so?"

"That's one thing that's not changed," Dakota said, bemused. "There are special ways for gay women to become pregnant, or they can adopt a child born to someone else."

Elizabeth furrowed her brow. "What are these special ways o' which thee speak?"

"Could I please cover that another day, Your Majesty?" Dakota put her hand on the back of her neck. "The main point is that men who love men and women who love women can live full lives as members of the community."

"It isn't as rosy as that everywhere, and it hasn't been that long that we could marry, just since 2004 in Massachusetts," Jeremy said. "And I sure hope that won't change." He shifted his weight.

"There is much for me to advise, Sir Jeremy. I must gather myself." Elizabeth sat down and leaned back into a pillow. After a few minutes, she spoke again. "Mayhap God's good heart welcometh love betwixt men, and I knew it not," she said, pursing her lips. "Certes, I heard o' dallianceth betwixt courtiers on an occasion. As long as they were loyal men o' good character, I cared not. "'Twas a private matter betwixt themselveth and God."

"You all are in intense conversation, I can see." CeCe sidled close to the trio. "But Teddy said that dinner will be ready soon, and we should take our seats."

"It smells delicious, by the way," Dakota said, glad to be done with a delicate subject, at least for now. "What are we having?"

"I'll answer that because I helped," Jeremy said. "We're having beef Wellington, scalloped potatoes, and asparagus for dinner, and homemade apple pie with vanilla ice cream for dessert."

"Oh my lord, I'm not going to fit in my jeans in a week if he keeps cooking like that," CeCe said, patting her abdomen.

"I'm going for a run tomorrow, CeCe. Come with me if you want," Dakota said.

"Why shalt thou run on the morrow, ladies?" Elizabeth looked from side to side at the two women. "Is a ferocious bear about?"

"Hah." Dakota tried—and failed—to hold back a guffaw. "Pardon me, Majesty. We run along the river for exercise. It helps us keep fit. Our muscles, that is."

"It keeps our hearts healthy too," CeCe said.

"I'm sleeping in, if anyone cares," Jeremy said.

"I wish to run to keep mine own heart healthy," Elizabeth said. "I look forward to running on the morrow." She glided toward the dinner table.

"Oh my effing God," Dakota said. "How are we going to take her running?"

"Nikes for the queen, please," Jeremy said. "We'd like little bejeweled gold ones." He did a flourish with his hand.

"Isn't the CTO of Reebok an AKA?" Dakota said.

"She certainly is," CeCe said. "And she just happens to be a good friend of a friend. I'll ask her to send a few pairs of size five running shoes to us ASAP. Texting her now."

"Or she can wear my extra pair of size eights," CeCe said.

"Or my size twelves," Jeremy said.

"Thanks, guys. That's super helpful," Dakota said. Ignoring their giggles, she said, "Jeremy, we need a break after dinner. She's exhausting. Can you figure out something we could all watch? It has to be something she'd understand."

"I'm so glad you asked. I already have something picked out," Jeremy said, grinning. "Elizabeth is gonna love it."

CHAPTER 28

April 10, 2027, Cambridge

"Who is this Brianna?" Elizabeth peered at the television to get a better look. "Is she a princess royal from the European continent? Mayhap she is the daughter o' a duke or at least a marquess." Elizabeth bent so close to look at the stunning young woman with bright blue eyes and flowing blonde hair that she obscured a good chunk of the screen. "I do not recognize her visage, yet she must be o' great and noble birth, else she would'st not have twenty suitors vying for her hand in marriage." Elizabeth adjusted her flowing saffron-colored cashmere sweater and returned to the sofa.

"I don't think she's actually a princess," Jeremy said with a smirk. "Perhaps she just plays one on TV."

Dakota elbowed Jeremy from her place on the couch. "We call this reality television, Your Majesty, because real people are put in unusual circumstances for the entertainment of the viewing audience at home. Brianna isn't a princess, right Jeremy?"

"Right. I just looked up her bio, and she's from Pittsburgh," he said. "Definitely not a princess royal."

"Like other stars of reality television shows, Brianna would have auditioned to become the Bachelorette," Dakota said. "Just as a player would for a stage performance, except that Brianna isn't reading lines."

"And the men would have done the same, auditioning for the chance to fall in love with her," Jeremy said, leaning over to look at Elizabeth. "On *The Bachelorette*, the woman chooses the man she wants to propose to her at the end of the series. It almost always ends with an engagement ring."

"What praytell is an engagement ring?" Elizabeth said, frown lines forming on her forehead. "Is it a gage o' fidelity from the woman to the man?"

"That's an accurate description of it, truth be told," CeCe said. "Many years ago, I expect it was a way for a woman to show that she belonged to her intended husband, so no one else could propose marriage to her."

"This is not so different from mine own time. The woman becometh the property o' the man, once married." Elizabeth sighed. "That is wherefore I could ne'er marry. It would'st not suit to have a man rule o'er me when I had already gaged myself to mine own people."

The doorbell chimed.

"Now who can that be?" Jeremy said, springing up to answer the door. "Hi, Gideon," he said. "Come on in. Did you have dinner? We have the most amazing leftovers."

"I'm famished actually," Gideon said. "I'm embarrassed to say that I napped all day, though I meant to get here much earlier." He walked over to Elizabeth and bowed deeply. "Forgive me, Your Majesty. I regret that I have missed the pleasure of your company these past hours."

Elizabeth put her hand out for him to kiss. "It matters not, Doctor Horn. It pleaseth me to see thee in company again," she said. "After thou hast supped, shalt thou join me for this evening's entertainment?"

"Rewind, people, will you, please?" Jeremy grimaced. "I just missed the backstory of the guy in the last limo," he said. "They're all so adorable. It's going to be hard to choose a favorite."

"I'll warm up a plate for you, Gideon," Dakota said. "You can sit by Her Majesty, and I'll bring it over when it's ready."

"And I'll help." Jeremy scooted off the couch and followed Dakota into the kitchen.

"Is it my imagination or is there some chemistry between Elizabeth and Gideon?" Dakota said in an undertone.

"She's got a certain something for a gal with black teeth," Jeremy whispered in her ear.

Dakota rolled her eyes at him. "Don't be so sarcastic, for a change."

"I'm serious," he said. "The air's so charged, I can feel my hair standing up." He ran a hand across his thick black hair. "I already look like Korean Billy Idol in the winter months. If this keeps up, I'm buying leave-in conditioner in bulk."

Dakota watched Gideon take his seat next to Elizabeth. When she handed Gideon his dinner plate, she realized they were speaking in an unfamiliar language.

"*Loqui latine pulchre,*" Gideon said to Elizabeth.

What the hell does that mean? "That's an interesting language," Dakota said.

"I just said that she speaks Latin beautifully," Gideon said, looking dreamy.

"Isn't Latin a dead language?" Jeremy said.

"Your Latin is o' excellent quality as well, Doctor Horn," Elizabeth said, ignoring Jeremy as she gazed at Gideon.

"You do me a great honor to say so." Gideon nodded. "Please, call me Gideon."

"Gideon, then." Elizabeth's easy laugh sounded like tiny bells. "Thee may call me Bess."

"Okay, ladies and gentlemen," Jeremy said. "Why don't we resume *The Bachelorette* in a few minutes? I can't wait to see what happens during the rose ceremony. So far, my money's on George from Seattle."

"He's stunning," CeCe said, over a bowl of ice cream.

"And his teeth are so white, they're blinding," Jeremy said.

"Are white teeth the fashion hither?" Elizabeth asked Jeremy. "They wert not so in mine own England."

"White teeth are considered attractive, Your Majesty, perhaps because people think they look healthy," CeCe said. "And we have doctors called *dentists* who specialize in the care of teeth."

"Are they like Doctor Robinson, who saw to my care with little pain? Or are they fearsome folk who pull teeth from one's jaw to cure an ache?" Elizabeth said. "I had a most troublesome tooth removed in such a way. I felt wretched for some days after."

"You had a tooth pulled without Novocain?" Jeremy put his hand on his jaw.

"They had no painkillers in Tudor England," Gideon said. "Some doctors used herbal remedies like cloves, but most used nothing at all." He turned to Elizabeth. "It took extraordinary courage to ask for help with a dental problem."

Elizabeth beamed at him, then covered her mouth with her hand.

"I have a wonderful dentist, Your Majesty," Dakota said. "Jim Nagerian. He's a good friend, and I'm sure he'd be happy to see you."

Elizabeth said nothing.

"I assure you that he won't cause you discomfort," Dakota said. "Dentists use analgesics to prevent that."

"From the Greek, *analgetos*, which means without pain," Elizabeth said. "What think thee, Gideon?"

"Do it not for beauty's sake, Your Grace, for you need no assistance on that count," Gideon said. "Do it rather for your health because that is of the utmost importance to us all."

"I suppose I shalt nev'r beest the Bachelorette again, though I wast once," Elizabeth said with a wry grin. "But I doth wish to taketh care of mine health. And if 't be true mine person is deemed attractive because of 't, so much the better." She raised her chin. "'Tis settled then," she said firmly. "I shalt see this dentist on the morrow."

What a relief. "I'll call Jim first thing Monday morning," Dakota said. Elizabeth blinked at her.

"Tomorrow is Sunday, and his office isn't open," Dakota said, gulping.

"Tomorrow is the Lord's day? I did doth not realize it." Elizabeth put her hand to her chest. "Praytell. Is thither a valorous Protestant church nearby?" No one spoke. "Ye are nay Catholics, I desire." She clutched her throat.

"I don't attend church services," Dakota said. She looked at CeCe, who shook her head. Jeremy examined his fingernails.

"We will find an Anglican church, Your Majesty…Bess," Gideon said. "For that's what we call Church of England—the church your father founded—in America."

Elizabeth patted him on the arm.

"Tomorrow's actually Easter Sunday," CeCe said.

"That's why the stores are full of Peeps," Jeremy said. "I have a love-hate relationship with those little guys."

"Marry!" Elizabeth leapt up. "I hath't did miss the Creeping to the Cross in its entirety. I desire yond God shalt not disfavor me for this act o' heedlessness." She placed her palms to her chest and collapsed onto the couch. She sat so close to Gideon that their shoulders almost touched. "'Twas November at which hour I did leave England. I did doth not realize yond we art in a diverse season, and yond the day of our valorous Lord's resurrection is nigh."

"I can see why that would be confusing, Your Majesty," Dakota said. "Our travel team—that's what we call Janet, Gideon, and Henry among ourselves—left our year of 2027 on Friday, April 2nd and returned with you on Friday, April 9th."

Elizabeth wrinkled her brow.

"Because with Tempus Fujit...that's what Kisai calls the time-travel...err...mechanism."

"Mechanism. From the Greek, *mēkhanē*, meaning machine or device," Elizabeth said, brightening. "Prithee continueth." She gestured to Dakota with a flourish.

Dakota cleared her throat. "With Tempus Fujit, we didn't need to match our time of year with yours," she said. "Our team left here in April and returned seven days after they had left because that's the number of days they stayed in November of 1588."

Elizabeth's face was turning red. It started with her nose and flushed across her cheeks. *Oh crud. This actually is confusing.*

"We arrived in thy time in April though we did leave mine time in the dark month of November," Elizabeth said, frowning.

"It shall become clear in time, Your Majesty." Gideon patted Elizabeth's hand. "We shall attend church together." He gave a small bow. "It would be my privilege to accompany thee."

"I grammercy for thy kindness, Gideon, and shall be prest on the morrow to celebrate this holiest o' holy days in thy company."

"Now that's settled, why don't we resume our entertainment?" Jeremy said. "Gideon, we just started episode one of the new *Bachelorette*. You know the gist of it, right? One gorgeous woman and twenty gorgeous guys. Who gets the roses, and who goes home? I bet you're a big fan."

"I've never seen it," Gideon said. "But I'm happy to do so." He edged closer to Elizabeth.

Twenty minutes later, Brianna had met each potential mate. "I'm changing my vote to Robert. He's smart and handsome," Jeremy said.

"Robert is a fine name for a favorite, but what is a software engineer?" Elizabeth said.

"Software engineer is a technical job that often requires higher education, at least it does at KODA," Dakota said.

"Is't prestigious to hold this position?" Elizabeth said.

"It is considered so, yes," Dakota said.

"Are any o' the other gentlemen o' noble birth?" she asked.

"There are few people of aristocratic birth in America so nobility is rarely part of our cultural hierarchy," Gideon said. "We tend to judge people by the type of work they do and by the amount of money they make. Lawyers and doctors, for example, are well-respected, as are company executives."

"Like Dakota," Jeremy said.

"Yes, Dakota is highly regarded, particularly as a self-made entrepreneur of significant financial means," Gideon said.

"How significant art that lady means?" Elizabeth said.

"She has about six billion means, I think," Jeremy said. Dakota shushed him.

"Six billion o' which coin?" Elizabeth said, arching her eyebrows.

"Six billion US dollars is about the same as five billion British pounds sterling," Jeremy said. "And one billion is one thousand million."

"God's blessed mother." Elizabeth grabbed her pearl necklace. "Lady Dakota's wealth exceeds that o' the entire European continent...in mine own day."

"It's just money," Dakota said. "It doesn't have anything to do with someone's value as a human being. That can't be quantified."

"It can't, but it does buy some nice vacations," Jeremy said. "Still, Dakota doesn't have a single family in Cambridge like some people I know." He pointed to himself and grinned.

Elizabeth sighed deeply. "I needeth a moment's privacy."

"Does anyone else need a bathroom break?" Jeremy said. "I do, and then I'm getting another piece of pie. Why don't we all take five?"

Once again safely ensconced in chairs and couches, the group watched Brianna show up for a group date wearing a sleeveless red mini dress with plunging decolletage. Elizabeth gasped. "'Tis scandalous. Doth maids bewray themselveth in such a manner to gentlemen not their husbands? Methinks Master Davidson a chaperone o' dram consequence, for Mistress Brianna displays that lady wareth for all to sample, withal dram regard for that lady chastity. 'Tis clear the lady is without a protector."

"Let's pause for a moment." Jeremy clicked the TV remote. "I'm starting to realize that I have a way to go until I understand your perceptions of our modern world, Your Majesty. *The Bachelorette* can get a bit racy, and I don't want to make you uncomfortable."

Dakota watched their exchange. *It's so touching when he shows he cares.*

"I appreciate thy sentiments, Sir Jeremy, for they bewray an affection o' which I wast uncertain," Elizabeth said, with a warm smile. "While our worlds are different, I am not naïve about the ways o' men." She raised her head as if holding court. "One o' mine own did trust courtiers, Sir Walter Raleigh, married one o' mine own dearest maids o' honor, Bess Throckmorton, without mine own consent. Didst thou know this?" Jeremy shook his head. "I learned yond lady wast carrying his issue, and this ere their feather-bed. This did doth break mine heart profoundly. I sent Sir Walter to the Tower, but only for a time, as I would'st not keepeth the lovers did part long."

"That must have been very painful," Jeremy said. "Sometimes when people fall in love, others are hurt in the process."

Elizabeth gave him a slight nod.

"If I may jump in, Your Majesty, I think Jeremy wants to forewarn you about what might happen on this show." Dakota leaned forward in her chair. "From what I've seen on other seasons of *The Bachelorette*—not that I watch *every* season like Jeremy..." She winked at him. "Brianna is likely to fall in love with more than one of the men."

"There will be kissing," Jeremy said. "For sure."

"Lady Dakota and Sir Jeremy, thou art moo attentive withal mine own feelings than almost any other in mine own long life." Elizabeth's eyes shone like liquid gold. "I grammercy for thy love, and I warrant thee yond I shalt not melt shouldst the kissing commence."

"I'm so glad, Your Majesty, because I do think you'll enjoy this show," Jeremy said. "It gives me hope because some of the men are so sweet, they only want to find someone to love."

"Your aspiration to findeth a partner is most commendable," Elizabeth said. "I hath't been did bless during mine own long life to findeth companions o' mine own heart, if't be true not a husband or a issue, and yet, I did love withal a volume o' humour."

Elizabeth's voice broke almost imperceptibly as she confided in Jeremy, but Dakota caught the change in her inflection. Could a woman leader have it all? Dakota still wasn't sure.

"Your life is far from over, Your Majesty," Jeremy said. "A woman your age may still find a partner who will stand by her side through thick and thin. In fact, I hope you do, although he'd need to be a most unusual man."

"An unusual woman needs an unusual man," Dakota said.

She almost missed the look Elizabeth gave Gideon. Almost.

CHAPTER 29

April 11, 2027, Cambridge

"Potage or pancakes. Hmm…whatever will I choose?" Jeremy flashed a smile at Teddy from his seat at the kitchen island. He had a front-row seat to the meal preparations of their new personal chef whisking a bowl full of batter.

"I expect the gentleman will have the pancakes with bacon," Teddy said, tucking a dish towel into the front apron pocket that rested against his slightly rounded man-belly. "After I graduated from the CIA, I took a Korean cooking course, and pork figured prominently into many of the dishes. Which is why I figured you liked bacon—if that's not a cultural stereotype."

"Stereotype away. I adore bacon." Jeremy grinned. "But what's this about the CIA? You're a chef *and* a spy? I'm so confused."

"Haha. CIA stands for Culinary Institute of America," Teddy said. "That's where I went to school." He leaned over to say something to Jeremy, but Dakota couldn't hear the exchange.

"I think I'll just have yogurt with fruit, if anyone cares." Dakota raised an eyebrow, like a Cantabrigian Spock. "I don't have Jeremy's metabolism so I can't start a day of three sit-down meals with pancakes."

"Same for me," CeCe said, who was wearing running tights and a long-sleeve Adidas shirt. "I'll get it myself after we go running."

"Sounds good," Dakota said. "But first, I need to check on Elizabeth since Ashley went to her boyfriend's house last night. I know Ashley bought a bunch of Lululemon at Saks, but I have no idea if Elizabeth knows what to do with it. She'll also need to try on the running shoes CeCe's friend sent over this morning." She looked at the stack of Reebok boxes in the corner of the room.

"She definitely has a lot of energy," Jeremy said. "But I'm thinking they didn't have spin class in Tudor England, so aerobic exercise might seem kind of foreign. Do you think she can do it?"

"I think she'll end up running circles around us," Dakota said. "She was very physical, from what I've read. She was an expert horsewoman, who rode vigorously every day until her late sixties. She did archery and crossbow, and she loved to dance."

"I just watched that Elizabeth movie from like twenty years ago," Jeremy said. "In this one scene, this stunning actress who played Elizabeth and the guy who played Robert Dudley did Elizabeth's favorite dance, the Volta. It was a lot of leaping and flinging, very athletic. She's going to leave you guys in the dust."

Dakota punched him in the arm.

"I'll go knock on her door," Dakota said. "Wish me luck."

She thought maybe she should get changed first. Or was that just procrastinating? *I'm totally procrastinating.*

"It's Dakota, Your Majesty," Dakota said with a knock. "Would you like to go running with CeCe and me before breakfast?"

The door swung open. "Come in, Lady." Elizabeth took Dakota's hands and kissed her on both cheeks. "Indeed I wish to join thee and Doctor Gibbons for the heart-healthy exercise of running. Praytell, what attire shall I wear for our outing?"

Dakota entered the walk-in closet that held Elizabeth's clothes on one side, and hers on the other. She skipped the gowns and dresses, passed the tops and pants (including jeans—would Elizabeth ever wear them?), walked by the neatly folded sweaters, and stopped in front of the Lululemon workout section. There were leggings of different colors and patterns, a variety of hoodies, sweaters, and t-shirts, all hanging up. She found hats, gloves, underwear, sports bras, and socks in the drawers. She paused to make her selections.

Folding a pair of black leggings, a winter-white fleece hoodie, and a moisture-wicking base-layer shirt over one arm, she wedged the hat, gloves, two different sports bras, and organic cotton boy shorts under her other arm. She laid the clothes out on the sofa for Elizabeth.

"This material is strange to me." Elizabeth picked up the hoodie and rubbed it against her cheek. "It is light in weight, yet it warms and comforts mine own body."

"I'm delighted that you like the fleece—that's what it's called. I'll wear my fleece sweatshirt when we run, and then we can be twins," Dakota said, with a giggle.

"I suspect not a one would sayest yond we wast born of the same mother," Elizabeth said, radiating genuine warmth. At five foot three, Elizabeth had to look up at Dakota, who loomed above her at five foot ten. The English queen was thin and lithe while Dakota was heavily muscled and just slightly overweight. Elizabeth was the dancer, and Dakota the rugby player. But both had lost their mothers young. There were more important things than physical resemblance. "With God's valorous grace, mayhap we shalt love each other as if 't be true we art sisters," Elizabeth said. "I should'st like to hath't a sister in whom I couldst trust and who is't couldst trust in me."

Dakota's heart was in her throat. "I would like that too, Your Majesty."

"Thee may address me as Bess." Elizabeth dazzled with her magnanimity.

"I will, gladly." Dakota's cheeks felt flushed. "Please call me Dakota."

"Dakota. 'Tis is an unusual name but one yond is pleasing to the tongue," Elizabeth said. She turned her attention to the clothes on the sofa. "Where hast thou concealed mine own dress for our running? I see only a pair o' men's hose, withal nay breecheth as their companion. Certes, thee cannot bethink me so ill-did breed to bewray mine own forks for all the ordinary to see."

"You're the most elegant woman I've ever met, Your Majesty… Bess, I mean," Dakota said. "I would never want you to feel uncomfortable, yet I can imagine that some modern attire resembles undergarments." She held up the black running tights. "These are *leggings* or *running tights*. And they're very much the fashion for exercise in public."

Elizabeth examined the tights and frowned.

"CeCe and I will wear something similar. You'll see, Bess."

Elizabeth sighed. "I gage to trust thee in this choice, and so I shalt," she said. "I hath't others o' this undergarment." She pointed to one of the sports bras.

"It's helpful to wear a sports bra," Dakota said.

"Mistress Ashley did doth clepe 't a 'brassiere,' and its purpose is to hold up the breasts." She pointed to her bosom. "It is an improvement beyond measure to the corset, and I am thankful for 't," she said. "The black lace brassiere I wear anon is preferential to me. These two art an offense to mine own eyes." She glared at the two boob-flattening sports bras.

"You may wear the lace, if that's what you prefer," Dakota said. "The sports brassieres are designed to provide better support, to limit the bouncing of the breasts, which comes from the up and down movement."

"I shalt contemplate 't in quiet at a future time," Elizabeth said. "Whither is Mistress Ashley? I would like that lady to dress me."

"Ashley stayed at her boyfriend's last night. She said she'd join us for dinner," Dakota said.

"Is a boyfriend a paramour? Or is he a sir withal whom one is cater-cousins?" Elizabeth said. "The word is strange to me," Elizabeth said.

Dakota thought for a moment. "In this context, Ashley's boyfriend is closer to a paramour. That is, they have a romantic relationship. I mean to say that she has a deep affection for him." *Could I trip over myself anymore?*

"'Tis as if 't be true clouds hath't veiled the heavens o' mine own mind, for I am bewildered by thy words." Elizabeth tapped her fingers together. "As Ashley is a maid and not yet did marry, for I did see nay wedding ring on that lady digit, I suppose yond that lady sleeping quarters art in the family home o' that lady boyfriend and yond last night of all the lady wast did attend by the boyfriend's mother all the while. What sayeth thee?"

"I don't know about her sleeping quarters, truth be told." Dakota started to sweat. "But in most cases, in this day and age, Ashley would have stayed at the home of her boyfriend, and not at his parents, since she's in her early thirties, and I'm sure he has his own place." Dakota swirled her foot in circles over the hand-knotted Tibetan area rug. "You may remember from *The Bachelorette* that courtship is very different in our time. Women are able to have intimate relations with men, even before marriage."

Elizabeth shook her head with vigor. "I cannot comprehend wherefore such conduct bears nay condemnation from a woman's father," she said. "Yond he would'st freely accept a sir who is't would'st forswear withal his daughter outside o' the feather-bed catch but a wink cubiculo astounds me." Elizabeth ran fingers through her ragged hair. "How can society's view o' intimate relations beest so altered at which hour the consequenceth o' such illicit unions shalt caterwauling for all the ordinary to see?"

"This has been one of the epic changes in human culture, at least in the Western world," Dakota said. "I'm not sure if it stems from the women's liberation movement of the 1970s—which I'd be glad to explain to you another time—or if it's a direct outcome of birth control."

Elizabeth sat on the couch and folded her hands together. "How can one possibly control the birth o' a issue, except to abstain from intimate relations? The anatomy o' sir and mistress cannot hath't did doth change."

"Medical science has freed women from the worry of pregnancy," Dakota said, as she sat down next to Elizabeth. "We have pea-sized pills that are ingested, as well as other devices that are worn inside the uterus, to prevent a woman from getting pregnant, should she not wish to do so. And there's something for men too, a type of barrier that's worn."

"Mercy." Elizabeth's face was red as beets. "Hath't thee—or any modern mistress—the merest understanding o' mine own fate as the virgin queen? I did deny myself intimate relations withal the sir I did love most wondrous 'mongst all others out o' the extremity o' fear, for I, as an anointed queen, couldst nay longer wear the coronet or liveth in mine own realm in valorous conscience if 't be true I did hath't becometh withal issue." Elizabeth was now yelling. "Neither couldst I marry any sir, for if 't be true I did doth, he would'st hath't been mine own king and ruler, and I couldst not abide thus."

"Bess, please." Dakota reached out to Elizabeth, who looked like she would throw the loveseat if she could lift it. Remembering that CeCe was always talking about the importance of validation, she said, "It must have been terribly frustrating, to have been in your position."

Elizabeth swallowed hard and nodded.

"I must confide that I never thought I'd marry," Dakota said quietly. "Most men wouldn't want a woman as successful as me." Elizabeth brushed her hand against Dakota's. It felt like a butterfly had landed there. The two powerful women stayed quiet for a minute. Then there was a knock on the door.

"Hello in there," CeCe said. "Are we ready to go running?"

"Could you just give us a bit more time? Bess is getting dressed," Dakota said.

"Okay. Just wanted to let you know that Gideon's here," CeCe said. "Church is at twelve, and it's ten now, so we should just run a couple of miles so Her Majesty—wait did you call her Bess?—has time to shower and get changed."

"That works, CeCe," Dakota said, ignoring the question about using Elizabeth's first name—and a nickname at that. "We'll be out there soon," Dakota said.

"Pray pardon me," Elizabeth said. "Wherefore would'st I bathe again ere I attend serviceth withal Gideon? I bathed just yesterday, and certes, can hath't nay needeth o' a second bath in so short a time."

"Ah. This is another cultural change that I should explain," Dakota said. "Most people take baths or showers once a day, particularly if they exercise." She looked at Elizabeth for a reaction, but there was none. "I, for example, sweat quite profusely when I exercise, so I shower after I workout." Blank stare from Elizabeth. "I like how it feels to be clean. I like putting fresh makeup on after I shower." Still nothing. "And I know I won't smell of perspiration, which is considered undesirable."

Elizabeth sniffed her shoulder. "I hath't a superior sense o' smelleth and can detect nay offense," she said. "Certeth. I hath't long disdained the odor o' humanity." She stood straighter. "I bathed oftener than others in mine own court. I did hath't mine own bath did doth endue withal me at which hour on progress so I would'st ne'er beest without." Elizabeth held out her running clothes to Dakota.

"You start with the tights. No, leave your underwear on, please," Dakota coached Elizabeth, who was not accustomed to dressing herself.

"I am did recollect to speaketh to Gideon about mine bathing for he attributed words to me which I ne'er spake." Elizabeth pulled on her socks. "In the booketh about mine own life, what wast its name?"

Heart and Stomach of a Lion: A Biography of Queen Elizabeth." Does she not remember the title of the book? I somehow don't think so.

"Yes, 'heart and stomach of a lion.'" Elizabeth looked bemused. "'Twas this July past yond I spake to mine own troops at Tilbury to exhort those folk in a time o' most wondrous expectation as we did knoweth not where the famed Spanish Armada would'st invade our shoreth. As this wast a most momentous nonce, I did doth not sayeth yond I did hath't the heart and stomach o' a lion. 'Twas the heart and stomach o' a king, is what I quoth." She frowned. "Mayhap mine own words wert recorded in error."

"I believe you were just talking about bathing," Dakota said, trying to return her to the matter at hand.

"Aye, I wast forsooth," Elizabeth said. "Gideon, or haply 'twas Professor Majors who is't did write 't so, attributed to me yond I claimed to bathe monthly, ere did need 't or not," Elizabeth harrumphed. "I ne'er quoth this, and I shalt advise when to bathe again after our running. I did sweat lightly, if 't be true at all."

"Goodness gracious, it's ten fifteen already," Dakota said, checking her watch. "We must be off for our run if we're going to get you to church on time."

"Leadeth on, Dakota. We art hence for the running."

Unbelievable. Dakota had just spent the past forty-five minutes talking with a sixteenth-century queen about bras, running clothes, birth control, bathing, and the Tilbury speech. Cool but unsettling.

"Hey, there. It's me again," CeCe said. "I have a few pairs of running shoes out here for Her Majesty to try."

Dakota opened the door. "We're ready."

But were they?

Dakota wasn't sure if they'd ever be ready.

CHAPTER 30

April 11, 2027, Cambridge

Thirty minutes later, Dakota limped to the door of her condo. CeCe dragged in after her and plopped herself down on the Berber area rug.

"Where's Her Majestic-ness?" Jeremy chortled.

"She took the stairs," Dakota said, pulling her damp sweatshirt over her head.

"I need a gallon of water and a snack," CeCe said. "I should have had the pancakes."

"You guys look like hell," Jeremy said. "What happened?"

"You'd think that a woman who's just traveled across space and time would be a little jet-lagged, but no. Our Elizabeth has cycles to spare," CeCe said. "When we were a few blocks from home, she started sprinting. Just a teensy bit competitive."

"More than a teensy bit," Dakota said. "But that's what we wanted, a competitor who will keep going against all odds."

"Pull up a seat." Jeremy gestured to the kitchen island. "I'll warm up some pancakes for you." He patted Dakota on the back. "Teddy's out grocery shopping. I'll ask him to pick up something with electrolytes."

CeCe put her head on Dakota's shoulder. "She asked me if she could go horseback riding later. Do we know anyone with horses?"

"There are no horses in Cambridge," Dakota said with a weak laugh. "If I'm not napping when Bess and Gideon go to church, I'll do some research on where to ride horses."

"You're probably going to have to buy a couple, Dakota." CeCe gave Dakota a kiss on the cheek. "I read that she had her own stable of horses."

"It's just like in *The Crown*," Jeremy said. "Those royals are always off in Scotland riding horses and stalking deer. Which are probably nice alternatives to sitting around looking haughty while wearing the crown jewels."

"I forgot to say that she asked for a dog, Dakota," CeCe said. "When we left you at the bridge..."

"Thanks for that, by the way. I had to tie my shoes."

"Sorry, but I didn't want to lose her, and I had this feeling she would have taken off, so I stayed close," CeCe said. "We saw someone with a giant dog—maybe a wolfhound? Elizabeth stopped to pet it and said she'd like to get a dog because she's always had dogs."

"We are not having a wolfhound in this condo," Dakota said. "We'd have to buy a separate house just for the dog."

"Let's get her something smaller," CeCe said. "I have a friend with Dachshunds, and she swears by them. I'll ask her for the name of her breeder."

A loud knock rang out. "She's ba-aa-ack," Jeremy said in a creepy, lilting voice. "Don't move. I'll get the door."

"Salutations," Elizabeth said. She pulled off her hat and gloves and tossed them on the carpet. "I so enjoyed running up the stairs that I decided to run up and down once again. Mine own heart and I both grammercy." She waved to them in a cascaded flourish.

"Good morning, Bess." Gideon rose from his seat on the sectional. "I'm glad to see you enjoyed your run," he said, eyes merry. "I look forward to taking you to church when you're ready. If it pleases you, we should depart in twenty minutes or so, if we'd like to arrive on time."

"I very much look forward to attending church serviceth withal thee," Elizabeth said. "I shall make myself presentable for our journey." She turned to Dakota. "I request thy wise counsel on mine own attire for church. Let us proceed to mine own chamber for the appointments."

"I need a few moments to eat these pancakes, Bess, and then I'll join you."

"Take a break. I got this," CeCe spoke to Dakota underneath her breath. "Your Majesty, or may I call you, Bess?" CeCe got crickets from Elizabeth, but she didn't miss a beat. "I would be delighted to help you dress for church," she said. "May I assist you in getting ready?"

"Certes, Doctor Gibbons. I shall await thee in mine own chambers." Elizabeth bounced off to the bedroom.

A few hours later, Dakota studied the lute of intricately carved blond wood that Maeve had brought to the condo when she was napping. The lute was a gorgeous instrument, and she hoped the Renaissance woman for whom it was intended would see it as authentic.

"I expect we'll be hearing music after dinner tonight," Jeremy said. "I picked up guitar a couple of years ago. Maybe we could play a duet." He winked at Dakota.

"Now there's an idea." Dakota sidled closer to him. "You do realize Janet and Gideon said she was an accomplished musician, right? Though I'm only just getting to know her, I'd venture a guess that she either played solo or with other expert musicians. Not that you're not an expert, of course." She gave him a gentle squeeze on the arm.

"Good point," Jeremy said. "She can be tonight's entertainment, at least until we all need a break from lute music. Then we should get her hooked on *The Crown* so she'll have that and *The Bachelorette* to watch, and so will we."

Dakota's phone chimed. "Who's texting you?" Jeremy said.

"Gideon. They're on the way up," Dakota said. "I'll ask him how church was." She texted him back. "Uh oh. He said, 'It's complicated.' I wonder what that means?"

"I expect we're going to find out," Jeremy said. "With everyone coming and going, will we all need keypad access to your place? I'm thinking the answer is yes. Or you need to buy us some condos in this building. I guess that could work."

"Keypad access it is," Dakota said.

Two minutes later, Elizabeth swooshed into the living room like a microburst. "Thee cannot imagine the callous disregard that I have just experienced. *Horrendum erat.* I have scarce recovered." She chucked her coat on the ground and sat next to Dakota.

Gideon picked up her coat. "We had quite a time of it," he said, his tone not giving anything away. "I'm making tea. Would anyone like a cup?"

Ignoring him, Elizabeth said, "I thought it not possible, to receive such ill treatment in the church mine own father founded." She pulled the gold-and-black Versace scarf from her head. One of the dozen ornate scarves Ashley had purchased during her Saks shopping spree, thinking Elizabeth would want to keep her head covered in public until they could regrow her thinning hair. Just one more thing on the list. *Stop getting side-tracked, Dakota.* She refocused on the conversation.

"Pray pardon me." Jeremy said in his best Early Modern English. "Your father founded Trinity Church in Copley Square?" He tilted his head at Elizabeth.

"Trinity Church is Church o' England, is it not, Gideon?" Elizabeth shouted to Gideon.

"It is an Episcopal Church, which is Anglican, and that's as close as we get to Church of England here in America," Gideon said.

"I speak in the broadest terms, Sir Jeremy, for as thee may know, mine own father founded our good Protestant church when he separated from the tyranny of Rome." She glared at Jeremy. "Mayhap if I explain the offense that took place at the Trinity Church, thee shall comprehend that I have substantial reason for displeasure."

"We're listening," Dakota said, folding her hands on her lap.

Elizabeth sat ramrod straight. "Gideon wast much delayed by the safekeeping o' the horseless carriage in the square o' Copley," she said. "Therefore, we arrived after the welcome but much ere the sermon."

"We were about ten minutes late," Gideon said, now cradling his cup of tea.

"I do try to arrive at a suitable time to the many events whereto I am invited." Elizabeth scraped her wet boot heels on the handwoven area rug. "Should I be delayed in transport, I expect nay activity shall commence until I am arrived."

"Respectfully, Bess, I wish to point out that the congregation didn't know you would be joining them today." Gideon sat next to her. "How, therefore, could they be expected to wait for your arrival?"

"There is reason to thy words," Elizabeth said. "Yet, wonder wherefore we did not make it known that I would'st join them on this day?"

"If we were in your England, please be assured that we would have done so." Gideon turned toward Elizabeth. "Here, unfortunately, people don't know your true identity, so we can't expect them to honor you in the manner to which you are accustomed."

"So the issue is that church started without you?" Jeremy said.

"It wast far worse than that, Sir Jeremy, far, far worse," Elizabeth said, glowering. "'Tis beyond the scope o' human perception." She touched her fingers to her forehead and gestured outward, like a modern-day person saying that her mind was blown. "My best playwrights could not have contrived a scene so heinous, for if they did, 'twould be a tragedy that would'st cause a profundity o' weeping."

Drama queen or what? Get out of my head, Jeremy.

"When we arrived, I escorted Bess up the aisle to look for seats," Gideon said. "Bess urged me to keep walking toward the front, near the altar. When we got to the first row, she asked a lady and gentleman to give up their seats for us."

"I asked them to make way, Gideon," Elizabeth said, darkly. "When they did not budge, I simply inquired if they knew me not. I expected them to recognize me, but they gave me nay respect." Her hands were in fists. "I should'st have liked to cuff them about the pate."

"I commend your forbearance, Bess, for this would not have gone over well at all," Gideon said. "Had you struck them, you could have been arrested for physical assault."

"What now?" Elizabeth growled. "Must I offer restraint when others are undeserving o' mine own good graces?"

"Alas, that is not the way of things now," Gideon said, placing his hand over hers.

"Very true," Dakota said. "Even a president must moderate her temper. She can't be seen as too angry or aggressive with others. Certainly, she can't use physical force to reprimand anyone. That would not be tolerated, not in a president—or in a queen."

"Unless you're Robert Vlakas, that is," Jeremy muttered.

"This augments mine own displeasure," Elizabeth said. "Maybe I have made a grave error in joining thee hither." She stuck out her chin and exhaled plumes of outrage.

"Please, Bess. We knew you'd need to make many adjustments to living here, and this is just one of them," Dakota said. "I, for one, have total faith you'll become more comfortable here over time. And as you know, we need you to help us, to help our country."

"This thou hast quoth to me, and yet I understand it not fully," Elizabeth said. "Upon mine own first acquaintance withal Gideon, Doctor Majors, and Master Henry at the home o' Doctor Dee, 'twas communicated onto me that Robert Vlakas…" She stretched out the "s" sound at the end of his name, making it sound like a hiss. "… who presideth o'er America is a vile miscreant who careth not for his own people. Nay more than that, he harms his people and threatens the very security o' his country. Sir Jeremy now suggests that Robert Vlakas, unlike an anointed queen or other pates o' state, is able to display his anger without censure." Her chest wast heaving. "I am confounded. How dost thou explain this?" *There's no way I can explain it.* "It's a mystery to me as well," Dakota said. "Robert Vlakas won enough votes to get elected because of our antiquated electoral system, which we'll explain to you another time because it's fairly complex."

"I managed to hold my crown for forty-five years, according to Gideon's biographical history, because I am well-practiced in managing complexity," Elizabeth said. "I await thy explanation." The look she gave Dakota could have burned stainless steel.

"I recognize your brilliance, and your ability to run a country. It's not that," Dakota held her hands, palm-side up, toward Elizabeth. "Rather, I, myself, have trouble understanding the electoral-college system and need to figure out how to explain it to you."

"This is well and good. I pray you continue," Elizabeth said, apparently satisfied.

"Vlakas has used fear to divide Americans from one another," Dakota said. "Don't trust people who don't look like you or think like you."

"Or worship like you," Gideon said.

"Remember when he called Hindus, Voodoos?" Jeremy said. "I thought I was going to lose it."

Dakota ignored him. "Our country was founded on freedom of religion, so publicly declaring some people dangerous because they worship a different religion violates one of our most important principles."

"I wast ahead o' mine own time regarding freedom o' religion, or so quoth Gideon in his book." Elizabeth pressed her hands together. "It mattered not if an Englishman wast a Catholic as long as he attended Protestant serviceth on Sunday." She paused for effect. "I welcomed Blackamoors to mine own court, and *they* were infidels. And I let it be known that 'twas safe for Jews to live in England during mine own reign. Thy might be amazed to hear that mine own royal physician wast a Jew." Elizabeth fastened her eyes first on Dakota and then on Jeremy. "This wast not so in the Catholic countrieth o' Spain, Portugal, Italy, or France." Every bit the experienced orator, she commanded their attention as her voice resounded through the room.

"Mine own sister, Mary Tudor—the people called her Bloody Mary, I have learned from the book—burned hundreds o' Protestants at the stake. Thee may recall this," Elizabeth continued. "I agree withal this freedom o' religion in America as long as mine own people worship their God.

Dakota felt a stab of panic. Who are her people and who is their God?

She recalled that Elizabeth had a contentious relationship with the Catholic church hierarchy. After Pope Pius V excommunicated Elizabeth as a "wicked" heretic in 1570, Elizabeth's spymaster, Sir Francis Walsingham, would torture the odd Catholic priest if he suspected involvement in an assassination plot against the queen. And while Elizabeth had Catholics fined for not attending Protestant services, by and large, her policy was one of "don't ask, don't tell."

As for the few Jews in England at the time, they weren't expressly persecuted, but many practiced their faith in secret while others converted to Christianity. Dakota remembered reading that Elizabeth's progressive attitude toward her Jewish doctor, Roderigo Lopez, hit a brick wall when one of her favorites, the Earl of Essex, accused Lopes of plotting to poison his most important patient. Once found guilty, Lopes met a gruesome death when he was drawn and quartered. *Didn't that happen after 1588?* Dakota wasn't sure.

Though Dakota wanted to push Elizabeth further on religious tolerance, it was too soon to do it now, so she said, "It's wonderful that you practiced religious tolerance. So very unlike Vlakas."

"Tolerance o' other religions. A welcoming o' refugeeth when they do not threaten the safety or the employment o' our citizens. These are the impetus for choosing me as thy champion?" Elizabeth said.

"Those are two of the reasons," Jeremy said. "But there's another big one you might find compelling."

Dakota elbowed Jeremy and then whispered in his ear. "This better be something we've already discussed," she said.

"We have, Dakota." Jeremy looked serious for a change. "It's Vlakas's abhorrent treatment of Jennifer Samson. It made me ashamed to be an American, seeing a presidential candidate treat her like that at his rallies." He turned to Elizabeth. "I'd like to show you some video footage on my phone. Would that be okay with you?"

Elizabeth shuffled forward on the sofa as Jeremy kneeled in front of her.

"Let's introduce her to Jennifer first, if you don't mind," Gideon said from his perch on the arm of the recliner. "Jennifer Samson was the vice president of the United States when she ran for president. She was also a former United States senator, and before that, a member of the House of Representatives.

"When she was running for president, Samson was the second highest-ranking political leader in the country," he said. "She'd already served in both houses of the United States Congress, which is a bit like the English Parliament."

"She was…I mean is…a highly accomplished politician," Dakota said. "I got to know her during the campaign. She was dedicated and intelligent, so ready for the job." She looked away from the others.

Jeremy jumped in. "Dakota held a big fundraiser for her." Seeing Elizabeth's blank stare, he said, "Candidates have to raise a lot of money to run for president, many millions of dollars. Your party raised a few million, didn't it, Dakota?"

"It was four million, not including my donation," Dakota said. "The point is that Jennifer Samson is an amazing person, and Vlakas's treatment of her was reprehensible. It felt like he put her on trial, and her main crime was just being a woman."

"He's a dreadful misogynist," Gideon said.

"*Misogynia* is from the Greek, to hate women." Elizabeth cupped her hand to her chin. "I ne'er ascribed such a harsh term to the men o' mine own time, though most all viewed women as intellectually inferior and emotionally weak compared to men."

"You proved them wrong," Gideon said.

Elizabeth rewarded him with a black-toothed grin.

"Jeremy, could you show Elizabeth a clip from a rally?" Dakota said. "Nothing too long because it'll make us sick to relive it. Just a snippet."

"Got it. Short but not sweet," Jeremy said. "I found one."

Jeremy showed Elizabeth a YouTube video of Vlakas standing on an elevated stage at some massive indoor arena, addressing thousands of his followers flying miniature American flags, and a disturbing number of Confederate flags. As he yelled, "Put her away. Put her away," they chanted back, "Don't give her another day. Put her away. Put her away." Vlakas waved his hands and laughed as the chanting grew cacophonous. As the camera panned the crowd, inflatable Samson "dolls" were tossed through the crowd like beachballs. Someone held a tall pole with a papier-mâché effigy of Samson hanging, a noose around her neck. *Jeezus. These people are terrifying.*

Elizabeth's face reddened and her mouth grew hard.

"He inciteth the crowd to violent fury," Elizabeth said. "And the one who opposed him, Lady Jennifer, she held a powerful role in government. Was she a member o' the president's Privy Council?"

"Yes. As VP, she was the president's second in command," Gideon said. "If the president died in office, she would have taken his place."

"She was also one of his chief advisors," Dakota said.

"Almost like William Cecil, your Baron Burghley," Gideon said.

"She sounds like a worthy rival indeed," Elizabeth said. "A highly capable politician, and a woman at that." She bent her forehead to her clasped hands, almost like she was praying. After a period of stillness, she said, "Mayhap Lady Jennifer Samson is as like an anointed queen as thou hast in this day," she said. "To mine own mind, when Robert Vlakas used his violent rhetoric to threaten her withal imprisonment, he imperiled her very health and safety. I know well the power o' slanderous words. They were as responsible for mine own mother's death as the headsman who took her life."

Elizabeth stood facing Dakota, Jeremy, and Gideon. She thrust out her chin and drew her shoulders back, filling the living room with her presence. Though she had only been with them for forty-eight hours, she looked like she could slay Vlakas in a debate with no problem.

Elizabeth cleared her throat. "My people, I say to thee that this is a weighty offense that shall not be tolerated by me or mine. I shall right this wrong." Elizabeth's chest heaved. "Now thee must tell me how."

CHAPTER 31

April 11, 2027, Cambridge

Elizabeth stared at the smart TV in Dakota's living room. "You say this woman shall anon become queen of England. When is her coronation date?"

"I think her coronation took place in the 1800s," Jeremy said, with a cheesy grin.

"You mock me," Elizabeth said, scowling. "This Princess Royal is in the bloom o' freshest youth. She cannot be more than twenty."

Jeremy looked up from his phone. "In season one of *The Crown*, Queen Elizabeth the second is only twenty-one when it begins, and she's not the queen yet. We're watching her wedding to Prince Philip, who must be like ninety-six million by now."

"He would be, if he were still alive," Dakota said.

"Oh right. He died a few years ago," Jeremy said with an air of nonchalance. "To be honest, I'd been so caught up in stories about him still driving his Range Rover in his late nineties, even when he was hitting the broadsides of barns while just popping out to the market for milk or whatever, that I forgot he had moved on."

"Maybe you forgot to pay attention because he'd lost his good looks," CeCe said with a smirk.

Ignoring her quip, Jeremy said, "Getting back to the current queen, here's what she looked like when she was old." He held up his phone, displaying a photo of the white-haired monarch wearing a wide-brimmed magenta hat with velvet maroon flowers, pearl-drop earrings, and an ornate gold-and-diamond brooch. Through creased eyelids, her blue eyes shone bright.

"She looks regal in this photo, wouldn't you say?" Dakota said.

"Why she is an aged crone o' advanced antiquity. 'Tis miraculous that she still stands. A strong wind could blow her asunder." Elizabeth clasped her hands. "I should'st like to meet her ere she joins God in the heavens above. Certes, she would'st enjoy such an opportunity, for thither are few queens o' England left, and she is mine own namesake." Elizabeth's eyes crinkled with good humor. "When may we go to England?"

"Unfortunately, Her Majesty, Queen Elizabeth won't accept a meeting with you because she, too, has died," Dakota said.

"She did live to a very old age, though," CeCe said.

"She died in 2022," Jeremy said, looking up from his phone. Probably a Wikipedia page.

"Mine own heart grieveth her loss." Elizabeth bowed her head. Seconds later, she said, "I should'st like to meet her heir. She doth have one, doth she not?"

"Oh does she ever." Jeremy gritted his teeth in a weird grin. "King Charles. Not quite as popular as Queen Elizabeth."

"Queen Elizabeth the second," Elizabeth said. "And wherefore is that?"

"You will learn all about it in *The Crown*," Jeremy said.

"I think they went too easy on him," CeCe said, scowling.

"I must agree," Jeremy said. "Once he became king, they must have rewritten all the bad parts about him."

"And there were a lot of bad parts," Dakota said.

"Especially when Princess Diana was killed," CeCe said.

"Who is this Princess Diana?" Elizabeth squinted at them. "Was she on *The Bachelorette*?"

Dakota coughed to cover a giggle. "No, she actually was a royal princess because she married Prince Charles when he was Prince of Wales."

"But their marriage did not end well." CeCe shook her head.

"Fie." Elizabeth waved at them dismissively. "I must needs meet King Charles. I pray you send an emissary to ask him to attend me here."

There was a knock on the door. Gideon had arrived. Ignoring the others, he greeted Elizabeth with a bow and said, "Even, Bess. Are you in the midst o' a discussion?"

"Though I had wished to meet her, I have learned that mine own namesake is withal our Heavenly Father," Elizabeth said, her mouth downturned. "As thy future pate o' state, I shouldst like to meet her son and heir, King Charles, as anon as it may be arranged." Elizabeth stood and paced the room. "Let us plan a sea voyage to England on my ship, which shall be powered by engine," she said. "I shall send a letter of introduction in advance—I shall use mine own Great Seal, which I remembered to bring in the single and tiny chest I was allowed to bring hither." At this she scowled. "And the new king shall honor my request as my true identity shall be made evident."

"You brought the Great Seal with you?" Dakota said, a hot flash engulfing her body. "We've got to return that straightaway."

Elizabeth ignored her and stopped dead in front of Gideon. "Shalt thou help me withal this?"

"I wish that I could, dear good Bess," Gideon said, "but King Charles will not meet you until you become president. And I regret that you cannot use your Great Seal, for the king would not believe it's authentic."

Elizabeth glowered at him.

"It's true. After you win the election in November 2028, you'll be able to meet the king," Dakota chimed in.

"Everyone will accept your invitation then." Gideon took her hands in his. "But as we touched upon last night, the election process is long and arduous."

"Still, we have every confidence that you will be victorious… with our assistance," Dakota said.

Elizabeth blinked her liquid brown eyes at Dakota. "What is the date on the calendar?"

"Today is April 11, 2027," Dakota said.

"'Tis many a month until I shall become president." Elizabeth returned to the sofa. She sat there, arms crossed and not saying a word. The mood in the room was tense until CeCe joined them.

"Hello, everyone," CeCe walked into the room and tucked herself into a chair. "What did I miss?"

"We just started watching *The Crown*, and we're right at the beginning, so we were talking with Elizabeth, Her Majesty, I mean. Am I still calling you by your title?" Jeremy looked at Elizabeth, who gave him a nod. "We're talking to Her Majesty about the true age of QEII."

"QEII?" Elizabeth laughed with gusto. "Is that what you called the old queen?"

"I think it makes sense in this case because how many Queen Elizabeths can we have in one room?" Jeremy chuckled. "Anyway, CeCe, *The Crown's* Elizabeth is about to marry Prince Philip."

"Oh good. I haven't seen *The Crown* before, so I'm glad to catch the beginning," CeCe said.

I'll have to tell CeCe later that her timing was perfect.

"You didn't miss much because we got sidetracked talking about QEII and King Charles," Jeremy said.

"Imagine, Lady CeCe, that this young English king would'st decline to meet withal me for he knows not o' mine own import," Elizabeth said. "There is great disappointment in these tidings."

Then she walked to the front of the TV and spun around to face them. "I should'st like to play lute in mine own room. I must have time for quiet reflection." She sighed deeply.

"Of course, Bess, we understand," Gideon said.

"And we'll stop the episode right here so you can watch it with us when you return," Jeremy said.

"I appreciate thy kindness," Elizabeth said. But instead of leaving them, she took a few steps closer. "Did the new queen, that is QEII, possess mine own jewels? Doctor Majors quoth that I could not take them withal me, else they would'st be lost to history." Elizabeth's voice was breaking.

Whew, Janet came through.

"I saw the Crown Jewels at the Tower of London when Janet and I were researching your legacy," Gideon said to Elizabeth. "As I recall, at least one of your diamonds is now in the coronation crown. I'm not sure about your other jewels."

Elizabeth eyes looked teary, and Gideon pulled out a handkerchief, which she used to wipe her eyes.

Elizabeth raised her head and straightened her posture. "Before we recommence the watching o' this television show, I should'st like to discuss how I shall become thy president," Elizabeth said. "Shall we meet after we break our fast on the morrow?"

"I have to go to the office for at least part of the day," Dakota said. "Jeremy and I have a client meeting at eleven, and since they're traveling from France, we can't reschedule."

"I do love the French accent," Elizabeth said, brightening. "Not the French themselves, of course, o' course, for as papists, they sit inside the pocket o' the prince o' Rome, and this hath made them most unkind to those o' the Protestant faith. Mayhap thou hast heard what betid to the Huguenots?"

"The Huguenots were French Calvinists who were heavily perse-cuted by the French Crown," Gideon explained to the group.

"'Twas Catherine de' Medici who set them alight, so to speak," Elizabeth said. "All fury and fire, that one, and not a pretty woman neither." Elizabeth sat next to Gideon. "I should'st like to converse withal thy French visitors."

Dakota hadn't noticed that Ashley had entered the kitchen. She hoped she'd had enough of a break—and that Elizabeth wouldn't ask her about intimate relations with her boyfriend.

Elizabeth swiveled her head toward Ashley. "Mistress Ashley. I am pleased at thy return. Could thou hast a horse made prest for mine own journey thither?"

"I think we're fresh out of horses, Your Majesty." Ashley cleared her throat. "Didn't you want to learn about the political process tomorrow?" She eyed Elizabeth.

"That wast mine own intention, but I have lately learned that members o' mine own court have other plans," Elizabeth said. "Dakota and Sir Jeremy shall be away in the morn and cannot serve as mine own tutors."

"I can do it, Your Majesty," CeCe said. "I helped Dakota plan that big fundraiser for Jennifer Samson. In fact, it was my good friend Eleanor—an AKA sister who's a total rock star, by the way—who tapped the vine to get us in with Samson's people during the campaign."

"Some friends come and go, but an AKA sister is forever...or so you've said." Dakota smiled at her friend.

CeCe squeezed Dakota's arm. "You're forever too."

"Who is this Eleanor, what is an AKA sister, and what is a rock star?" Elizabeth glanced around.

"That's a lot to unpack, Your Majesty, but I will try." CeCe took a deep breath. "Eleanor Smith is a friend of mine from the AKA chapter of my undergraduate university," CeCe said. "AKA stands for Alpha Kappa Alpha, and it's the most influential sorority for Black women in America. I joined AKA when Dakota and I attended MIT, which stands for Massachusetts Institute of Technology."

"And rock star is a vernacular phrase, one of many idioms that you will hear," Gideon said with good cheer. "A rock star is someone who stands out in his or her field, someone to be greatly admired. Someone like yourself." Gideon gave Elizabeth his most gorgeous smile.

Elizabeth processed for a moment. "I did not realize that thee spake Greek," she said to CeCe.

That's her takeaway from all of that? "She doesn't speak Greek," Dakota said. "Sororities call themselves Greek institutions, but that doesn't mean that members speak that language."

"And they're not actually institutions. They're more like service organizations," CeCe said.

"I always thought they were more like party organizations," Jeremy said.

Dakota gave him the hairy eyeball.

"Let us summarize together," Elizabeth said. "Doctor Gibbons and Lady Eleanor Smith are members o' Alpha Kappa Alpha, which thee clepe AKA, and this is a service organization that useth a Greek name but 'tis not, in fact, Greek, nor do those who belong to it speak Greek." Elizabeth brought her tented hands beneath her chin. "Lady Eleanor Smith is a celebrated personage."

Elizabeth cleared her throat with gusto. "I shall restate, I am curious as to the process by which I shall become president. I await thy explanation." She tapped her foot on the carpet.

"The campaign is many monthslong process through which you, and those who support you in becoming president, tour the country to influence people to vote in your favor," Gideon said.

"The common people select their president?" Elizabeth wrinkled her forehead. "How very strange." She rose and returned to her post in front of the TV. "How can the common people be entrusted withal a task so weighty? Do they possess education, breeding, social connections, all that is required to choose their own government?"

"We have a government for the people and by the people," Gideon said.

"Do we?" Jeremy said, flicking a crumb off his shirtsleeve. "Our Houses of Congress are heavily influenced by lobbyists. These are people paid to advocate for a cause or a commodity, like oil. And they give tons of money to people in Congress to try to influence their votes."

"Which has nothing to do with the election process." Dakota scowled at him. "It's an unfortunate reality of our government's dysfunction, and we'll cover it, but not tonight."

"Well slap me with a speeding ticket." Jeremy folded his arms across his chest. "I have been cancelled."

"Sorry about that," Dakota said to him. "I don't want to overwhelm her with a process that even I find confusing."

"And sometimes absurd and unfair," Jeremy said.

"Yes, those too," Dakota said. "It makes total sense that you have many questions about the political process in America, Bess." She walked over to Elizabeth. "Given the complexity of the process, perhaps Gideon and Janet could explain it to you tomorrow?"

Elizabeth glared at Dakota. "My stated preference is to begin mine own study o' this topic this evening," she said. "There is much for me to apprehend."

"Alas, I am sure that Janet will want to participate in your political education, but she must lack your energy, as she was too tired to join us this evening," Dakota said, being fast on her feet. "Could we not wait until tomorrow for Janet as I'm sure she would be saddened to miss any part of this discussion?"

"I would'st be gratified to attend until she is refreshed," Elizabeth said. "Mayhap we should'st see what taketh place for QEII upon her marriage to Prince Philip?"

On the TV, the actress Claire Foy beamed at her handsome prince—and Elizabeth beamed at Gideon.

Dakota sighed. All was well in the world—at least for one night.

CHAPTER 32

April 12, 2027, Cambridge

"I comprehend that thither are three brancheth of the national government," Elizabeth said, her voice tightly coiled. "What I cannot abide is the balance o' power among them. As the pate o' the executive branch, the president should'st have control o'er the laws o' her nation, should'st she not?"

"The balance of power is central to the concept of a democratic government," Janet explained. "The one, no matter how powerful, cannot dictate the laws of the many."

Having left work a few hours early so she could tune in to Janet and Gideon's politics 101 tutorial with Elizabeth, Dakota nursed a blueberry yogurt flax smoothie from her perch on the sectional. She was close enough to the dining table to pick up most of the conversation.

"One of our most beloved presidents, Abraham Lincoln, is famous for saying, 'government of the people, by the people, for the people, shall not perish from the earth,'" Gideon said.

"Democracy. From the Greek, *dēmokratia*," Elizabeth said. "'Tis an old concept, and not one that can be fully realized without an educated class o' people who are empowered to make beneficial decisions for those less fit to govern themselveth."

Oh boy. Janet and Gideon have their work cut out for them. Dakota pulled her Bose noise-cancelling headphones over her ears as she reviewed Sumiko's projections on that week's top cyberthreats. Lots of activity from Russia. *No surprise there.* China, Iran, North Korea.

Same old, same old. I wonder what they're talking about now? She pulled down her headphones.

"The Republicans and the Democrats. Are they akin to ruling houses, as in the Medici, the Habsburgs, and...the Tudors?" Elizabeth said.

Stop listening, Dakota. She pulled up her headphones and read through the needs assessment of the French client, the Ministry of Foreign Trade and Economic Attractiveness. The Russians were hacking through the Ministry's defenses daily, screwing up the country's supply chain of fine wine and expensive perfume, jeopardizing both revenue streams and their reputation. The French were not pleased. Which was bad for the French but good for business because she and Jeremy had rocked it at the pitch meeting that morning. Where was Jeremy, anyway?

Teddy told her he'd have dinner ready at about 6:30, and Jeremy wouldn't want to miss that...or him. She'd try to concentrate until it was time for Teddy's Yankee pot roast with mashed potatoes and gravy, roasted parsnips and carrots, and wilted Swiss chard with bacon—which he was busily preparing in her kitchen. Knowing how much wealthy Elizabethans had prized meat, she'd asked Jeremy if Teddy could prepare at least one kind of animal protein at every meal. At least for now. At some point, they were all going to need a break from so much heavy food or they'd have to start serving statins with dessert.

After an hour and half of reading reports and answering email, Dakota took a mini break to get a glass of water. Stretching her arms over her head, she heard another familiar voice. *Oh good. CeCe's back from her place.*

"Sure. I'd love to hear you play lute now," CeCe said. "We can watch *The Crown* again after dinner."

"I wast most captivated by Princess Elizabeth's wedding ceremony. She did look gladdened by it," Elizabeth said. "I find myself eager to watch her coronation. Dost thou know if we shall see it this night?"

"Jeremy's the expert on that so I'll need to look at the list of episodes. I'll just be a minute," CeCe said.

How are they talking about The Crown *again?* As Dakota walked into the kitchen, she stole a glance at the notes Elizabeth had been making on her padfolio. Her script was elaborate, with sweeping curlicues and vaulting capital letters. It was also hard for the modern eye to read. Add that to the list: teach Elizabeth legible writing.

"We still have a few episodes until the coronation, Your Majesty, so you'll either have to wait or we'll binge-watch it," CeCe said.

"Binge-watch is a very modern term, Bess," Dakota said. She was trying to stay out of Teddy's way as she drew water from her magnificent stainless-steel Thermador refrigerator. "With on-demand viewing of shows, we now can watch an entire season in one or two sittings. Not too long ago, people waited until their favorite show was broadcast once a week on television, so what would have taken twelve weeks for twelve episodes now takes only twelve hours, in some cases."

"It may be difficult for some to show forbearance when a table o' sweetmeats is ere them," Elizabeth said. "I shall measure withal care mine own consumption o' the television." She brought her clasped hands to her chin. "Before we recommence our discussion on politics, I am curious to know if there is a television program about mine own person."

Jeremy emerged from the direction of the powder room nearest the kitchen. *Wait. I didn't hear him come in either?* Her headphones really did drown out the noise.

Jeremy began heading toward the kitchen island but pivoted to greet Elizabeth instead of parking himself on one of the kitchen stools where he could watch Teddy cooking. "Good evening, Your Majesty," he said.

"Jeremy, mayhap you canst help us withal something," Gideon said. "Bess asked a question about television shows," he said. "As our resident expert on popular culture, I thought thee might be able to answer." Gideon randomly stuck Early Modern English words into his vocabulary. *I wonder how long that will last?*

"'Tis true, Sir Jeremy, I find myself inquisitive, knowing that a magnificent program is dedicated to QEII, and *she* did not defeat the Spanish Armada." Elizabeth raised her eyebrows and gave a tinkling chuckle. Dakota didn't think she'd ever tire of Elizabeth's laughter. It was the aural equivalent of rainbow sprinkles on ice cream.

"We seem to have drifted off topic." Janet removed her reading glasses and rubbed the bridge of her nose."

Elizabeth gave Janet a look that could freeze all the glaciers in Alaska.

Jeremy carried on. "I'm glad you asked, Your Majestic-ness."

Jeremy's calling that to her face? In 1588 he would have earned a cuff on the ears for that little quip. *Is she already adapting?*

"Because there have been at least two fabulous television series about you and a couple of feature films," he continued. "Emma Winters played you in the movie, *Elizabeth*, and she's one of my favorite actresses. Let me show you some photos." He pulled out his Surface and crouched between Elizabeth and Gideon.

"I'd like to see too." Dakota joined the group now crowded around Jeremy's screen.

"Here's Emma as Elizabeth. This is from 2000." Jeremy showed them a young Emma Winters, wearing a burnt-orange gown with seed pearls embroidered in flower shapes, her long strawberry-blonde hair flowing around her shoulders. "And here's what she looks like today." There was a *Vanity Fair* cover of Emma wearing a lacy black sleeveless dress. The actress was still stunning, but much older. Her emerald eyes sparkled beneath a short but stylish haircut, and her full red lips framed her brilliant white teeth.

Elizabeth studied the *Vanity Fair* image. "The artist must have embellished much the second portrait of Mistress Winters, for she appears to have scant aged with over five and twenty years gone past." She grunted. "Mayhap his progenitor was Hans Holbein," she said lightly. "You may recall that mine own father, the king, was enraptured by the countenance of Anne of Cleves in the Holbein portrait. Alas, the painting and her true visage were not matched."

Jeremy beamed. "Emma looks damned good for fifty-eight, doesn't she?"

"Fie. She is not eight and fifty." Elizabeth waved a dismissive hand. "For I am five and fifty, and I seem more her mother than her sister."

"I can understand your surprise, Your Majesty," Janet said. "But the truth is that women age differently now because we have access to more specialized care. We have aestheticians to give us facials, colorists to take the gray out of our hair, personal trainers to help us keep fit."

"And dentists to care for our teeth," Jeremy mumbled.

"How many years have you, Lady CeCe?" Elizabeth said.

"I'm fifty-three and fabulous." CeCe did a quick twirl. "But Dakota's fifty-four."

"I hate to remind you, darling, but we're almost the same age," Dakota said.

"I believed you to be no more than five and thirty." Elizabeth said to Dakota, placing her palms on her chest. "I am most parched. May I have some refreshment?"

"I'll make us some tea," Gideon said, padding off to see Teddy in the kitchen.

"Lady CeCe and Dakota, thy skin appears luminous, and thy hair shows not a strand o' gray. Do the two of thee visit an aesthetician?" Elizabeth said.

"I have one, Your Majesty," Janet said. "Would you like to know my age?"

Elizabeth ignored her.

"What's the name of that place on Newbury Street where you get your facials, Dakota?" CeCe said.

"I go to Bon Visage on Newbury Street," Dakota said, referring to a day spa on Boston's most fashionable street.

"That place is so old-school pretentious, Dakota," Jeremy said. "The Spa at the Mandarin Oriental is *so* much better. You'd think it would be intimidating, but it's not. The practitioners are fantastic and friendly, and the atmosphere is relaxing. Should we book you an appointment, Your Majesty?"

"Will I look as young as Mistress Winters?" Elizabeth said.

"Ummm…Ashley just texted to say she's on her way up," Jeremy said. "Seems like a good question to ask her because isn't she your stylist, Bess?"

Elizabeth squinted at him. "Do you intend to call me by my given name, Sir Jeremy?"

"Oh, sorry about that, Your Majesty. We're more casual in our forms of address, as you can probably tell," Jeremy said.

"'Tis mine own observation that thou art on the most intimate terms withal one another," Elizabeth said. "There seems to be a want o' station in thy social structure." She rubbed her chin. "'Tis as if you are o' egal rank, withal nay semblance o' an aristocracy."

"That's an astute observation," CeCe said. "We treat each other as social equals, and that's pretty typical of Americans."

"Even in the business world, my employees call me by my first name, although I'm the highest-ranking person in the company," Dakota said.

"How about the person who cleans thy privy or the person who cooks thy food?" Elizabeth said.

"That's true of the people who clean our office," Dakota said "And it's true of Chef Will, who runs our café. We're all on a first-name basis."

"I do not want to be viewed as fashioned from an ancient cloth," Elizabeth said. "I suppose thee may all clepe me Elizabeth. And I shall clepe thee by thy first nameth." She extended an arm in a sweeping motion toward Jeremy, CeCe, Janet, and Teddy as she uttered the first of many pronouncements to her new Privy Council.

"She's here," Jeremy said when Ashley opened the door. "We were just talking about things that should interest you." He took Ashley by the hands. "First, we are all on a first-name basis now so you may call Her Majesty, Elizabeth." He grinned. "And Elizabeth is interested in a makeover of sorts. Facial, hair, and let's get some nice makeup. Shall we start booking and keep buying?"

"Let me just put my coat away, and I'll talk with you about making the arrangements. Would that be all right with you..." Ashley gulped. "Elizabeth?"

Elizabeth stared blankly at Ashley.

"Bess, I realize that you had many servants who cared for you back in England," Dakota whispered in Elizabeth's ear. "But Ashley is completely unfamiliar with that world. She's never been a servant, and I am grateful that she quit her job to work as your stylist. Could you please ask for her help? I think she's been a little unhappy, and this would go a long way toward building your relationship."

"This is a most unusual request indeed," Elizabeth whispered back. "Yet thy modus operandum differs so greatly from mine own that I shall accept your recommendation."

"Welcome, Ashley. I am delighted that thou hast joined us this evening," Elizabeth said. "We have been discussing mine own rejuvenation. This cometh from the Latin *re*, which means again, and *juvenis*, which means youth." Elizabeth smiled sweetly. "Would thee be so gracious as to assist me in this matter?"

Ashley's mouth hung open briefly. "Your Majesty…that is to say, Elizabeth. I would be most gratified to assist you. Now, where shall we start?"

Twenty minutes later, Ashley was mumbling something about weekly microdermabrasion and restorative facials over the phone. Amazingly, she scored a ninety-minute appointment for Elizabeth at the Mandarin Oriental for the following day.

Ashley also told Dakota that she'd leave a message for a friend she met when she was getting her degree at FIT. When some 7th Avenue stylist had managed to give her orange highlights instead of blonde ones, Ashley had made an appointment at Oscar Blandi Salon NYC. She'd walked away from the appointment with a newfound appreciation for color-correction specialists and had made a lifelong friend, who just happened to move to Boston a few months ago. So Ashley would cover Elizabeth's face and hair, but the dentist? That was all Dakota.

While Ashley used Jeremy's laptop to show Elizabeth ideas for hairstyles—she wanted one like Emma Winters's but needed to grow her hair in first—Dakota headed to her study for some privacy. It was almost six-thirty so she decided to call Jim Nagerian on his mobile. He'd probably be driving home to Concord. She was going to have to read him in.

"Hi, Jim. Is this a good time?"

"Yes, dahlink, I always have time for you," Jim said, in his warm, melodious voice. "What can I do you for?"

"I have a friend who needs a considerable amount of dental work, Jim. In fact, I'm not sure she's ever seen a dentist."

"What is this, the fourteenth century? What do you mean she's never been to a dentist? Did she grow up on Mars?" Jim said, with a laugh. "I find that statement highly suspect."

"I'm going to have to meet you in person to discuss this or you will never believe me," Dakota said. "In fact, I think we'll have to meet at KODA because you're going to want some proof points."

"Proof points for a friend who needs a lot of dental work? Can't we just discuss her case—with her express permission in accordance with HIPPA?"

"You're going to need to see some video of my friend, and the footage is in a lab that's only open to specific employees and very special guests."

"Ooh. You're making me feel very special, bubbeleh, which is good, because you are very special to me."

"I'm glad that we are special to each other, Jim." Dakota said. "I need you to get your special self to KODA. When would that be possible?"

"Thursday's my day off this week so I could pop in then."

"I'll text you with a couple of times, and you can get back to me when you get home."

"It'll be lovely to see you. Bye for now."

Dakota sighed and walked to the kitchen/dining area. Dinner was ready, and everyone except Teddy and Jeremy was seated. Teddy was plating food in the kitchen, and Jeremy was giving Teddy glowing looks each time he picked up a new plate to bring to the table. It had been years since Jeremy had been serious about anyone, and

Dakota liked Teddy's calm, confident demeanor. It didn't hurt that Teddy was a stellar chef, and Jeremy's favorite pastime was eating.

Dakota noticed that Elizabeth was digging into her pot roast while the others were still getting served. In the English court, etiquette would have dictated that the queen needed to start eating before her courtiers could take a bite. And who were they if not Elizabeth's courtiers? She supposed she was like Elizabeth's lord chamberlain. The only problem was that she was also CEO of a powerful cyber-security firm on which serious enterprises and national governments depended. It was going to be a helluva balancing act, supporting a former sixteenth-century queen in her quest to become president and maintaining her business at KODA.

But Dakota was never one to shy away from a challenge—even one as monumental as putting a Tudor in the Oval Office.

CHAPTER 33

April 15, 2027, Charlestown

"Jim actually said that the whole thing was whackadoodle?" Jeremy's head was so close to Dakota's that their hair touched. They were curled around a table for two at the KODA Café.

"We started at seven this morning, so he was probably a bit sleep-deprived to start off," Dakota said. "Things started off slow. When Maeve and Henry showed Jim their visit to Ebbets Field, he was convinced I'd hired a special-effects artist who put Henry and Maeve on a green screen. He was less than impressed," Dakota sipped her iced tea. "But when they showed him the footage of their first meeting with John Dee, I thought he was going to faint." She giggled.

"The poor guy, Dakota. He's a dentist not a sci-fi writer," Jeremy said.

"Right. And although I know it's all real, I sometimes have to remind myself that we actually have Elizabeth the First at my condo. And at this very moment, she might be playing lute or learning to apply the entire La Prairie skincare line I bought her."

"Or the Chanel makeup. Or the Christian Louboutin lipstick that Ashley got her. How much was that lipstick anyway?"

"One tube is ninety-five dollars, but Ashley bought five because she wasn't sure which colors Elizabeth would like." Dakota looked bemused. "Elizabeth went gaga over them. Instead of a cap on the top, they have crystal crowns. Definitely fit for a queen, and priced for one too."

"You just got sidetracked on lotions and potions, and that was fun, but let's get back to Jim," Jeremy said. "First, though, one more sidetrack. Get yourself some of that Louboutin lipstick. I bet they have some colors that would look dazzling on you. You're also one of the few people on the planet who can actually afford the stuff."

"Ashley already bought some for me. I guess she figured that what's fit for a queen is fit for a CEO." Dakota grinned. "Honestly, I've never spent anything near that on lipstick so it feels indulgent."

"Nice." Jeremy flicked some blueberry muffin crumbs off his sweater sleeve. Then he propped his head on his hands, elbows on the table. "You now have my undivided attention. Tell me about Jim."

"When Jim saw John Dee with Henry, Gideon, and Janet, he realized the footage was authentic," Dakota said. "He was so overcome that he cried. But then he wrapped me in his bearpaw arms and told me that he couldn't wait to meet Elizabeth."

"I bet he's going to be seeing a lot of her. Or her teeth, to be exact."

"I'm bringing her at six tomorrow morning." Dakota said. "He's coming in early and is rescheduling his other appointments so can dedicate himself to Elizabeth's teeth."

"How are you planning to get Elizabeth to sit in a dentist's chair all day? She's hardly the world's most patient person," Jeremy said. "And remember she's going to be freaked out because there was no dental care in merry old England, save untrained louts with dirty hands yanking out teeth by their roots."

"That's what I asked Jim." Dakota scrunched her brow. "He said he does sedation dentistry for some patients, and even without meeting her, he's pretty sure Elizabeth will fall into that category. He already knows that she'll need an extensive amount of work, and we can't minimize her prior experience of having one of those louts pull a tooth without Novocain."

"Hey, it's almost six." Jeremy looked up from his phone. "Teddy just texted to say he's serving dinner at seven so we should get going."

"I hope things are calm at home because I'm pretty wiped out," Dakota said. "If we didn't have the marvelous Teddy cooking for us, I'd say we should get Chinese tonight. I would love some Kung Pao chicken."

"As much as I adore what he's been serving, even I am getting tired of so much meat. Maybe we could get takeout tomorrow and invite Teddy over for a relaxing evening."

"Chinese food for our English queen. I hope she likes dumplings."

"And pork buns. And bean buns. Maybe some Szechuan chicken, a little beef and broccoli, a few servings of Peking ravioli."

"It's official. I'm starving. Let's go home." Dakota took a look at her phone. "Oh my God. I must have fifteen text messages from CeCe. She said the dogs aren't house-trained yet so I should pick up some puppy pads on the way home." She gestured to Jeremy. "Dogs? What dogs?"

"Umm…I may have heard CeCe talking about puppies last night and forgot to tell you. So I'll tell you now," Jeremy said. "CeCe was on the phone with her friend's breeder, and the breeder just happened to have two Dachshund puppies available. Sounds like she may have picked them up for Elizabeth."

"You can't be serious. CeCe wouldn't bring little peeing-pooping animals into my home without telling me first. Would she?" Dakota grasped her chest. "I need a glass of wine. Or three."

"It's not all bad," Jeremy looped his arm through Dakota's. "CeCe said four months old so they're pretty good for puppies."

Twenty minutes later Dakota and Jeremy opened the door to the sight of CeCe, Ashley, Gideon, Elizabeth, and Janet sitting on the living room carpet, oohing and aahing over two chestnut-colored longhaired Dachshund puppies, who seemed to have their own collection of little plush animals, squeaky balls, and pull toys.

"Are they the cutest or what?" CeCe picked one up and kissed him. He gave a tiny yelp when he nipped her on the nose. "I am in love."

Elizabeth was beaming as she petted the other one. "We have had the most wonderful day, haven't we, mine own hounds?" Elizabeth picked up one of the puppies and held him out to Dakota. "I should'st like to introduce thee to Dudley. His brother Raleigh is just yon." She pointed out the wriggling dog next to CeCe and Janet, who was nuzzling the puppy with her nose. *Janet likes puppies?*

"Are they not delightful?" Elizabeth said.

"They are sweet." Dudley licked Dakota's nose. "This little guy smells good." Dakota picked up Dudley and held him to her chest. *I think he just sighed.* "These dogs are going to have a lot of aunts and uncles. I just hadn't expected to come home from work to find them."

"Thanks for understanding, Dakota." CeCe gave her a sheepish grin. "When the breeder said she had two puppies, I took Elizabeth and Gideon to see them. We just couldn't resist bringing them home." She touched Dakota's shoulder. "I promise, you won't regret it."

Dakota rubbed the back of her neck. "I guess it will be nice to have a different mammal species in the house."

"What is a *species*?" Elizabeth asked with furrowed brow.

"Did Darwin invent the word species?" Janet asked.

"Who, or what, is Darwin, may I inquire?" Elizabeth said.

"Charles Darwin was a nineteenth-century scientist who wrote a famous book called *Origin of the Species*, which is still the foundation of modern evolutionary biology," Gideon said. "Darwin was the first person to claim that some types of animals are not just closely related to one another, but that they descended from one another over millions of years."

"Like humans descended from apes," Jeremy said.

"God's teeth," Elizabeth yelled out. "Humans wert made by our Heavenly Father in His image. We are not cousins o' the jungle gorilla. 'Tis blasphemy to say so."

"That was the reaction of many people when Darwin's book was first published, and for some years after that," Gideon said. "Yet, I can assure you, his claims were based on real science. This doesn't mean that we're the same as gorillas, but we do share common ancestors from millions of years back."

"Fie. I cannot, I shall not, believe it so." Elizabeth folded her arms across her chest.

"I can understand why you'd find this a shocking claim. Yet, it's not a subjective one," Janet said to Elizabeth. "It's been empirically proven."

"It's also not something we'd expect you to believe the first time you hear it." Gideon drew close to Elizabeth. "There will be time enough to process this information when you are ready."

"Excuse me, all, but dinner is ready," Teddy said with a flourish. "Please take your seats and my assistant Jeremy…" At this he smiled. "…will bring your meals to you."

"Excellent news. I'm famished," Jeremy said. "What's on tonight's menu?"

"Medallions of pork tenderloin with mushroom sauce, scalloped potatoes, roasted Brussels sprouts, and caramelized beets," Teddy said. "And since the meal is on the heavy side, I made lemon granita for dessert."

"My ass is getting bigger as we speak," CeCe whispered into Dakota's ear.

"Right," Dakota said. "I'll ask Jeremy if Teddy can make some lighter meals, so we don't have to buy new wardrobes."

"Go ahead and start without me," CeCe said, scooping Dudley and Raleigh into her arms. "I need to feed the puppies and then take them for a pee before I put them in their playroom." She pointed to a large wire playpen that Dakota hadn't noticed.

Dakota looked around the room. There were eight table settings at her farmhouse dining table. A lute was propped up on the sofa near the TV. A giant puppy playpen now overlooked the floor-to-ceiling windows in what used to be her quiet place in the common area. She hoped it was easy to get puppy pee off her reclaimed Douglas fir flooring. It was all crazy and wonderful and off-putting at the same time.

"Dakota," CeCe called out on her way out the door with the now-leashed puppies. "Wait until you see Elizabeth's virginals, just arrived this morning from London."

"She said she'd play for us after dinner," Gideon said from his seat at the table. "We just need to move the instrument from her bedroom to the sitting area. That way we can all enjoy an Elizabethan concert." He gave Elizabeth an adoring gaze.

Virginals? Is that bigger than a harpsichord? How big is a harpsichord?

"That sounds just lovely," Dakota said. "Dinner and music on a Friday night. Just what I always wanted."

Dakota sighed deeply, sat down, and stared at the steaming plate of pork tenderloin before her. She used to keep the food on her plate separate. Her chicken never touched her vegetables, her omelet never brushed against her hash browns. But now, she could see that the sauce from the pork was all over her Brussels sprouts, and the potatoes were blending into the beets. It wasn't the worst way to eat...or live.

CHAPTER 34

April 16, 2027, Belmont, Massachusetts

"Jim, please meet my good friend, Elizabeth Rex," Dakota said. It may have been the crack of dawn on a Friday morning, but Elizabeth still dressed to impress. She was wearing her new Dolce & Gabbana black cashmere sweater with its embroidered laurel wreath and large silver crown across the chest. Ashley had bought it on sale for $1,995. At $400 off the list price, she said it was a deal for a D&G sweater that Elizabeth just "had to have" when she'd seen it online. *Must remind Ashley to browse privately, or it'll cost me thousands every time Elizabeth looks over her shoulder.*

Somehow dashing in his blue scrubs, Jim bowed his six-foot-two frame like a courtier greeting his monarch. He took Elizabeth's extended hand and kissed it. "It's my greatest pleasure to meet you, Elizabeth. I only hope that my skills as a dentist will bring as much delight to your heart as you've brought to mine by coming to see me." Jim's black eyes sparkled from behind his tortoiseshell glasses. "May I invite you to join me?"

"I am delighted to make thy acquaintance, Jim," Elizabeth said, giving him her best royal smile. Dakota noted Jim's swift intake of breath at his first glimpse of her teeth. She hoped Elizabeth hadn't registered it.

"Let me escort you to the treatment room, if I may." Jim offered his arm to Elizabeth. With his back to Dakota, he looked over his shoulder and said, "Oh, and Dakota, please join us as well." *Geez. Glad he invited me too. I've only been his patient for a decade.*

When they got to the room, Jim gestured to the winter-white recliner on the hydraulic lift. The clamshell light on the swivel arm was moved away from the chair, as was the small round tray that typically held the dental instruments. When Elizabeth sat down, Jim pulled a cream-and-silver faux fur throw from the back of the door, and gently handed it to Elizabeth, who draped it over her legs.

"This is an improvement indeed o'er the first time I wast attended to by a dentist," Elizabeth said. "I could not tell when he had last washed as the smell from his person seared mine own nostrils, and the hand tool he used to pull the tooth from mine own gums had not seen cleansing o' late either." Elizabeth clamped her mouth shut.

Jim shook his head in disgust. "The person who attended you last was a charlatan, and an affront to the dental profession," Jim said with a growl. "I assure you that I will do everything possible to keep you comfortable while you are in my care." His chest rose and fell as he took a deep breath. "With your permission, I will ask Eva, my dental assistant, to join us. Pardon me for a moment, please. And Dakota, would you accompany me?"

"What do you think, Jim?" Dakota said, as they walked down the corridor.

"I think you should go home and get a book because we're going to be here all day," Jim said, exhaling through puffed cheeks. "I'll need to do a proper exam and take X-rays, of course, but from the little I've seen, I think we're talking at least one root canal and some fillings. And if she wants the smile I think she deserves, she'll need a full set of porcelain veneers."

"Sounds like a big project," Dakota said.

"And an expensive one. Does she have dental insurance?"

"She doesn't even have a birth certificate...yet."

Jim cleared his throat. "Okay then. If I had to guess, I'd say that we're looking at twenty to twenty-five thousand for everything."

"I'll cover it." Dakota took Jim's hands in hers. "Whatever you do, I don't want her to feel it."

"Agreed," Jim said. "We're going with some light sedation. You'll need to be here to walk her around every hour or so and make sure she drinks water, but it won't be uncomfortable for her, and that's the goal."

By four that afternoon, Jim looked exhausted but happy.

After charging $22,100 to her AmEx Platinum Card, Dakota escorted the still-dozy Elizabeth to her Tesla. She carefully tucked Elizabeth into the front seat and clicked her seatbelt in place. She was hoping Jeremy would be at the condo for dinner but wasn't sure since it was Teddy's night off. But Teddy and Jeremy were watching *Bridesmaids* at her place when she got home, and they were having pizza and Greek salad for dinner. Nice.

On the twenty-minute drive from Jim's office to her condo, Dakota congratulated Elizabeth for her bravery—and told her that she'd see Jim again the following Tuesday. Elizabeth was less than thrilled. But when Dakota said that her teeth would be dazzling after just one more appointment, Elizabeth reluctantly agreed to go. Still groggy from treatment when they got home, Elizabeth retired to bed with the set of instant ice packs that Jim had given her. Dakota, for a change, had the night off.

Saturday, April 17 was a glorious early spring day. The sun reflected off the Charles River like a hundred thousand beads of light, and billowing sailboats floated on the water. Dakota was the first one awake, and the condo was peaceful. For five minutes.

CeCe came tearing out of the bedroom in her pajamas, puppies barking behind her.

"Dudley has to pee. I can tell because he just nipped my nose to wake me," she said. "Dakota, could you please take Raleigh and him out for a quick walk? You're the only one dressed."

"That's exactly what I wanted to do," Dakota said drily. But when Dudley and Raleigh saw her, they wagged their tails and sprang for the couch. She bent her head down, rubbed their ears, and kissed them on their brown puppy heads. "God, I love these little guys, weird as that is for me." She threw on a sweatshirt, stuffed some poop bags in her pockets, and leashed them.

Elizabeth materialized and greeted the dogs, who typically traveled back and forth between her room, and Dakota and CeCe's during the night.

"I should'st like to go riding today," Elizbeth announced. "I shall have an energetic steed who shall run through field and forest withal me. When may we go?"

"Dakota's taking the dogs out, so I'll look into horseback riding," CeCe said.

"That is well and good," Elizabeth said. "I shall now make some coffee for us. I shall prepare an espresso upon your return, Dakota." She padded off to the kitchen in her Chanel bathrobe. Dakota felt her heart jump. She couldn't tell if it was happiness or menopause. *Maybe I should switch to decaf.*

It had been quite a morning, finding a place to go horseback riding, but CeCe had located some stables that would accommodate two riders. In this case, Gideon and Elizabeth. Dakota agreed to drive them to the bucolic town of Concord, about thirty minutes west of Cambridge. As the site of one of the first Revolutionary War battles, Concord was well aware of its role in early American history. From the whitewashed clapboard buildings in the quaint town center to the First Parish, a Unitarian-Universalist church with roots in the seventeenth century, Concord was the quintessential Yankee town.

As Dakota was pulling into the parking area of Rockledge Stables, Elizabeth bounded out of the still-moving car and strolled over to where an older blonde wearing a biffed-up leather jacket, knee-high breeches, and riding boots was walking a chestnut horse with cream-colored mane onto the dirt riding track. Dakota and Gideon had to run to catch up with her.

"Hello, mine own good woman. I am Elizabeth Rex, hither to ride thy best horse." Elizabeth walked over to the horse and took her by the bridle. "This mare might suffice, though she is on the small side. What do you call her?"

"This is Lady Jane, and I am Sharon Whitecliff, the owner of Rockledge," Sharon said, taking the bridle back from Elizabeth.

"I knew a Lady Jane Grey once, but therein ends the verisimilitude." Elizabeth showed Sharon her already improved smile. "I should'st like to take her for a long ride on some hillocks. Hast thou any nearby?"

"We are fresh out of hillocks, as it turns out," Sharon said with a smirk, "so you'll need to ride her around the track like my other customers." Sharon pointed to the fenced-in elliptical track.

Elizabeth frowned for a microsecond but quickly changed her expression to neutral. "'Tis not mine own custom to do so, but if that is all that thee offer, I shall partake," Elizabeth said. "But this saddle shall not do. I must have a side saddle."

"You can't be serious," Sharon said, laughing. "No one's ridden side saddle for the past one hundred years. You'll have to go astride."

Dakota glanced at Gideon, whose mouth hung open. *I feel you, Gideon. This woman has no idea who she's dealing with.*

Dakota watched Elizabeth's face bloom scarlet, starting at the tip of her nose and flaring out toward her cheeks. Instead of voicing her displeasure, Elizabeth quietly walked over to Lady Jane, hoisted herself onto the saddle, put her feet in the stirrups, and began to trot around the elliptical dirt track. Trotting became cantering, and cantering became something much, much faster. Sharon's eyes grew wide as she yelled at Elizabeth to slow down.

Dakota felt like she should do something—wave to Elizabeth to stop?—but before she could manage any useful gesture, Elizabeth's horse leaped over the wooden fence around the track and took off down the lane toward God knows where.

"Goddamn it, people," Sharon screamed at Dakota. "What the Christ does she think she's doing with my horse?"

"We'll get her back, Sharon." Dakota sounded calmer than she felt as she grabbed Gideon by the hand and pulled him toward her car.

"Damn straight you will." Sharon's face was mottled with red splotches.

"How the hell are we going to find her?" Dakota asked Gideon as she tore away from the stables like a Formula 1 racer. "I meant to get her a phone just for the location-tracking, but it slipped my mind. I'll get her a company phone on Monday."

"We'll just have to drive around until we see her," Gideon said, swiveling his head right and left as he searched for Elizabeth.

"She can't have gone far, can she?" Dakota said.

"I don't know about that. She was an accomplished horsewoman who used to ride for hours at a time," Gideon said. "And the fact that the proprietor of the stables tried to clip her wings is going to make her ride that much harder."

"So she might be riding back to Cambridge then."

"If she knew the directions, she very well could."

"I feel sick. That nasty Sharon is probably going to sue me for letting Elizabeth run off with her horse." Dakota's phone rang through the car's sound system.

"Hi, Sharon," Dakota said, gulping.

"Get that crazy lady back here with my horse now, and I frickin' mean it!"

Two hours and thirteen Sharon calls later, Dakota and Gideon were walking aimlessly around Concord Center when Dakota saw a chestnut horse tethered to a tree on Concord Green.

Which wasn't the only thing she saw. Musket-holding men wearing knee-length red coats and plumed hats with white feathers were lined up, facing other musket-holding men wearing brown jackets and black tricolor hats. Why were British soldiers and colonial minutemen on the green? Patriot's Day—the Massachusetts holiday that celebrated the battles of Lexington and Concord on April 19, 1775—wasn't until Monday. It was like the high holy day of colonial reenactors.

And where was Elizabeth? Dakota scanned the crowd of bystanders but didn't see her.

"I found her." Gideon waved his hands in the air at Elizabeth, who was on the corner of the green talking with a British soldier. *I hope she's not asking him for a uniform so she can inspire the troops like she did when she gave the Tilbury speech in 1588.*

"Elizabeth. We've been so worried about you." Gideon embraced Elizabeth, then quickly let go.

Elizabeth gazed at him and squeezed his arm. "I regret having caused thee any concern, Gideon."

"What were you thinking, running off like that?" Angry tears welled in Dakota's eyes. "We had no idea where you'd gone, Sharon's furious, and I was terrified that something had happened to you."

Elizabeth thrust out her chest and spoke in her lowest register. "Thou are not my keeper. I am accountable to none but mine own self."

"Don't you understand that we were frightened for you?" Dakota said. "You're still a foreigner in a strange land. It's a land that we hope will one day be your own, but you've only just arrived, and you need to take more care with yourself." Dakota sucked in a sniffle.

Elizabeth put her arms around Dakota and held her for a few moments. Then she kissed her on the cheek. "I offer apologieth for causing thee distress, mine own dear friend," Elizabeth said. "I am indeed grateful for the many kindnesseth thee extend to me."

"I was most worried too," Gideon said, with the slightest of pouts.

"Thy love is most welcome, good sir, and I am thankful for it." Elizabeth brought Gideon's hands to her upper chest. It was hard to miss his blush. "I should'st like to observe these players as they perform their battle on its natural stage," she said. "One o' the Englishmen told me that this battle took place two hundred and fifty years ago, when America wast a colony o' the British crown." Elizabeth glowered. "What could have caused these young colonials, chartered by their king to bring civil society to a barbarian land, to foment rebellion against their protector? I cannot comprehend its logic."

"Let's find a place to sit, and I'll explain it to you," Gideon said.

"And then could you explain to me why they're staging the battle of Concord on this random date?" Dakota said.

"The player to whom I spake quoth this performance is a rehearsal for a holiday that shall take place two days hence on a state holiday for patriots," Elizabeth said.

"Got it. They're probably trying to make sure they out-do Lexington—that's the town next door," she said to Elizabeth. "I hear Concord's fife-and-drum rivalry with Lexington is more intense than Texas football." She giggled, then remembered herself. "Wait. Before we sit, I'll call Sharon about her horse."

"Lady Jane Grey. She's a fine beast. I should'st like to own her, if you can arrange it withal her spleeny, weather-bitten owner," Elizabeth said. "Had I found such a woman in mine own court, she would'st have been chambered near the cesspit."

"Now there's an idea." Dakota swallowed hard. "I think I'll just call her to let her know where her horse is and to pay her an exorbitant surcharge for her pains."

By 4:30 that afternoon, Gideon had explained why the American colonials had revolted against their mother country. Or he tried to explain it. Elizabeth couldn't help but side with the English crown.

At least Sharon had behaved better than expected. The thousand-dollar bonus Dakota paid for Elizabeth running off with Lady Jane Grey more than eased their exchange. Dakota didn't broach the subject of buying the horse, but it did give her pause.

When they returned to the condo, it was nearly 6:00 p.m., and thankfully, almost time for dinner because Dakota was starving. Elizabeth was taking a long bath, Gideon was asleep on the couch, CeCe was having dinner at the house of an AKA sister she'd befriended at MIT, Teddy was in the kitchen, Ashley was staying at her boyfriend's, Janet was getting a facial, and the puppies were on the bed in Elizabeth's room. So the place was quiet for a change, giving Dakota time to sit down with Jeremy.

"You look stressed, D. What happened out there?" Jeremy said.

"A typical day with Elizabeth," Dakota said, sighing. "She ran off riding someone else's horse, and Gideon and I couldn't find her for hours. When we finally discovered her, she was enmeshed in a historical reenactment of the Battle of Concord on Concord Green, and she still had the horse." Dakota took a gulp of wine. "Which did not please the horse's owner so I paid her a massive amount of money so she wouldn't sue me." Dakota nibbled the tips of fingernails. "After that, Gideon explained the purpose of the American Revolution, but

Elizabeth couldn't relate because she thinks the colonials should have advocated for parliamentary change instead of fighting the British."

"Sounds super relaxing." Jeremy put his arm around Dakota. "And also eventful. No wonder you're tired."

"That's not all," Dakota said. "Elizabeth asked if I could buy the horse for her."

"I think it might make your condo feel a bit cramped," he said. "And smelly." He wrinkled his nose.

"Right. But it gave me an idea."

"You're building stables at the Esplanade?"

"Not quite. I'm thinking it might be time to buy a home in the country."

"Say what?" Jeremy brought his hands up to his face in mock horror. "Are we going to be like the English Royal Family in *The Crown*, off in Balmoral all the time, riding horses and playing board games?"

"We're running out of space here," Dakota said. "Elizabeth is used to living in palaces, and while my condo is nice, it's not a country estate. If we had a bigger place, she could have a music room and stables. And I could have my own room again."

"You mean you're not enjoying sharing a bedroom with CeCe?"

"CeCe snores," Dakota said. "And although I never saw it when I visited her house, she's a mess. She leaves her clothes all over the place, and I like putting things away where they belong."

"It sounds like you've made a decision."

"I wanted to get your opinion on it first. What do you think?"

"I'm thinking we should get a room for Teddy there too. Or maybe we could share." Jeremy grinned. "But first, do you know where we're going?"

"I was just looking at real estate in Concord on my phone," Dakota said. "It's a beautiful town that's rich in history, Elizabeth likes it, and it's only thirty-five minutes from KODA."

"On a good day."

"Right. It depends on traffic, but I figure we'll be working remotely as much as possible, just going into the office for meetings. And at some point, we're going to need to expand the team by hiring a campaign manager, so that's one more person in the mix, even if he or she doesn't live with us."

"I know one thing for sure," Jeremy said. "I am so buying riding boots. Not that I've ever ridden, but the boots are awfully stylish, and now I'll have a good excuse to wear them."

"Riding boots all around, I think." Dakota chuckled. "But first, I've got to buy a place to live. And a horse."

"Or maybe two or three horses, and you'll need someone to take care of them."

"And I'll need to talk with CeCe and Ashley."

"I'll talk to Teddy. As long as the place has a nice kitchen, I think he'll be happy."

"And you'll be there so that'll make him happy." Dakota kissed Jeremy on the cheek.

"Awww. Love you back," Jeremy said. "And don't forget about Gideon. You should just get him his own room since he's around all the time."

"Got it. A room for Gideon," Dakota said. "I'll tell the realtor we're looking for a what…?" She counted on her fingers. "A six- or seven-bedroom house with spacious grounds and room for horses. And lots of bathrooms. I want my own, and it's got to be at least as nice as Elizabeth's."

"Umm…we forgot about Janet," Jeremy said.

"I didn't forget about her." Dakota looked directly at Jeremy. "I just don't think she'd fit in."

"She's a buzzkill."

"We'll let her come over for tutorials and the odd dinner," Dakota said. "That's about all I can manage."

She closed her eyes for a moment. She never imagined that she'd have a home in the country, but then again, she never imagined that she'd be living with a lute-playing, horseback-riding, Latin- and Greek-speaking, sixteenth-century English queen, who would, if all went according to plan, one day become the forty-eighth president of the United States.

CHAPTER 35

May 8, 2027, Dakota's new manse in Concord, Massachusetts

There was nothing like springtime in Concord. Birds chirping, flowers blooming—and Elizabeth holding a dead rabbit by its feet. Not the best way to meet the new campaign manager—for that's what Dakota was hoping she'd found—but at least Vince Caiozzo and his wife, Diana Drummond, knew Elizabeth's true identity.

But they hadn't known about her for long. Dakota had first met Vince and Diana in DC on Wednesday, and today was only Saturday. Still, she'd felt an immediate click with Vince, whose knowledge of the DC political scene and tightly coiled kinetic energy fascinated her. The fact that Jeremy had found Vince through an unnamed source at NSA—who'd said that Vince was "unnervingly good" and the most creative tactician he'd ever met in Washington politics—made him sound promising. She didn't know what unnervingly good meant, but she wanted to find out.

So here they were in Dakota's expansive wood-paneled living room at the new "family residence" in Concord. They rose to meet Elizabeth, who only tilted her head, while seeming to study them.

Ruggedly handsome with textured dark-brown hair and thick almost-black eyebrows, Vince had retained the stocky build of his football-playing days at Columbia. As a physical type, Diana was his foil. Tall and slender, and almost as fair as Elizabeth, Diana's long blonde ponytail and striking blue eyes made her look like a thirty-something Disney princess. Based on Dakota's limited experience with her, she was also just as sweet.

Vince, on the other hand, was not so sweet. But he was very charming, and he'd need that in spades to deal with Elizabeth.

"Wow. There's something you don't see every day," Vince said, wincing at the sight of the tawny rabbit wobbling in Elizabeth's grasp. Dakota's heart lurched at the sight.

"Good tidings. We have had a most fortuitous ride," Elizabeth said, her cheeks rosy. She was not always the best at reading the room. "Lady Jane Grey wast in good form, and Gideon is becoming an accomplished horseman after just a few short weeks of riding. He spied a hare in one of our fields, and I dispatched it with mine own crossbow." Elizabeth held up the rabbit for all to see.

"The spirit of Elmer Fudd is among us," Jeremy said.

Ignoring Jeremy's quip, Dakota said, "Good to know that you've found a use for your crossbow." She forced a grin. "Elizabeth and Gideon, I would like to introduce you to Vince Caiozzo and Diana Drummond."

Vince and Diana bowed to Elizabeth, who gave them a cursory nod. Gideon shook their hands with vigor.

"As you know, Vince comes highly recommended by Jeremy because of his depth of experience in political campaigns," Dakota said. She didn't mention that Vince was ex-INSCOM, the army's intelligence and security command, which Elizabeth would have liked. Or that he'd been one of Jennifer Samson's most trusted advisors until he left the campaign right after Samson clinched the Democratic nomination. That worried Dakota. When she'd expressed her concern to Jeremy, he'd tapped his sources to try to learn why Vince hadn't stayed with Samson through election night. Wasn't he her chief strategist-slash-campaign manager? Had he left of his own accord or had he been dismissed? Dakota was convinced

Jeremy knew the truth, but he wasn't talking. And that was alright with her. He'd proven himself on the corporate battlefield so many times over the years that he had more than earned her trust.

When Dakota had pushed for more information, Jeremy stayed tight-lipped. "This guy is brilliant, experienced, and ruthless," Jeremy had said. "We need all three if we're going to win."

Dakota had put her fears aside and reached out to Vince. Just days after buying Elizabeth's new home, an eight-bedroom/eight-bath, eleven-thousand-square-foot Georgian estate with working stables and formal gardens, Dakota had hopped on a plane to DC to meet Vince. Charismatic, smart, and funny, Vince was the kind of guy you liked from the start. Even upon that first meeting, she was surprised at how much she wanted him to like her in return.

She thought back to her breakfast with Vince at The Hay-Adams hotel. The suite she'd rented overlooking Lafayette Park offered a discreet but elegant meeting place where many confidential conversations had taken place over the past century. Theirs was just one in a long line of many.

When breakfast began to run into lunchtime, Dakota had invited Diana to join them. From Jeremy's briefing document, Diana's background was more clear-cut. She was a well-regarded attorney who'd left a public policy firm on Constitution Avenue to teach legislative and administrative law at Georgetown. Which sounded good to Dakota because navigating the dangerous waters of a presidential campaign without a lawyer seemed ill-advised. The way Dakota saw it, Vince and Diana could fill two critical spots in the campaign.

Dakota took a deep breath and returned to the present. "As you know, Elizabeth, Vince and Diana are visiting us from our nation's capital, where Vince works in government policy, and Diana is a professor at Georgetown Law," Dakota said.

"That sounds very impressive," Gideon said, beaming light in Elizabeth's direction. "Doesn't it, Bess?"

"Indeed." Elizabeth brushed some of the rabbit fur off her sleeve. "I look forward to o'er discourse over dinner, for which I must now refresh myself else the scent of horse and field may follow me." Elizabeth began to walk away.

So that's what she does when she's done with the conversation.

"I'm so pleased to meet you, Elizabeth," Vince said, with a slight bow to Elizabeth's back. "I take it we have much to discuss to get you ready to run for office."

"I was not aware that I needed thy…rather your…assistance in that matter." Elizabeth's voice sounded strained as she turned back toward Vince. "However, I expect to make a more informed decision after we are better acquainted."

Ouch. That's icy.

"But I thought we were going to…" Vince started to speak, but Diana finished his sentence.

"We were going to enjoy a leisurely conversation over dinner at the loveliest home I've ever seen," she said with a curtsy.

"You are a native of mine own England." Elizabeth's face brightened when she heard Diana's accent. "Where is your family residence?"

"I was born and raised in Richmond," Diana said.

"I have a residence in Richmond." Elizabeth's eyes sparkled. "'Tis the most beautiful of all mine own palaces in England. Have you had the occasion to see it?"

"Alas, I don't think it's there anymore," Diana said. "But I'm sure it was remarkable."

Elizabeth looked down at the floor. "The only thing inevitable in life is change."

Time to change the subject. "Where did you meet Vince?" Dakota said.

"Here in Massachusetts," Diana said, smiling.

"I was getting my master's at the Kennedy School, and she was just down the street at Harvard Law," Vince said. "I saw this stunning woman pouring over her constitutional law book at Starbucks, and I just had to say hello." Vince squeezed his wife's hand.

"Your attraction to the book as well as to the woman seems to have led you down a sunny garden path," Elizabeth said. "How fortunate for one still so young."

"I'm not as young as you may think," Vince said, knitting his black eyebrows together. "I'll be thirty-nine next month."

"I meant nay offense, young sir," Elizabeth said. "Jeremy has been telling me of your many, many accomplishments. Thusly, I am surprised that one who is not quite forty has achieved so much. We shall speak further during our evening meal." Elizabeth turned and handed the rabbit to Jeremy. "Could you please bring this to Teddy as he may wish to prepare it for us?"

"This has always been my dream," Jeremy said, taking the rabbit.

"Perhaps we should hunt for stag upon our next outing," Elizabeth said. "Venison is a viand I have long enjoyed."

"You need a license to hunt deer, and I don't think it's the season," Vince said.

"'Tis always the season for deer when I am the huntress." Elizabeth glared at him.

"Why don't you enjoy your bath, Elizabeth? We'll discuss the deer later." Dakota gave her a tight-lipped smile.

Later that evening, Dakota led Vince and Diana into the formal dining room. Elizabeth sat in her usual spot at the head of the reclaimed cherry wood table, which Dakota's interior designer had called "modern organic." Featuring neutral colors and organic fibers, comfortable seating, and nature-inspired décor, Dakota's country estate was even lovelier than her Cambridge condo, as hard as that was to admit. Elizabeth's room was an outlier. Featuring an ornately carved seventeenth-century canopied bed from England, an eighteenth-century baroque walnut desk from Italy, a nineteenth-century walnut inlay bench also from Italy, a nineteenth-century carved mahogany prie-dieu from France, and a claret-colored velvet settee from Ethan Allan—because you couldn't find a comfortable one on the antiques market, it seemed—Elizabeth's room was fit for a queen.

Once again, Dakota caught herself daydreaming. But as soon as Teddy served dinner, she snapped back to the present.

"This smells amazing, Teddy," she said to him.

"Would you like to tell them what they're having, dear?" Jeremy said to Teddy.

"Tonight's dinner is braised beef ribs with mashed potatoes, Swiss chard, and garlic cream." Teddy brushed his beard with his fingers. "It's Julia Child's recipe."

"She must be a fine friend indeed to have shared her recipe with you." Elizabeth took a bite. "I find it most delicious," she said. "What came of the rabbit I sent to thee…you? Is that our next course?"

"I have it roasting in the oven," Teddy said. "There will be enough for all to taste."

Elizabeth's smile blazed across the table. She picked up her glass of red wine and held it up to toast. "I thank God in the heavens above for the company of such dear friends," she said. "I wish ye good health, long life, and much laughter." She took a hearty sip.

"I'm relieved she turned up the charm-offensive," CeCe whispered to Dakota. "I was getting seriously worried."

"She's like a queen holding court tonight, and our guests have noticed," Dakota said. "Take a look at Vince." She nodded to the only man at the table wearing a suit and tie. He was staring directly at the sun, with no fear of getting burned.

Gideon turned to Vince and Diana. "I remember the first time Dakota approached me and my colleague Janet Majors about her vision, to bring Queen Elizabeth I to our time so she could run for president of the United States in 2028," he said. "I was gobsmacked, and that was *after* I'd seen the footage of Henry and Maeve from 1947." His eyes twinkled. "How did you come to believe that not only is time-travel real, but that the Elizabeth sitting at this table is actually the last Tudor queen?"

"Now that's a good story," Vince said, his eyes merry. "When Diana and I met Dakota in DC, all we knew was that she wanted to support a candidate to run against Vlakas. I thought we'd be talking about Evie Howard, since I'm pretty sure she's preparing to run, at least that's what her chief of staff told me when he called."

Dakota gulped. "I didn't realize Governor Howard had reached out to you."

"Her chief of staff was one of my professors at the Kennedy School, so I've known him for years," Vince said. "He asked me if I'd like to interview for campaign manager."

"I hope that you declined his invitation." Elizabeth sat tall in her chair. "For I shall expect your sworn loyalty...rather your exclusive attention..." She corrected herself. "...dedicated to me and mine own candidacy should we come to an agreement on this vital position," said with a huff. "And I shall not under any circumstances have any person in my company represent a one from the Howard line."

"She's not of that line of Howards," Gideon said to Elizabeth.

Scary how Gideon knew what Elizabeth was thinking before anyone else caught on. But it made perfect sense. Elizabeth assumed that the Howard family into which Henry VIII married when he took his sixth wife, Catherine, were the ancestors of Governor Evie Howard, who would perhaps become Elizabeth's rival for power. Though the Howards were a powerful family of their time, they weren't powerful enough to prevent the twenty-two-year-old Catherine from losing her head, making her the second of King Henry's two wives to suffer such a death.

Running for president wasn't quite as bad as the often deadly political battles of the Tudor court—but it was, unfortunately, pretty darned close.

Before Elizabeth could run down the wrong path further, Vince deftly changed the subject.

"While we've only just met, Elizabeth, I can assure you that I've met many politicians over the years, and not one of them commands a room like you," Vince said. "From what I've observed, you offer that rare combination of the intelligence, wit, and ferocity of spirit required to win the presidency."

"You take the measure of a man with such ease, and aptly so," Elizabeth said. "This will prove foundational to our political strategy, I do not doubt it."

Maybe he's not such a longshot after all.

Vince took a deep breath. "I suppose I should get back to the story of how Diana and I first learned of Elizabeth," he said. "Dakota said that she had a very surprising candidate, one who could shake up the race, someone with more than thirty years of governance, who was also an unknown in Washington. I had no idea how that could be possible."

"It's impossible, but we're doing it anyway," Dakota said, grinning.

"Right," Vince said. "But I didn't believe it at first because I couldn't think of anyone like that, unless it was a mayor of some small city." Vince raised his eyebrows.

"That's when Dakota said we'd have to take a major leap of faith, and she asked us to hear her out," Diana said.

"She said she had a secret time-travel lab at KODA, and her team had convinced Queen Elizabeth I of England to travel from 1588 to this past March so Elizabeth could run for president in 2028," Vince said. "I almost fell on the floor."

"You lost all the color in your face, dear," Diana said.

"Though I still wasn't as pale as you under normal circumstances," Vince said with a laugh. "I was ready to walk out the door at that point, but Diana told me we should at least listen."

"Dakota showed us some video from your two trips to England, Gideon," Diana said. "When we first saw John Dee in his study, I thought it was an elaborate ruse."

"But you looked so sincere, Dakota, and here you are, one of the most successful technologists on the planet, that I wanted to give you the benefit of the doubt," Vince said. "So Diana and I kept watching."

"And then you showed us Gideon, Janet, and Henry meeting with Elizabeth at John Dee's," Diana said. "That's when I started thinking there was a chance this was real."

"An infinitesimal chance. A miniscule chance, but a chance nonetheless," Vince said. "We must have watched that footage for an hour."

"Which was fine with me because you were open to the idea that this unimaginable journey—and a meeting with England's greatest queen…" *She loves it whenever we say that.* "…actually took place," Dakota said.

"Which it most certainly did because I remember it well," Elizabeth said. "Had Doctor Dee not prepared me for the meeting, I would have dismissed it as mere folly, but thy story was proved by Gideon's biography of me, though not every detail in the book was accurate." She winked at Gideon.

"I had so many questions for Dakota," Vince said. "How can we present a candidate with no historical record in our time? She has no public presence because she didn't exist until last month."

"I assured you we would have an American birth certificate for Elizabeth," Dakota said.

"Which I already have for her," Jeremy said. "And her Social Security number."

"Jeremy's been amazing," Dakota said, patting his hand. "He and CeCe have created a current history for Elizabeth. She was born on the way to the small local hospital in Hadley, Massachusetts, because her mother refused to stop working on the mysterious Voynich Manuscript—which she was convinced she was decoding. She *was not*, in fact, deciphering the unknown language in the manuscript…"

"But she *was* going into labor." Jeremy finished the sentence for her. "You talk about work ethic." He gave an appreciative whistle. "That's impressive."

"Wait. Why was she trying to decode this manuscript?" Vince said. "Was it some kind of a hobby?"

"Not at all. It was her profession." Dakota turned a serious eye on him. "Elizabeth's parents were linguistic anthropologists," she said. "They were adjunct professors at Hampshire College."

"Which was perfect for our purposes," Jeremy said. "Because that school is one random-ass hippie mess." He smirked. "It was easy to mess with the records of Elizabeth's parents, so we created their personas with fake academic histories and a ridiculous research area that would take them to remote parts of the planet.

Elizabeth frowned at him. "You shall not speak ill of mine own parents," she said with a huff. "Mine own father was a formidable king, and my mother was well-educated and a patron of the arts." Then she looked at the window and spoke just above a whisper. "She was remarkable, I have been told."

"My apologies, Elizabeth," Jeremy said, sounding oddly sincere. "In real life, they would have had me for lunch."

290

"Fie, Jeremy," Elizabeth said, her tone fiery. "Mine own parents were not cannibals."

"Jeremy doesn't think so either, Bess," Dakota said in her most soothing voice. "It's an expression that means one person is tougher than another." Elizabeth was still scowling.

"It means your parents were braver and more fierce than I could ever be," Jeremy said, his voice soft.

"It is one of your many colloquial expressions then," Elizabeth said. "I learn new vernacular every day, it seems."

"Back to Elizabeth's modern history," Dakota said. "As linguistic anthropologists, Elizabeth's parents traveled frequently so they could study rare living or undeciphered ancient languages. As their only child, Elizabeth traveled with them, and was educated by tutors."

"She had no school records until university," Jeremy said. "That was my idea." He pointed to his chest.

Dakota noticed that CeCe was tapping her foot on the floor. And it was getting louder. "CeCe had some great ideas too," Dakota said, wanting to avoid a battle over the false personal history of Elizabeth Rex.

CeCe shifted from annoyed half-smile to human speech. "I suggested that Elizabeth graduate from the University of Massachusetts at Amherst because it's such a large school, making it plausible that none of the graduates in her class remembered her," she said. "Plus." She raised her index finger in the air like a prosecuting attorney on a television show. "Elizabeth can say that she took classes at the five-college consortium of which U. Mass Amherst is a part."

"Which was very clever of CeCe." Jeremy was back again. "Because she could, theoretically speaking, have attended classes at Amherst College, Smith, Mount Holyoke, and Hampshire as well, making it even easier to evade questions about why her classmates didn't remember her."

"I was exceptionally studious, you may know," Elizabeth said with a sly grin. "A true scholar, some say. And oftentimes, I spent more time with mine own books than with people." *Oh good. She's playing along.*

"I can't believe I'm saying this, but it seems very plausible," Vince said, looking bemused. "Still, we need to know what happened to her parents."

"Oh, it's very sad," Jeremy said. "They both died of malaria when they were living in a remote part of the Amazon. They were buried there when Elizabeth was still in college."

Elizabeth's face dropped. "How I wish I could have known mine own mother at the very least."

"I understand your sentiments, Elizabeth," CeCe said, her eyes soft and warm. "But we had to concoct a personal history that would keep your parents out of the picture."

"So now we have an outstanding candidate with extensive political experience and zero skeletons in her closet," Dakota said.

"How refreshing," Vince said with a grin. "A candidate with minimal public history and no social media footprint will seem like she's blasted from nowhere," he said. "She'll need to master our political system in a short time to secure the highest elected position in the country, of course, but I like a good challenge." He gave them a vigorous nod.

"I wish to inquire something of Vince," Elizabeth said. "How shalt you make me known to those who matter? Surely, I must make a lasting impression on the people who vote in this election or I shall not win it, a possibility that I cannot abide. What shall you do to elevate my presence?"

"First, we'll do some foundational work," Vince said. "We'll build a profile for you and a platform for your candidacy." His dark eyes flashed with intensity. "Then we'll need to write policy statements that are ready to share publicly when the time comes. We'll also need to fund the campaign. It's going to be very expensive one." He glanced at Dakota. "From there, we'll begin to introduce Elizabeth Rex to some of the power-players who matter."

"I am no neophyte in the political realm." Elizabeth's cheeks were turning red, and it wasn't just the effects of the wine. "The power-players of whom you speak may influence the minds of the people, but it is the people themselveth who shall cast their votes for me. I repeat my question: How shall you make me known to my people?"

"Vince is known for his social media strategy," Diana said. "That's why the Howard campaign approached him. He can build a sustained following for Elizabeth's campaign, and no one else will come close."

"We have spent scant time on social media during our tutorial sessions," Elizabeth said. "There have been topics of far greater import to cover." She waved a hand dismissively.

Note to self: Elizabeth doesn't understand social media.

"I understand why learning about social media comes in a distant second to grasping over four hundred odd years of history," Vince said. *He's showing sensitivity. Good.*

"May I add something to our discussion?" he said to Elizabeth. She nodded "yes."

"Thank you, Elizabeth." Vince bowed his head slightly. "Social media is the most effective way for you to connect with the millions of people we need to vote for you," he said. "But you're absolutely correct that it's not the only thing we need to do to make you visible to your people. I have an idea to put you on the road to connect with average people in ways that other candidates don't or can't do. We'll amplify these connections through the press and, yes, social media." He gave a slight smile. Then he reached toward the ceiling like an old-time movie director explaining the plot of his next film.

"Just imagine Elizabeth Rex hunting deer with a factory worker from Pennsylvania or holding an archery contest in a small town in Iowa. We'll create memorable events that will stick in people's minds," he said, his voice bouncy. "Her memes will be all over the internet."

"And this will make me known to all, just as your reprehensible President Vlakas is known to all?" Elizabeth said. *Oh, thank goodness she didn't ask about memes.*

"All of that will help, but we'll need something to catapult you onto the national stage, and not just that, onto the global stage." Vince's eyes were shining. "We'll need to create an opportunity for you to capture the attention of people everywhere. We're going to come up with a launch platform that will define you as a candidate, and not just as a candidate, as a person." Vince was now breathing heavily.

"Perhaps we could hold a grand ball?" Elizabeth said. "Or I could dress in full regalia and speak to my military men?"

"Those are very good ideas," Vince said. Elizabeth winced. "I mean those are excellent ideas, but I think we need one launch event that will get covered by every major news organization in the world."

"Perhaps we could have it where world leaders are already gathered?" Diana said. "A forum that's already on the global stage."

"Are thither many such gatherings of important global leaders such as myself?" Elizabeth said. "Perhaps thither is a one to occur in mine own England." She looked around the table hopefully.

After a few minutes of everyone but Elizabeth searching on their phones, Diana said, "I don't see anything in England, unfortunately."

"But I do see something in Switzerland," Vince said. His eyes gleamed with intensity. It was almost frightening.

"What do the Swiss have other than chocolate?" Jeremy winked at him.

"You can't mean what I think you mean." Diana picked at her pearls.

"January 24th through 28th. We're going to Davos 2028, baby," Vince said. "It's late in the election cycle, but I think it could work." He tapped the table with both hands. "Want to hear my crazy idea?"

CHAPTER 36

May 8, 2027, Concord

"Davos, as in the World Economic Forum in Davos, Switzerland?" Dakota leaned over her decaf espresso to get a direct line of sight to Vince. "What could that possibly have to do with Elizabeth's campaign?"

"It doesn't have anything to do with her campaign...yet," Vince said. "But it's a powerhouse of an event. You've got heads of state, NGOs, CEOs, and the international press all attending the same conference in a small city in the Swiss Alps. It's the kind of environment where we could make a big splash, given the right opportunity."

"I should like to ask a question." Elizabeth spoke more quietly than usual. "Do the Swiss now have their own land?"

Vince did a double take. "Umm. You've never heard of Switzerland?"

"Switzerland didn't exist as a country in the sixteenth century," Gideon said. "It was an association of rural and urban cantons called the Swiss Confederation." He looked over his glasses at Vince. "It wasn't until the mid-nineteenth century that Switzerland became a sovereign nation." He opened his phone for Elizabeth. "Let me show you where Davos, Switzerland, is. And on Monday during our tutorial, I'll show you a map of all the countries in modern-day Europe."

Elizabeth turned her brilliant white smile on Gideon, and he gave her a gooey look in return.

Elizabeth's regimen of weekly facials, hyaluronic-acid serums, revitalizing lotions, and restorative hair treatments—which had recreated Elizabeth's warm-ginger hair, but in a face-framing cut that curled behind her ears—had made Elizabeth very attractive. Combined with her regal carriage and gorgeous attire, she'd stand out in any room.

"Why do such influential people meet in one location, leaving their own countries unprotected?" Elizabeth said. "If King Charles is in Switzerland, what would prevent the Spanish from attacking England?"

Dakota took a gulp of water and hoped that Gideon would explain. He did.

"As you know, global politics have grown very complex, Elizabeth," he said. "Not that they were simple in your day, of course." Gideon cleared his throat. "But world powers don't attack one another without cause, or if they do, they generally stage a covert operation rather than an overt act of war."

"Vlakas could attack another country at any time," Jeremy said. "He's such a lunatic hot head. He probably has nuclear weapons pointed at China at this very minute."

"You make a good point," Gideon said. "There are exceptions, but even Vlakas would be unlikely to launch missiles against China without some type of Congressional approval."

"I am gladdened to hear that there are some limits on Vlakas's power as so often when our group speaks of him, it sounds to mine own ear that he is a tottering bunion who threatens the world at the slightest provocation," Elizabeth said. "Before we continue our discussion, I would appreciate clarification on a word." She directed her question to Gideon. "What is a missile?"

"A missile is a weapon of war that causes a level of destruction that was unknown on Earth until the twentieth century," Gideon said in his matter-of-fact instructional voice. "World War I and II are on our syllabus for the week after next. We'll review weapons of mass destruction shortly."

Elizabeth barely batted an eyelash. *She's going to need extra support that week, whether she knows it or not. I'll talk to CeCe later.*

"I have an odd question for Elizabeth," Vince said. "Why do you pronounce the name Vlakas as you do, with an 'ah' sound at the end, not a double 's' as in Vlah-kass?"

"I spake it as you do until I first saw its written form," Elizabeth said. "I assure you that my pronunciation is the correct version because Vlakas derives from the Greek, *vlaka*, and it is a very fitting surname indeed." Her belly laugh rang throughout the room. She laughed so hard that she began to cough. Gideon handed her a glass of water. When she'd recovered enough to speak, she said, "Vlaka means *idiot*, as in a horse's ass, in the original Greek."

Gales of laughter broke out around the table.

"Oh, that's rich," Dakota said.

"It's perfect," CeCe said.

"I see a Randy Rainbow video in our future," Jeremy said.

"I see another weapon in our arsenal against Vlakas," Vince said.

"And horse-butt stuffed animals," Jeremy said. Dakota giggled.

"Why would you vote for a horse's ass when you can elect a gorgeous lass?" Gideon said, with a lingering moony-eyed look at Elizabeth.

"Courtly love or something more?" Dakota whispered to Jeremy.

"Methinks it's something more," he said.

"Umm. We'll get to campaign slogans later," Vince said. "You made an important point when I brought up Davos earlier, Elizabeth," Vince said. "Having so many powerful people in one place makes them vulnerable." His eyes gleamed. "I think we can contrive an event that will take advantage of that vulnerability."

"I know that look, Vince, and it's making me nervous," Diana said.

"Don't worry. It'll be a small-scale event but a significant one," Vince said. "And if we pull it off, every single person at Davos, along with anyone in the world who follows the news, will know the name of Elizabeth Rex."

"Now you're freaking *me* out, Vince." Dakota bit her bottom lip. "You've also piqued my curiosity, so tell us what you're thinking."

"We need to make Elizabeth into a hero," Vince said. "She does something remarkable." He tapped his fingers together. "She saves someone's life, or we make it seem like she does."

"That's genius." Jeremy clapped his hands. "It sounds morally and legally questionable, but I'm good with that."

"Want to hear my idea?" Vince said. He didn't wait for an answer. "Okay good. I'll tell you."

"Wait." Dakota held up her hands. "Before we go further, we all need to take an oath of confidentiality. And that's on top of the NDA, which doesn't cover things quite this weird," she said. Jeremy nodded his approval. "Let's all pledge that whatever we discuss is never shared with anyone beyond this room."

"I do so enjoy spy craft," Elizabeth said. "Did you know that mine own Lord Burghley William Cecil and my trusted secretary Sir Francis Walsingham were known as the first modern-day spymasters? You wrote that in your book, Gideon."

"I did indeed," Gideon said. "Their spy networks were without precedent, and their good work helped keep you safe, my dear."

Spoken like a man in love.

"I can see we're all in agreement." Dakota watched the heads nodding. "How do we do this, Vince?"

"First I have a question for Elizabeth," Vince said. "I know you use a crossbow. From this morning's rabbit." He swallowed. "How good of a shot are you with a bow and arrow?"

"I am much practiced at archery," Elizabeth said. "We have an archery target beyond the stables. Would you like to see me shoot?"

"So you're good at archery?" Vince said.

"She could make the Olympic team," Dakota said. "And when I say that, I mean the US team, and she could win the gold medal."

"She never misses the center of the target," CeCe said.

"As in, never ever," Jeremy said.

"Excellent. I'm glad to hear that," Vince said.

"I can't imagine what's going through your mind, and I'm not sure I want to," Diana said. "What are you thinking?"

"I'm thinking we're going to need those NDAs," Vince said.

CHAPTER 37

December 31, 2027, Charlestown

"The monogrammed towels were a stroke of genius." Jeremy looked across the Italian walnut desk in Dakota's office. "She seems to love anything with 'ER' in gold embroidery," he said. "And unlike that damned necklace, those towels didn't cost you a quarter of a million dollars."

Dakota looked up at him from her walnut-framed forest-green leather armchair and shuddered. "Must you keep reminding me?"

"I must," he said, putting his hand flat against his heart as if taking a sacred pledge. "But seriously, I think they were her favorite Christmas gift."

"The bejeweled dog collars from you were a close second, though," she said. "Now we always know who's barking at us, Dudley or Raleigh. Otherwise, I can't tell them apart." She looked over her reading glasses at him.

"Vince can tell them apart," Jeremy said. "Remember when Elizabeth and Vince had their first disagreement?" He used his fingers to make air quotes around "disagreement." "When she first heard Vlakas had withdrawn US troops from South Korea—which she knew would leave them far too exposed—she told him she wanted a televised debate with Vlakas. No honorable country would abandon its allies to a madman. I remember her saying that."

"She was right, by the way." Dakota frowned. "About the US withdrawal, I mean, but not about the debate."

"Vince told her she'd need to win the Democratic nomination to debate Vlakas. That it was impossible to arrange before that," Jeremy said.

"I've rarely seen her so angry." Dakota clasped her hands and shook her head. "She called him something horrible."

"A milk-livered foot-licker." Jeremy chuckled. "She has the best insults."

"Then she called in her *hounds*, and I'll be damned if those little dogs didn't come running into the living room," Dakota said. "I thought they were going to bite his ankles off."

They belly-laughed so hard tears ran from their eyes. When they'd recovered, Dakota said, "When was that again? I'm trying to remember."

"June," Jeremy said. "So much happens in a week, I find I'm losing track of time."

"God, me too," she said. "We're so lucky that Vince came back the next day."

"That's because you made her apologize to him."

"Actually, it was Gideon," she said. "When he explained the debate process to her over dinner that night—you were out with Teddy so you didn't hear the conversation—I could tell she knew she'd messed up." She took a sip of water. "I doubt she apologized much— if ever—when she was queen, but Gideon told her that a leader has to admit when she's in the wrong, if she's to maintain respect."

"And she definitely wants respect," Jeremy said.

"I'm trying to remember when Vince decided that she was too far behind the other candidates to win the Democratic nomination." Dakota scratched her head.

"I remember it," Jeremy said. "Because it was our Fourth of July cookout at the house."

"That's when she said her hotdog wasn't fit for an actual dog to eat." Dakota started laughing again. "She literally threw that hotdog, which cost about nineteen dollars a pound from Formaggio Kitchen, by the way, across the patio. Then she ran to retrieve it before one of the dogs could pick it up." They both started heaving.

"She wasn't in the best of moods when Vince said she couldn't win the Democratic nomination—so she'd have to run as an Independent," Dakota said. "Although that one decision will free us to run the kind of campaign we want."

"Without having to worry about the long tendrils of the DNC," Jeremy said, finishing her sentence as usual.

"Let them run their same-old strategy, have a good female candidate or two in the running, and settle on an old white guy once again," Dakota said. "Talk about archaic." She sighed as she looked out the window at Boston Harbor. Christmas lights decorated one or two of the big ships that moored there all winter. Which reminded her of her mother, who used to say, "Even in the darkest times, there will always be light." Dakota shivered.

"I can't believe it's New Year's Eve." Jeremy leaned back in his chair as he looked at the ceiling. "The past twelve months have been nuts."

"Remember when she learned about World War II?" Dakota sipped her iced coffee. "I was really worried about her."

"That was awful." Jeremy had a slurp of his kombucha, which he was always asking Dakota to try again because, even if she didn't like it at first, it was an acquired taste that she would appreciate over time. "The only person not panicking then was CeCe," he said. "She told me it wasn't just the subject matter that had disturbed Elizabeth, though it was that. It was the scale of the killing that put her over the edge."

"And the visuals." Dakota rolled her eyes. "Gideon gave her a lecture that Friday afternoon, and we watched *Schindler's List* that night. Even *I* had nightmares after that movie. I somehow managed not to see it when it first came out in theaters."

"Gideon couldn't find her that morning." Jeremy scratched his chin. "When was it, in May?"

"Right after Mother's Day, which was another thing that upset her." Dakota frowned. "When Elizabeth woke up that Sunday morning—which was only hours after our first dinner with Vince and Diana—she asked Gideon if he was taking her to church in Concord. I explained that Gideon, CeCe, and Ashley would all be with their mothers that day because that's what people do to honor their mothers on Mother's Day, even if *is* just a Hallmark holiday."

"Because it was invented by a greeting card company," Jeremy said, smirking.

"You know me so well." Dakota sighed. "I told her it wasn't my favorite day either since it made me miss my mother. She told me she had only a few memories of her mother, though she could still recall her dark brown eyes and beautiful face. Then she ran to her room to show me that Chequers Ring."

"Which she wasn't supposed to bring with her because it's one of a kind and might be missed wherever it is now," Jeremy said.

"True. But it's the one remembrance of her mother from her own time," Dakota said. "It must be very meaningful, to have her mother's face on one side of that locket ring, with hers on the other." Dakota studied her hands. "I can understand why she couldn't bring herself to part with it."

"I don't remember that day at all."

"That's because you were with Teddy at his mother's house." Dakota swallowed hard. "Anyway, the World War II tutorial started the Friday after Mother's Day," she said. "That Saturday morning, she went out riding for hours," Dakota said. "Then she practiced archery."

"Then she played lute."

"Then she played virginals."

"And then she had a panic attack." Dakota rubbed the back of her neck. "I'll never forget her gasping for air like that. She looked like a fish out of water," she said. "I thought we were going to have call an ambulance."

"I found a new respect for CeCe that night." Jeremy puffed out his cheeks and blew air through his lips. "She put those instant ice packs under Elizabeth's eyes and held her hands."

"Who knew CeCe always carried Atomic Fireballs in her purse?" Dakota widened her eyes. "We've been friends for thirty years, and I had no idea," she said. "I remember her popping one into Elizabeth's mouth. It was weird to give someone candy at a time like that, but somehow it helped Elizabeth calm down."

Jeremy laughed. "But that was after she swore a blue streak at CeCe."

"Yes. After that."

"Then CeCe explained how the cold packs triggered Elizabeth's parasympathetic nervous system," Jeremy said.

"And the Fireballs activated one of her other sensory systems, distracting her from feeling so panicked."

"It must have been hard on Elizabeth." Jeremy stretched his arms overhead. "I think of her as indomitable, bullet-proof, but she clearly has her vulnerabilities."

"She has a history of trauma," Dakota said. "Her father had her mother beheaded when she was only three years old. She spent a few months in the Tower of London when her sister suspected her of treason. If that wasn't enough, the one stepmother who was actually nice to her, Katherine Parr, married that creep Edward Seymour after Henry VIII died." Dakota took a deep breath. "Seymour made moves on Elizabeth when she was living with him and Katherine Parr, and Elizabeth was only fourteen years old."

"I'd like to have seen him try that when she reached adulthood," Jeremy said with disgust. "She would have nailed him up by his balls."

"Then she would have made it a Hallmark holiday."

They sniggered together.

"Elizabeth was shaken, though, right?" Jeremy said. "I seem to recall watching a lot of *Poldark* for a while."

"She watched all five seasons by the next weekend," Dakota said. "We are careful curators of Good Queen Bess." Dakota grinned.

"I can't say that I minded," Jeremy said. "I'll watch Aidan Turner take his shirt off any day of the week. Mmm mmm good." He licked his lips.

"He is quite gorgeous, that curling black hair, those smoldering eyes," she said.

"Keep distracting me, and you'll never hear my bit of gossip," Jeremy said.

"Ooh. Do tell." Dakota clapped her hands.

"When Teddy got up this morning, remember how he wanted to get fresh lobster from Gloucester for dinner? Well, he left the house by six." Jeremy rubbed his hands together. "Who do you think he saw leaving Elizabeth's room at that ungodly hour?"

"No." Dakota clapped a hand to her forehead. "You're not telling me…" She shook her head. "Are you intimating that we no longer have a virgin queen?"

Jeremy wiggled his eyebrows.

"Flirtation is one thing, but this…. This is something completely different," she said. "I hope Elizabeth can handle it."

"I hope Gideon can handle it," Jeremy said. "She'll be fine. She had all those courtiers fawning all over her when she was queen. She's used to male attention."

"Hmmm...I don't think she was used to *that* kind of attention."

"I like the way you talk about sex like it's a subversive activity—or a disease," Jeremy said. "When's the last time you had it, by the way? Was it like, 2017?"

Dakota ran around the desk and tried to grab Jeremy, but he was quicker. She chased, and he dodged around the office furniture for a few seconds until they dissolved into laughter and collapsed on her couch.

"This has been a fun little journey down memory lane," Jeremy said. "But it looks like it's getting dark, and I need time to dress for dinner."

"Women in gowns. Men in tuxes. Formal attire for Elizabeth's first New Year's Eve with us," Dakota said. "And it's going to take me longer than usual to get dressed because Ashley's doing my makeup. And CeCe's and Elizabeth's, so we have to give her enough time." Dakota frowned. "I don't even like getting that dressed up."

"We had to let Elizabeth have that, don't you think?" Jeremy said. "After she came downstairs a couple of weeks ago wearing that Bulgari Beating Heart around her neck like she was going to the Met Gala, all because we said we were taking her to the theater."

"She said she saw the young queen wearing her good jewelry to the opera on an episode of *The Crown*," Dakota said. "Elizabeth thought she'd finally get the chance to dress as 'meets a woman of her station.'"

"She looked so disappointed when she saw you wearing jeans," Jeremy said. "Even Gideon was wearing a sweater, not a sport coat. I felt bad for her." He made a baby-face pout. "You were really kind, telling her that the holidays were coming up, and we'd have a formal evening at the house."

"Here we are, at that formal evening." Dakota pulled Jeremy to standing. "We can all toast 2028 at midnight. It'll be the first day of the year that Elizabeth Rex will become president-elect of the United States."

"That's right, baby. Keep your eye on the prize," Jeremy said.

"I won't take my eye off until she wins it," Dakota said. "And I can sleep knowing that that paunchy, beetle-headed canker blossom will be kicked to the curb, where he'll fall through the storm grate and into the sewer."

"He will end up a collection of cells in a wastewater treatment plant," Jeremy said.

"He will end up something too poisonous for sludge. The sludge with his cells will need to be hermetically sealed and sent into space on a Jeff Bezos rocket," Dakota said.

"Then the rocket will combust, and his sludgy cells will be obliterated into atomic particles."

"Hey, Jeremy, it's almost five." Dakota looked up from her watch. "It's time to ready our finery, for the lady of the manor awaits us."

"We better hoof it or she's going to give us serious attitude," he said as he was walking out the door.

"But at least we won't be turned into sludge. Never sludge." Dakota laughed to herself.

She glanced out the window, then turned off her office lights. It was so quiet in the dark of her office. And she had so little quiet these days. She hoped it would be worth it.

Dakota stilled herself as she closed her eyes and imagined. A woman of five foot three with a radiant visage and glowing smile. Arms made taut by archery, and legs made fit by horseback riding.

And her spine? Her spine was made of steel—which is exactly what she'd need when they got to Davos.

CHAPTER 38

5:58 a.m., January 25, 2028, Davos, Switzerland

*W*here the hell is she? It's freezing out here.

Dakota pulled the hood of her parka around her face as she squatted on the fourth-floor balcony of Waldhotel Davos. She stared through her night vision goggles, watching Elizabeth fire arrows at the archery target that the fitness director had set up on the grassy area to the side of the footbridge. Amazing what hotel management would do for a guest willing to pay a few thousand extra for the privilege of practicing archery during the World Economic Forum Annual Meeting at Davos.

At face value, Elizabeth was an avid archer and special guest of the billionaire cybersecurity genius Dakota Wynfred. The two friends were sharing one of the penthouse suites at the venerable old hotel that had seen better days but was still one of the official conference hotels for Davos 2028.

Dakota didn't have butterflies in her stomach. She had marbles.

She'd been struggling with the ethics of using a less-than-conventional mechanism to launch Elizabeth on the world stage since the New Year, and now it was go-day.

January 25, 2028, the second day of Davos. It would be the public debut of Elizabeth Rex. Though months of planning had gone into the staged event that would make Elizabeth headline news, Dakota had been plagued by doubt over whether she could go through with it.

She'd called Jeremy in a panic the night before, and he'd talked her off the ledge. "It's going to be worth it, Dakota," he'd said. "Our plan is rock-solid, and Elizabeth can absolutely pull this off."

But can I? Would my parents agree with me, that the end justifies the means? My mother wanted me to use my privileged position for the better—and that's what I'm doing. Still, if this thing goes up in a ball of flames, I'll be like a piece of popcorn in a modern-day Vesuvius. Only the charred kernel of Dakota Wynfred will remain.

Dakota knew that if her plan were exposed, she could lose everything. Her freedom, her reputation, her company. She'd spend the rest of her life in some prison for white-collar criminals, pining for the life she could have lived. A chill wriggled down her spine.

She'd never imagined herself a modern-day Machiavelli, yet she was convinced that the risk was worth the reward. Because if she didn't risk it, what would happen? Abortion was illegal in half the states already. Covert "overground railroads" had sprouted to transport pregnant women to states where abortion was still available. But when officials in the illegal-abortion states discovered plans for an "illicit" abortion, they often pursued that fleeing woman—or girl—within an inch of her life. Some states prosecuted the women, then forced them to bear their children in prison. It was like living in an alternate reality.

And that wasn't all. Transgender rights. Environmental protections. Affirmative action. Book-banning. Hell. She'd be surprised if the US Supreme Court allowed women to keep the right to vote. She snorted in disgust.

Was her fear justified or unjustified? That's what CeCe would be asking. *Hmmm.* Dakota ran her fingers through her hair. *Justified.*

After she visited her mother in November, Dakota had thought long and hard about whether she was the right person for the job. To save America, or the promise of America, because parts of America were becoming unrecognizable to her. But could she, one of the few people rich enough and smart enough, and with a decent set of values, pull this off? Was she somehow power-mad? Or was she taking the greatest moonshot of all time to preserve what was still good in America—and to correct what was not?

Jeezus. If her neck and upper-back muscles got any tighter, they'd have to put her in traction. She chewed the inside of her cheek.

Just thirty minutes ago, Dakota had done the final run-through of project "Rising Phoenix"—Jeremy had insisted on the code name—with Elizabeth and Vince. The most powerful English queen in history was now outside firing arrows in the near-dark at an archery target that was many meters from where she was standing.

Dakota felt reassured that Vince was in Davos with them, but she had no idea where he was staying. Like a ghost, he remained invisible while running his operative, Rick Roberts, a former US Navy SEAL whom he'd hired to play this morning's attacker. Given Vince's extensive preparation for everything he did—Jeremy called it "fanatical"—she assumed he'd been working with his "assassin" before they went live.

But where was German chancellor Marion Bäcker? Dakota wished that they'd planted a mini GPS tracker on her.

According to the intelligence Jeremy had covertly gathered, Chancellor Bäcker always took a brisk morning stroll during Davos. Accompanied by a security guard, she'd walk from the Steigenberger Grandhotel Belvédère, the elegant white stucco hotel where she stayed year after year, down the restaurant-lined promenade and up the hill to Waldhotel Davos. She'd cross the footbridge that led to the hotel's second-floor side entrance, stroll through the lobby, pick up a Pfaffenhüatli—a nutty, crumbly hazelnut pastry popular in Germany—then exit the front door, and walk back down the hill.

If the chancellor were feeling particularly jaunty that morning—which in her case meant an almost-discernible smile instead of a tiny frown—she might pose for a selfie in the lobby with one of the early risers who fell all over themselves trying to get within a few feet of her.

Oh, how Dakota wished she only wanted a selfie with Chancellor Bäcker, whom she viewed as one of the greatest politicians of the modern age. Unfortunately, Dakota needed much more from the chancellor that day, for it was the regularity of Marion Bäcker's morning routine that made her the best target for Rising Phoenix.

"It's almost six-thirty. Shouldn't she be here already?" Dakota said aloud to herself.

She peeked around the corner at Elizabeth, who was gamely shooting arrows dead center into the target that was illuminated by the outdoor floodlights that Dakota hadn't noticed when they'd arrived two days ago. The sun wouldn't rise until almost eight, so Elizabeth needed those lights or she wouldn't be able to hit the broad side of a barn.

Rick Roberts—if that was his real name—was stationed on the balcony two floors below Elizabeth's and her room. She knew Rick would be outfitted in black from head to toe. The only part of him that would be exposed to the security cameras around the hotel would be his eyes. If all went according to plan, once he jumped down the two floors to roll onto the snowy verge, project Phoenix Rising would be completed in less than two minutes.

Rick would then take a high-speed snowmobile a half-mile through the towering evergreen forest at the back of the hotel to a helicopter parked on the open field near the Bobbahnstrasse. He'd fly the helicopter twenty-two miles south to St. Moritz, where he'd check into a private medical clinic to have his arm—Dakota hoped it would just be his arm—stitched up.

But would all go according to plan?

Ugh. Fifteen minutes had passed, and there was still no chancellor in sight.

Sweat beaded down Dakota's back. She tried to lick her lips, but her mouth was so dry she felt like she'd been encrusted in salt and baked at 350°F for two hours. Then it all happened in the blink of an eye.

Marion Bäcker, flanked by a towering security guard, swung her arms as she crossed the footbridge to the Waldhotel.

"Who the hell is that?" Dakota's heart pounded as she watched a person wearing a pom-pom hat bounce toward the chancellor from the opposite side. She hoped it was a jogger and not a real assassin. You never knew what would happen at Davos.

Dakota watched the security guard block the jogger with his hands. Like an offensive lineman in a football game, he pushed the jogger up the hill and away from the chancellor. The jogger must have gotten the message because he or she turned away from the guard and sprinted up the hill.

A split-second later, Rick vaulted over the balcony's railing and rolled to standing as he hit the ground. The security guard didn't even have time to draw a weapon. Rick took him out with a flying kick to the chest and a punch to the head. Then he grabbed Chancellor Bäcker from the back, held a knife to her throat, and shouted in German. Dakota couldn't hear what he yelled, but they'd rehearsed it enough times that she knew it by heart. "Deutschland ist für Deutsche." *Germany is for Germans.* Just like Vlakas's horrible anti-immigrant slogan, *America for Americans.* She hoped people would make the connection when the news stories rolled out.

Elizabeth reacted to Rick's vocal queue exactly as practiced. She shifted a floodlight toward his voice, drew her bow, and shot a metal-tipped arrow into Rick's right arm. He dropped his knife and took off for the snow mobile while Elizabeth ran the twenty or so yards to Chancellor Bäcker, embracing her in a protective hug. Dakota exhaled.

No longer stunned, the security guard ran over to Elizabeth, pulled her away from the chancellor, and then pushed her to the ground. For God's sake, the man was kneeling on Elizabeth's chest. *Please don't let him hurt her.*

At least the chancellor had her head on straight. She placed her gloved hands on the guard's shoulders and forcefully pulled him off Elizabeth. Then she extended both hands to Elizabeth and pulled her to standing. She draped an arm over Elizabeth's shoulders, and they walked in tandem toward the hotel's side door.

It was 6:48. Dakota texted *Rising Phoenix* to Vince, who was watching through his infrared goggles from an unknown location, and then to Jeremy, who was stationed in the Core because he wanted to work from a secure environment where Vince or Dakota could contact him if needed. After that, she took a moment to steady herself against the balcony railing. *I can't believe we did it.* She opened the slider to the suite and collapsed on the caramel-colored leather couch. She hugged the sheepskin throw against her chest and stared at the ceiling. *I have just orchestrated the first illegal action of my life, and it was a doozy.*

By now, Jeremy would have wired one million each from new accounts in three different countries—the Cayman Islands, Bolivia, and Antiqua—to Rick's bank in Switzerland. *I have sold my soul for three million dollars to catapult Elizabeth Tudor to the US presidency. I think I'm going to throw up.*

Dakota's hands felt cool on the marble tile as she retched bitter bile into the porcelain toilet bowl in her en suite bathroom. Her phone rang. It was Elizabeth.

"Oh, dear lord, Bess, are you alright?" Dakota wiped her mouth on her sleeve. "I was terrified that the damned security guard was going to hurt you." She gulped. "I had this sick feeling he was going to shoot you in the head. I can't tell you how many times that's happened in America." She used a piece of toilet paper to wipe a smudge from her eyes. "Good thing it was you, not someone like CeCe down there. I doubt she would have fared so well."

"I am in good health, my dear friend. Be not afraid," Elizabeth said, sounding hale and hearty. "Notwithstanding my natural vigor, it was rather unpleasant to have the chancellor's guardsman accost me, as one would a common criminal, when I had just rescued his charge." Elizabeth sniffed loudly. "The chancellor is a very pleasant sort of woman," she said. "Her body is sturdy, much like an English peasant. Her mind, though, it veritably sparkles with intelligence. And when she speaks, 'tis with purpose. Nary a word is wasted."

"Thank you for calling to let me know." Dakota exhaled through her mouth. "I don't think I've ever been this nervous."

"We shall talk further in mere moments," Elizabeth said. "I must avail myself to Chancellor Bäcker. She beckons me to her." The phone went quiet.

Did Elizabeth just hang up on me?

Dakota splashed water on her face. The face in the mirror showed dark circles under the eyes. *Maybe I'll feel better after I have a shower.*

Dakota was just pulling a winter-wheat cashmere sweater over her head when Elizabeth burst into her bedroom, breathless.

"Dear lady. You cannot imagine the morning that I have had." Elizabeth clapped her hands. "Marion—she asked me to call her by her first name, and I told her she could call me Elizabeth—has invited me to dine with her this evening. She said it would be an intimate dinner with just a few friends." Elizabeth threw herself onto the raspberry velvet armchair opposite Dakota's double bed. "Would you like to venture a guess on the identity of those friends?"

"I cannot imagine," Dakota said. "Am I invited too?" She cocked her head to the side.

"Heavens above." Elizabeth covered her mouth. "I afear that I was so taken by the excitement of the moment that I did not inquire as to whether I could bring a guest."

"I understand completely." Dakota's heart sank, but she tried not to show she was crushed. "You've made a new and important friend, and it is for you to cultivate the relationship." She smiled weakly. "Who are the other guests? You haven't told me yet."

"I shall meet some other heads of state," she said. "President Thibault of France, Prime Minister Buonanotte of Italy, and Prime Minister Socorro of Spain." Arms outstretched, she twirled in place. "It feels like hundreds of years since I have dined with a Spaniard. I hope this one is more amiable than his forebears." Her eyes glittered. "Though we shall explore the climate crisis during the course of our conversation, there may be time enough to become acquainted with the men—and the woman—who will become my peers."

"I'm so pleased for you, Bess." Dakota's jaw tightened. "And now you have some big decisions to make: Whatever shall you wear?" She forced another smile.

"'Tis an important decision, to be sure," she said. "I must do a video chat with Ashley to solicit her advice on whether to wear the floral Dolce & Gabbana midi or the midnight blue Chanel gown. I shall phone her promptly."

Dakota shook her head. "It's way too early to call Ashley," she said. "It's six hours earlier in Massachusetts, which is about one in the morning Ashley's time. You'll have to wait until at least 1:00 p.m. our time."

Elizabeth frowned. "I must take rest before this evening," she said. "'Twas an eventful morn, as you may know." She huffed out of the room. *Wait until she gets famous…again.*

The house phone rang. "Hello," Dakota said.

"People are asking for Miss Elizabeth Rex." A German-accented man's voice warbled at her. "Is she available to speak with them?"

"Umm…what people, may I ask, and to whom am I speaking?"

"Pardon me," the voice said. "I am Mr. Klauser, the manager of Waldhotel." He cleared his throat. "The people are from the news. There are so many television crews in the lobby that one simply cannot move," he said. "And not just television. Radio. Newspapers, they are from everywhere. *The New York Times*, they are okay, but *Le Monde* told *Die Welt* that café au lait is superior to kaffe-crème, which started all the French and Germans shouting. If Miss Rex does not come down soon, I cannot guarantee the safety of the journalists. Could you please speak with her and let me know when she will be ready for the interviews?"

Dakota called Vince. "It has begun," she said. "What the hell do we do now?"

CHAPTER 39

January 25, 2028, Davos, Switzerland

The room phone had been ringing off the hook during her entire call with Vince. She picked it up. "We're moving everyone to the ballroom." Dakota heard a crash and a scream over the phone. "*Mein Gott.*"

"That didn't sound good," Dakota said. "Are you all right, Mr. Klauser?"

"I am fine, thank you." He was breathing hard. "But Miss Abdi of CNN is not. A cameraman collided with her. But do not be concerned. We will get her some ice." Dakota heard footsteps. "Please, Miss Wynfred, please. Could you have Miss Rex come to the ballroom on the second floor? There are too many journalists in the lobby for personal interviews. She must hold a press conference."

"Wow." Dakota noticed her quads were tight. "You've put together a press conference that quickly?"

"We have a lectern and a microphone for Miss Rex. My staff are setting up chairs as quickly as possible." Mr. Klauser was panting. "When may we expect her to join us?"

"I'll alert her that people are waiting, but she may want to freshen up," Dakota said.

"The seconds tick by, Miss Wynfred. As they do, the journalists become more hungry," Mr. Klauser said. "They're like small children who have not had their snack. If they are not fed soon, they will begin to eat one another, and then I will need more ice."

Dakota gulped. "I understand," she said. "I'll have her down there as soon as possible."

Elizabeth was still wide-awake when Dakota knocked on her door. When Dakota told her she was needed immediately, Elizabeth said she wanted a stylist sent up "to attend her," but since Dakota couldn't manufacture one out of thin air, she offered her version of hands-on assistance.

"I can do hair in a pinch," Dakota said. "I did my own on New Year's Eve, if you remember."

Elizabeth didn't say a thing.

"Well, then, why don't you freshen up, and we'll get you to the ballroom as soon as possible?"

"I shall need time for my toilette, for this is a momentous occasion," Elizabeth said. "How much time may I have?"

"Can you keep it to fifteen minutes?"

"'Zounds!" The door flung open. "I must bathe, apply cosmetics, select a gown and accompanying adornments." Elizabeth arched her eyebrows. "I must have at least one hour before I introduce myself for all the world to see."

"While that would be ideal, we don't have that kind of time, Elizabeth," Dakota said.

"Be that as it may," Elizabeth said with a harumph. "I shall attend to my own person." She began to shut the door.

"Please, Bess. The hotel manager is in a state of panic." Dakota's heart pattered. "The press are beginning to get vicious with one another."

Elizabeth paused to listen.

"The French and Germans are yelling about coffee, and one famous reporter from CNN got injured."

"I have no wish to begin my reign with a war."

"Excuse me?"

"That is, my brand—as Vince would describe it—I balance strength and peace." She clasped her hands as if in prayer. "My platform cannot be tainted by early acts of aggression."

"I'm so glad you understand," Dakota said. "And one more thing. Vince thought you would make a more powerful statement by staying dressed in your fitness wear."

Elizabeth blinked twice.

"You saved the chancellor during archery practice. An athlete. A competitor. A champion." *Ah, that one landed.*

"I acknowledge and appreciate your good counsel," Elizabeth said. "This is good strategy, and I have decided to honor it."

Whew. "And do you think you could be ready soon, my dearest Bess?" Dakota made her best puppy-dog eyes.`

Twenty minutes later, Elizabeth emerged, a picture of vitality. Her brown eyes were perfectly accented by the earth tones of her eye makeup, her tinted moisturizer and blush made her complexion appear flawless, her rosy lips were almost plump. *The old fox is about to charm the chickens.*

Down the elevator they went.

Attired in a winter-white Helly Hansen Lillo sweater that showcased her glorious red hair, Elizabeth walked around the throngs of seated journalists, still wearing her black leather ankle boots.

Dakota, on the other hand, felt hot and dizzy as she blinked into hundreds of flashbulbs. Fortunately, Mr. Klauser was there to escort her to a chair at the front of the room while Elizabeth took her rightful place behind the wooden podium. As Elizabeth gazed upon the audience, her smile was brilliant—almost blinding in its intensity. Hook her up to a lightbulb, and she could have powered it up. Or a refrigerator. Or a small city.

Dakota adjusted herself in her seat and listened.

"I hear that some of you have questions for me." Elizabeth's eyes shone as she surveyed the crowd. "Before we begin, I should like to say I am grateful that I could be of service to Chancellor Bäcker. I have long admired her leadership and am pleased to have made her acquaintance at a pivotal moment in time." She bowed her head for a few seconds. "Let us begin. Gentleman in the blue suit and yellow tie. What is your question?"

"Stefano Georgeopoulos of ABC News, Miss Rex. Who are you and where did you come from?"

"Who am I, Mr. Georgeopoulos?" Elizabeth said, bemused. "I am Elizabeth Rex from Concord, Massachusetts, and I work for Dakota Wynfred in a special capacity."

"What does that mean, special capacity? Are you some sort of female James Bond?" Stefano said with a wink.

The audience tittered.

"Nay, I am not James Bond, but I do much admire spycraft," Elizabeth said, grinning.

Oh, thank God we included Skyfall *in her cultural education.*

"Yes, to the lady in the pearls and the radiant red jacket," Elizabeth said.

"Thank you, Miss Rex. Nia Zuri for NBC News. Could you say a few more words about the work you do for Dakota Wynfred?"

"It would be my pleasure to do so," Elizabeth said. "My expertise is in cyberwarfare, and in that capacity, I have long worked with Dakota. It is because we collaborated on her presentation, 'A Secure Cybersphere for a Secure Tomorrow,' that we are in company at the World Economic Forum. Dakota will present at 14:30 this afternoon at World Congress Centre. I hope to see you there."

Nia nodded and sat down.

"Hello to the lady in the charcoal-gray pantsuit. You may ask a question," Elizabeth said.

"Kinsley Madison, MSNBC. I was incredulous when I heard that you shot the chancellor's attacker with an arrow. How is that even possible?" Kinsley pushed her tortoiseshell glasses up off her nose.

"I fully understand your incredulity, Miss Madison, and I shall do my best to explain," Elizabeth said. "I enjoy the sport of archery and practice it whenever it is possible. That is why we arranged with the wonderful staff of this hotel to accommodate my interest in early-morning practices, before the conference day begins."

"It was dark when the attack took place, wasn't it?" Kinsley scowled. "How could you possibly know what was happening in time to respond?"

"These are excellent questions, Miss Madison," Elizabeth said. "It is indeed dark here at Davos in the morning, which is why the hotel used spotlights to illuminate the greenspace. Thus, I could see my target perfectly at a distance of forty meters." She looked directly at one of the television cameras. "I was just about to draw my bow when I was alerted to someone yelling. I shifted the spotlight nearest me toward the vocalization." Elizabeth thrust out her chin. "I saw the attacker's arm around the neck of the chancellor. He was behind her, but I could not see what he had in his hand, so I shot his free arm. After this, he fled."

An angular woman wearing a black V-neck dress stood and waved. "Eva Quinn, PBS News Hour, Miss Rex," she said. "What was it that he yelled?"

"I did not know it at the time, but Chancellor Bäcker told me that the attacker said, '*Deutschland ist für Deutsche.*' A most offensive statement, do you not agree?"

The crowd gasped.

"Yes, Germany for Germans." Elizabeth's eyes grew dark. "A xenophobic declaration, if I am not mistaken." Elizabeth pointed to a silver-haired man with a small American flag and a black AR-15-shaped pin over his lapel.

"I'm Pauly Pappnase of Fox News, but I bet you already knew that." He stuck out his pointy chin. "You're expecting our viewers to believe that you can hit an archery target from forty meters away? Are you practicing for the Olympic team?" He pulled his lips taut in a mirthless smile.

"Olympic distance is much farther, Mr. Pappnase, at seventy meters, a detail that pales in comparison to the continued good health of Chancellor Bäcker." Elizabeth glared at him. "I should hope that we can dispense with such trivialities."

"There's no need to give me attitude, lady," Pauly snarled. "I'm just doing my job as a journalist."

Dakota realized she was clasping her hands so hard, her fingers hurt. *Don't engage, Bess. We can't afford to have him get to you.*

Well-practiced in the art of ignoring petulant men, Elizabeth drew a hand over her brow as if searching for a particular person. "Is Miss Mira Abdi among you?" she said. "I heard that she may have sustained an injury preceding this press conference, and I should like to inquire if she is well."

A hand shot up in the back of the room. Mr. Klauser ran over with the only portable microphone.

"I am here and in one piece, Miss Rex, and I thank you for your concern." CNN's chief international correspondent grunted as she rose to standing. "Could you please tell me what happened after you shot the attacker with an arrow?"

"It all took place very quickly, but I shall try to recall." Elizabeth stood tall behind the podium. "I saw him run away from the chancellor and up the hill toward the forest. He was wearing all black so I lost him before long." Elizabeth took a deep breath. "I noticed a man on the ground and ran toward the chancellor. That man, as I now know, was her security guard. I learned later that the attacker had temporarily disabled the guard."

A man sporting black stubble on his chin waved at Elizabeth. "The guard disabled you next, I have heard. Is this so, Miss Rex?"

"You have the advantage of knowing my name, sir, and yet I know not yours. Could you please share your affiliation?" Elizabeth said.

"I apologize for this." The man pointed to his chest. "Guillermo Abril from *EL PAÍS* in Spain."

"Ah, it is good to speak with a true Spaniard." Elizabeth gave him a small smile and answered in Spanish. Guillermo's jaw literally dropped open at her reply.

"Umm…what was that in English?" Kinsley said.

"I said that the guard, to his credit, brought me to the ground, as he perceived me as a potential threat," Elizabeth said. "He did not use excessive force, which I appreciated. Chancellor Bäcker soon… corrected him. I then made her acquaintance."

Hands flew all around.

"Gentleman in the white shirt and black jacket."

He's handsome. No surprise Elizabeth called on him.

"Luc Bronner of *Le Monde*. Do you speak French as well?" he said, raising his eyebrows.

"*Bien sûr, je parle Français*" Elizabeth blinked her lashes. "*Mais c'est plus facile pour les autres en anglais.*" She beamed at him.

"Yes, of course, English is easier for the others." Luc beamed back at her. "Now that you are the hero of Davos, what will you do next?"

"I must dedicate serious thought to such a question, monsieur," Elizabeth said. "And as soon as I have the answer, you shall be one of the first to know." She winked at him, and the typically hardboiled journalists seated before her actually laughed.

Elizabeth waved a queenly goodbye and spoke a few parting words into the microphone. "I hope we shall have the occasion to speak again one day." She smiled with her eyes and stepped away from the podium.

Dakota had changed so much for the red-haired rocket who stood before her. She'd moved from an urban life in Cambridge to a bucolic estate in rural Concord. She'd created an intricately threaded team of specialists to form a new "Privy Council" for Elizabeth. And unless she were focused on KODA business, her thoughts and hopes—and fears—were entangled in whatever Elizabeth needed. Which included her participation in this morning's carefully choreographed "rescue" of the German chancellor.

There was no longer a question of what Dakota would change for Elizabeth. She felt a chill run down her spine.

CHAPTER 40

2:20 p.m., January 25, 2028, Davos, Switzerland

"Since the ancient Egyptians first scrambled hieroglyphs nearly four thousand years ago, we've been using ciphers—which you may know as *secret codes*—to protect our communications from unintended eyes." Dakota looked into the bathroom mirror and took a deep breath. "At first ciphers were relatively simple, like the letter-substitution cipher invented by Julius Caesar."

She rubbed the back of her neck and continued practicing her opening remarks. "Over the centuries, they grew so complex that codebreaking helped preserve governments and win wars. By cracking the ciphers in the letters of Mary, Queen of Scots, Queen Elizabeth I's spy network thwarted a plot to overthrow one of history's greatest rulers. More than three hundred and fifty years later, Alan Turing built the machine that broke the Enigma code used by the Nazis and their allies during World War II, marking the start of modern cryptanalysis." She wiped her sweaty palms on her Alexander McQueen Prince of Wales pantsuit.

"I was always fascinated by the history of cryptography, but it wasn't until I started my graduate work in 1998 that I realized people and institutions needed a much better way to secure our data. The day after I left MIT with a doctorate in computer science, I began work on my new cyber cryptography platform. After six months of working night and day from my tiny studio apartment in Cambridge, KODA was born."

She glanced down at her note cards. "And now it's in the cybersphere, rather than in the physical sphere, that we must apply our intelligence to protecting all facets of modern life, from our personal financial information to our most guarded state secrets." *Not bad for a practice run.*

Backstage, Dakota gazed at her reflection in the bathroom mirror. She fumbled pulling her lipstick out of her TUMI laptop bag but managed to get ahold of it long enough to apply a shimmering cranberry coat to her pursed lips. She wanted to look good when she addressed her first audience at the World Economic Forum. She sucked in her cheeks and returned to the waiting area backstage.

Why am I so nervous? When she'd first entered the small auditorium, she'd seen rows of empty seats. But that was twenty minutes ago, and now, a few minutes before she was supposed to take the podium, she heard the clamor of voices and the sound of chairs scraping against the floor. *I'll just peek out to see what's happening.*

Dakota moved the curtain by a fraction of an inch. Elizabeth still sat dead center in the front row, but she was no longer alone. Her new "bestie" was seated so close to her, their heads were almost touching. What's next, three-day weekends in the South of France with Marion Bäcker? *Get over it, Dakota. Your girl is growing up.*

Dakota scanned the auditorium, seeing some of the same journalists from the morning press conference. His hairy black eyebrows visible as he bent his head to type on his tablet, Stefano Georgeopoulos was smushed between the handsome French reporter from *Le Monde* and a woman scribbling ferociously in her notebook. But they were far from the only news media in the auditorium.

Photographers adjusted their lenses. TV cameramen checked their angles. The place was alive with the energy of people hoping for a one-on-one interview with Elizabeth. At least that's what Dakota assumed, for it was hard to believe that the press had come in droves for a story on cybersecurity. Still, it was nice to have a full house, whatever the reason. And aligned as she was to the rising star that was Elizabeth, the attention would also be good for KODA. Aside from her session running behind schedule, things were still going according to plan.

Until they weren't.

A din from the back of the room caused heads to turn. Four beefy besuited men wearing earpieces plowed down the center aisle between the rows of seats, one in front and back, and one on each side of a florid-faced, round-bellied man, who stage-whispered his interest in a "very important talk by another great American." Vlakas. *Yuck.*

Wrapped in a blanket of Secret Service men like a gypsy moth in a cocoon, the American president would soon burst forth to consume all life in his vicinity. But first he needed a place to sit.

Vlakas seemed oblivious to the fact that all the seats in the front of the room were already occupied. He stood with his back to the stage for a few minutes, scowling at the audience. Then he walked over to Elizabeth, grabbed for her hand, and shook it vigorously. *He's probably trying to dislocate her shoulder.* Dakota had never seen Elizabeth recoil like that. She looked like Maggie Smith with dog poop on her lap. Jeremy would have loved it.

Vlakas tapped the shoulder of a bearded man seated on the other side of Marion Bäcker. Did he expect the man to vacate his seat because the most powerful man in the world, no, in the entire universe, had asked him to do so? The man shook his head "no." Too bad. The narcissist in chief was out of luck.

Vlakas's late arrival must have sent the conference organizers scurrying to accommodate the great and powerful Oz because a man in a navy-blue jacket and yellow polka dot tie soon race-walked to the front of the room carrying a chair, which he placed in the center aisle for Vlakas. So much for the fire code.

Vlakas parked his sizable ass in the gray plastic chair and unbuttoned his suit jacket. He squeezed his lips together as he scanned the audience to his left and right. Then he nodded at a pod of photographers standing near the stage. Not a single flash bulb went off in his direction. Must be weird for him not to be the center of attention. *Get used to it, baby.*

"Ms. Wynfred." Someone tapped Dakota's shoulder. "We've been running a bit late, but it is now time for your presentation."

"I'm ready," Dakota told the elegant woman in a sea-green silk dress. "But first, I'm curious about something."

"I will answer if I can."

"Almost no one was in the audience until the last minute, and now it's standing room only. Do you have any idea why that might be?"

The woman sighed. "The American president was scheduled to speak from 14:00 to 14:30, and your talk was scheduled for 14:30," she said. "This timing was too close for some people, especially the media, who left his presentation a little early so they could make it to your talk. At least, that's what I surmise." She touched her fingers to her chin. "I have volunteered on the conference committee for the past eleven years, and I have never seen this happen. Forum attendees do not leave their seats before the speaker has finished, especially a head of state."

Dakota bit back a smile. "It does seem unusual," she said. "But then again, cybersecurity is a hot topic at the moment, so that may be what drew them here."

"And it may not be." She placed a hand on Dakota's elbow. "Let us not keep them waiting further."

Dakota rolled her shoulders back and took a deep breath. *Go time.* She stepped up to the microphone and delivered her opening remarks.

The minutes flew by. And just before she spoke to the last slide of her presentation, Dakota stole a glance at Elizabeth. While she wasn't smiling with her mouth, Elizabeth's gold-brown eyes beamed rays of light. Dakota was always amazed at how Elizabeth could express her emotions without moving a muscle. Her eyes said it all. They revealed when she was happy, sad, angry, approving, critical, scornful, offended, joyous. But to read Elizabeth's emotions, you had to know her intimately. The ability to cloak her true feelings from all but her inner circle must have served her well. As a queen long courted by a collection of suitors whom she never intended to marry, she'd mastered the art of juggling the intentions of countless men without actually offending them. What a magnificent skill to take to her political career.

Dakota clicked to the end and summarized her key points. Time for the Q&A.

"Could you please tell us when you first met Elizabeth Rex and in what context?"

Definitely not a question about her presentation. But Vince had foreseen this possibility, and she felt well prepared to answer the woman—who looked remarkably like Claudette Vinet, head of the European Central Bank. The heavy hitters were in the room.

"I didn't actually meet Elizabeth Rex at first. I'd read a paper she'd written about cyberwarfare, and I was so impressed that I reached out," Dakota said. "That was about fifteen years ago, and she came to work for me shortly thereafter."

Dakota pointed to a tall man in the left-front section. "Dakota, now that Miss Rex is known to the world, can we expect her to be in the public eye?"

"That would be up to Miss Rex." Dakota smiled. "Now does anyone have a question about *my* presentation?"

"What a phenomenal presentation. It's good to know that America has smart, really smart people working in the cyber area." It was Vlakas, and he was plodding up the stairs to the stage.

"Do you have a question, Mr. President?" Dakota said, using her body to block him from reaching the podium. He pushed forward and draped a hulking arm around her shoulders. *Eew. Remove that arm before you lose it.*

"May I help you, sir?" Dakota clenched her jaw so hard her teeth felt locked in place.

"Yes, absolutely. We're gonna be on the same team," Vlakas said. "Because I've had my eye on you, yes, I have." He mock-pouted. "No, not that way, Dakota. You're not my type." He squinted his eyes in a smarmy smile. "It won't be long before KODA is part of the United States government, and you'll be working for me. What do you think about that?"

I think I'd like to punch you in the head. "I'm not sure where you got your information, Mr. President, but I would know if there were any truth to that statement," Dakota said, choosing each word with care.

"Then let me be the first to tell you. We're gonna do it, and it's going to be an amazing thing, an incredible thing, just outstanding," Vlakas said. "We're gonna have the best, the strongest, the safest. I mean the very best-protected computers in the world because that's what I do. I'm the man who keeps America safe."

The crowd gasped. Dakota tried to blink away the blinding flash-bulbs as Vlakas squeezed her harder. She thought she was going to projectile-vomit in front of the prestigious attendees of the World Economic Forum. Then she looked down at the podium and tried to breathe. Not a second later, she felt a gentle touch on her arm. Elizabeth was now standing next to Dakota.

"Mr. President, I must interject before you proceed down a path that is paved with falsehoods and fallacies." Elizabeth put her arm around Dakota's back, pulling her away from Vlakas. She stepped closer to the microphone. "I am compelled to correct your misstatements. KODA is now and shall remain a private company, with Dakota Wynfred as the majority owner."

"I'm supposed to believe that some little lady with a weird, and I mean weird as in disturbing, accent has access to the privileged information of the United States government?" Vlakas curled the corners of his mouth and raised his eyebrows. "I didn't give you any security clearance."

"'Tis true," Elizabeth said. "It seems that you reserve such secure clearances for your immediate family, and we are no relation, sir, nor ever shall be." Her eyes burned black as she enunciated every word.

"You think you know security? You know nothing about security. You know less than nothing about security." He leaned over Elizabeth, angry spittle flying from his mouth as he spoke. "I know more about security than anyone in this room, than anyone at this conference. But you don't have the brain power to understand that."

Elizabeth calmly shook her head. "I shall not contend the issue further as I have no desire to descend to the foul invective in which you so regularly indulge." Elizabeth folded her hands on top of the podium. She paused to look at the gaggle of photographers crowded just below the stage.

Talk about grace under pressure.

"You think you're so cool? You wouldn't last a day in my job. Not a minute. Not even a second." Vlakas overemphasized each consonant in "second," making the word itself into a taunt. Elizabeth didn't bite. Instead, she took Dakota by the hand and started heading offstage.

"Are you kidding? You're gonna turn your back on me? I'm the president of the United States." He puffed out his chest. "It's not exactly an easy job, in case you were wondering, but it's *my* job, and *I* make the rules."

"Perhaps you should cease from doing so." Elizabeth turned back toward Vlakas, who was crowding the podium. She deftly navigated around him until she was in front of the microphone. "Because the contract that the president has with the people of the United States is sacred, and in accordance with the United States Constitution, that venerable document on which our political system is founded, the president represents one of *three* branches of our federal government to ensure the balance of power. The president is not a dictator nor a divine right monarch. He, or she, is subject to the will of the people, and must govern in accordance with their wishes."

"Now you're gonna lecture me about the Constitution? Give me a break." Vlakas crunched his eyes together in fury. "I guess I don't need to worry." He sneered. "It's not like you're ever gonna be president."

Elizabeth stood stock-still and said, "Do not presume to know my plans, sir." She stared steel-tipped arrows at him. "Having now witnessed the manner in which you comport yourself, I am convinced that America needs, nay deserves, a chief executive who shall guide her with a hand that is steady, thoughtful, fair, and above all, one that adheres to the rule of law rather than sets himself above it."

"You, running for president? This has to be a joke." He rolled his eyes at her. Elizabeth did not respond.

Dakota watched Elizabeth leave the stage, shoulders out and chin up as she walked down the stairs. The daughter of Henry VIII and Anne Boleyn, educated to the highest standards, an expert in machinations and political intrigue, and here she was, having gone toe to toe with a powerful, dangerous man without blinking twice. *That's my girl, ready for whatever's next.*

Elizabeth stood with her back to the stage and gave the people her best smile.

And they, the people, smiled back.

~~Queen~~ Bess:
A Tudor Comes to Save America

Book Group Questions

1. Why do you think ~~Queen~~ is crossed out in the book's title?
2. Why do you think friendships are so important in Dakota's life?
3. Think about how you'd adapt this book into a film. Who might you cast in the leading roles and why?
4. From your point of view, what were Dakota's primary motivations in the book? How did they change over time?
5. Why Elizabeth Tudor? What makes her a good presidential candidate?
6. If you were a member of Elizabeth's inner circle, what would worry you about her becoming president?
7. If you could bring any historical figure to the future — so he or she could run for president — whom would you choose and why?
8. If you had a time machine, how might you use it?
9. Elizabeth had to adapt to life in the twenty-first century. Is there anything in your life or in current events that might require a similar adjustment?
10. Do you think a compelling independent political candidate could be successful in the United States today? Why?
11. What do you think happens next for Queen Bess and Dakota?

Acknowledgments

I'd like to thank a core group of people who helped me to realize QB. My spouse Helen Privett and daughter Stella for your steadfast support during the whole long process of bringing this idea to life.

My agent, Maura Phelan of Green Light Media + Literary, who championed QB from her first read. And for Merry, Green Light's "secret weapon," who improved the manuscript immeasurably.

My editor at Regalo Press, Adriana Senior, for embracing the work of a first-time author.

My friend, Stella D., for her invaluable feedback and for letting me borrow her last name for one of the characters.

My phenomenal book coach, Dawn Ius, who taught me how to write fiction and talked me off a cliff when the journey got hard and scary.

Bev Wilson, who divulged essential beauty secrets that only another redhead would know.

The author, Diana Renn, who provided touchstone support along the journey.

Jein Park, for introducing me to the Haenyeo of Jeju island in South Korea, and who schooled me on the correct Korean swear words for Jeremy.

Anja-Maria Hastenrath, for renaming both the German chancellor and the pastry the chancellor loves most.

About the Author

Maria Vetrano tried to save the whales when she was nine years old. It didn't quite work. But that didn't quell her desire to ease some of the world's ills in some small way, even if only through fiction. She is the mother of one young adult daughter and currently lives with her wife and animal family in Massachusetts. When she's not writing, Maria is the principal of Vetrano Communications, the PR and marketing firm she founded in 2004 that specializes in tech clientele. Maria is also a lounge singer who's entertained audiences in Boston, Cambridge, and Provincetown. Along with her wife, she created Against the Tide, a fundraising event to fight breast cancer. She is a graduate of Colgate University with a BA in English literature.